For my friend Tom Jackson

I hope my story brings magic to people the way you brought magic into the lives of everyone who knew you.

D1614425

Acknowledgements

Thank you to my sister Anne-Marie and my good friend Teresa for patiently reading my work and giving me honest feedback and to my family and friends for their support and encouragement. And thank you to Brian Cook for proving that characters don't only exist in books.

PREFACE

He put his mouth to my ear, and his words sent waves of fresh terror through me. "I am going to savor you, little Sara. I had planned to have you now, but why rush when we can take all the time we want later."

"No..."

"But I think a taste first to whet the appetite." His face lowered as he forced my head to one side, baring my throat. His lips touched my skin, and his tongue lapped at the spot where my pulse beat. Blackness swam before my eyes.

"What is this?" he murmured and sniffed as if he was trying a new wine. His tongue touched my skin again. "You taste like – " His head whipped up, and his eyes glittered like he had just been served his favorite dessert. "You're a – "

1

"Y ou're late."

Malloy huffed as he slid into the booth across from me. "Don't get your panties in a knot. I got other business to tend to besides yours, you know."

I scowled and tapped my watch, and he threw up his hands. "I'm sorry, alright? Jesus, you're an impatient one."

"You're not the only one with places to be."

He harrumphed as if he could not imagine what someone my age had to do that was so important – if he only knew. I schooled my expression to hide the anxiety gnawing at me.

"Alright then. Where is it?" he asked.

I patted my chest where the small lump lay inside my coat and lowered my voice so no one outside our booth could hear it above Lynyrd Skynyrd blaring from the jukebox. "Half an ounce, as promised."

Malloy's brown eyes widened, and he leaned forward to rest his forearms on the table. Shorter than me by a few inches with a small pinched face and dull brown hair, he reminded me of a little brown field mouse. Not that I was fool enough to be taken in by his harmless appearance. You didn't survive in this business by being nice.

"Well, let's have it then." His eyes swept the dimly lit bar before settling back on me. I could have told him not to worry; the patrons at Jed's were good at minding their own business, which was why I'd suggested the biker bar in the first place. That, and the fact that Jed kept a wooden bat and a .44 behind the bar in case of trouble. No one was stupid enough to start something at Jed's.

I reached inside my coat and pulled out a rolled up paper bag. Malloy grabbed for it, but I pulled it out of his reach and put on my business face. "Payment first."

"Ah, yes." He made a sour face as he put a hand inside his jacket. His hand stilled. "This wasn't easy to come by, you know. Maybe – "

"We had a deal, Malloy." Damn it, I should have known he would try to pull this again, and on the one day I didn't have time for games. My cell phone was lying face down on the table. I picked it up.

"What are you doing?"

"What do you think?" I didn't look at him as I scrolled through my short contact list. "Half an ounce is worth ten of what you're paying for it, and you know it. But if you don't want to do business, I'll have to go through someone else." I bit my lip. I really didn't want to go elsewhere, and I was running out of time. If I had to wait even one more day to get what I came for, it wouldn't matter anymore. A day? Hell, hours was more like it.

"Excuse me. I need to make a call." I moved toward the edge of my seat, hoping he didn't see through my bluff.

"Wait." He sighed and pulled out a small square package wrapped in dirty gray cloth. Laying the package on the table, he covered it with his hand and slid it toward me. I did the same with the paper bag, and we made the exchange at the halfway point. I stifled a sigh of relief when my fingers closed around the package.

I lifted the cloth-wrapped package to my ear and shook it before I sniffed it to confirm its contents. Satisfied, I tucked it into an inside pocket and picked up my soda, taking a long sip to hide my eagerness to get out of there. It was never wise to appear desperate or hurried to people like Malloy; you might as well paint a big red target on your back.

Malloy tipped the paper bag and spilled a small glass vial onto his palm. His eyes glittered as he rolled the vial of yellowish-brown liquid between his fingers.

"Kid, I'd give my left gonad to know how you managed to get your hands on this stuff... and lived to tell about it."

I let out a short laugh to hide my nervousness. "Who said I'm telling?" I set my glass back on the table and inclined my head toward the vial. "I wouldn't show that off too much in public." What I really wanted to say was, "Put that goddamn stuff away before you get us both killed," but I refrained because it would not do to lose my cool.

"You don't need to tell me how to handle my affairs," he retorted, but at the same time he made the vial disappear with a sleight of hand that would do a magician proud.

"There is no way anyone can trace that back to me, right?" Malloy had a wide network and a reputation for discretion. But the contents of that vial could bring a lot of unwanted attention.

He sat up straighter. "Like I told you last time, I wouldn't be in business very long if I gave away my suppliers. And I got to protect my own head, too. I move my stuff through some middlemen who'd take the names of their business contacts to the grave. Ain't no profit in talking. And those guys have no idea where I obtain my merchandise. You can be sure I ain't telling anyone."

"I'm glad to hear that." I slid out of the booth. I'd stayed here too long already.

"Wait! I have some other items you might be interested in – if you can get more of this stuff, that is."

I stood and put my hand over the small bulge inside my coat. "I got what I came for. If I need anything else, I'll be in touch."

He shook his head. "You know, you are way too serious for a girl your age. You ought to loosen up, have fun every now and then."

I turned toward the exit. "Yeah, I get that a lot."

The sun's glare blinded me after the bar's gloomy interior, and I blinked a few times, sagging against the heavy wooden door. *God I hate this.* My hands trembled as I pulled up my sleeve to glance at my watch. "Damn it." I pushed away from the door, cursing Malloy for running late. My business with him would all have been for nothing if I stayed here much longer.

I pulled my short coat together and set out to meet Remy, making it to the bus stop two streets away just in time to catch the next bus. Sinking gratefully into a seat in the back, I leaned against the window and watched the streets and buildings flash by. We passed a football field where a practice game was in progress, and I watched a group of cheerleaders waving red and white pompoms. My hand went to the lump in my pocket and the weight of the responsibility I carried made me feel years older than the girls on the field.

The bus line ended near an old brewery that had gone out of business two years ago, and I jumped off in front of the padlocked gates. *No Trespassing* signs hung along the wire fence, and the whole place had a sad, deserted look about it. My nose twitched as it always did at the smell of sour barley that lingered there as I hurried past it.

Behind the brewery was an older subdivision of duplexes and two-story houses, most of them needing a fresh coat of paint. Five years ago this was a thriving neighborhood, before the brewery shut down along with the automotive parts plant that had employed half this area. Now, the lawns were overgrown and the cars in many of the driveways were badly in need of maintenance. A country song blared from someone's stereo, and in another house a young couple argued until a baby started to bawl loudly. I passed a group of younger kids playing road hockey, but they largely ignored me. I did stop for a moment to rub the head of a familiar lab-shepherd mix that trotted up to greet me, but when he started to follow me I shooed him back. He stared after me forlornly, but I was too busy to play today.

At the last stop sign, I turned right and jogged down an empty street lined with tired looking, boarded-up old houses and yards that backed up to the woods. I slipped between the last two houses and ducked under a broken board in the fence of the last house. Grass and weeds had taken over the backyard, while ivy strangled the ancient swing set and covered the back of the house. I followed a narrow path through the grass to the back door where I gave a quick look around and then slipped inside.

"Remy, you here?" I called softly.

It was dark in the house, except for the dusty bands of light that spilled in between the boards over the windows. Thankfully, I knew the house pretty well and I didn't need much light to find my way around. I left the kitchen and walked down a short hallway. On my right was the empty shell that used to be a living room, and on my left was the closed door to the den. I pushed the door, and it swung inward on creaky hinges.

"Remy?" I whispered loudly, trying to see through the dense shadows of the room. Silence greeted me. *Where the hell is he?* I spun around to go back the way I'd come.

"Argh!" I found myself face-to-face with a thin, pale gray face with large, round violet eyes and a mop of shaggy gray-brown hair. I stumbled back, and he reached for me, grabbing my shoulders in a strong grip that belied his slender build.

"Jesus, Remy!" I slapped a hand to my chest as he steadied me. "Are you *trying* to give me a heart attack?"

The troll gave me a lopsided grin, revealing a row of short sharp teeth. "You too young for heart attack," he said with a fierce little smirk that would send a chill through anyone who did not know him.

"You late," he chastised me.

"I'm sorry. Malloy was twenty minutes late, and I got here as fast as I could. How are they doing?"

"Not so bad. Fren worried, but I tell him if Sara say she get medicine, she will." He gave me an expectant look.

I smiled and pulled the package from inside my coat to lay it in his eager hands. "Have I ever let you down?"

Remy immediately turned and headed to the kitchen with me close on his heels. Curious about the contents of the package that had come at such a high price, I watched as he removed the cloth to reveal a small. rectangular wooden box. He lifted the lid and poured the contents out into a large, shallow stone bowl, then picked up a smooth rounded stone and began to grind whatever was in the bowl. I moved closer and saw pale golden crystals the texture and color of coarse cane sugar. As Remy ground the crystals into powder, the smell of rotten eggs and ammonia I'd gotten earlier grew stronger. I waved a hand in front of my nose. Definitely not sugar. Remy had called it *Baktu* when he asked me to find it, but he hadn't been too clear on exactly what it was, just that it came from some place in Africa.

He quickly reduced the crystals to powder; then he spat in the bowl several times and stirred the mixture with a smooth wooden stick to make a thick paste. "Come," he said at last, taking up the heavy bowl and heading for the stairs. I followed him quietly. My part was done, and the rest was up to my friend now.

In the first room at the top of the stairs, a pallet of rags had been laid on the bare wooden floor, and a small dark shape lay curled up on the rags, whimpering. The upstairs windows were not boarded up so I could make out the creature's rounded body and long spindly limbs. Kneeling by the pallet was a second creature, and his ugly squashed face looked at us hopefully when we entered the room. I gave him a smile and pointed at the bowl in Remy's hands, and he grunted softly to his mate, who replied in kind. I had no idea what they were saying because I didn't speak Boggie, but it didn't take much imagination to guess that he was reassuring her.

Remy knelt beside the pallet, and I stood behind him where I could observe but not get in the way. He laid the stone bowl on the floor and grunted at the boggies in their own language. Then he gently repositioned the female boggie until she lay on her back with her swollen belly bared to us. Boggies lived in bogs – as their name implied – and they were usually covered in mud. The female was unusually clean, and I wondered if Remy had done it in preparation for the procedure.

Fren, the male boggie, moved closer and took one of his mate's small hands in both of his. His large eyes brimmed with love, but it could not hide the fear I saw on his face. I wanted to tell him it would be okay, but he could not understand me and I wasn't sure if everything *would* be alright. According to Remy, boggies normally have easy births, but Mol's pregnancy had been very difficult. After being ill for months, she was very frail and her baby refused to come. Boggie pregnancies were not like human pregnancies where the baby came after nine months. If the mother was sick or weak, the body would not go into labor. If the baby was not delivered, both mother and child would die.

I watched as Remy began to smooth the paste over Mol's extended belly with gentle hands. She stiffened and made a weak mewling sound. This close to her, I could sense her pain and fear, and a familiar urge awoke in me – the need to go to her and try to take away the pain. But I trusted Remy, and right now he was Mol's best chance of getting through this. I just clenched my hands and observed.

He finished applying the thick paste and laid the bowl aside. Then he spread his long hands across Mol's belly and applied the slightest pressure against the bulge that was her unborn child. He started to chant in troll tongue, and I only recognized a handful of words, but they were enough to tell me that he was praying. Trolls were deeply faithful to their god, and they mixed prayer with their magic in whatever they do. I had seen enough of Remy's abilities to have great respect for his faith and his magic.

The paste soon dried to a brittle shell, and I noticed that Mol seemed to be in less pain now and able to bear the weight of Remy's hands. Was it working?

Mol's scream made the hair lift on the back of my neck. I fell to my knees beside Remy as Mol's stomach began to contract so violently that her whole body shook from it. "What's wrong?"

"This normal," he replied, lifting his hands from the boggie. "Baby coming."

"It's coming?" I asked dumbly. Mol looked like she was being ripped apart from the inside, not about to deliver a baby. But then I had no idea what was normal for a boggie birth. Like most of the People, boggies were secretive and shy of humans. It was a sign of their gratitude and respect that I was permitted to stay and witness this event. Tears filled my eyes as I watched nature take over and Mol's body find the strength it needed to bring her baby into the world.

Fren was there to take the infant when it arrived. The little brown body was incredibly small and doll-like and made no sound when its father cradled it in his arms. Fren stared at his newborn and ran his fingers over the infant's face as if he could not believe it was real.

"Shouldn't the baby be crying?" I whispered to Remy, trying not to disturb the boggies. Fren cooed at the baby, and Mol lay there with her eyes closed, too exhausted to even look at her child.

Remy nodded, his face grim.

That's when I felt it, the familiar pulling sensation drawing me toward the baby like steel to a magnet. I gasped softly. "He's sick, so sick..." The first icy tendrils of death brushed my skin, and I knew we were too late. If I'd only gotten here earlier.

I yanked off my coat. "Give him to me! Hurry, there's not much time." Already I could feel the new life draining away.

Remy reached for the baby, but Fren shook his head, holding the little body to his chest. Grunting forcefully, Remy leaned forward again. Whatever he said to the boggie worked because Fren relinquished the infant to him. I held out my hands, and Remy placed the naked, wrinkled little body in them. It was no bigger than a week-old kitten, and as soon as I touched it, I felt the weak fluttering heartbeat and the coldness already settling into the tiny limbs. "Try to hold on, little one," I murmured as I pulled him to my own chest and covered him with my hands. Then I reached inside of myself and opened the wall holding back my power.

It was like opening a furnace door. Heat flared in my chest and roared through my veins like a spark following a fuse. I didn't have to tell my power where to go; it always knew. My body buzzed like a live wire as currents of energy raced along my nerve endings toward my hands and chest, any part of me touching the dying creature.

Normally I released the power in a controlled stream, letting it flow gently to find the source of injury or illness. It was so strong, so forceful that I worried it would shock my patients and kill them outright. But when a body was shutting down and preparing to die, a jolt to the system was sometimes the only thing that could help it. It was kind of like those defibrillator paddles they used in emergency rooms, only mine worked on the whole body instead of just the heart. That was the only way I knew how to describe it; my power didn't exactly come with an operations manual.

The heat pooled in my hands until they gave off a pale white glow. Hotter and hotter, the fire burned until it felt like I was grasping a hot metal pipe, but I didn't stop. I bit my lip to keep from crying out and held on, waiting for the power to grow to the right intensity before I released it.

Power exploded from my hands, pouring into the little body. I felt it race through veins and bones and weave through tissue, saturating every cell like a spring storm soaking the earth. My power was an extension of me, so I felt it coiling around the failing heart, pulsing and surging. With each push it sent a spike of energy through the heart, causing the creature to jerk and spasm before it went still again. I sent wave after wave of power into the body, praying that each would be the one to fix the damaged heart.

I lost track of the minutes but at least ten passed before I was forced to accept that I could not save the boggie. My power was the only thing making his heart pump, and I could not keep it up much longer. One of the earliest and cruelest lessons I had learned about my power was that sometimes I couldn't save someone, no matter how much of myself I poured into them. I held the baby away from me and felt a painful tug at my chest when I looked at its lifeless face. *I'm so sorry, little one.*

A broken sob rent the air. I opened my eyes to meet Mol's stricken stare as she grieved for the baby she had never held in her own arms. My heart ached for her. No one should watch the one they loved die.

It's not fair! We had done everything right. Mol's baby deserved to live.

I pulled the power back to me until my hands grew hot again. The pain lanced through me, but I barely felt it buried beneath the anger building inside me. I sent power shooting back through the baby with the force of a lightning strike. That much energy could stop a heart completely, but there was nothing to lose now.

The power drained away. I was used up and vaguely aware of Remy and Fren breathing and Mol sobbing as the little heart pressed against mine gave a long irregular flutter and stopped.

There was only silence.

Then... lub-lub, lub-lub, lub-lub.

Then the slightest of movements as tiny lungs expanded with their first breath of air.

Then the tickle of a tiny foot moving against my chest.

I lifted the infant cupped in my hands and watched in wonder as the squashed little face quivered and the tiny mouth opened. It started as a faint wheezing sound that quickly became a mewling wail, and suddenly my hands were full of a squirming, crying, healthy baby boggie.

I laughed and cried at the same time as shouts filled the room. Mol grunted anxiously and held out her arms, and I lay her baby boy on her chest. I watched as mother and father touched their child with awe, exploring the baby they both thought they had lost.

I sat back heavily and then lay down on the dusty floor. Healings always drained me, some more than others, and normally I just needed a few minutes of rest to put me right again. But bringing back a life from so close to death was very hard, and my body felt like I had run half a marathon. No matter how many times I used my power, it did not get easier.

I was six when I discovered what I could do. In the beginning, I often overdid it, until I learned not to drain myself too much. It was easy to overlook your own welfare when you were trying to save a life. I had to learn how to lock my power away unless I needed to call on it. Otherwise, every time I came within a few feet of a sick or injured creature, the energy got sucked right out of me. Now when I healed, I let out just enough to do the job.

Releasing a torrent of power like I'd just done for the boggie was almost like overloading a circuit, except there was no breaker to reset my energy. My power always replenished itself; it just took a little while.

A cool hand touched my arm. "You okay, Sara?" I heard the worry in Remy's voice, and I gave him a weary smile.

"I'll be fine. You know how I am. Just need to rest a bit."

"Yes, you rest." He gently lifted my head and stuffed my folded jacket beneath it. I heard him talking to Fren and Mol and sounds of movement, but it all became muffled as I drifted off.

Somewhere between wakefulness and sleep I felt a familiar stirring in the back of my mind. After expending so much power, I was not surprised it was on the move. It was always active after a healing when my power was low. Not that it would get far. Even exhausted, I had enough left in me to push it back down.

I called it the beast. It used to scare me having this dark thing inside my head, even though I knew it came with my power. I read a quote once that said, "When you light a candle, you also cast a shadow," and I wondered if the same was true for me. My power was the candle – bright and warm – and the beast was its shadow – sullen and dark. Remy said that most power was a balance of good and bad, and I should not be afraid of something that was a part of me. I did not embrace the beast, but I had no choice but to learn to live with it.

The room was quiet when I woke up, and the long shadows told me it was late afternoon. Turning my head to the side, I saw I was alone. The boggies had most likely gone home, but I knew Remy was still here. He would never leave me alone while I recovered.

I groaned as I got to my feet. My body ached, partly from the intense healing and partly from lying on the hard floor, and I stretched several times to get the kinks out. Then I picked up my coat and went downstairs where I found Remy looking out through the cracks in one of the boarded-up living room windows. I walked over and leaned against the wall, ignoring the peeling wallpaper that snagged my hair.

He smiled down at me. "You sleep deep this time. Feel better?"

"That was a hard one," I admitted. "But worth it." I heard laughter outside, and I peered through the crack at a group of teenage boys hanging out down the street. Remy had been watching them in case any of them decided to venture this way while I slept. I wondered what they'd do if they came in and found a troll waiting for them. Probably wet their pants. If I didn't know my fierce friend, I'd probably do the exact same thing.

"Mol and the baby are okay?" I asked.

"Yes. Fren and Mol take baby home to show family. They say you have big magic. Ask if you are sorceress."

"Hardly." If any magic had happened here today, it had come from Remy, the way he'd helped Mol deliver her baby. Though he didn't have my power, he was as much a healer as I was, and his knowledge of medicines never failed to amaze me. In troll years he was still a teenager like me, but he already knew more than I could hope to learn in a lifetime.

He looked at the street again. "It get dark soon."

"Not for another hour. And I'm not afraid of the dark."

"Uncle will not be happy if you stay out late."

"Nate's not happy about most things I do," I quipped. Remy shot me a disapproving look, and I said, "You know it's true. I love Nate, but we're just so...different. He wants me to be someone I'm not. He wants a normal niece who has girlfriends and joins the band or the cheerleading squad or whatever. That's not me, and it never will be."

"That not true. He just want you to be happy."

I raised an eyebrow. "Since when are you an expert on human parents?"

"All good parents want children to be happy." He pushed away from the window. "Come. Boys leave."

I poked him in the back as I followed him to the back door. "You know, you're getting kind of bossy these days."

He let out a gravelly laugh. "Not even trolls boss you."

"That's right! I'm a strong, independent woman, and don't you forget it."

We crossed the yard and slipped through the fence. Remy turned to me. "You do good today."

"*We* did good," I said. "By the way, you never did tell me what Baktu is."

"Baktu is winged serpent from desert lands."

My brows drew together. "Huh? How does a serpent turn to crystals?"

"Crystals not serpent. It dried Baktu droppings."

"Droppings? You mean poop?" I wrinkled my nose. "Ugh! That's disgusting, Remy!"

Remy laughed and started for the woods. "Baktu is poisonous serpent. Droppings make strong medicine."

Before I could reply he disappeared. I envied the way trolls could melt into their surroundings like vanishing into thin air. It'd be a handy skill to have at times.

The streets were empty when I walked back to the bus stop. Even though it was a Saturday evening, not a lot of people were headed into town, so there were plenty of seats to choose from on the bus. The same driver always drove this route on weekends, and he nodded at me when I dropped my change in the farebox.

At least I could relax on the return trip, because Remy and I had done what we'd set out to do. I'd helped save two lives today – how many girls my age got to say that? Not that I enjoyed hanging out in smoky bars, doing illicit business with people who were the underworld equivalent of drug dealers. Just because I had enough wits to keep a cool façade and act like I knew what I was doing did not change the fact that I was in way over my head. But I couldn't stop now, not when lives depended on me.

When Remy asked me two years ago to help him find powdered chimera horn to help a dying kelpie, I had no idea there was an actual black market for that, and practically anything else you can think of – if you could pay. Since then I'd found half a dozen other items for him, and I also got pretty good at negotiating since none of them were cheap or easy to find. It's not like you could buy hydra scales or hansling teeth on Amazon or eBay. Well, not yet anyway.

We were lucky Remy could afford to buy pretty much anything. Of course there were some things more valuable than even money, like the contents of the vial I'd given Malloy, rare and nearly impossible to obtain. He'd sell his own mother to know how I'd gotten my hands on it, but I'd never tell him – or anyone else. It was dangerous enough just letting someone like Malloy know that I had some to trade. People killed for a hell of a lot less. And if Remy's people ever found out what we were up to... I shuddered at the thought.

Troll bile was a potent drug and priceless, not just because of what it could do but also because there were few brave enough to try to get it. Trolls were not only secretive and elusive; their vicious reputation kept humans and nonhumans alike from seeking them out, let alone trying to take something from them.

It disgusted me when Remy first told me about it. But if you could get past the ungodly smell and not think about where it came from, it had incredible regenerative properties. It could slow aging and degenerative diseases such as Alzheimer's or Parkinson's, and it could reverse balding. I heard it could even fight certain types of cancer. I knew from experience that it couldn't fix *every* injury, but half an ounce, like what I'd given Malloy, could stop someone from aging for up to five years if used properly. It was basically the fountain of youth, and there were people who would pay almost anything to get their hands on it.

The younger the troll, the more potent the bile, but trolls were so protective of their young that it was nearly impossible to get close to them without meeting a horrible end. Remy gave me his own bile to barter with on his behalf, but his people would be furious if they ever got wind of what we were peddling. Trolls didn't like humans, though for some reason the elders tolerated Remy's friendship with me. But I didn't kid myself about where I stood with them. I was still just a human.

The bus pulled up to my downtown stop in front of the post office, and I waved to the driver as I exited by the rear door. Market Street, the financial and commercial hub of New Hastings during the week, was quiet now except for the people heading to Subway or Antonio's. I crossed at the light and cut through the small parking lot between two buildings to come out on the end of the waterfront near the wharves. South of me were the pier and the shops and restaurants that lined the waterfront. Almost home. After the day I'd had, all I wanted was to curl up in bed with a book for the rest of the night.

When two boys emerged from between the buildings ahead of me and ran across the waterfront to disappear down the bank by one of the fishing wharves, I recognized them right away. I knew they were probably up to no good, but I was too tired and hungry to care. *Let someone else deal with them.*

Out of sight, one of the boys let out a familiar laugh and yelled, "Don't let it get away."

I stopped walking.

"Look at it, Scott. It's half-dead."

"Ah hell!" I swore and turned toward the wharf.

2

I looked down at Scott Foley and Ryan Walsh on the beach below me. Tall and good looking with straight dark hair, Scott stood with his back slightly toward me. Ryan, who was a few inches shorter than Scott, stood several feet behind him, looking like he would rather be somewhere else.

"Leave it alone." Ryan ran a hand through his blond curls. "This is not cool, man."

"Dude, when did you turn into such a pussy?" Scott scoffed. "I'm only having some fun, and like you said, it's half-dead already."

My fists clenched, and I scoured the beach for whatever animal they were talking about. Seeing nothing, I moved closer to the edge of the bank to get a wider view.

I let out a yelp as my foot slipped out from under me, sending me tumbling down the four-foot embankment to land in an undignified heap at the feet of the two startled boys. Not exactly the entrance I would have chosen.

For a moment neither of them moved. Then Ryan crouched and peered at my face through the curtain of dark hair that had come loose from my ponytail. "Whoa. You okay?"

"I'm fine." I pushed my hair back out of my face and got to my feet, wincing at the pain in my left ankle. I put my weight on it to test it. A light sprain maybe. Great.

I faced the boys and found Scott's wide-eyed gaze fixed on me. He narrowed his eyes when he realized who he was staring at. "What do you want?"

My eyes left his to scan the beach. What the hell were they after? "You guys look like you're searching for something. Anything I can help you find?"

"No," Scott retorted. His eyes went to a spot behind me, and I followed his gaze but saw nothing but a pile of old fishing nets.

"Are you sure, because – ?" I broke off when the nets made a plaintive mewling sound. In the fading light I saw them move as a scrawny gray tabby emerged. The cat was a sorry sight. Its ribs stuck out painfully, and it walked unsteadily for a few seconds before sinking down on its hind legs.

I whirled on Scott and Ryan, my eyes blazing. "You were going to hurt that cat!"

"No." Ryan could not meet my eyes. "I wouldn't…"

Scott shifted from one foot to the other. "Yeah right. Like we'd waste our time with that flea bag."

I stepped between them and the cat. Scott and I had known each other since elementary school, and if I knew one thing about him, it was how to tell when he was lying. "This is low, even for you, Scott."

A flush crept across his cheeks. "I told you I couldn't care less about a stupid cat. And what's it to you anyway?"

"You think I'll let you hurt a defenseless animal?" My voice rose. Scott always managed to irritate me, but for some reason I was having trouble keeping my anger in check this time. "Is this how you get your kicks on a Saturday night? Does this make you feel big and manly?"

"Shut up!" Scott glared at me, and for a second I thought I saw something else in his eyes that looked like regret, but it was gone as soon as it appeared.

Scott and I had been friends for a time way back in elementary school. He was the first person to approach me when I moved here, even though his buddies teased him about making friends with a girl. Our friendship was short-lived, ending the day I caught him and some other boys throwing rocks at an injured crow outside the school. I'd yelled at him, pushed him to the ground, and told him I could never be friends with someone like him. Any feelings of friendship he had for me quickly changed to animosity after I embarrassed him in front of the whole school like that.

"Make me shut up." Even as I said the words, I wondered what the hell I was doing. Why was I goading someone who had six inches and at least forty pounds on me – and who already couldn't stand me?

Scott's face darkened. "If you know what's good for you, Grey, you'll get out of my face."

"Or what?" I took a step toward him. "You going to beat me up, too?"

"Whoa! No one's beating anyone up." Ryan laid a hand on Scott's arm. "Come on, Scott, let's go. This is not worth it, man."

Scott shook off Ryan's hand. "No one talks to me like that."

Try to stop me. The thought flitted maliciously across my mind. Another voice told me to calm down and step back, but I ignored it. Instead, I let out a mocking laugh. "Come on then, and shut me up if you can. If you're man enough, that is."

Scott's eyes glittered dangerously as he took a step toward me.

"Dude, you can't fight a girl." Ryan sounded scared now.

"Shut up, Ryan," Scott and I said at the same time. I gave Scott a cheeky grin, and his nostrils flared.

I glanced down at my coat and let out a sigh. "Just try not to bleed too much, okay. It's a bitch to get blood out of this thing."

Scott made a choked sound, and Ryan yelled something as Scott raised his right arm. I didn't know if he intended to strike me. I wasn't even sure Scott knew what he was going to do.

Roaring filled my ears and a strange prickling heat spread through my body. It felt nothing like the fiery power I'd released a few hours ago. This fire held no healing, just rage and wild exhilaration like a lion set free from its cage. In the back of my mind the beast stretched and swelled with joy. I blinked, and it was like a veil lifted from my eyes, bringing the world into startling focus.

My right fist connected with Scott's cheek before he even realized I had swung. I barely registered the pain in my knuckles as I watched him stagger back several feet from the force of my blow. *Again*, cried the beast, and my other hand curled into a fist.

Scott recovered faster than I expected, and I ducked just in time to avoid the brunt of the powerful fist that would surely have knocked me senseless. I felt a sharp pain in my lower lip as his fist clipped it, and a coppery taste filled my mouth.

"Scott!" Ryan yelled, his voice muffled in my ears. "What the hell are you doing?"

Moving faster than I could have believed possible, my left fist plowed into Scott's chin and spun him off balance. I pivoted on the foot I was sure I'd sprained just a few minutes ago and delivered a well-aimed kick to his midsection, a move I had never even attempted before. He doubled over with an agonized moan that made my lips curl into a wicked little smile. The beast crowed with glee.

Scott roared and came at me like an enraged bull, but I sidestepped his charge and he stumbled past me. Behind me, I heard Ryan smother a laugh, but that only seemed to anger Scott more. He turned and came at me with both arms raised.

My hand moved so fast it seemed to blur as my fist met Scott's nose with a sickening crunch. He fell to his knees with both hands over his face. "You bitch!" he wailed. "You broke my nose!"

Standing over him with my hands on my hips, I savored the delicious triumph at seeing my opponent brought low. I reveled in how easy it had been to take down a boy who was bigger and stronger than me. Heady with power, I spat, "You're lucky that's all I broke, you asshole."

"Jesus, Sara!"

I felt Ryan's eyes on me, and I took in his stunned expression as his gaze moved from me to his moaning friend. It was like a bucket of cold water in my face. The rage drained out of me along with the bizarre heat that had enveloped me a few minutes ago. *What am I doing?* I thought as the world around me returned to normal and I stared aghast at Scott's bloody face. His nose was swelling grotesquely, and bruises were already beginning to show around his eyes. I was no angel, but I had never inflicted this kind of beating on another person. The knowledge of what I'd done made my stomach churn.

"Scott, I – "

"Stay away from me, you fucking lunatic!" he growled, throwing a hand up to keep me from coming near him. As he spoke, a spray of blood dotted the rocks in front of him.

I backed away, sick with remorse as he staggered to his feet. What the hell had come over me and made me go all berserker on him? I was mad about the cat, yes, but Scott would have gone on his way if I had left well enough alone. I'd baited him and deliberately made him angry, and I had struck first. The memory of my fist hitting his face filled me with disgust. It was as if I'd been possessed, and if Ryan hadn't spoken and woken me up, there was no telling what I might have done.

"We were just messing around. You know he wouldn't have hurt the cat, right?" Ryan asked, forcing me to look up and meet his gaze, to see the truth on his face.

He turned away to help Scott climb the embankment. As soon as I was alone I sank down to sit on the ground, pulling my knees up and wrapping my arms around them. It was the beast. I always kept a tight grip on it, but whenever I used up some of my power for a healing, I felt it stirring, pressing against the walls that imprisoned it. Today I'd depleted my power so much that I lost control of it – and look what had happened.

I hadn't fought since I was ten and never with such intent to hurt someone. Hell, I'd never *moved* like that before. No wonder Ryan had looked at me like I was some kind of circus freak.

A weak meow intruded upon my unhappy thoughts, and I lifted my head to see the scrawny little cat sitting beside me. Up close he looked even more pitiful with half a tail, one ear in tatters, and his whole body wavering like a breeze would blow him over.

"Hey there, kitty." I reached out to stroke the back of his head. He hissed but didn't try to run away, which told me how sick he was. Animals were drawn to me, especially the sick ones. I think they could sense my power even when it was locked away. Even so, the feral ones needed a little encouragement to get past their natural fear of humans.

I opened my power to let a wave of soothing calm sweep over him, and within thirty seconds he stopped hissing and leaned against my leg. As soon as my fingers made contact, I sent a stream of healing energy into his frail body and he immediately laid down. My hand moved down his back, feeling the bones almost poking through his skin as I sought out his injuries. He had mange and his fur was full of fleas, but there were no broken bones. I got rid of the fleas and mange, took care of a few cuts and scrapes and knocked a respiratory infection out of his lungs before I pulled back my hand, satisfied he would be okay.

"There. You're still one of the sorriest looking things I've ever seen, but I think you'll make it." I stood slowly, a little drained from my second healing today. "Stay away from those mean boys from now on, you hear me."

The cat's amber eyes met mine, and he let out a sad yowl.

"None of that," I warned him as my heart felt a little tug. "I can't take you with me. I'm not supposed to bring home any more strays."

He got up and walked unsteadily over to rub his thin body against my calves. Even through my jeans I could feel the outline of his ribs.

"No fair." I sighed and bent down to scoop him up. He began to purr as soon as I cradled him in my arms. "Okay, you can come home with me for now, but I can't guarantee anything. My uncle's not exactly a cat person, and he still hasn't forgiven me for the last houseguest I brought home."

The steel door swung open noiselessly on well-oiled hinges, and I slipped inside, easing it shut behind me. Silence greeted me. I started to smile, but it turned into a wince when the split in my lip stung. Eyes watering, I crossed the storeroom to the far wall and set the cat on the floor. I climbed one of the sturdy shelving units to the ceiling where I stuck my hand under one of the tiles and pulled out a small, black metal box. Inside the box were a few hundred dollars and a tiny vial of troll bile half the size of the one I'd given Malloy. The bile was my own personal stash that Remy insisted I keep on hand for emergencies. I usually healed very fast and hardly ever got sick – a benefit of having healing power – but it wouldn't do for Nate to see me with a fat lip.

I uncorked the bottle, tipped it to wet my finger and dabbed the pungent liquid to my swollen lip and bruised knuckles. There was an instant burning sensation, then blessed numbness as the sting faded away. I didn't need a mirror to know that my lip was already mending and in no time it would be healed completely. The bile didn't heal broken bones, but it made cuts and bruises disappear in minutes. I dabbed a bit on my knuckles and watched the redness fade from them, trying not to think of Scott who was probably having his nose reset right now. I corked the vial and put the box back in the ceiling, thinking that if anyone should have the bile right now it was him.

"Come on, cat." I picked him up again and headed for the stairs.

Nate and I had a whole building to ourselves, which was actually pretty cool. Years ago the first floor used to house a bookstore, but it went out of business when the large chain stores came to town. After that, Nate decided that being a landlord was too much hassle. He didn't really need the rent, so he decided not to lease the space again. We lived in the two-story apartment upstairs, and the bottom floor was mostly used for storage now and Nate's home gym.

I dragged my tired body up the stairs and slipped quietly into the apartment. Sounds from the den told me Nate was at work on his computer. I crept past the open door, hoping he was too involved in his work to notice my entrance.

"You missed dinner again."

I backtracked and stood in the doorway wearing an apologetic smile. "Sorry, I lost track of time."

Nate looked at me over the top of his monitor, and I met his green eyes that were so like my own. With the same chestnut hair and golden skin we resembled each other so much that people often mistook us for father and daughter. Nate's hair was already streaked with gray, making him look a little older than his thirty-nine years, but I thought the gray suited him. Or maybe I told myself that to feel better about being guilty of putting some of that gray there.

His hair was mussed, and the shadows under his eyes told me he wasn't getting enough sleep again. He had been working night and day on his latest book, barely coming out to eat and sleep; he always got like that when he was near the end of the first draft. Nate wrote military suspense novels, and he was on the fourth book in his series. His work was very good. He didn't know it, but I read all his books.

"What on earth have you been up to? You look like you've been in a fight." There was no accusation in his voice, just disappointment. I opened my mouth in denial, but he said, "You have blood on your coat."

"Oh." I frowned at the spots of dried blood on the front of my tan coat. "This is my favorite one, too. I'd better put it in cold water."

"Sara," he said in warning tone. I stopped, and he sighed heavily. "What happened?"

I made a face. "You say that like I'm out there brawling every other day."

"So you were in a fight."

Busted. "I had a perfectly good reason." I held up the cat so he could see it over his monitor.

Nate stared at the scrawny bundle of fur in my arms. "Is that thing alive?"

"Of course it's alive!" I stroked the cat's head, and he purred loudly. "Do you think I'd be walking around with a dead cat?"

"Do you want me to answer that?"

I made a face. "Didn't I tell you? I'm into voodoo now, and I thought I'd start with zombie cats." I wondered what he'd think if he knew there were people out there who really could reanimate corpses.

He stared at me like he was trying to decide if that was a joke. I used the opportunity to try to slip away.

"Not so fast. You still didn't tell me what happened. Sit."

I took the chair in front of the desk and laid the cat on my lap as Nate maneuvered his motorized chair around the desk. He parked it two feet from me and said, "Spill it."

I told him about seeing Scott and Ryan chasing the cat and how I followed them to the beach. With as little detail as possible, I related the altercation between me and Scott, making the fight sound more like a shoving match than a fight. I still felt so ashamed and afraid of what I'd done that I really didn't want to relive it.

"So where did the blood come from?"

"Um... this poor little guy is all scratched up. It must have come from him."

He cast a suspicious look at the cat. "Speaking of your new friend – what do you plan to do with him?"

"I don't know," I said honestly. "Clean him up and feed him for now."

Nate was silent for a long moment. I waited for the double scolding – one for fighting and the other for bring home yet another stray. My uncle wasn't an animal hater. He just liked order in his home, and animals weren't exactly the tidiest roommates.

As if on cue, Daisy, our three-legged Beagle, limped into the room. I don't know how she lost her leg. I used to see her around the waterfront, and it amazed me how well she moved on three legs. One day, six months ago, she didn't move fast enough and got hit by a car. Healing her took a lot out of me, but I saved her. Nate was not happy when I came home with a dog, but who could put a three-legged dog out on the street? Now Daisy was his almost constant companion, and though Nate would never admit it, I knew he liked her company.

Daisy came over to me and sniffed, and the cat let out a warning hiss. Chastised, the dog sat back on her haunches to watch the newcomer from a safe distance.

"Sara, you're seventeen, too old to be fighting with boys down at the wharf no matter what the reason." I tried to speak up, but he held up a hand. "You spend too much time alone when you should be going out with your friends, having fun. And you should be dating boys – not fighting with them."

I squirmed on my chair. I was pretty sure no other teenage girl had a parent telling them to go out to parties and date. "I have friends," I argued weakly. Okay, maybe I had never dated and I wasn't a social butterfly, but I did have friends. As for girls, well they didn't seem to warm up to me much. I didn't know why. It wasn't that they hated me; they just didn't seem comfortable around me.

Nate scoffed. "Friends like Greg, you mean? There's a model of good behavior. I suppose that's where you learned to fight."

"Greg is not a bad guy – and no, he didn't teach me to fight. Just because he's a biker doesn't make him a criminal." There was that *one* thing, but I didn't think juvenile records counted once you reached eighteen. And I wasn't about to bring that up to Nate.

"He might not be a criminal, but he's no angel either."

I had to suppress a smile because Nate was right about that. Greg was definitely no angel. A year older than me, Greg was already the school badass when I started high school and met him for the first time. He grew up working in his uncle's bike shop, and he was tougher and brawnier than half the senior boys and not afraid to show it. There was something about the roguish tilt of his head and the gleam in his green eyes when he smiled – or scowled at you – that either drew you in or scared the heck out of you. I wasn't sure if it was the way he did his own thing without a care for anyone's opinion or the fact that he could have bullied anyone in school and chose not to, but I liked him immediately. He didn't really associate with the other students, so I wasn't sure why he'd decided to befriend me. One day he just started sitting with me at lunch, and when he got his first bike he gave me rides and took me to Jed's with him and his friends. I'd even had a crush on him for a short while until his friend Mike told me I reminded them of Greg's younger cousin, which put a damper on any romantic notions I had for him.

I missed Greg. He and Mike had moved to Philadelphia right after graduation to work for Mike's uncle who owned an automotive parts plant. It wasn't the best job in the world, but as long as it paid the rent and kept his bike running, Greg was happy. We kept in touch through email, but it had been over a week since I'd last heard from him.

"Greg moved to Philly, remember? I haven't seen him since June."

"Well, I won't pretend to be sad about that." He tapped the arm of his chair. "What about Roland? I remember when you two used to be inseparable. And Peter, too."

"We still hang out. We just like to do some different things now; that's all." It wasn't that Roland didn't try to include me, and I *did* go to an occasional party with him. I just wasn't into partying as much as my best friend. Roland understood that even if no one else did.

"It seems like you've become more closed off the last few years. It's not healthy to shut everyone out." He ran a hand through his hair. "It's my fault. I left you alone too much when you were younger. I know I'm not your father... I just wish I knew how to get through to you." He gave me a pleading look. "You spend so much time alone or off doing God knows what. I have no idea where you are or what you're doing."

"Nate, I – " I faltered, because we always seemed to end up here. I mean, what was I supposed to say? *"Hey, Nate, guess what? I saved a life today. I have this amazing power that lets me heal things. But I can't fix your spine because it doesn't work on humans. By the way, can I invite my troll friend over for dinner?"*

He pressed a button on his chair, and it began to back around the desk again. "Go get some dinner. I left lasagna in the oven for you."

I carried the cat to the kitchen and found a can of tuna for him, making a mental note to pick up some food for him tomorrow. Daisy followed us, and I poured some food into her dish before I popped my own dinner in the microwave.

Nate's lasagna was one of my favorite foods, but I could have been eating cardboard and not noticed it with the myriad of emotions swirling through me. What had happened to me on the beach? In the span of a few hours I went from saving a life to hurting someone. Seeing what I was capable of freaked me out more than a little.

To top it all off I had lied to Nate again. I sat quietly at our small kitchen table, pushing my food around with my fork. I hated deceiving Nate, but there were too many things in my life that I couldn't tell him about. It was easier to let him be disappointed in me than to try to tell him the truth.

I wished there was a way to bridge the distance between us. He was all the family I had, and I knew my dad would have wanted us to be close. It wasn't Nate's fault; he had been a good parent to me after my dad's death. I was pretty messed up when I came here, and I never opened up to him as much as I could have. And then I discovered Remy and the real world, and suddenly I had all these secrets I couldn't share with anyone.

It's not that I didn't care, because I loved Nate more than anything in the world. We just had so little in common. Nate was one of those people who didn't believe in the paranormal or supernatural or anything that did not have a solid scientific explanation. He never read fantasy fiction or watched supernatural movies or TV shows. It drove him nuts when I watched *Buffy* reruns, so I usually watched them in my room. In some ways, he was more closed off than I was, and I wasn't sure he could handle learning about my power and the real world around him.

I rinsed my plate and retreated upstairs with the cat in my arms. The top floor of our building was split into an attic and an open space that served as my bedroom, kind of like a loft apartment without the kitchen. On one side stood my bed, dresser, and desk. Beneath the large window on the other side was a faded green couch that was barely visible under the clothes and books strewn across it, and beside the couch were two tall overflowing bookcases. My dad had been an English teacher, and he had loved books, especially the classics. He used to say "No man can be called friendless who has God and the companionship of good books." I looked it up a few years ago and found that it came from Elizabeth Barrett Browning. Sometimes I'm not too sure about God, but I agree with my dad and Browning about books. I've read all of his books and added my own to the collection. I think he'd be pleased to know I grew up to share his passion for reading.

The walls of my room were bare except for a few pictures of my dad and some of me, Roland, and Peter. Roland called the room depressingly empty and lamented the fact that I refused to replace my dad's old stereo with a newer one. But I liked my space. It was private and I had my own bathroom, even if it was the size of a closet. The best part was that the room had lots of windows with a wide view of the bay. What more could a girl want?

"Alright cat, let's get you cleaned up before you go anywhere near my furniture." I grabbed Daisy's shampoo and a towel and proceeded to wash the filthy animal from head to toe. He was too lethargic from his meal and the healing to put up much of a fight, and he purred like a little engine when I toweled him dry. I set him down on an old blanket on the couch, and he stretched happily and curled into a ball, completely at home.

After I set up the litter box used by our last feline guest, I left the cat to his nap and jumped in the shower, hoping the hot water would wash away more than the grime from today's events. But nothing could cleanse me of the memories of what had happened with Scott. I had always thought of myself as a good person, but only a monster would relish hurting a person the way I had. I shivered despite the hot water flowing over me.

My thoughts went to the little boggie family as I dried myself, and I wondered how they were doing. Instead of grieving the loss of a child tonight, Fren and Mol were at home with their new baby. I had saved a life today – that had to count for something. Was that enough to redeem me for the awful thing I'd done after?

Dressed in a cami and my favorite pajama bottoms, I popped in a Fleetwood Mac CD and carried my sketchbook over to the bed. I'd inherited my dad's CD collection, along with his love for seventies rock. It was one of the few things Nate and I had in common – our taste in music – and he even borrowed CDs on occasion. I shook off my regret as I flipped open the sketchbook to a clean page. If it wasn't for this whole secret life thing I had going on, my uncle and I might have been a lot closer than we were.

I thought about the boggies, summoning an image of the tiny boggie infant I'd held in my arms. My pencil flew over the paper as I tried to capture his likeness. I drew him in my hands because that was my clearest picture of him, the moment he opened his mouth and bawled for the first time. When I was finished, I smiled at the drawing of the little creature, his squashed face scrunched up unhappily and his tiny mouth open in a silent cry. I was no da Vinci, but my sketches weren't half bad. It wasn't like I shared them with anyone anyway.

A tapping at one of the windows drew my attention away from my sketch, and I ran over to open the window to admit a large black crow. He cawed and flapped around the room a few times before landing on my outstretched hand.

"Harper, it's about time you came home," I scolded him, stroking the soft feathers at the back of his neck. He'd been gone for two days, and I was worried he'd gotten into trouble. Technically, he didn't live with us, but he liked to hang out here, especially on the roof. He had kind of adopted me after I saved him from Scott, but he still liked to go off and do his own thing.

"If you're hungry, there's food in your dish," I told him when he shifted restlessly, a cue that he wanted a treat. I wasn't surprised when he left my hand, flew out the window, and headed for the roof. More than once I'd suspected he understood me when I talked to him. I read that crows were very intelligent, and Harper had gotten a good dose of my power when I'd healed him. Who knew what other effects my power had on animals?

I left the window open for him and sat down at my laptop to check out the online activity. Today was the second time I'd used troll bile to purchase medicine for Remy, and I was paranoid as hell that someone would trace it back to me, and especially to Remy. It was the main reason I dealt only with Malloy. For all his crafty ways, Malloy was very discreet about his business. In his line of work he had to be if he didn't want to end up gutted in an alley.

The message boards were busy. There was no mention of troll bile, but another thread caught my eye – one about vampire activity in Portland. Vampires were the most common topic discussed on the boards, and there were always tons of posts about vampire sightings, though it was pretty easy to distinguish the real deal from the hype. I'd never seen a vampire, but I knew plenty about them, mostly learned from Remy, and my education had taught me that Hollywood and fiction writers had absolutely no clue.

Vampires usually kept to large cities where their hunting could be camouflaged by the higher crime rate. They lived in covens and liked to hunt in small packs, and while they were mostly active at night, mature vamps could handle exposure to daylight as long as it wasn't direct sunlight and not for long periods. Younger vamps, those less than a hundred years old, were not strong enough to withstand even a minute of daylight. Most vamps, young and old, wouldn't risk the chance of meeting the sun, so they stayed hidden during the day.

And there were no solitary vamps wandering the earth with tortured souls waiting to be saved by true love. Vampires were pure evil, and their only redeeming quality was that they could be killed with the right weapons. Unfortunately, if a human got close enough to see a vampire in the flesh, chances were they would not survive to talk about it.

The posting about Portland caught my attention because Portland was a little over an hour from New Hastings, and I used to live there with my dad. There usually wasn't that much talk about the Portland area because its population was not big enough to hide unusual activity. So when I read that four teenage girls, all seventeen and eighteen, had disappeared in the last two weeks, a chill went through me. All the girls were reported as suspected runaways, though they had taken nothing with them and none of their friends believed they would run away. None of the girls knew each other, and the police had no leads. The poster said it looked like a vampire was at work in the area.

Bile rose in my throat. Vampires took great pleasure in torturing their victims before they drain them. And what they left behind... A shudder passed through me as an image came unbidden to my mind. I closed my eyes, but the scene had been seared into my brain.

I gritted my teeth and waited for the old fear and pain to pass. At times like this I wanted nothing more than to climb into bed and hide under my covers. But I didn't. If there were vampires in Maine, I had to know.

The rest of the thread did not offer any more information other than the girls had all disappeared at night. The user who had started the thread was a regular on the site, and we talked often. He really knew his stuff, so I pinged him and asked for a private chat. Within minutes, he popped up in a separate window.

Wulfman: Sup, PG? Been a while.
PixieGirl: Yeah, been busy. Reading your post. Vamps in Portland?
Wulfman: According to my sources. Weird though. Not their usual scene.
PixieGirl: Wonder what brings them back to Portland.
Wulfman: Back? What do you know?
Pause.
PixieGirl: Knew someone killed by vamps ten years ago.
Wulfman: Wow. I never knew. Sorry.
PixieGirl: You remember any activity back then?
Wulfman: I wasn't on the scene then. I can check my sources and get back to you.
PixieGirl: Thanks.
Wulfman: It would help if I had the name of your friend who died.
Long pause.
Wulfman: Still there?
PixieGirl: Yeah. His name was Daniel Grey.

3
___

The sparrow twitched restlessly in my hands, so I opened them and watched him take flight, his newly healed wing moving like it had never been broken. I giggled as he circled my head happily a few times then flew up to perch on a branch above me.

"I hope you're more careful next you see that old tom cat," I told him as I stood and brushed dirt off my jeans. I pulled on my mittens and set off across the small park at the end of our street. The sky was heavy with gray clouds, and I could smell snow in the air. If we got enough snow this time, Daddy promised to take me sledding. My pace picked up, and I hurried home.

I could hear our neighbor's basset hound, Charlie, baying from halfway down the street, and I wondered what had upset him. Charlie was old, and he didn't even bark at squirrels or cats anymore. When I reached our neighbor's house I walked around to their backyard to see what Charlie was making so much noise about. It surprised me to find him straining at his wire run, barking and howling at my backyard. Something about the way his hackles were raised made the hair on the back of my neck stand up.

I ran back out to the street and up the walkway to our front door. "Daddy, I think there's something wrong with Charlie," I called, opening the door. I tossed my mittens and cap on the bench in the hallway. "Daddy?" I called again.

No answer.

Where is he? The house was filled with the aroma of pot roast, so he had to be here. He would never leave with the stove on.

Something did not feel right. Then I felt the cold draft coming down the hallway.

He must have gone out back to see why Charlie was barking and left the door open. I shook my head. He was always scolding me for doing that.

I smelled it just before I reached the kitchen, a warm coppery scent that made my stomach lurch and my pulse quicken. A cry burst from me when I stepped inside and saw the spray of red across the white cupboards and the trail of blood that disappeared out through the open door.

Fear exploded in my chest. "Daddy!" I cried, running for the door. My boots skidded on the slick blood, and I flailed as I fell through the doorway, landing hard on my hands and knees on the back step. My head came up, and I saw the bloody steps, the broken railing, and...

"No!" I crawled frantically toward the figure lying at the bottom of the steps, his favorite blue shirt shredded and bloody. I felt it then, the horrible pulling sensation of a life draining away. "No, Daddy, no!" I threw myself on him, begging him to stay with me as I poured my power into him until there was nothing left to give. It was not enough. His green eyes stared sightlessly at the gray sky as the first snowflakes touched his ravaged face.

"No!" I came awake with a cry and stared blindly in the dark with my heart thudding against my ribs. Reaching up a trembling hand, I swiped at the tears on my cheeks and pushed damp strands of hair out of my face. I lay there for several minutes as my heart rate returned to normal and the last vestiges of the dream left me.

The curtain fluttered, drawing my eyes to the pale light coming through the window. Far out in the bay a buoy clanged, and closer to shore a sea otter whistled. Soothed by the familiar noises, I threw off my covers and went to push the window open wider, letting cold morning air fill the room. I took a deep calming breath of ocean air as I listened to the muted sounds of the bay and let myself think about the dream.

In the beginning the nightmare came every night, the same paralyzing dream that ripped me from sleep, screaming in terror. Time after time Nate tried to get me to tell him about the dream, to talk about what I'd been through, but to speak of the horror out loud and relive those moments was more than I could bear.

I'd seen the police reports. Our neighbor called in the disturbance, and when the police responded they found me lying on top of my father's body, both of us covered in snow. At first they thought I was dead too, until one of the policemen checked and found a pulse. I was rushed to the hospital, suffering from shock. The child psychologist who examined me later said I suffered from "severe psychological trauma from witnessing her father's brutal murder." She recommended a few weeks in a child psych ward.

Nate's response was "Absolutely not." My uncle knew something about post traumatic stress. He was twenty-three when he was hit by shrapnel in Bosnia that left him in a wheelchair. He said I needed to be with family, and since my grandmother was too ill to care for a child, he brought me here to live with him. I knew it wasn't easy for him, a single man in a wheelchair suddenly faced with raising a traumatized kid. But he did it anyway, and I loved him for it, though I could not find the words to tell him what it meant to me. Sometimes I thought of us as a pair of damaged bookends. We both had our flaws, but we belonged together even if there was always something between us, keeping us apart.

My alarm clock said six o'clock, so I knew it was useless trying to go back to sleep. Instead, I drew the covers up over my bed and headed for the bathroom to get ready for school. I splashed cold water over my face and studied my pale complexion and my eyes that were still haunted by the lingering effects of the dream. I released a shuddering breath and started the shower. *What a way to start the week.*

"I heard her bike gang did it. He's lucky he's alive."

"Seriously?"

"Yeah, I think Greg McCoy just got out of prison or something."

"I had no idea she ran with such a hard crowd."

"You guys are all way off base. I say she did it herself, and knowing him, he deserved it."

I glanced up from my book, and the whispers died as the students at the surrounding tables suddenly found their lunch trays interesting. Resisting the urge to roll my eyes, I dabbed a french fry in ketchup and popped it in my mouth. I should have been used to it by now. When you keep to yourself, people will fill in the details about your life themselves. But a bike gang? Really?

I looked at the end of my table where Jeffrey Crumb sat eating his hamburger and fries. He gave me a lopsided smile, sharing in my amusement over the gossip before he bent over his own book again. Blond and painfully thin, Jeffrey was two years younger than me, and he lived with his grandparents, one street over from me. I heard his mother was a serious drug addict who had gotten pregnant at eighteen and Jeffrey was born with a bunch of health issues. He was pretty smart but small for his age, and he found it hard to talk to other kids. We started sharing a table a few years ago because we both liked to read at lunch, even when Greg chose to sit with us. No one dared mess with Jeffrey after that, most likely because they were afraid I'd sic

Greg on them. Greg might be gone now, but it looked like some of his reputation had rubbed off on me. I didn't mind if it kept people from bothering us.

I wondered how word got out about the fight because I knew Scott and Ryan would not tell anyone. I'd gotten a glimpse of Scott in Chemistry second period, and I'd had to suppress a gasp at his black eyes and swollen nose. Apparently no one was buying his story about swerving his car to avoid hitting a deer, but how on earth had they connected his bruises to me?

I gave a mental shrug and went back to my well-worn copy of *Jane Eyre*. As long as they left me alone, they could think whatever they wanted.

The chair across from me scraped over the floor as someone pulled it out and sat down. I didn't bother to look up. "Go away. I'm busy."

A hand snaked out to grab one of my fries. When I didn't object, it reached for another one. I pushed the plate toward the hand. "Help yourself."

"Hmm, I don't see any bruised knuckles. What did you do, take a baseball bat to him?"

I lifted my gaze to Roland Greene's laughing blue eyes. He leaned toward me, and his dark bangs fell over his forehead. "So?" he asked, pushing his hair back. It was a useless gesture. I kept telling him he needed to cut it, but he said the girls liked it that way. Based on the number of girls making cow eyes at him right now, he was probably right.

"So what?"

Roland snorted. "Don't even go there. What happened?"

I picked up my Coke can and took a long swallow, debating whether or not to tell Roland the truth. He wouldn't repeat it if I asked him not to, but there was no way he'd be able to hide his gloating and that would just confirm everyone's suspicions. Scott wasn't on his favorites list either.

"Hey, did you guys see Scott Foley's face? I heard some gang beat him up." Peter Kelly took the chair next to Roland, his cheeks flushed and his rusty hair sticking out at all angles as usual. His green eyes flashed as he leaned in and lowered his voice. "Of course that's not half as interesting as the other story I heard." He gave me a meaningful look.

I shook my head. "Sorry to disappoint – "

"Sara almost made him cry."

My mouth fell open as I swung my head to stare at Jeffrey.

Roland smirked at me and slid his chair over next to Jeffrey. "Is that so? Why don't you tell us about it?"

I shook my head. "You weren't there, Jeffrey."

"Ha! So you did do it," Roland crowed.

Peter's eyes widened. "You really beat up Scott Foley? How is that possible?"

"Hey!"

"No offense, Sara, but Scott is way bigger than you and... well, you're a girl."

"Gee, thanks for pointing that out."

"She's the best fighter I ever saw," Jeffrey declared. "I was on the wharf, and I saw it all. She was super fast, too."

Roland grinned wickedly and moved back across from me. "So now are you gonna tell us what happened?"

"I hit him. He hit me. We went our separate ways."

"Nice try. We want details," Peter said.

I took another sip of Coke, wondering how much I could tell them. "Scott was tormenting a cat," I said in a low voice, not wanting to share with the whole cafeteria. "I overreacted a bit and hit him. There's really not much to tell."

"She kicked him in the privates, too," Jeffrey piped in loudly, making Roland and Peter wince. I heard snickers from the table closest to us.

Peter looked at my hands. "How is it you hit him hard enough to break his nose and your knuckles aren't even red? And I don't see any bruises on your face either."

"You know I hardly ever bruise. Besides Scott barely touched me." *And I have the world's best first aid kit at home.*

Roland shook his head. "I don't know what it is with you and Scott. He always gets weird around you." He chewed another fry. "He's never going to live down getting his butt kicked by a girl. Sorry, Sara, but it's true. I'd feel bad for him if he wasn't such an ass."

I could only shrug because I wasn't proud of what I'd done. It was true that I didn't like Scott, but I'd attacked him, not the other way around. And I knew, even if Scott didn't, that it wasn't exactly a fair fight.

I glanced at my watch. I still had about twenty minutes left before English, but I had no desire to sit there and relive the whole Scott thing again. "Well, boys, it's been fun, but I gotta run."

"Wait." Roland laid a hand over my book before I could take it. "Friday night Pete and me are going to hear Dylan's new band play at the Attic. You want to come?"

I made a face. "Is he still doing that rap thing?"

"Nah, his new band is more rock... kind of like Pearl Jam. They're pretty good."

"I don't know."

Roland tilted his head to one side and gave me a dimpled smile. "Come on. We haven't hung out in ages."

I rolled my eyes at him. "You know that doesn't work on me, right? Besides, don't you guys have camping or something this weekend?" For the last few years, Roland and Peter had been going on weekend outdoor trips with their cousins once a month. Their families were close, and they did a lot of things together. Roland complained about having family always up in his business, but I envied him. My dad and I were close like that before he died.

"We just got back." Peter shook his head at Roland. "I can't believe we were gone a whole weekend and she didn't even notice."

Roland put on a wounded expression. "That hurts."

I grinned at their lame antics. "After a weekend in the woods, I'm surprised you don't have a date lined up for Friday night already, Roland."

"Sara, you know you're the only girl for me." He laid a hand over his heart. "I'm just passing time until you realize that."

Out of the corner of my eye I saw two girls at a nearby table watching his display with equal expressions of jealousy and dismay. "Yeah, okay. Cool it, Romeo," I said, laughing. "Before you break every heart in here and start a lynch mob after me."

"What?" he asked innocently.

I shook my head because I knew Roland was not as clueless about his effect on the opposite sex as he let on. Girls had started chasing him around long before he began to notice them. Then he went through a growth spurt in eight grade and bam – instant heartthrob. His casual disregard for rules added just enough bad boy to his image to make the entire female student body lust after him. I couldn't fault a guy for having good genes, but I often thought Roland was a little insensitive where girls were concerned. He dated a girl a few times, and as soon as she started to get serious, he ended it. He was always nice about it, which probably made it even worse for them. Whenever I said anything about it, he argued that no one's heart gets broken after two dates. But I'd seen the pining faces more than once. I loved my friend, but he was an idiot when it came to matters of the heart.

"I'll cool it if you say you'll go to the Attic with us. Come on, we'll have a blast."

"I'll think about it," I said, taking my book from him and stuffing it in my bag.

I left the two of them finishing my plate of fries. No one else spoke to me as I made my way to the door, but I heard the whispers. Already, Jeffrey's comments were circulating the cafeteria.

The door swung open just as I reached it, and I had to step back to avoid getting whacked in the face. The malicious smile on the face of the pretty blond standing in front of me told me she had been aiming for me. I wasn't surprised. Faith Perry and I weren't friendly on a good day, and I didn't expect her to be happy after what had happened to her boyfriend.

"Excuse me." I started to walk past Faith, but she moved to block my way. I groaned inwardly as the cafeteria fell silent behind me. It was only the second week of my senior year, and already I was wishing for graduation.

"Are you happy?" she hissed, her venomous green eyes glittering.

I pasted an innocent expression on my face. "About what?"

Faith tossed her long, straight hair back over her shoulder. "I'm talking about Scott."

At that moment, I spotted Scott and Ryan coming down the hallway toward us. They stopped walking when they saw me and Faith. Scott's eyes flashed angrily then looked away as if he couldn't face me.

I shrugged. "Seriously, Faith? You honestly think I could have done *that*?" I spoke loud enough for my voice to carry to the people behind me. "Do I look like I was in a fight?"

That brought her up short, and she stared at me as if she noticed my lack of bruises for the first time. I felt Scott's gaze on me, and I knew he must be wondering how I didn't have a fat lip today.

"How the hell do I know?" Faith scoffed. "For all I know you had those loser biker friends mess him up. I wouldn't put it past you."

I bristled. If anyone here liked to hurt other people it was Faith. She'd been a bully ever since we were little kids, and she'd only grown worse as we got older. When I started school here, Faith was not happy that Scott wanted to be my friend and did everything she could to make my life miserable. I was already devastated from losing my dad, and she might have broken me if it wasn't for Roland. His friendship had filled some of the aching void inside me and gave me the strength to stand up to Faith. I'm not sure what made her dislike me more – not being able to hurt me anymore or the fact that Scott had liked me first – but she'd hated me ever since. I usually kept my distance from her because it was just not worth the hassle.

"You know what, Faith?" I took a step toward her, and she stumbled back. I leaned toward her, and I could sense everyone in the cafeteria craning forward in their seats. "If I were you," I whispered in her ear, "I'd be less worried about whether or not a girl beat up my boyfriend and more concerned about why my boyfriend wasn't with me."

Faith's mouth fell open. It probably wasn't wise to stir her up like that. After years of crushing on Scott, Faith had finally gotten him, but she was very jealous where he was concerned. If she weren't such a bitch, I would have told her not to worry because she and Scott were made for each other.

I pushed past her, leaving behind a room full of curious onlookers. More people had stopped in the hallway to hear our exchange, and I ignored their stares as I walked past them. Scott stepped aside when I reached him and Ryan, and our eyes met briefly. I could see the confusion and suspicion on his face, and I knew he was wondering why I'd denied hitting him when I could have totally humiliated him in front of half the school. I just walked by because I had no desire to explain my actions to him or anyone else. Let him think what he wanted.

The rest of the afternoon was quiet. There were no more run-ins with Faith, and Scott kept his distance as well. Neither of them was going to forgive or forget any time soon, but I had a feeling Scott would keep a wide berth from me for a while. I hoped they both did because I didn't like the person I became around them.

I was on Market Street on my way home after school when I started to feel like someone was watching me. It was an eerie sensation, but I shook it off and cut though the small parking lot between the pub and the antique store, emerging on the waterfront. Our place was the seventh one down at the end of the row.

Just as I passed the pub, the feeling of being watched came over me again, stronger this time. Was someone following me? I stopped and listened for footsteps, but this close to the beach the gulls and waves drowned out a lot of noises. It was the middle of the afternoon so I was not afraid, but I was growing annoyed.

"Scott or Faith, if that's you, you'd better turn around and go home right now if you know what's good for you," I called, not really expecting an answer.

After a few seconds I resumed walking. It was a warm afternoon, and there was barely any wind, save for the light breeze on my ankles. I watched absently as leaves from the lonely maple tree in front of the coffee shop swirled around my feet then tumbled ahead of me like a playful puppy all the way home.

"What the – ?" I came up short when I rounded the corner of our building and came face-to-face with a mini whirlwind of leaves and dirt hovering directly in my path. I stood and watched the leaves spinning faster and faster as the little cyclone picked up more of them and began to form a blurry outline about three feet high. My mouth fell open, and I snapped it shut as a creature I had only heard about took shape before me. I knew about elementals of course, but I had never dreamed I'd see one up close in my lifetime. I didn't know whether to be scared or excited by the rare appearance.

"Um, hello," I said hesitantly.

The sylph made a movement that looked like a bow, and not knowing the proper etiquette for elementals, I bowed in return. That seemed to please her because she moved closer until I could hear a soft whispery sound, almost like the wind in the fireplace flue during a storm. When I listened closely I could pick out words. "Hello, Sara Grey," she said in a breezy voice. "I am Aine."

I swallowed and sat down hard on the bottom of the stairs to our apartment. She knew my name. Why would an air elemental know my name? A lot of the People in these parts knew me for my healing, but I doubted a sylph needed my help in that area. I wouldn't even know where to start anyway.

"Do you need my help, Aine?" I asked, and I heard a whispery laugh.

"I have watched you and seen your power and how good you are to the People. You are a kind child."

"I'm almost eighteen."

The sylph laughed again, and I could not help but smile. She had lived countless lifetimes, and compared to her I was an infant.

I didn't know a whole lot about elementals except that they were super powerful and they pulled their power from the earth. They were highly revered by the People, including the trolls. Remy talked about elementals sometimes, but even he had never met one.

"Aine, do you know where my power comes from?" If anyone could answer that question, it was an elemental. Maybe she was here to give me the answers I desperately wanted.

Aine moved closer until I could feel her brush against my legs. I wanted so much to lean down and touch the distorted shape, but I was afraid she might vanish.

"All power comes from the earth," she answered cryptically. She moved away again. "Why do you heal the People, little sister?"

The question caught me off guard; no one had ever asked me that before. "I don't understand. Why *wouldn't* I heal them?"

"Humans fear the People. You do not."

"No. Some of them are my friends."

"And what of the ones who don't wish to be your friend? Do you help them?"

I wished I could see the sylph's face clearly to understand the reason for her questions. "I've never had to make that decision, so I honestly can't say what I'd do. I guess I would help most creatures."

Aine seemed to hang in the air in front of my eyes. "Most – but not all?"

"Well, I'm not going to heal something that will turn around and kill humans, if that's what you mean. I know there are some who aren't nice, but they aren't evil either. I'd help them if they asked for it."

"And you decide who is evil and who is not?"

I let out a short laugh. "I think the evil ones are easy enough to identify."

A long moment passed before the sylph nodded. "You are wise for one so young. I am glad I came to meet you."

"I'm glad, too." This was one of the strangest conversations I'd ever had, and I half expected to wake up in my bed and find out it was all a dream.

"I think we will meet again, little sister." The swirling mass of air began to move away until it suddenly dissipated, leaving a loose pile of dirt and leaves on the ground.

An elemental. I just met an elemental!

I sat on the steps for a good ten minutes after she disappeared because it took me that long to recover from the shock of my encounter. Elementals were extremely elusive beings, and I could not fathom why Aine would come here just to talk to me. I had a little power, yes, but it was nothing compared to her immense magic. And she said she had been watching me? For how long and why?

Nate was in his office when I finally schooled my face into a somewhat normal expression and went inside. I grabbed a blueberry muffin from the kitchen to tide me over until dinner and went upstairs, calling hello to Nate as I passed his door. Throwing my backpack on my bed, I changed my clothes, put on some Carly Simon, and sat at my laptop. I was dying to know if Wulfman had found out anything for me. It was probably too soon to hope for something, but I felt like anything was possible after my encounter with Aine.

To my surprise there was an email from Wulfman in the mailbox I used for the message board. I opened his message, curious about what he'd found out already.

It looks like you were right. There were several suspicious deaths in Portland about ten years ago. Your friend was one of them. I'm still waiting to hear from all my resources. Hope to get back to you in a few hours.

I stared at the screen. In a few hours I could be closer than I'd ever been to getting answers about my dad's murder. All these years the biggest question tormenting me was why him? He was a good person, and we had lived a very quiet life. What drew them to that neighborhood, to our little house that looked like every other house on the street? That question was a fire inside me, and it would never stop burning until it was answered. The truth would not help me get over what happened to him, but maybe it could bring me some kind of closure.

Grabbing the muffin, I nibbled it as I paced the room, my eyes going to the laptop with every turn on the floor. The cat lay across the back of the couch watching me as I walked back and forth, his head following me around the room. I tossed him a small piece of muffin and he watched it bounce off the couch in front of him, but he made no move to catch it before it fell to the floor.

"Two days ago you would have been glad to get that," I scolded softly as I bent to pick up the crumb.

A tiny shuffling sound behind the attic wall caught my ear, and I smiled behind my hand. Breaking off a large piece of muffin, I unlatched the small attic door and set the food on the floor in front of it. Then I retreated to the couch to watch. It took a few minutes, but I was rewarded when the door squeaked and a tiny pale arm reached out from the shadows to snatch away the piece of muffin. I heard a gleeful snicker as the little fiend retreated with its prize.

"You're welcome, you ungrateful little wretch," I called after him.

The only response I got was a muffled burp from inside the wall. Little buggers never said thank you.

I shook my head and finished my muffin. Some houses had mice – mine had imps. Imps were the vermin of the supe world, notorious thieves and the devil to catch. For a while I couldn't leave anything of value lying around or it would disappear – until last fall when one of the little beasts got caught in an old mousetrap in the storeroom. I freed him and fixed him up even though he tried to bite me in the process. Remy said I was nuts, but I couldn't stand to see a creature in pain. I guess one good turn did deserve another because nothing had gone missing since that day. Of course, the imps weren't any friendlier, but what could you expect from six-inch tall kleptomaniac demons with sharp teeth?

I forced myself to do homework for an hour before I finally gave in and went to my laptop to check my email. Nervous excitement twisted my stomach when I saw a message requesting a chat. I clicked *okay*, and Wulfman responded immediately.

Wulfman: Have something. Not sure it's what you want.
PixieGirl: What is it?
Wulfman: One of my sources lost a friend when you lost yours. Same M.O.
PixieGirl: And he thinks it was vampires?

Wulfman: He's sure of it. He knows a lot.
PixieGirl: So what now?
Wulfman: He wants to talk to you. But it has to be in person. You up for that?
PixieGirl: You trust him?
Wulfman: 100%
PixieGirl: Ok but it has to be very public.

My cell phone vibrated where it lay on the desk. The corner of my mouth lifted when I saw the text message from Roland. **Fri night?**

PixieGirl: I think I know of a place. Have him ping me and we'll talk.
Wulfman: Will do. Let me know how it goes.
PixieGirl: Thanks, I will.

I leaned back in my chair. Was I insane to agree to meet a total stranger even if he might know something about my dad? I'd heard enough stories about girls disappearing after going to meet someone they met online. But then this wouldn't be the first time I'd made contact with someone this way. It was how I met Malloy the first time, and there were several others I'd dealt with before him. I was always careful, and it wasn't like I'd be alone with the guy.

And it might be my only chance to learn the truth about what had happened to my dad. After all these years, there was no way I could pass up this opportunity. I was willing to take a few risks to finally get the answers I sought.

My mind made up, I picked up my phone. **I'm in.**

4

By the time Delilah's Crush began pelting out their last set, my temples were pounding and I wished I could heal myself. Roland was right – Dylan's new band was great – but I liked my music more rock and less metal. I didn't think Delilah's Crush knew exactly what type of music they wanted to play, so they went somewhere in between. Roland and Peter were having a great time, cheering and moving with the rest of the crowd. My sigh was drowned out by the music. Maybe it was me; I just didn't know how to enjoy myself like a normal teenager.

The truth was that I was disappointed and more than a little annoyed that my reason for coming here tonight had not shown up. NightWatcher, the guy I'd talked to online this week, was supposed to be here at ten o'clock, and it was almost eleven with no sign of him. We had agreed that I would wear a silver cross in plain sight where he could see it, I guess because vampires couldn't touch silver. My fingers went to the cross to make sure it was still hanging outside my shirt, and I almost smiled at the idea of anyone mistaking me for a vampire. It looked like that didn't matter now since he hadn't even bothered to show, or if he had, he was not approaching me for some reason.

I scanned the room again, and this time my gaze fell on a dark-haired man who looked more out of place here than I felt. Leaning against a wooden column at the edge of the dance floor in dark jeans and a snug gray knit top, he looked more at home in a Calvin Klein ad than here at the Attic. It wasn't just his clothes or the way his dark eyes swept the room lazily that drew my attention; he was just too . . . beautiful, like one of those androgynous male models. In a room full of teenagers and college students wearing T-shirts and jeans, he stood out like a beacon.

It took me a few seconds to realize that Mr. CK's eyes were staring into mine. The boldness of his gaze brought heat to my cheeks, and my eyes darted away from his seductive smile and the invitation I saw in his stare. I had little – okay, zero experience with the opposite sex – but I'd have to be comatose not to understand the signals coming from him. What I couldn't understand was why he was turning his attention to me with all the attractive girls here trying to catch his eye. Not that I think I'm unattractive; I'm just not what you'd call alluring, and I'm certainly not used to hot guys giving me the "come hither" look.

A little breathless, I shifted my attention to the stage where the drummer was revving up the crowd with an awesome solo. I moved forward and nudged between my friends, dancing along with them. Five minutes later I stole a glance at Mr. CK, and I smirked when I found him engaged in conversation with two shapely blondes who were almost comical in their attempts to out-flirt each other.

The band finished the song and started another, and everyone on the dance floor began dancing again, except for me. After downing two bottles of water in two hours, what I really needed was to find the restroom. I tapped Roland on the arm and mouthed "restroom" to him to let him know where I was going. He nodded, and I headed for the ladies' room where I stood in line for five minutes before I got inside. I was washing my hands when the two blond girls I'd seen with Mr. CK came in.

"I saw him first, Shelley," one of them said, pulling a tube of dark red lipstick from her handbag.

"You always say that, Trish," the other girl replied with a scowl. She started retouching her makeup. "This one is mine."

Trish checked her perfect hair in the mirror. "If you think I'm letting you walk off with this one, you're nuts."

"Letting me?" Shelley's voice went up a notch.

I shook my head and left the restroom before they started brawling over the guy. There was no arguing the fact that Mr. CK was incredibly hot, but no guy is worth fighting over, especially one you just met in a bar.

Apparently, Trish and Shelley disagreed with me. I barely made it ten feet from the restroom when I heard them coming behind me in a heated argument that drew amused looks from the people nearby. I slowed and stepped sideways to let the angry pair pass me. *It's no wonder I don't go out much.*

I heard Shelley shout "You bitch!" a second before she gave Trish a hard shove that sent Trish stumbling backward into me. "Umph!" I grunted as one of the girl's elbows got me in the stomach before we went down in a tangle of arms and legs. I saw stars when my head hit the hardwood floor. It didn't help that I had cushioned the bigger girl's fall.

Someone pulled Trish off me, and a girl asked, "Is she alright?" I assumed she was talking about me because I was the only one still lying on the floor, a little dazed and not sure whether I was more embarrassed or pissed.

A hand waved in front of my face, and I realized someone was bending over me. "Are you okay?" he asked in a deep voice that carried the trace of an accent I could not place. The ceiling lights behind him made it impossible to see his face, but from his voice I guessed he wasn't more than a few years older than me.

"Um, I think so," I said, moving to get up. The man reached down and took my hand, and I gasped at the warmth that rippled through me. I stared at our clasped hands as he helped me to my feet, and I stood there for a moment before I realized I still held his hand. I let go and looked up at him with a sheepish smile. "Thank – "

He stood so close I could reach out and touch him. His face was no longer hidden in shadows, and I found myself gazing into a pair of steel gray eyes that looked at me with such intensity I almost forgot to breathe. Mutely I stared at him while my stomach twisted with a sensation I could not put into words, and I felt a touch against the back of my mind like the flutter of butterfly wings. I experienced the strangest sense of recognition, though I knew I had never seen him before, and deep inside me something stirred like a cat uncurling from a long nap.

The man blinked and took a step back, breaking the spell that held me. Remembering to breathe again, I glanced down to steady myself then looked back to find him watching me with a slightly confused expression that probably matched my own. My eyes moved up his handsome face taking in his square jaw, firm lips, aquiline nose, and black hair that fell across his brow in careless waves with a few strands curling around his ears. His skin was lightly tanned, and the shadow of a beard played around the curves of his jaw.

I suddenly realized we were staring at each other, and I smiled to cover my embarrassment. "Sorry, I must have banged my head harder than I thought."

My words did not elicit the reaction I expected. His whole body stiffened, and his eyes suddenly blazed as if I had slapped him. I took a step back, stunned by the hostility in his stare, especially after his kind assistance. "Okay... well, thanks for your help," I mumbled and fled.

I slipped through the crowd until I spied the door that stood open to the deck, and suddenly I was in desperate need of fresh air. *What the hell was his problem?* I stewed as I leaned against the rail and stared at the dark building across the street. This night just kept going downhill. First my contact didn't show, and then I got dumped on my butt in front of a room full of people, and on top of that I acted like a total idiot. I cringed, remembering how I'd stood there like a fool staring at him. What had gotten into me, going all slack-jawed over a hot guy? *God, I'm as bad as Trish and Shelley*, I groaned inwardly and closed my eyes, letting the night air cool my burning cheeks.

"I believe this is yours."

The voice so close behind me made me jump because I hadn't even heard him approach. I turned to see a silver chain dangling from his fingers, and my hand went to my bare neck. I reached out gingerly without looking at his face, and he laid the necklace in my hand. "Thank you." I ran my finger over the cross then put it in my front jeans pocket. The chain was broken, but I was glad to get it back. It had been my grandmother's, and Nate had given it to me last year on my birthday.

I expected the man to leave then, but he stared at me for a long moment, studying me. It felt like he was sizing me up, trying to figure me out as if I was a weird piece of art he couldn't understand. There was nothing suggestive in his look. If anything, he looked at me with something akin to dislike.

"Are you done?" I finally asked after I'd had enough of his rudeness. His eyes widened a little, and I got the distinct impression he wasn't used to being rebuffed, especially by the opposite sex.

"You're a bit young for this place," he said brusquely, ignoring my barb.

I bristled at his tone. "I'm sorry but I don't think that is any of your business."

"You can't be more than seventeen or eighteen. You shouldn't be here alone."

"You're not much older than me," I shot back. "And I'm not here alone."

"I'm older than I look." His voice was cool, but his eyes burned into mine and the beast in my head stirred again. After what had happened to Scott, I clamped down tightly on it until it was silent. All I needed was for that thing to get loose again. Besides, this guy might be aggravating, but I didn't sense any real danger from him.

He ran a hand through his dark hair and looked out at the city. I could not help but think that he really was gorgeous. Not like Mr. CK, who was way too pretty for my taste. No one would dare call the guy in front of me *pretty*. There was an edge to him – serious, almost guarded.

"Nikolas," said a voice from the doorway. We both turned to face a blond man who gave my companion a "raised eyebrow" look, as if he wasn't surprised to find his friend alone with a girl. "Ready to move out?"

I wasn't sure if Nikolas's frown was for me or his friend. He gave me another searching look then nodded. "Be out shortly, Chris."

I expected him to say something else to me, but he only stood where he was for a long moment before he strode to the door. He swung toward me again before he stepped inside. "Stay with your friends. This part of town is not safe for a girl alone at night."

"I'll keep that in mind, thanks."

And that wasn't weird at all. It was definitely my week for strange encounters.

I waited another minute then made my way back to Roland and Peter. They were still dancing where I'd left them, and Roland had made a new friend. A petite brunette girl had taken up my spot, and she was rubbing against him like a cat on a post. I was beginning to wonder if the girls in this place had never seen a good looking guy before.

When Roland saw that I had returned he beckoned me closer, earning me a glare from the brunette, which I chose to ignore. The band had almost finished their last set, and I was ready to leave. My head was pounding even harder after my fall, and I was a little wigged out from the whole encounter with that Nikolas fellow. I wasn't sure what bothered me more; his behavior or my reaction to him. He was gone now so it didn't matter, but I couldn't put it out of my mind.

The band finished their last song to loud cheers and shouts for an encore. Peter hooted at them then turned to me and Roland. "That was sick! Did you hear Samson's solo?"

"It was hard not to," I said with a laugh. My ears were ringing.

"I told you they were good," Roland said, nudging me with his arm. "Dylan's gotten a lot better since the last time you heard him play."

"Yes, he has," I agreed.

Peter punched Roland's arm. "They're starting to pack up. Let's go." They both looked expectantly at me, and I waved them off.

"Go on. I want to sit down for a bit anyway. I'll be over there." I pointed at pair of leather chairs being vacated by a couple of girls. Roland nodded, and he and Peter headed for the stage with the brunette in tow. I snagged one of the chairs and laid my head back with my eyes closed, trying to will my headache away. It was a little better now that the music had stopped. I listened to people milling about, content to sit there quietly until Roland and Peter came back for me.

Someone took the chair across from me. I opened my eyes, expecting to see one of my friends, and I was more than a little surprised to find Mr. CK sitting there watching me. He was alone, and I wondered how he had managed to slip away from Trish and Shelley.

He was maybe nineteen or twenty, and up close he was even more beautiful – if that was possible – with ridiculously thick lashes and full lips that parted in a disarming smile. I could not help but smile back.

"Did you like the band?" he asked in a voice so silky it was almost a caress. For a moment I forgot to answer.

"They weren't bad. You?"

He gave a small shrug. "They're decent, but the next one is much better. The Furies, have you heard of them?"

"No." I found it a little hard to believe that he was into hard rock. The Attic and this type of music really didn't seem to suit him. But then what did I know?

The leather chair creaked as he leaned forward with his elbows on the armrests. His bottomless indigo eyes bored into mine. "You should stick around to see them. You won't regret it."

I felt an inexplicable urge to lean forward too, to get closer to those mesmerizing eyes, but I stopped myself before I did. Wow, this guy was good. I wondered if he was aware of the effect he had on the opposite sex. I almost laughed out loud. He definitely knew.

I gave a mental shake to clear my head. "We only came to hear our friend play," I told him, pointing to Roland, Peter, and Dylan. "We're leaving as soon as they finish packing up."

He seemed puzzled for an instant, but then he gave me a small smile of resignation. "That's too bad." He leaned closer and spoke in a soft voice. "You're not like the other girls here. It's quite refreshing."

Not sure how to take that, I quipped, "If the girls here don't suit your tastes, maybe you're looking for women in the wrong place."

His eyes flashed in amusement, and he settled back in his chair. "I think you may be right."

I saw Roland waving me over. "Looks like my friends are ready to leave." I stood, and my companion stood, too. "It was nice talking to you."

The corners of his mouth turned down slightly. "Are you going to run off without leaving me a name to put with your lovely face?"

Smooth. "I don't give my name to strange men."

He raised his eyebrows and gave me a beguiling smile. "Not even a first name."

"Sara," I replied without thinking. I immediately wanted to kick myself.

"Sara." He said my name like he was tasting an exotic fruit. "I'm Eli, and it has been a pleasure. I hope to repeat it sometime."

I doubted the likelihood of that ever happening, but I smiled anyway. "Well, enjoy your band." I turned toward the stage, blinking several times to shake off the feeling of lethargy that had stolen over me while I sat. *I must be more tired than I thought.*

"You ready to go?" Roland asked when I reached them. I saw with some amusement that the brunette was hanging off Samson now and the blond drummer was looking around helplessly for someone to come to his rescue.

I glanced over at Eli as we headed for the exit and saw that the seats around him had already been snatched up by some new girls who were vying for his attention. He gave me a slight nod as we passed, and I returned a polite smile.

The Attic was on the second floor of a converted warehouse, and we had to descend a set of stairs to get to the street. Music had started playing inside the building again, and it wafted down the stairs after us.

I yawned. "That was fun, but I'm pooped all of a sudden."

"You guys stay here, and I'll go get the car." Roland set off running to the parking garage at the far end of the street. I sat on the bottom of the staircase while Peter called someone on his cell and started raving about the band.

I took out my own phone to call Nate and let him know we were leaving the club and I'd be home in an hour or so. Nate was pretty cool about me staying out late as long as I let him know where I was. Before I could dial, the stair above me creaked and Eli appeared beside me. I tried to hide my surprise and dismay. I hoped he didn't think I'd been flirting with him upstairs because I hadn't been; at least I didn't think I had. It was not exactly my area of expertise.

"Have your friends abandoned you?" he asked, and I felt a little tremor pass through me at his nearness. Really, what was this guy's secret?

"No, Peter's right there..." My voice trailed off when I realized that Peter had wandered off. I could still hear him talking on his phone so he wasn't that far away.

"I thought you were leaving," Eli said, his breath warm against my cheek. Too close for comfort.

I shot to my feet, not caring what he thought. Okay, enough of that. "We are. My friend went to get the car, and we're waiting for him." I knew I was babbling, but I wanted to put some distance between me and Eli. Something didn't feel quite right about him, and he was starting to make me nervous. I started toward Peter until I felt a hand on my arm. It wasn't restraining me, but it still set off alarm bells in my head. Nikolas's earlier words rang in my head. *Stay with your friends. This part of town is not safe for a girl alone at night.*

"You seem to be in such a hurry to leave all of a sudden. Nothing I have done, surely?"

"No, no, it's nothing like that. I just think I hear my ride coming." I tried to swallow, but my mouth was dry. Where was Roland?

"You are a terrible liar, you know," Eli said softly. He moved so fast he was standing right in front of me before I knew what was happening. "But you are such an intriguing creature that I will forgive you for it."

My mind struggled to grasp what my eyes were seeing. *How did he...?*

The truth hit me like a truck, knocking the air from my lungs and sending spikes of fear into my brain. I opened my mouth to call for help, only to find myself rendered mute by a hard hand. The street blurred, and I found myself in the alley, pressed face-first against the building and unable to move or call out.

"Sara," he hissed against my hair. Terror threatened to choke me as the image of my father's mutilated body swam before my eyes. *Oh God no. Please, not like this.*

I screamed into Eli's hand and struggled wildly to twist out of his hold, but his grip was like steel bars holding me fast. He laughed softly in my ear and pressed his body against my length. "You're a fighter. I like that." I could hear the excitement in his voice, and his body responded to my fear. My heart threatened to explode from my chest.

"As soon as I looked into those beautiful green eyes of yours, I knew I had to have you. Those other girls, they simper and fawn, and they would do anything I asked of them. But you... you are different. You are an orchid in a field of dandelions." He ran his free hand along my throat, and I whimpered. "Now, you are mine, little flower, and I cannot wait to taste your sweet nectar."

His words sent shudders of revulsion through me. Pinned between him and the wall, his scent assailed my nostrils, and I almost gagged at the sickly odor that permeated his skin. It had been faint at first, camouflaged by expensive cologne, but the longer he held me, the stronger it grew. I found a fox once with a badly infected cut. Eli reeked of that same stench of rotting flesh and death.

"I just have to know one thing first," Eli whispered and spun me around to face him while keeping me silenced with his hand. In the weak light of the alley I could see him as he smiled at me almost tenderly. "How did you do it? How did you break the compulsion? No one has ever resisted my will before."

He started to lift his hand from my mouth, and I sucked in a deep breath to scream my head off. He tilted my head, forcing me to look into his eyes. "One thing, little flower. If you call out, I will rip your little boyfriends to shreds. You don't want that, do you?"

My eyes widened even more, and I shook my head frantically.

His lips parted in a smile, and I watched in horror as two curved snake-like fangs grew from his mouth, gleaming in the pale light. In that moment I knew what a mouse felt like when it looked into the eyes of a rattlesnake. The mouse knew it was going to die, but it was too mesmerized with fear to move.

When Eli lifted a hand to my face I tried to jerk away from the inch-long black claws where his fingernails had been. He touched my cheek lightly, and I shuddered at the feel of the cold, hard claws on my skin.

"Now tell me how you resisted me and I promise your friends will not be harmed."

"I–I don't know."

He sighed impatiently, and his clawed hand moved down to brush against my throat. I swallowed convulsively. "I'm not lying. Please... I don't know what you want me to say."

Eli's eyes narrowed, and he stared down into mine. "I think I believe you. Hmm, can it be that you don't even know what you can do? It makes me wonder what other charming little talents you might be hiding." He licked his lips and gall rose in my throat at his meaning. "What a delight you are. To think I almost settled for one of those insipid blondes."

He put his mouth to my ear, and his words sent waves of fresh terror through me. "I am going to savor you, little Sara. I had planned to have you now, but why rush when we can take all the time we want later."

"No..."

"But I think a taste first to whet the appetite." His face lowered as he forced my head to one side, baring my throat. His lips touched my skin, and his tongue lapped at the spot where my pulse beat. Blackness swam before my eyes.

"What is this?" he murmured and sniffed as if he was trying a new wine. His tongue touched my skin again. "You taste like – " His head whipped up, and his eyes glittered like he had just been served a favorite dessert. "You're a – "

"Now that is no way to treat a young lady," said a deep masculine voice from the other end of the alley. The voice was cold and menacing and the sweetest sound I had ever heard.

Eli moved so he was backed against the wall with me dangling in front of him like a ragdoll. "You are very brave, my friend, but you will move on if you know what's good for you."

"I have been told that I don't heed orders well." The shadows shifted, and a tall shape moved forward into the meager light. He wore the jeans and navy blue sweater I'd seen him in earlier, but over them he now wore some kind of leather harness that crisscrossed his muscled chest, holding an assortment of knives. Behind his right shoulder I could see the handle of what looked like a sword strapped to his back. I was so happy to see him that I almost sobbed his name.

Eli stiffened and let out a hiss. "Mohiri!" Fear crept into his voice, and my dazed mind wondered what on earth scared a vampire.

Nikolas chuckled, and I felt a tremor run through my captor. "I see there is no need for introductions. Good. I hate to waste time on formalities."

"Stay back or I will rip her apart." Eli's hand was at my throat now, the icy claws biting into my skin. I was afraid to breathe and risk being sliced open. I froze and focused on Nikolas's face, praying he would save me from this nightmare. For a second his eyes met mine, and I saw barely controlled rage in them. I glimpsed something feral and lethal simmering below the surface.

"A bit melodramatic, don't you think?" Nikolas quipped, but steel laced his voice. He took a step forward, and Eli jerked in response.

"Her death will be on your hands, Mohiri." Eli's claws pressed tighter against my throat, and warmth trickled down my neck. He shuddered at the scent of warm blood beneath his nose, and I could tell he was about to lose it. Nikolas would never reach us before those fangs tore my throat out.

Nikolas's expression never changed. His voice grew deeper, colder, and I shivered at the power radiating from him. "Do it and it will be your last act, vampire."

Eli quailed, but he did not loosen his grip. I could sense the struggle inside him. He was afraid, but he craved my blood. Would he stay and fight for his prize or run for his life?

"Brother, how like you to sneak off and sample the sweets by yourself," drawled a male voice from above. "And look at the trouble it has brought you."

Dread filled me as I looked up at the figure standing on the fire escape above our heads. Eli's grip on my throat loosened, and he sighed with relief against my hair.

"Come now, Joel. You know I always save some for you," Eli's voice rang with triumph, and the hope I'd felt a minute before died. What chance did we have against a pair of vampires?

Joel laughed and leaned against the metal railing. "I think I deserve a little more than a nibble this time. Mmm... she looks like a tasty little bit."

Eli caressed my cheek. "This one is mine."

"No!" I shouted, twisting out of his hold. For a second I was free, and my eyes immediately flew to Nikolas. His body tensed to spring.

Eli snatched me back against him just as Joel landed softly beside him. I found myself flanked by two snarling monsters, and my newfound courage floundered.

Nikolas drew a long lethal sword and faced them with no trace of fear on his face. In that instant, I knew that no matter what happened, he would not desert me. For whatever reason, he had risked his own life for mine, and live or die, we were in this together.

"You can't take us both and save her," taunted Eli. "She will die, and your efforts will be for naught."

A ghost of a smile passed over Nikolas's face. "Then I will have to settle for killing only you."

If Eli reacted to that statement, I did not see it. But I thought I detected a small quiver in his voice when he said, "Bold words for one outnumbered."

Before Nikolas could reply, a new voice cut through the tension in the alley. "Sara?" called Roland, followed by Peter shouting, "Sara, where are you?" My heart constricted, and I had to bite my lip to keep from calling out to them. I couldn't drag them into this and watch them die beside me.

Eli's head jerked a little, and Joel's eyes darted from Nikolas to the alley entrance.

Nikolas laughed harshly. "Do you smell that my friends? I believe the odds just changed."

I shot him a horrified look. Was he planning to use Roland and Peter as decoys to draw the vampires away from us? I would rather die than watch my friends get hurt because of me.

"Come, brother. There are sweeter meals to be had," Joel said, not taking his eyes off Nikolas.

"No," Eli spat. "I want this one."

Nikolas shifted, and his sword gleamed wickedly. "Release her or die, your choice. And you'd better make up your mind very soon."

"Sara, damn it where are you?" Roland sounded frantic. They were closer, almost at the mouth of the alley.

Eli's hold tightened convulsively, and I let out an involuntary cry.

One of my friends shouted, but I couldn't tell who it was. I heard a commotion in the street, followed by a growling noise that made my hair stand on end. *Oh God, what is that?* I didn't want to think about what horrors Roland and Peter could be facing now, too.

I couldn't see the street, but I heard something big run into the alley. Eli let out a screech unlike anything I'd ever heard and lunged for the fire escape, pulling me with him like I weighed nothing. When he reached for the metal ladder, my gut twisted because I knew if he made it up the fire escape I was dead. Once he reached the roof he could easily jump to the next building, and there was no way Nikolas would catch him. I'd rather die here in this alley than be tortured at the hands of a vampire.

Behind us, I heard snarls and the sounds of a battle as Nikolas engaged the other vampire. There was no time to wonder who was winning that fight because I was fighting for my own life. I scratched and kicked and struggled futilely to break free from the vise-like arm around my waist. Eli's other hand snared the ladder and pulled it toward us.

He made it almost to the first landing before he shrieked in pain and jerked backward violently. Hanging from the ladder with one hand, he lashed out with his feet at whatever was coming at him from below. He could have thrown me at his attacker to save himself, but he held on, determined to keep me while I screamed and clawed like a wild cat. The ladder groaned as the thing below tried to pull the vampire to the ground. Eli kicked at it with a force that would have killed a human, but it held on. Whatever it was, it was as strong as a vampire. The thought of something that powerful terrified and thrilled me at the same time, and I twisted my body to see what it was.

The creature had to be almost seven feet tall, even while slightly hunched over. It stood on two legs, and it was covered in dark, bristled hair with broad shoulders and clawed hands and feet. My eyes lifted to its face, and I sucked in a sharp breath at the yellow eyes, short pointed ears, and long snarling snout that revealed the biggest teeth I'd ever seen.

Werewolf! My mind struggled to come to grips with what my eyes were telling it. I was face-to-face with a real live werewolf. I knew vampires and werewolves were mortal enemies, but what were the chances of me ending up in the middle of a battle between the two in an alley in downtown Portland?

The werewolf's terrifying gaze met mine, and I saw savage intelligence in his amber eyes as his powerful jaws clamped down on Eli's calf. As the deadly fangs tore through his flesh and bone, Eli screamed in pain, and his arm around me tightened until I gasped for air. With a bloodcurdling roar, he kicked at the werewolf with his other foot, and the force of the blow sent the wolf staggering backward. It was all Eli needed to pull us both up to the metal landing.

He lay there panting for several seconds before he struggled to stand on his ravaged leg. Through the grate, I saw the werewolf recover and jump at the ladder again. Eli saw it, too, and pulled me toward the stairs. I looked at the distance between us and the wolf, and my heart plummeted because I knew it would never reach us in time. Werewolves were powerful creatures, but their bodies were not designed well for climbing. And once we got to the roof, Eli would have healed enough from his leg wound to carry us both away from here.

Eli sped up the stairs. I grabbed for the rail to slow our ascent, but he was too strong. At the last landing he paused to adjust his grip on me. "Now it's just you and me," he said with a triumphant leer as he started up the narrow ladder to the roof.

We were almost to the top when Eli let out a pained screech and stopped climbing. I looked down, hoping to see the werewolf latched onto Eli's leg again, but the creature was two landings below us. Eli gasped and struggled to hold onto me and the ladder with one hand while his other hand tried to reach something behind him. My eyes followed his movements until I saw the silver hilt protruding from a smoking hole in his side. I watched him grasp the handle of the knife, then yank his hand away, screaming as the pure silver scorched his skin.

The fire escape shook below us as the werewolf drew closer. *Please hurry,* I begged him silently, and I could have sworn he looked right into my eyes and sped up.

Eli saw him coming and abandoned his attempts to remove the knife. He reached for the roof two feet away. I did the only thing I could think of to stop him. I stretched out my hand and grasped the hilt of the knife. Pulling it free, I twisted and swung at the vampire. I didn't aim. I just tried to make contact, anything to slow him down, and I felt a bolt of satisfaction when the knife sank into the soft flesh of his shoulder.

His scream of rage and pain was like a thousand nails on a chalkboard. He shook me violently, and I dangled away from the fire escape, three stories above the ground. Far below, I saw Nikolas's furious face as he reached for another knife. At his feet lay the decapitated body of the other vampire.

Nikolas drew back his hand to throw the knife, but he stopped when he saw me hanging above the ground. He was afraid Eli would drop me if he wounded him again.

"Do it!" I screamed. I didn't want to die, but I would rather fall to my death now than let this monster carry me away to rape and torture me. My voice turned pleading. "Nikolas... please."

His arm moved so fast I barely realized the knife had left his hand before it whistled past me to embed itself in Eli's other shoulder. The vampire moaned in pain and scrabbled to maintain his grip on the ladder. He looked up at the roof, then stared fearfully down at the werewolf who was now at the bottom of the ladder directly below us. He was out of time.

The fury and hunger in his eyes when he glared at me sucked the air from my lungs. "I will have you," he rasped right before he let me go.

Time seemed to stand still. In one suspended moment I was dimly aware of the werewolf's roar, of shouts below me, and the smoking dagger in my hand before time sped up again.

5

_____

"Sara! Sara, can you hear me?"
　　"Is she – ?"
　"She's breathing."
　"Christ! Did you see what he did?"
　"I-I couldn't reach her, Pete."
　"Forget that now. Let's get her out of here."
　Strong arms picked me up and cradled me against a warm chest. I opened my eyes to see a familiar face above me.
　"Roland?"
　"She's awake," Roland said hoarsely, and I heard Peter whisper, "Thank God."
　Roland sat me on a bench at the bus stop near the building and knelt in front of me. Peter sat next to me, and I let myself lean against him. The world was coming back into focus and along with it, my memory. I pulled my knees up against my chest as my whole body shook, and I began to sob uncontrollably. I hadn't cried in front of another person in years, but it now felt like a long-sealed dam had burst open.
　Roland rose and sat on my other side. He put an arm around my shoulders, pulling me against his warmth. "You're safe now."
　I let him comfort me for a minute before I pulled away from him. My dad used to hug me all the time, but since his death I shied away from most physical contact. It provided comfort, but it also gave you a false sense of security. I used to feel safe when my dad held me, like nothing could ever hurt either

of us. Letting someone get that close to you only opens you up to more pain when they're gone.

"No one is safe," I croaked between hiccups. I was such a fool. I knew what was out there. I knew there had been vampire sightings in Portland, and still I came and nearly got all of us killed. I shuddered and buried my face in my hands, wondering if I'd ever feel safe again.

"Shit, Sara, I'm so sorry," Roland moaned. "If I had any idea something like that would happen, I never would have brought you here."

"It's my fault." Peter's voice was full of regret. "If I had stayed with her..."

Roland glared at Peter. "I was gone for five minutes. What the hell happened, dude?"

"It–it's not his fault." What could a teenage boy have done against a vampire? Then I remembered Nikolas fearlessly facing down two vampires, armed with nothing more than a sword and a bunch of knives.

"Where is Nikolas?" At Roland's confused look I said, "In–in the alley. He saved my life."

"I'd say. He ran over and fucking caught you!" Peter exclaimed. "You fell thirty feet, and the guy caught you."

"I remember falling, but that's it." How was it possible to catch a person falling from that height? How was I still alive after that?

"Probably better if you don't remember." Roland's eyes took on a haunted look. "Seeing you fall like that... I never want to feel like that again."

"So he caught me and left?" I could not keep the tremble from my voice. He'd saved me from a fate worse than death then just... disappeared?

"Yeah, he went after the um..."

"Vampire. You can say it, Peter."

Roland and Peter exchanged looks, and Roland's tone gentled like he was speaking to a child. "You've been through a lot and you're in shock right now. We should talk about this later."

"I know about vampires, Roland," I said wearily. I heard Peter's sharp intake of breath as Roland's mouth fell open. Another time I might have found their reactions comical. "Of course, I know more about them now than I ever wanted to."

"How do you – ?" Roland broke off as a group of people left the club and came down the stairs. It felt surreal to see people laughing and carrying on after what I'd just experienced, and I had to force down another wave of tears.

Roland jumped to his feet. "We should leave. We can talk in the car."

"Okay." I stood with him, but I pulled back when I remembered vampires hadn't been the only creatures in the alley. "Wait! What happened to the werewolves?"

He paled and looked around nervously. "Werewolves?"

"Don't tell me you didn't see them. Or hear them." My mind was still a bit fuzzy, but I'd never forget those yellow eyes or that massive jaw. "I only saw one, but I think there were more. For a minute there I was sure they got you. How could you not have seen them?"

"It was pretty crazy in there. I'm not sure what I saw," Peter replied slowly, and right away I knew he was hiding something because his face grew flushed. He never could lie worth a damn.

"Oh come on. You were – "

"I really think we should get out of here," Roland cut in, and I heard the urgency in his voice. "Vampires normally travel in groups. There could be more of them around here."

I pulled back. "Wait, how do you know that? How do you know about vampires at all?"

"We'll explain later, but right now we have to get out of here in case there are more." Roland tugged on my arm.

The thought of encountering another Eli sent a tremor through me, and I almost ran to his mother's blue Toyota Camry parked across the street. Roland waited until I had buckled myself into the front passenger seat before he went around to the driver's side and got behind the wheel. Through the windshield, I saw Peter pull out his cell phone and make a call. Peter's worried eyes met mine as he spoke into his phone, and I wondered who he was talking to at this hour.

Peter hung up and climbed into the back seat. He looked troubled when he leaned forward and rested his elbows on the backs of our seats. "Dad said we need to bring Sara there before we take her home. He's pretty pissed at us."

"Take me where?" I asked apprehensively. "Why does your father want to see me?"

Peter and Roland shared a look before Peter answered. "To the farm. Dad will explain it all to you when we get there."

"Why don't you guys explain it to me now?" I unbuckled my seat belt and turned in my seat to face them. Neither of them could look me in the eye, and that made me nervous. "Roland, what is going on?" I demanded.

Roland gave me a pleading look. "Please, Sara, let's just get out of here. I promise we'll tell you everything."

"I don't understand. What do you mean...?" The question died on my lips when something brushed softly against my mind just as my eyes fell on the dark figure striding down the empty street toward us, light glinting off the knives strapped to his chest. I remembered how he had walked out of the dark and faced down the vampire without a trace of fear, and a shiver went through me. I wasn't sure if it was pleasure at seeing my savior or fear; maybe a bit of both.

"Stay here," Roland ordered before he and Peter jumped out of the car to intercept Nikolas.

"Yeah, I don't think so," I muttered, already reaching for the door handle. After what I'd been through, I had no intention of staying put. And something told me that Nikolas had not come back to see my friends.

"... hunter doing around here?" Roland was saying to Nikolas as I approached them. "This is not Mohiri territory."

Hunter? Mohiri? Eli had used the word *Mohiri*, too. There was obviously a whole lot more going on here than I knew about.

Nikolas looked past my friends at me. "Hello again. You seem to have recovered quickly from your adventure." He wore a wry smile, but I thought I heard admiration in his voice.

He waved a hand at Roland and Peter. "So, these are the friends you spoke of earlier," he said with less warmth. "It's no wonder you were attacked, with nothing but a pair of pups to protect you."

Peter scowled. "Hey!"

I pushed between my friends to face Nikolas. Saving my life did not give him the right to talk to my friends that way. "It's not their fault. How could they have known something like this would happen?"

Nikolas's brows rose. "How indeed?"

"What do you mean? What's going on here?" I'd have to be blind and deaf not to notice the thinly veiled animosity between my friends and Nikolas. When no one answered, I turned to Roland. "Roland? Do you know this guy?"

Behind me Nikolas made a sound that told me he did not like being referred to as "this guy." I ignored him and glared at Roland until he shook his head. "I've never seen him before."

"But you know something about him? What does *Mohiri* mean?"

"I am Mohiri," Nikolas said. All traces of mockery were gone from his expression.

I faced him again. "And you hunt vampires." That much was kind of obvious when you figured in his attire and the headless vampire in the alley, but I wanted to hear him say it.

"Among other things." He had the same expression he had worn on the deck, like he was trying to figure me out. *God, was it really only an hour ago?*

"What about your friend from the club? Is he a hunter, too? Why didn't he help you?"

"Chris scouted the area for more hostiles while I handled the situation here."

The *situation*. That's what he called battling two bloodthirsty vampires in a dark alley? I shook my head. "So what happened? Did you get the short straw or something?"

"Or something," he drawled as his gaze burned into mine. Warmth curled in my stomach, and I dropped my eyes in confusion.

"What about the other vampire? Did you get him?" Peter asked.

"Chris is tracking him."

"He got away?" Roland's voice echoed my alarm. Eli had vowed to have me. Was he going to come after me again?

"He's injured, so he won't get too far. Don't worry. He won't stick around here now that he's being hunted."

"We should put some distance between us and this place all the same," Roland said, and I silently agreed with him.

"You live in Portland?" Nikolas asked, and we shook our heads. "Good. The farther you get from the city the better. It's not safe here right now."

"No shit." Roland took my arm. "We need to get out of here."

We made it ten feet before it hit me. *I haven't even thanked him.* I spun back to face Nikolas and found him watching me with that same impassive expression. "Thank you... for what you did. If you hadn't come when you did..." My voice cracked. After the night I'd had, the last thing I needed was to start blubbering in front of a complete stranger.

Nikolas's expression softened for a moment, and I saw a flicker of something raw and turbulent in his eyes. It pulled at me like it was an invisible cord attached to my chest, and I almost started walking toward him. But in the next moment, it was gone and I was left wondering if I had imagined it.

"Just doing my job."

"Oh...okay, well thanks anyway." His clipped words stung after what we'd just been through. It was the second time tonight he had suddenly gone cold toward me for no apparent reason. It shouldn't have bothered me because it wasn't like I'd ever see him again. But for some reason it did.

I didn't look back this time as I walked to the car. I got into the front seat again and laid my head wearily against the headrest while I waited for Roland to get in and start the engine. When I felt the car move I looked up, but the street was empty.

"Oh God, I need to call Nate." Eli had shown up before I could call Nate. "What am I going to tell him?"

"Well, I don't think you want to tell him the truth," Roland said, and I shook my head. He thought for a minute. "Just tell him we're going to hang at my house for a while. It's what we would have done anyway."

Nate, not surprisingly, was still up working on his book. I told him I was going to Roland's, and he just said not to stay out too late. It weighed on me after I hung up how easily the lie had flowed from my lips. Nate was good to me, and all I ever did was deceive him. But I honestly could not see any way to tell him the truth.

No one spoke as Roland drove us through downtown Portland. We passed a few bars with people lined up to get in as taxis of more people arrived for a night of partying. It was Friday night and the night life was in full swing. At one stoplight I watched a group of laughing young women crossing in front of us, and I couldn't help but think how that had been me a few hours ago. Was there another Eli watching them right now, selecting one to meet the fate that could have been mine tonight?

God, I'm nothing more than a statistic now. I read stories online all the time about vampire sightings and people disappearing. I'd always felt bad for the unsuspecting victims who had no idea what was out there. Until tonight, I believed I was smarter than them, more prepared because of what I knew. It was scary and humbling to know that I was just as vulnerable as everyone else.

As soon as we hit the interstate I heard Roland let out a sigh of relief. None of us were sorry to put Portland behind us. Roland fiddled with the radio until he found a classic rock station, and an Eagles song filled the car. We all relaxed a little after that, but none of us seemed inclined to speak. I knew they were keeping something from me, but my brain was too tired to process anything else right now.

A little more than an hour later, Roland took the exit ramp to New Hastings, but instead of heading into town, he drove toward the rolling farmland on the outskirts called the Knolls. He and Peter lived in the Knolls, and when we were kids I used to come out here all the time. I couldn't count the hours I'd spent on their Uncle Brendan's farm. As we passed the sign for the Knolls, it hit me that I hadn't been out here in almost a year. Had it really been that long? Up until two years ago, not a weekend passed when I wasn't with Roland and Peter. It was around that time that they began doing some "male bonding" thing with their cousins, going off on their outdoor excursions. I was hurt at first that they excluded me from their fun, until I started spending more time with Remy. Eventually, I stopped coming out here at all.

It was funny, now that I remembered it, that Roland had agreed to spend so much time with his cousins, especially Francis who was four years older than us. Roland and Francis had never gotten along, and as far as I knew, they still didn't. Francis didn't like me, and he never hid his feelings, which angered Roland. In fact, they'd had a huge fight – and I mean a bloody brawl – right before they started to hang out. We were at the farm when Francis came by and asked if I had a home to go to instead of always being underfoot. I would have told him where to go if Roland hadn't punched him first. Next thing I knew, the two of them were tearing through Brendan's cornfield, making a God-awful racket like two wild dogs trying to kill each other. Then Peter's father, Maxwell, showed up and roared at them until they'd slunk out of the damaged corn like scolded puppies.

My mouth fell open. *No!*

Do you smell that, my friends?

It's no wonder you were attacked with nothing but a pair of pups to protect you.

A large furry body jumping to catch me…

"It can't be." My hand clutched the seat belt that suddenly threatened to choke me.

Roland glanced at me. "Sara?"

I would know, right? All the days, the hundreds – no thousands – of hours together, I would have seen some sign. It wasn't like I was ignorant of the real world. Sure I'd never seen a werewolf in person until tonight, but a person would never be able to hide the obvious drawbacks of lycanthropy from people close to them. That was why most werewolves were reclusive. Like vampires, they couldn't touch silver, and it would be pretty hard to explain how you got second-degree burns from a silver fork. And werewolves were predators, they had to hunt. They couldn't live among humans unless they transformed and hunted live animals at least once a month…

My hand flew up to cover my mouth. "Stop the car."

"What's wrong?" Roland asked in alarm.

"Stop the car!"

Peter leaned forward. "Dude, I think she's going to hurl. Pull over."

Roland let off the gas and eased the car over onto the shoulder in front of a dark field. As soon as the car stopped moving, I opened the door and ran to the fence where I bent over, trying to suck air into my lungs. Behind me, car doors opened and leaves crunched as my friends came after me.

My best friends, the werewolves.

Roland spoke hesitantly. "Are you okay?"

The worry in his voice penetrated the ache in my chest. I took a deep breath, but I couldn't face them. "Why didn't you tell me?"

"Tell you what?"

"I was in shock back there, but my head is clear now." I gripped the top fence rail, and the rough wood dug into my palms. It was solid, more real than anything else tonight, and I clung to it. The desperate words I had heard as I woke up came back to me. *I couldn't reach her.* "It was you on the fire escape, wasn't it, Roland?"

Silence.

"Sara, I—" Roland began weakly.

"Shit," Peter muttered.

A breeze soughed through the trees and ruffled my hair. Close by, a small animal rooted through the underbrush. It was so dark and quiet here, and so calm compared to the city. I took a deep, tremulous breath of the country air as I tried to think of what to say.

"Please don't be afraid," Roland said in a rush. "We would never hurt you."

I turned to face them. "I know that. I'm not afraid of you. I'm upset because I had to wait for a vampire to attack me to find out the truth. And even then you tried to cover it up."

I felt like a hypocrite as soon as the accusation spilled from my lips. I was yelling at my friends for keeping a secret from me when that's exactly what I had been doing as long as I'd known them. My not-so-righteous indignation drained out of me, and I sagged against the fence, cold and tired.

Roland slowly walked toward me. "I'm sorry," he said softly, his voice heavy with regret. "We had to hide it from you. We were bound by our laws."

"And when my dad lays down a law, no one disobeys," Peter added earnestly. "We wanted to tell you, but humans are not allowed to know about us."

"Your father?"

Peter grimaced. "He's the pack leader."

Of course. Who else but Peter's imposing father, Maxwell, would be alpha? "So both of your families, all your cousins, you're all werewolves?"

"Yes," Peter replied.

My breath came out in a whoosh.

"I know you're upset, but please hear us out before you hate us," Roland implored.

"I could never hate you guys." My voice cracked. "It's just a lot to take in after..."

Roland reached for me, but I put up a hand to keep him from trying to hug me again. Instead, I took his warm hand in mine to let him know my feelings for him hadn't changed. He was still the same Roland I'd always know. Nothing would change that.

"Guys, my dad is waiting for us, and I bet he's not alone. We should probably go."

"Pete's right." Roland squeezed my hand. "You up for this?"

I nodded, and we walked back to the car. The mood during the rest of the drive was subdued. Roland and Peter kept shifting restlessly like they wanted to talk but couldn't. I had a ton of questions for them, but it looked like I wasn't going to get any answers until we saw Maxwell.

For the first time in my life, I was nervous about visiting the farm, and I felt a stab of apprehension as we turned onto a narrow lane and I saw the large white farmhouse looming ahead. Every window was lit up, and I saw Maxwell's Jeep parked next to Brendan's big Chevy pickup.

I rubbed my forehead as Roland pulled up behind the pickup and shut off the engine. He reached across the console to lay a hand on my arm. "You okay?"

"Yeah, it's just been a long night. Guess we should get this over with."

Peter leaned forward. "It's not that bad… depending on how you look at it. I mean, you just faced a couple of vampires. Can't be as bad as that, right?"

"Pete, you're not helping," Roland said sharply.

A shadow appeared in one of the windows, and I knew they were waiting for us to come in. I took a deep breath and reached for the door handle. Peter was right. I'd just survived a vampire attack. A pack of werewolves should be a piece of cake.

I followed Peter as he opened the front door and entered the house. The first person I saw in the archway to the living room was Maxwell. Tall and sinewy with a hardened face, graying reddish brown hair and beard, he watched us with a shuttered expression as we filed inside. As many years as I'd known Maxwell, I had never gotten used to his austere ways. Not that he had ever been mean to me. But he was the only person I'd ever met who could intimidate the heck out of me. Of course, knowing that he was the alpha of a werewolf pack put things in a bit more perspective. It took a tough person to fill that role.

Standing next to Maxwell was his younger brother, Brendan. The two men were matched in height and had similar features, but Brendan was stockier with receding hair and a rounder face that gave him a less severe appearance than his brother. The serious, contemplative look he gave us made me nervous, and I almost turned and ran back out the door. I didn't know if I could cope with another confrontation tonight.

Maxwell opened his mouth to speak, but a woman's voice cut him off. Roland's mother, Judith, was tall and slender but still inches shorter than her son. They had the same dark brown hair and blue eyes, though at forty-five Judith's hair was speckled with gray. I'd never met Roland's father because he died when Roland was a baby, but I always figured my friend had inherited his father's size. He sure as hell didn't get it from his mother.

"Not now, Max," Judith said in a voice that brooked no argument. "Give the girl a few minutes." She took my arm and led me to the stairs, calling over her shoulder, "Roland, go put the kettle on."

I wasn't used to having someone coddle and fuss over me, but it felt kind of nice to let Judith take charge. She bustled me up the stairs to the bathroom and told me to shower while she went to get me some fresh clothes.

After Judith closed the door behind her, I looked at myself in the mirror and gasped at the disheveled girl staring back with tangled hair, tearstained cheeks, and a dirty ripped shirt that was spotted with dried blood. It was like looking at a stranger.

I tilted my head to the side to see the four small claw marks on the left side of my throat. My fingers went to touch the marks, and a shudder passed through me as I remembered Eli's hands on me. My stomach turned over suddenly, and I retched violently in the toilet as hot tears streamed down my face.

I would have curled up in a ball right there on the floor if Judith hadn't knocked softly on the door and roused me. "Are you alright, sweetheart?"

"Yes," I called weakly. I flushed the toilet and grabbed some tissue to blow my nose. "I'm just getting in the shower." I tore off my dirty clothes and left them in a pile on the floor, then slipped under a blissfully hot stream of water. I stood there for a good five minutes letting the water cascade over me, soothing my aches and pains. It did little for the hurt inside me, but that would need some time. The water washed away a few more tears before I finally turned it off and stepped out.

A clean pair of jeans and a soft red sweater had been left on the vanity along with a steaming cup of tea that smelled like chamomile and peppermint. I sipped the tea gratefully while I dried myself and got dressed. Brendan's daughter Lydia was away at college, and I knew these must be some of her things because I had to roll up the legs and sleeves.

I towel dried my hair and combed out the tangles before I headed downstairs with the empty cup in my hand. At the bottom of the stairs, I heard Maxwell's raised voice coming from the kitchen. "... can't believe you took her to a club in Portland with everything going on," he said harshly. "And how could you be so careless? Where was your training?"

"But you said yourself this week that they had moved on," Roland protested.

"And we've been to the Attic loads of times. No one's ever messed with us," Peter chimed in. "We figured – "

"Of course no one messed with you!" Maxwell sounded even angrier if that was possible. "So you two idiots not only endangered Sara, you exposed us to a human."

"But Dad she – "

"I won't tell anyone about you."

All conversation stopped when I walked into the kitchen. Judith sat at the table with Maxwell and Brendan, and Roland leaned against the refrigerator. Peter stood by the back door looking liked he wanted a quick escape from his father's wrath. I walked over to the sink, rinsed out the cup, and laid it in the dish rack. Then I steeled myself and turned to face the room, aware that every pair of eyes was watching me.

Judith pushed out the chair next to her. "Sara, why don't you sit and we'll talk. You must be pretty confused right now."

"I'd rather stand if that's okay." I was amazed at how steady my voice sounded.

Maxwell cleared his throat, but Judith laid a hand on his arm. She nodded at me and gave me an understanding smile. "We know you've been through a lot tonight, so take all the time you need."

I didn't need time. I needed answers. Surprisingly, the first question on my lips was not the one I'd intended to ask. "Why did you let us become friends? Weren't you afraid that I'd find out what you were, spending so much time here?"

It was Maxwell who answered. "There were some in the pack who thought it a bad idea, but if we are to live among humans, we can't shut ourselves off from people. And we have ways of concealing what we are."

Apparently. Until tonight, I hadn't the slightest clue that my friends were anything but human. I wondered about the people who'd been against my friendship with Roland and Peter, and I could name at least one of them. Francis had never hidden his dislike for me. Now I knew why.

"I know you guys go hunting once a month, but Roland and Peter have only been doing that for a few years. Why didn't they go when they were younger?"

Maxwell's eyebrows shot up, and he sent a scorching look at Roland and Peter. Peter raised his hands in defense. "We didn't tell her anything, I swear."

"It wasn't them. I know werewolves have to hunt or... bad things can happen." I glanced around at the faces showing various degrees of surprise.

"See, I told you. She *knows* things," Peter piped in.

"How do you know this?" Maxwell asked.

"I – " How much could I tell them without giving away secrets I was not ready to share? I thought about what I was going to say before I continued.

"I've seen things, and I talk to people online." At Maxwell's look of disapproval, I said, "It's mostly message boards, but I do chat with some people. I've been doing it for a long time. I'm not sure if you guys know this, but there are a lot of people – humans – who know about the real world. We just don't go around telling everyone about it. Who would believe us, right?"

Maxwell's scowl softened. "You said you've seen things. What kind of things?"

Oh, you know, vampires, trolls, elementals. "Um... imps."

"Imps?" Judith repeated.

Her startled expression was so funny that I almost laughed for the first time since the attack. "Our building is infested with them."

Roland wrinkled his nose. "Ugh! You know there's a remedy for that. Pete and me can take care of them for you."

I shook my head. "I know they're a bit of a nuisance and no one likes them, but they're not so bad once you get used to them. They love blueberry muffins, so I leave them a few treats every now and then and they leave my stuff alone. They're great at catching rats, too."

Brendan coughed into his hand.

Peter's brows drew together. "I've never heard of imps infesting a human home. Is that normal, Uncle Brendan?"

Brendan shook his head. "No, but then how many human homes have you checked for imps? Guess it had to happen eventually with towns and cities growing and all."

Maxwell looked pensive. "You say you've known about our world for a long time. How long, exactly?"

My fingers gripped the edge of the counter behind my back. The only person I'd ever told this to was Remy, but there was something about my fierce friend that made it easy to tell him my troubles. Telling people who were like family to me was a different matter.

"I've known ever since my dad was killed and I saw... what they did to him." I swallowed hard. "No human could have done that, no matter what the police said. It took me a few years to figure it out."

"Vampire," Peter said, and the word hung in the air between us.

Roland straightened. "Jesus, Sara. I had no idea."

"No one did." I toyed with the hem of my borrowed sweater. "It's not like I could tell Nate or the police. Who would believe it?"

Maxwell rubbed his fingers through his beard. "We suspected. We have friends on the Portland PD, so we knew there were several suspicious deaths around that time. You were so young. I had no idea you saw it or that you knew the truth."

A chair scraped the floor, and I found myself in Judith's warm embrace. "You brave girl. I can't believe you had to deal with this alone all these years."

I hadn't been hugged so much since before my father died. I wanted to pull away, but that seemed rude somehow so I let her hold me.

She stepped back and cleared her throat. "I think I need some tea. Anyone else?"

I moved aside so she could fill the kettle. "Is it true that werewolves hunt vampires?" I asked Maxwell, who nodded.

"I can't believe I never caught on to what you are." All the days I'd spent out here, all the sleepovers with Peter and Roland and dinners with the family, and I had never seen a single clue that they were different in any way. I certainly never would have pegged them as vampire hunters.

Maxwell smiled for the first time. "We're very good at keeping our secrets. I'd be very put out if we couldn't hide them from one little girl."

Roland snorted, and his uncle shot him a dark look. "You won't find it as funny when you're running drills for the next month."

Roland's face fell, and I almost laughed at his pitiful expression. To save him from Maxwell's glare, I said, "So, is that how you know that guy, Nikolas? What's his story anyway?"

"The Mohiri are a warrior race of vampire hunters who have been around probably as long as there have been vampires. They are very secretive, and they hardly ever communicate with other hunters, though our people cross paths with them sometimes. We don't care for them and they don't like us, but we're on the same side so they leave us alone."

"Why don't you like each other?"

Brendan had been quiet since I came downstairs, but he spoke up now. "The Mohiri don't only hunt vampires. They hunt anything that is a threat to humans. A long time ago, our kind was not as... civilized as we are now, so they were hunted, too. We changed over time, but every now and then there is an incident. The Mohiri don't trust us, and there are still some hard feelings among werewolves for them."

The kettle began to whistle, and Judith lifted it from the burner and poured hot water over teabags in two mugs. The scent of jasmine wafted toward me as she slid one of the mugs across the counter to me then carried her own cup to the table. I let mine steep for a minute before taking a sip. I loved Judith's teas; she grew and dried the plants herself and stuffed the dried leaves in little mesh bags she bought at an Asian market in Portland. She always seemed to know the best tea for a situation.

"You didn't answer my question about why Roland and Peter didn't start hunting until a few years ago," I reminded Maxwell.

"We don't get the urge to hunt until sometime after puberty starts," he explained. "It's different for everyone."

"Yeah, and we also have to train… a lot," Peter added.

I looked at my friends, still finding it hard to believe they could become the terrifying creatures I saw tonight. "Have you ever hunted vampires?"

Roland shook his head. "Not until we're eighteen." A satisfied gleam entered his eyes. "Not many of us get to tangle with one before our first vampire hunt."

Maxwell shot him a withering look. "It's nothing for you to crow over. If that Mohiri hadn't been there, we might be having a different conversation right now."

The kitchen grew quiet as the weight of Maxwell's words hit us. If Nikolas had not shown up when he did, Eli would have taken me away before Roland and Peter knew I was in any danger. No one would ever have known what had happened to me, just like those other missing girls. And Eli had left no doubt about the horrors he planned for me in the last hours of my life.

Pain and guilt crossed my friends' faces. I couldn't tell them the things Eli had promised to do to me or how close I had come to never seeing them again. They already blamed themselves; I would not add to it. And if there was one thing I was good at, it was keeping secrets.

"Sara, you seem to be handling this well, all things considered," Judith observed.

I blew on my tea. "You didn't see me two hours ago."

Maxwell turned to Brendan. "We'll have to call a meeting in the morning. It looks like we're not done in Portland after all."

Brendan nodded grimly. "Wish we knew what's keeping the suckers there. They're brazen bastards to go after a girl with two pack members and a couple of hunters nearby."

I thought about Eli's determination to have me. Could he really have become obsessed just because I rejected his advances and I could not be compelled? That raised another question – why couldn't he compel me? Did it have something to do with my power? Maybe there wasn't enough room in my head for the vampire with the beast already lurking there.

"Whatever their reason, I won't tolerate them in my territory any longer. We'll add more patrols here around town and send a team to go over every inch of the city. They'll leave or die." Maxwell's voice rumbled with authority unlike anything I'd ever heard from him, and I shivered in spite of the cup of hot tea in my hands. I stole a glance at him, expecting to see glowing amber eyes, but his face was unchanged.

"I think this discussion can wait until tomorrow," Judith said firmly, obviously not in the least intimidated by her alpha brother. "Sara, why don't you stay at our place tonight? You still look too shaken up to face Nate."

I almost said no to her offer because all I wanted was my own room and my own bed. But she was right about me not being ready to see Nate. One look at him and I'd probably dissolve in tears, and there would be no hiding it from him then.

I looked over at Roland, who nodded, his eyes hopeful. I could tell he was afraid tonight had changed how I felt about them and I wanted to reassure him that nothing would ever come between us.

"I'd like that, thanks," I told Judith. Roland smiled.

Judith stood and went to rinse her cup. She took mine and washed it, too. "Alright, I think it's time we head home and let you get some sleep. You must be exhausted."

"I don't know if I'll be able to sleep tonight." I knew that as soon as I closed my eyes I'd see Eli's face.

"Then we'll keep each other company," Roland said, following us.

Peter caught up to us. "Me, too."

Judith turned around to confront them. "This is not a slumber party. Sara's been through a lot, and she doesn't need you two keeping her up all night, no matter what she says."

"You boys can stay here tonight if you want," Brendan offered, and Roland's smile faltered. It wasn't hard to read his emotions because I was sure the three of us felt the same thing. After going through such an ordeal together, none of us wanted to be separated from each other right now.

"I'd feel better if they came with us," I said, unable to keep the slight quiver out of my voice. Judith gave me a concerned look, and I hoped she wasn't going to hug me again because I was afraid I might get weepy this time. I'd cried enough tonight.

Judith smiled in understanding, and I thought for the thousandth time how lucky Roland was to have her for a mom. "Okay. Roland, you can drive."

Roland reached out and squeezed my hand as we headed for the door. "Later," he mouthed to me, tilting his head toward his mother. I gave him a small nod back. When we used to have sleepovers, he'd wait until his mother went to bed then come get me. All we did was hang out in his room and watch movies or talk until one of us started to fall asleep, but it was always the best part of my stay.

I suddenly longed for those days when the monsters were still faceless things I'd only heard about. Thanks to Eli, I'd probably never feel safe again, and I fervently hoped that Nikolas and his friend had tracked the vampire down and sent him straight to hell where he belonged.

6

"Remy, please stop glaring at me like that. You're scarier than the vampires when you make that face."

"This not funny," he scolded, pacing the mouth of the small cave we had claimed as ours years ago. His tone was angry, but I could see the worry in his eyes. "You almost die. Why you not tell me you going to city?"

I turned away from him to stare at the waves crashing against the rocks below. We both knew why I hadn't told him. He would have fussed and made me promise not to go, and it's hard to say no to a troll when he sets his mind to something.

Trolls don't fear vampires or much else for that matter, but Remy worried about me a lot. I had some amazing supe friends and the power to heal things, but I was still just a human. I had never felt more mortal than when I thought I was going to die in that alley.

I'd been tempted to not tell Remy what happened because I knew exactly how he would react. I forgot that my troll friend had the nose of a bloodhound. He'd smelled the vampire on me as soon as he got within a few feet of me. The knowledge that after three days, I still carried any scent of that monster made me want to jump into the ocean and scrub it away.

But the ocean couldn't clean the images from my mind or the memory of those cold claws pressed against my throat. I saw them whenever I closed my eyes, and at least once a night I woke in a cold sweat, still seeing Eli's snarling face and hearing his parting words, *I will have you!*

Other times I dreamed of falling, only to be caught by a dark-haired man with granite eyes. He never smiled and his eyes were cold, but I felt safe in his arms. I woke from those dreams feeling oddly bereft, but they were infinitely better than the nightmares.

The hardest part was hiding everything from Nate. I stayed upstairs most of the weekend, coming down to eat and do my usual housework chores. I felt Nate's questioning stares when we ate together, but thankfully he didn't bring it up. Roland texted me a few times to see if I wanted to do something, but I just wanted to hide in my room and lick my wounds. The animals seemed to sense my distress and made it their mission to keep me company. The cat, who I'd named Oscar, took every opportunity to snuggle up next to me, purring like a little motor boat. Daisy left Nate alone and spent the weekend sleeping at the foot of my bed. Even the imps were oddly subdued. Usually I could hear them shuffling behind the walls, but for the last two days they had been quiet except for an occasional chirrup.

After so much time alone with my thoughts, I had looked forward to getting back to school today, but I found it almost impossible to focus on classes. School seemed trivial compared to what I'd been through, and I didn't feel like the same person who had walked out of school on Friday. How do you go back to everyday life after experiencing something so life-altering?

"You know city not safe. Best to stay here with uncle."

Remy hated the idea of me leaving New Hastings, but someday I'd have to if I ever wanted to go to college or see the world. Or find out the truth about my father.

"I had to go. If there's a chance of learning more about my dad, I have to take it." I still didn't know why NightWatcher hadn't shown up at the Attic, and he hadn't been online since then either. Wulfman said it didn't sound like his friend and he'd see what he could find out. I did tell Wulfman that two vampires had been seen at the Attic so he could warn others, but I asked him not to quote me as his source. His post had shown up last night and caused quite the stir. PixieGirl was not mentioned.

"Knowledge not bring father back. It not make you less sad."

I picked up a pebble and tossed it into the waves. "I need to know, Remy. He was everything to me." I looked up at him. "What would you do if it had been your mother or father?"

Remy came over to sit beside me, his longer legs dangling beside mine. "I not lose anyone yet so I not know how you feel," he admitted. "It different with us. Humans alone, but trolls always stay together. If one killed, all trolls rise up and find killer. Protect our own."

The thought of a horde of angry trolls made me quail inside. There is a good reason why everyone fears trolls. It all started about five hundred years ago. Trolls and vampires hated each other because trolls mined silver and silver can kill vampires. One day, a vampire hunting party came upon four troll children unprotected in the woods and they slaughtered all but one, who escaped. The trolls went on a bloody rampage and literally destroyed every vampire within two hundred miles. Since then, no vampire will mess with a troll.

"Promise you not go back to city," he implored.

I watched a gull dive toward the water and rise up with a wriggling fish in its beak. "You know I can't promise I won't ever leave here. But I will promise to stay away from Portland for a while. The werewolves are hunting the vampires now, and they said the city will be safe again soon."

Remy nodded. "Werewolves not as strong as trolls, but they good hunters. Good you have werewolf friends."

"Oh yeah, about that." I faced him. "Why didn't you ever tell me? And don't say you didn't know, because you must have smelled them on me."

"Not my place to tell," he said unapologetically. "Trolls respect other Peoples. Other Peoples respect trolls."

"Does that mean my friends know about you?"

"No. Werewolves know trolls live here but keep distance." He gave me a shark grin. "You braver than pack."

I laughed, and he joined in. I wondered how Roland and Peter would react if they ever came face-to-face with a troll. What would they say if they knew about me and Remy? Maybe someday I could bring them all together and find out. That would be something to see.

I glanced at my watch and got to my feet. "I'd better head home. It's my turn to make dinner." Which meant we were having tacos. I could make three meals well: tacos, spaghetti and meatballs, and hamburgers. It was a good thing Nate liked to cook, or it would have been ground beef every night.

Remy stood and patted his shoulder. I climbed on his back and wrapped my arms around his neck. The cave was halfway down the face of a one hundred foot cliff and partially obscured by a couple of sturdy little trees growing out of a crevice in the rock. You could climb down to it if you were brave enough and knew where all the hand holds were. But the fastest way was on the back of a very strong troll. Remy started bringing me here when we first met, and it was one of our favorite hangouts because no one could see us here. This was also the ideal place to hide the troll bile because it was too dangerous to keep it at my place. At that moment we had three small vials tucked away in a hidden crevice at the back of the cave. Even if someone managed to stumble on the cave, they would not find the bile.

My stomach did a little flip when Remy grabbed a jutting rock and swung us out over the boiling waves. It always felt like this would be the time he lost his grip and sent us falling to our deaths. But he quickly scaled the cliff, never faltering once.

At the top, I slid off his back and picked up my bike helmet, which I'd tucked under a lone stunted pine tree. We crossed a small meadow and entered the woods to start the short trek to where I'd hidden my bike. Neither of us needed a trail to find our way to the road. Remy and I had explored every inch of the woods and cliffs south of town, and we probably knew the area better than anyone.

"Sara! Sara!" a high voice thrilled as we trekked through the woods. I stopped and peered through the trees because I knew that voice. Suddenly, a small body landed on my back and a pair of thin arms slid around my neck.

I reached up to swing the little troll around into a hug. "Hey, Minka, what are you doing out here alone?" The trolls lived in a network of underground caverns somewhere south of here and they did not allow their young ones to go far from the clan. That rule did not contain some of the more adventurous young trolls like Minka. Remy had been just like her at that age.

Remy's little cousin gave me a sweet smile that would one day make grown men quiver with fear. "I not alone. You here."

"Minka, you not allowed out here," Remy scolded. "You go home now."

Her lip quivered, and tears welled in her round eyes. "Not yet, Remy, please. Sara fix Nog first."

I gave Remy a questioning look. "What's a nog?"

He made a face that suggested he didn't care much for it, whatever it was. "Nog is his name. He one of the People."

One of the People? Curiosity overcame me. "If he's hurt, we should help him, shouldn't we?"

Remy sighed heavily and nodded. "Show us," he said to his cousin.

Minka slid down from my arms and ran ahead of us. "This way!" she cried. "Not far."

It was only a few minutes before we heard voices up ahead. We came to a small clearing where we found Minka's brother, Haba, and their cousins, Creah and Sinah. The three little trolls were gathered around someone huddled on the ground.

"I got Sara!" Minka yelled happily, and the others cheered and ran over to greet me. I was pretty sure the elders would not be happy to know the youngsters were this familiar with me.

Strong little hands grabbed mine and pulled me forward. "You fix Nog?" Sinah asked.

I smiled down at him. "I'll try."

"Oh!" I stared at their friend, Nog. The creature on the ground was about two feet tall with walnut-colored skin and wild yellow hair that came to his shoulders. His face was long with owlish eyes, a long nose, and a mouth that was turned down either in a scowl or in pain; I couldn't tell. On either side of his head, a pointed ear stuck straight out. He wore a crude vest and short pants made of some kind of animal hide.

He was not happy to see me. As soon as I approached him, he started thrashing and making a screeching sound that hurt my ears. I backed up a few feet into Remy.

"Remy, is that what I think it is?" I turned to him. "Is that a gobel?"

Remy nodded, and I held back a gasp. Gobels – or goblins as they are commonly called – were rumored to have died out a long time ago. Horrid creatures, they stole, liked to torment children, and were known to eat any small animal they could catch, especially cats.

"I thought there were none left," I said over the screeching.

Remy shrugged. "Not all gone. Nog live here many years. He stay away from most other People. They not like him."

I rubbed my ears. "Gee, I wonder why. Is his name really Nog?" It seemed more fitting for a Disney character than a real-life goblin.

"His real name too long to say in human tongue."

"Oh. Nog it is then."

Remy stepped past me and spoke to the goblin in what I assumed was Nog's language. He gestured toward the goblin's leg and then pointed at me, which only set the creature off again. Then Remy raised his voice, something I rarely heard him do, and spoke very forcefully. Watching the goblin suddenly calm down and glower at me sullenly, I was reminded of how Remy had talked to Fren that day in the old house. Very few could stand up to a determined troll.

"Come," Remy said. I followed him cautiously, not wanting to upset Nog again. Remy pointed at the goblin's leg, and I saw blood around his calf. "He caught in trap. Little ones free him, but his leg hurt."

I gave Nog what I hoped was a comforting smile and knelt beside his legs. "I'll need to touch his leg."

Remy spoke to the goblin again and then said, "Fix now."

I reached out tentatively and pulled the pant leg up over the wounded leg. The cut wasn't as bad as I had expected, but there was a lot of swelling and I suspected the bone was broken. When I laid a hand gently across the swelling, Nog made a growling sound and bared his teeth at me. *Of course he has to have a mouthful of needle-sharp teeth.*

"Is he going to bite me?"

"No," was Remy's response. I trusted him, so I set to healing the goblin's leg. The heat filled my hands and quickly found the fractured bone. I heard the creature gasp as my power did its work, fusing the bone together until it was whole again. Soon after, the swelling shrunk and the last of the heat seeped out of my hands.

I sank back on my heels. "All fixed," I said, and the younger trolls cheered.

"I knew you fix him," Minka said, running over to give me a rib-crushing hug.

Remy spoke to Nog, and the goblin got to his feet slowly, testing out the leg. He peered at me for a long moment then said something to me that I could not understand. I looked to Remy for help.

"He say you smell bad and now he smell bad like you for days."

"Not big on gratitude, is he?" I retorted, and Remy grinned. I turned back to the goblin, who had already started walking away. "Next time you get caught in a trap I hope a bear eats you," I called after him.

"Gobels not know how to say thank you," Remy explained. "This just their way."

I let him pull me to my feet. "It's no wonder they almost went extinct."

Remy chuckled. He ordered his little cousins to go home. Then we resumed our walk to my bike. We took our time so I could regain my energy. Strangely, I didn't feel as drained as I normally did after mending a broken bone.

"So what's Nog's story? Does he have family here?"

"No family. He like to live alone. Gobels not like other People much."

"He seemed friendly enough with your cousins," I said as we reached my bike where I'd hidden it behind some bushes.

Remy made a snorting sound. "Little ones think he funny. When they grow older they not like him so much."

"Yeah, everything looks different when you grow up." I strapped on my helmet and grabbed the bike's handlebars to stand it up. "By the way, I've been keeping an ear out and no one's mentioned the bile. I think we're safe. But we should probably lay low for a while."

"Okay. We wait some time before we make more trade."

"We'll have to wait a few months, maybe longer," I reminded him. For someone wise in so many ways, Remy knew very little about technology or the resourcefulness of humans. He did not understand that someone determined enough could track trade patterns in this area. I'd used the bile twice as currency, and I always tried to be as vigilant as possible, trading only with Malloy. But there was no telling who was paying attention out there.

"You feel strong to ride?"

I wheeled my bike up to the road. "I'm fine. It's only a few miles."

The road was little more than a gravel path with grass pushing up in the center. A long time ago there used to be an old silver mine down this way, but that had closed up back in the forties. Now the only vehicles that came down here were the occasional ATV or dirt bike. There were a lot better trails out past the Knolls and up near the old lighthouse.

It was a rough ride until I reached the main road. I thought for the hundredth time that I really needed to get my license. Nate had a Honda Element that fit his wheelchair, and he'd probably let me borrow it sometimes if I could drive. Roland was always offering to teach me; maybe it was time to take him up on it.

Once I hit the main road, I moved to the shoulder to avoid the evening traffic. Halfway home a sleek black Ducati roared past me, and the wind almost knocked me sideways. "Watch it!" I yelled at him as if he could hear me. For a moment, he started to slow down and all I could think was *Oh crap!* But he apparently changed his mind and kept going. Hanging around Jed's I'd seen a lot of bikers and most of them were decent guys, but there were always a few troublemakers. The way my luck was going lately, I didn't want to push it.

Needless to say, I was taken off guard when I reached the waterfront and saw a black Ducati sitting in front of the coffee shop next door to our building. It could have been a coincidence – there are lots of black motorcycles – but something told me that wasn't the case. I considered cutting between the buildings to Market Street and going the long way around to our building, but I dismissed that idea. Eli had made me suspicious of strangers, but I wasn't a coward and I would not start acting like one now.

I changed my mind when I spotted the tall figure leaning casually against the side of the coffee shop. Wearing jeans and a black leather jacket over a gray T-shirt, Nikolas appeared to be waiting for someone – and I didn't need three guesses to figure out whom.

As I drew near him, I felt the stirring in the back of my mind, the same faint tickle of recognition I'd experienced the moment we met. My stomach fluttered as I remembered our first encounter in the club and then how he had faced down two vampires to save me. But then I remembered his strange behavior. One minute he'd looked at me with something akin to hostility, and the next he was swooping in to save my life. Then he was back to being cold and distant again. Which Nikolas was waiting for me now? More importantly, what did he want?

I was tempted to ride past him, but curiosity got the better of me. "How did you find me?" I asked brusquely. After the way we'd parted the other night, I didn't see any need for niceties.

The corners of his mouth turned upward, and amusement flashed in his gray eyes. "What, no hello after everything we've been through together?"

He could turn that charm on someone else, because it was wasted on me. "Hello. How did you find me?"

If he was bothered by my less-than-friendly greeting, he didn't show it. "I tracked your friend's license plate."

I wasn't sure whether to be impressed or disturbed; maybe a bit of both. "Why?" He hadn't exactly left on a friendly note the other night, and I could not think of any reason for him to come looking for me. He didn't strike me as a guy who made house calls.

My question seemed to make him pause for a moment before he pushed away from the building. "We need to talk."

His tone had lost some of its teasing, and I instantly felt uneasy. I tightened my grip on the handlebars. "Talk about what?"

Nikolas raised an eyebrow. "You look ready to flee. I don't bite, you know."

"Yeah, that's what I thought about the other fellow," I replied dryly, and he surprised me by chuckling. His face lost its hardness, and his sensual smile made my stomach flutter before I gave myself a mental shake.

"You sound like you're well recovered at least." His eyes met mine unwaveringly. "I'm not here to harm you, and we really do need to talk."

"What could we have to talk about? I don't even know your last name."

"It's Danshov, and your last name is Grey. Now that we're acquainted, can we talk?"

He sounded sincere and we were out in the open, so I didn't think I was in any real danger. Plus he *had* saved my life. I should hear what he had to say; I owed him that much at least. "Okay."

"Is there somewhere we can talk privately?"

I thought for a moment. "We can go down to the wharves. They're usually pretty empty this time of day."

"That will work."

I told him I'd be back in a minute. Then I wheeled my bike around the corner of our building and hid it behind Nate's car. When I came back he was standing in front of his motorcycle waiting for me. Neither of us spoke as we started walking toward the wharves. I wondered if he felt as awkward as I did. No, guys like him probably never feel uncomfortable. His every movement emanated confidence, and he had the added advantage of size. At five-five, I felt dwarfed by him as we walked side by side.

He was silent until we passed a stack of lobster traps and began strolling along one of the deserted wharves. "How long have you been friends with the werewolves?" he asked.

The question confused me until I remembered what Maxwell had said about the werewolves and the Mohiri disliking each other. If Nikolas had a problem with my friendship with Roland and Peter he would just have to get over it. "A long time."

"And your parents don't mind?"

"It's just me and my uncle, and he likes my friends but he doesn't know what they are. He doesn't know about any of this," I said pointedly.

He nodded. "Do you mind if I ask about your parents? How did you come to live with your uncle?"

"My parents are gone. My mother left when I was two, so I don't remember her. My dad died when I was eight." I swallowed the familiar lump and stared straight ahead. "Uncle Nate is his brother."

"Do you know your mother's maiden name?"

I stopped walking and looked at him. "Why do you want to know about my parents? What do they have to do with anything?"

His face gave nothing away. "Answer my question, and I will answer yours."

I turned away in a huff and resumed walking. "Her name was Madeline. I think her maiden name was Cross or something like that. She abandoned us. I don't really care who she was."

It took me a few seconds to realize Nikolas was not beside me. I turned to look back at him and saw an odd expression on his face. "What's wrong?"

"Madeline Croix? That was her name?"

"It could be. I'm not sure. Why are you looking at me like that?"

He stared out at the water. "I just haven't heard that name in a while. If she is the Madeline I knew, it explains a lot to me."

"Well, it doesn't tell me anything, so why don't you fill me in? You said you would answer my question if I answered yours."

He gave me a small smile as he walked toward me. "I will." We were almost at the end of the wharf where two large lobster boats were moored. Nikolas pointed at some overturned crates. "Let's sit. This is a good place to talk."

I sat on one of the crates. Nikolas took the other and turned it so he was facing me. This close, his eyes were like liquid mercury, and I tried to ignore the funny twisting in my gut.

"You didn't know who the Mohiri were before the other night. How much do you know about us now?"

I lifted a shoulder. "I know you guys are vampire hunters, and you and the werewolves don't like each other. That's pretty much it."

"I imagine your friends don't talk about us any more than we do about them. Would you like to know more about the Mohiri?"

"Yes." I had no idea why he was telling me this, but I was curious about him and his whole race.

My response appeared to please him because he smiled. "You seem very familiar with our world, but how much do you know about demons?"

"Nothing, except to stay as far away from them as possible."

"What if I told you there are thousands of types of demons and that vampires are one of them?"

I narrowed my eyes at him. "I'd ask you if you are deliberately trying to scare the hell out of me."

He leaned forward with his elbows resting on his thighs. His eyes held mine with the same intensity I'd felt when we first met. "I am not here to frighten you."

I tore my gaze from his and looked down at my hands. *Too late.*

"Do you still want to hear about the Mohiri?"

I looked at him again, glad that whatever I'd seen in his eyes a minute ago was gone. "Go ahead."

"You sure?"

I gave him an encouraging smile. "Yes. I want to hear this."

He looked out at the bay. "It all started two millennia ago when demons learned how to leave their dimension and walk the earth in corporeal form. Most of them were lesser demons, and they were dangerous but not a major threat to humanity. But then a middle demon called a Vamhir appeared. It took a human host and gave the human immortality... and the thirst for human blood."

"The first vampire," I whispered, feeling a mixture of revulsion and fascination.

Nikolas nodded. "The demon soon learned how to make more like him, and before long there were thousands of vampires. The earth's population was small back then, and ancient civilizations were virtually defenseless against the vampires' strength and bloodlust. If left unchecked, the vampires would have eventually overrun the earth and wiped out humanity. So the archangel Michael came to earth to create a race of warriors to destroy the vampires. He took a middle demon called a Mori and put it inside a human male and had the male impregnate fifty human women. Their offspring were half human/half demon and they had the speed, strength, and agility to hunt and kill vampires. They were the first Mohiri."

He stopped and looked at me, waiting for my reaction. But I was still trying to absorb the part about a demon impregnating women without squirming off my seat. It finally hit me what he was saying, and I couldn't help the incredulous look I gave him.

"The Mohiri are demons?"

"Half demon," he corrected me. "Each of us is born with a Mori demon in us."

I felt the color drain from my face. "You mean you live with a demon inside you like... like a parasite?"

"Exactly like that," he said as if it was no big deal. "We give the Mori life, and in return, it gives us the ability to do what we were created to do. It is a symbiotic relationship that benefits us both."

It was too much. I got up and walked to the edge of the wharf, struggling to grasp what he was telling me. Demon parasites? I peered down at the water, and I could just make out a few tomcods and a sculpin below the surface. The water looked deceptively shallow here, but I knew it was over fifteen feet deep at this end of the wharf. Nothing in this world was what it appeared to be.

"You're not planning on jumping, are you?" There was amusement in his voice but also something that sounded like concern.

I sucked in a fortifying breath and faced him. He was still sitting on the crate, watching me expectantly. What was I was supposed to say to him? Everything I'd ever heard or read had taught me to fear demons and keep my distance from them. Now Nikolas was telling me that he was a half-demon warrior who went around protecting humans by killing other demons. I didn't know how much more weirdness I could handle.

"Why are you telling me all this?" Somehow I didn't think he had tracked me down just to educate me on demons.

He stood and walked toward me, stopping a few feet away. "Because you need to hear it."

"Why? What does this have to do with me? Or my parents?"

Nikolas's face grew more serious. "I'll get to them in a minute. First, tell me, haven't you wondered why you're different from everyone else you know?"

"D-different?" How could he possibly know about that? "I don't know what you mean."

"I think you do."

"Listen I – "

His gaze captured mine again, his eyes turning a deep charcoal gray. Before I could contemplate how a person's eyes could have so many different hues, I felt the softest brush against my mind. Some unseen force pushed gently against my walls, testing them, and in the recesses of my mind the beast stirred in response. Panic flared in me, and I reached for my power, suddenly feeling like I was locked in a battle of wills. The comforting strength of my power coursed through me and slammed against the foreign presence, flinging it away from me. Gasping, I whirled away from him. *What was that?* I'd never felt so exposed and vulnerable in my life, and it terrified me.

"Sara?"

I can't do this. I wasn't sure what *this* was, but I suddenly knew I didn't want to hear anything else he had to say. "I have to go," I uttered, moving to go around him.

"Running away won't change anything, Sara."

I didn't answer, just kept walking.

"I didn't take you for a coward."

His taunt brought me to a halt, but I didn't turn around. "You don't know anything about me."

"I think we both know that's not true."

I spun back to him because there *was* one thing I wanted to know. "What about my parents?" I demanded. "Did you know them?"

"Not your father. But I knew Madeline Croix for many years."

I shook my head. "You're only a few years older than me."

His face was unreadable. "I'm older than I look."

"So what are you trying to tell me?" I asked weakly. "How do you know Madeline?"

There was no softness in his voice, only truth. "I watched her grow up."

I stared at him mutely, and his words hung in the air between us. No, it wasn't possible. Madeline Croix was a terrible wife and mother, but she was not... one of them. Because if she was then that would make me...

7

"No!" I spun away from him, and this time I didn't stop when he called my name. I bolted for the waterfront, afraid to hear whatever he started to say next. It wasn't true – it couldn't be true. There had to be more than one woman named Madeline Croix, and for Nikolas to make such an assertion after our one encounter was insane.

He appeared in front of me, feet apart, blocking my only means of escape, and I skidded to a stop inches from him. My hands flew up to brace me from slamming into his hard chest.

"How – ?" I panted.

"Demon speed, remember?"

I winced and backed away. "Someone could have seen you."

He gave a small shrug. "You and I both know that people see only what they want to see and believe what they want to believe." He took a step toward me, forcing me to take another step back. "But just because a person chooses to not believe something, doesn't mean it's not real."

I hugged my arms to my chest. "How can you be so sure?" I asked, hearing the desperation in my voice. "There must be more than one Madeline Croix."

Nikolas's sigh sounded almost regretful. "I was sure of what you are before I heard her name. As soon as I saw you the other night, I knew." He averted his gaze as if he knew I would not like his next words. "My Mori recognized yours."

The air left my body. "What?"

"Mori can sense each other when they are near. It is how one Mohiri always recognizes another." He glanced at me, and he must have seen the denial forming on my lips because he added, "They are never wrong."

"I…" I had no idea how to respond.

Nikolas's dark eyes swept over my face as if he was searching for something. "You felt it, didn't you?"

I thought about that night and the weird sense of déjà vu that hit me when I first looked into his eyes. There had been an instant where it felt like I knew him somehow, even though I was sure we had never met. The same feeling I'd had when I saw him waiting for me by the coffee shop.

My nod was almost imperceptible. "This can't be happening."

One corner of his mouth lifted. "There are worse fates, you know."

"You're telling me I have a demon parasite inside me, and I'm supposed to be okay with that?"

"It's not as bad as you make it sound."

"No, it's worse." All these years I'd fought with the beast in my head, and now I discovered it was something far worse than I could ever have imagined. Nausea curled in my stomach.

He made no move toward me, but I heard a softening in his voice. "I know this is strange and frightening, but you are not the first orphan we've found. You will adjust as they have."

"Orphan?"

"It's just a term we use for young Mohiri who were not born to our way of life. They have no idea who they really are until we find them."

"Then there are others like me?" The thought that someone else had gone through this gave me a small measure of comfort.

"Not exactly like you." His brow furrowed. "The others have been much younger."

"What does that matter?"

He looked away briefly, and his expression was serious when his gaze returned to me. "Our Mori need us to survive as much as we need them, but they are still demons and they have certain impulses and wills of their own. We learn from a very early age to control those urges and to balance our human and demon sides. Otherwise, the Mori will try to become dominant. Orphans who are not found young enough to be trained, grow up with deep mental and emotional problems, tormented by their demon sides. The worst cases become severely schizophrenic and end up in institutions… or they kill themselves."

I inhaled sharply as I thought about the thing in my head and the dark elation I'd felt as I punched Scott. It had always felt like another consciousness lived in my head, one that would take over my mind if I let it. A shudder passed through me when I thought of where I'd be if I hadn't learned to control it. I would have ended up just like those kids Nikolas was talking about. Maybe I still would.

"How old was the oldest orphan you ever brought in?"

"The oldest reclaimed was ten, and she was the exception. The others were no more than seven."

"Ten," I squeaked. If what he was saying was right, I should be insane or dead by now. Maybe he was wrong about me. Maybe I wasn't one of his orphans after all.

"I know what you're thinking; I see it in your face. You are Mohiri. I know that with one hundred percent certainty." He took another step toward me, his eyes searching mine. "What I don't know is how you learned to subdue your demon without training. I've never seen control like yours. Your Mori is practically dormant."

Warmth spread through my belly at his nearness, and something fired in my brain. I backed up a step to keep several feet between us. I knew it was that *demon* inside me reacting to another of its kind, but that didn't make me feel any better about it.

"Is that why I'm not fast or strong like you?" I asked to cover my discomfort.

"That and we reach maturity around nineteen or twenty, which is also when our Mori reaches full strength. You should already have noticed some of your abilities starting to show by now, but you'll have to learn how to use your demon side to enhance your physical abilities."

My demon side. A shudder went through me. I didn't want this.

"Are you okay?"

"No," I told him honestly. "It's just so much to take in."

He nodded in understanding. "It will take time."

My throat was dry when I tried to swallow. "So, what else can you do besides move really fast and catch people falling off buildings? What other powers do you have?"

"Powers?"

"You know, can you compel people like vampires do or read minds or heal things? Stuff like that."

He chuckled. "No special powers or compulsion or anything else. We have the speed and strength to fight vampires. That is all we need."

"Oh." Not the answer I expected. If my healing ability did not come from the Mori, where did it come from?

"You sound disappointed."

"No, I'm just trying to understand it all." The sun was low in the sky now, and it suddenly bathed his perfect face in golden hues. "How old are you? And I don't mean how old you look."

I thought he wasn't going to answer until he said, "I was born in eighteen twenty."

My jaw fell open, but I did not care. It wasn't hard to do the math; he was almost two hundred years old. And he looked twenty, twenty-one at the most. Then the impact of his answer hit me. "Am I...?"

"Yes. Once you reach maturity, aging will stop for you, too."

"Oh," I said faintly. People were always searching for the fountain of youth. Even I had wondered what it would be like to live many lifetimes and see how the world changed. But suddenly being faced with the prospect of never aging, while Nate and everyone else I loved grew old and died, filled me with a sense of loss so great it almost sent me to my knees.

"That upsets you?" His voice held a note of surprise, and I guessed most orphans were happy to learn they would live forever.

I nodded mutely. A cool breeze came up, and I rubbed my arms, thinking that fall was just around the corner. I almost laughed hysterically at my thoughts. Here I had just discovered I was immortal, and I was thinking about the weather.

"You're cold." He started to remove his jacket, but I waved it away, not sure I could deal with kindness from him.

"I'm fine thanks." I stared down at the worn boards of the wharf then back at him. "What if I don't want to join the Mohiri?"

His brow furrowed. "You don't join. You *are* Mohiri."

"What if I don't want to live with them and I just want to stay here? You said yourself that I can control this demon thing better than anyone you've ever seen, so I don't need your training." I'd gotten by okay so far, and I didn't want to leave Nate, Remy, Roland, and Peter. I was grateful to Nikolas for saving me, and I couldn't deny I felt some strange attraction for him, but it wasn't enough for me to turn away from the only life I knew.

"You don't belong here anymore. What will you tell people when you stop aging? What will you do when everyone you know here grows old and dies? You need to be with your own people."

Nikolas's words hurt, even though I'd had the same thoughts a few minutes ago. "These are my people."

"That's because they are all you've ever known. Once you get to know the Mohiri – "

"No! I knew a Mohiri, remember? All she did was abandon me and my father." He opened his mouth to speak, but I blazed on. "My *loving* Mohiri mother deserted us, and my dad was murdered by vampires. Where were my people then?"

His face registered his shock. "Vampires killed your father?"

I laughed bitterly. "Pathetic, isn't it? You'd think someone like me would be a lot less likely to be taken in by a vampire, considering my past and my genes. Some warrior."

I pushed past him, and he didn't try to stop me. Instead he kept pace beside me. "That vampire, Eli, knows what you are now. He'll be looking for you. Vampires love nothing more than draining Mohiri orphans. We deprived him of that pleasure, and he will not forget it."

My step faltered, but I kept going. "I thought you said he wouldn't get away."

"He was more resourceful than most."

"Well if he does come back, he'll think I'm in Portland, right? There's no way he'd know to look for me here. Besides, this is werewolf territory and the werewolves are doing sweeps of Portland to find the vampires."

"The werewolves might not catch him either."

I shot him an angry look. "Are you *trying* to scare me?"

"No, but I will not lie to you either." Nikolas sounded sincere, and for some reason that annoyed me even more. I wanted to go home and put him and the Mohiri behind me, to go back to the life I knew and understood.

We reached his motorcycle, and I stopped and faced him. "I don't want you to think I'm not grateful for you saving my life because I am, more than I can say. But your way of life, your people – I don't belong with them."

He did not look happy. Obviously most orphans were willing to give up everything they knew for the Mohiri. I was not one of them.

He reached inside his jacket and pulled out a white card containing only a phone number. "This is my number. Call me if you need me or when you reconsider your options."

I took the card and stuck it in my back pocket, knowing that it would end up in a drawer somewhere and I'd never use it. "I won't reconsider."

"One more thing." Nikolas put his hand inside his jacket again and withdrew a sheathed dagger. He turned the knife over in his hand and thrust it toward me handle first. "You may feel safe here now, but as you found out Friday night, danger can find you when you least expect it."

I tried to refuse the weapon, but he pressed it into my hand and my fingers closed around the handle of their own accord. When I pulled the knife free of its sheath the silver blade gave off an almost ghostly gleam in the fading light. It looked like the one I had stabbed Eli with, only smaller, and the intricately carved handle was made of a dark polished wood. It fit my hand like it was made for me.

He donned his helmet and swung a leg over his motorcycle. "I'll be seeing you, Sara," he drawled before the Ducati purred to life.

"No, you won't," I replied, but it was drowned out by the roar of the engine as he sped away.

I moved like a sleepwalker as I made dinner. It was a good thing Nate was too busy working on a big scene to eat with me because I was incapable of making normal conversation. After I finished my tasteless meal, I escaped to my room where I watched TV, read a book, even did homework – anything to avoid thinking about the weapon hidden in the back of my closet and the train wreck that was my life. No matter what I did, the truth hovered over me like a wave of misery about to crash down and suffocate me, and there was nowhere to hide and no way to outrun it.

I paced the floor of my room like a lion in a cage, except I could not roar out my anguish with Nate downstairs. How could I tell him what was going on and who or what I really was? I pictured the revulsion on his face if he learned that I was part demon. My skin tightened and my stomach rebelled whenever I dwelled on the fact that a demon parasite was burrowed inside me. I wanted to scream and rip the ugliness from me so I could go back to feeling human again.

But I never was human, was I? My whole life was a lie. Did my dad know what Madeline was? Did he die knowing his daughter had a monster living inside her?

I stared at my face in the bathroom mirror, looking for signs, anything that would give my horrible secret away to the world. But all I saw was a normal, seventeen-year-old girl. I'd always scoffed at the kids at school for not being themselves, for trying to be something else to fit in. Jock, cheerleader, bully – they were all masks that hid the real people. But now I knew that I wore the biggest mask of all. I was a demon wearing a human face.

How could I live like this, to endure this knowledge for the rest of my life – my immortal life? I put a hand over my mouth to smother the sob torn from my throat. Nate, Roland, Peter, even Remy, everyone I loved would die someday, but I would live on. I could never have a normal relationship because everyone around me would eventually grow old and die. The thought of such a dismal existence brought on a swell of loneliness so fierce I almost doubled over from the pain in my chest.

Sleep was impossible, and the next morning I was bleary-eyed and hollow as I got ready for school. I managed to avoid talking with anyone all morning, and instead of going to the cafeteria at lunch, I holed up in the library. I had no appetite, and I couldn't bear to face Roland and Peter yet. The werewolves had made it clear they did not like the Mohiri. What would my friends do when they found out I was Mohiri? I couldn't keep something like this from them, but I needed more time to prepare myself. I needed a few more days to pretend my life was not being ripped apart from the inside out.

The week passed in a blur of classes, skipped lunches, and tormented nights. On Thursday after school, Roland caught me before I could slip away and asked me if I was sick because I was pale and even more withdrawn than usual. I mumbled an excuse about the flu and escaped before he could see through my lie.

At home it was easier to hide my turmoil. Nate worked long hours on his book, trying to meet a deadline. When he wasn't writing, he was on the phone or going out to meet with a group of local environmentalists who were concerned with rumors about some oil company suddenly showing interest in the area. Fishing and tourism were the main industries in New Hastings, and any kind of energy exploration could be damaging to both of them. I liked my town just as it was, and I hoped the oil companies would leave it alone. It was easy to forget my own misery for a little while when I thought about the animals and other creatures that could be hurt or displaced if such a thing came to pass.

I stayed close to home on Saturday and Sunday, except for a walk down to the wharves. On Saturday afternoon, I spent a few hours on the roof with Harper who strutted around, upset that I'd neglected him lately. Normally, spending time with him relaxed me, but nothing could ease my mind now.

Roland texted me on Friday night and again on Saturday to see if I wanted to do something with him and Peter. Both times I replied that I wasn't feeling well yet. I knew I was a coward and it wasn't fair to my friends, but I still didn't know how to tell them and see our friendship end.

On Monday, Roland and Peter ambushed me in the parking lot after school. "All right, Sara, what's up with you?" Roland demanded after they pulled me out of earshot of everyone else. "And don't give me that crap about being sick, because you've hardly been sick a day in your life."

"I – "

"Is it us?" Peter asked with some hesitation. "Are you freaked out about... you know... what we are? We're still friends, right?"

"Of course we're still friends." I saw doubt on their faces and realized I had been so caught up in my own misery that I hadn't seen how my sudden reticence affected my friends. While I was trying to gain the courage to tell them the truth, they were worried that I didn't want to be around them anymore because they were werewolves.

"That doesn't bother me. It's…" I bit my lip and looked down to hide the dread in my eyes. *How can I tell them?*

Peter moved closer. "You alright?"

I started to nod, but I shook my head instead. I couldn't count how many times someone had asked me if I was okay since last Friday and I always said yes, but the truth was, I was far from okay. In the last week my world had changed so much that I felt like I had stepped into someone else's life without a script. I didn't know how to think or act anymore.

"Come on." Roland touched my arm and pointed to his old red pickup. "Let's get out of here."

None of us spoke as we piled into the cab of his small Chevy truck. Roland pulled out of the parking lot and headed north. I didn't pay much attention to where we were headed. I stared at my hands most of the way and tried to find the words to tell them my awful secret when we got to our destination.

The truck slowed, and I looked up to find that we were at the old Signal Point lighthouse. The lighthouse had been decommissioned years ago, and it used to be a favorite teenage hangout. They still threw the occasional party up here because the police didn't bother with it for the most part. The sight of the peeling white tower surrounded by the faded white picket fence brought back a lot of good memories but did little to ease the weight on my chest.

Roland opened his door. "You want to go inside?"

The wind was surprisingly calm up here today so I said, "Let's go sit on the bluff."

We strolled through the grass until we neared the edge of the bluff. The three of us sat in a circle, obscured from the rest of the world by the tall grass. Overhead the blue sky was dotted with small white clouds, and below us the surf broke against the rocks in a familiar rhythm. In this peaceful setting it was almost hard to believe that bad things could happen.

"Nikolas came to see me last Monday."

"What the hell did he want?" There was no mistaking the dislike in Peter's tone, and I cringed inwardly. Would he feel the same way about me soon?

"He told me some things that kind of freaked me out. I'm not sure how to tell you about it." I looked from Peter to Roland and saw the mingled curiosity and concern on their faces. "This is really hard, so let me finish before you say anything. Okay?"

They both nodded. I took a deep breath and started at the point where I came home and found him waiting in front of the bookstore. I told them how he had tracked Roland's license plate and how he'd asked about my parents and told me he had known my mother. When I told them that Mohiri can sense each other and Nikolas had recognized me as one as soon as we met, Roland made a small sound but didn't say anything. He did not speak until I said that Nikolas told me I should be with the Mohiri.

"What did you tell him?" he asked in a tight voice.

I clutched my hands together. "I told him I belong here with you guys and Nate."

"Good."

"I thought... that since you guys hate the Mohiri you wouldn't want anything to do with me when you found out I was one of them."

"Is that what you were upset about all week?" The hurt in Roland's eyes made my own sting. "You honestly think that we would do something like that."

"No – I don't know. After what Brendan and Maxwell said about them and you two didn't hide how you felt about Nikolas – what was I supposed to think?"

Roland let out a long breath. "We don't like the Mohiri, but we don't consider them our enemy. And you being one of them doesn't change who you are."

"I guess I was just so upset that I didn't think of it that way."

"So your mom was one of them?" Peter shook his head. "All this time we were friends with a Mohiri and never knew it."

Roland could not hold back his smirk. "I bet he wasn't happy when you told him you'd rather stay with a bunch of werewolves."

I remembered Nikolas's expression when I told him I didn't want to go. "He wasn't."

"What happens now? Will they leave you alone?" Peter asked.

"I don't know. Apparently finding orphans is a big deal to them, and I'm a lot older than the other orphans they bring in. They want me to join them, but I won't let them force me into anything I don't want."

Roland swiped at an insect near his ear. "Why are you older than the other orphans?"

I bit my lip. I'd deliberately left out certain details about the Mohiri because I wanted to see how my friends reacted before I laid the whole thing on them. "What do you guys know about the Mohiri – other than that they're vampire hunters?"

Peter lifted his shoulders. "Not much. Like Dad said the other night, they're like some kind of secret society. They're super fast and strong and – " He grabbed my arm. "Hey, that means you can move like them."

I shook my head. "Nikolas said I'm suppressing that side of me. In order to be fast like him I'd have to stop holding it back."

"Then let it out. What's stopping you?" Roland said.

I tugged at a tuff of grass, unable to look at them. "I can't do that."

"Why not?"

There was never going to be an easy way to say it, so I blurted it out. "It's a demon."

Roland let out a choked laugh. "What?"

"The Mohiri are half demon." I looked up, waiting for the realization to sink in, waiting to see the same revulsion I'd lived with for a week. The only sound was the crashing of waves against the rocks. I looked away from the shock and disbelief in their faces and waited for the inevitable reactions.

"Half demon? How is that possible?" Roland's voice sounded dubious instead of repulsed, but I still couldn't look at him.

"It's called a Mori demon. The Mohiri were created specifically to kill vampires, and each one of them is born with a Mori inside. They have to learn to live with the demon side and control it, and it makes them able to fight like they do. Orphans have to be found really young so they can learn to control their Mori. If not, the demon drives them insane. Nikolas says my Mori is practically dormant, and he has no idea how I'm doing it. Otherwise, I'd probably be locked up in a mental ward right now."

Peter let out a long low whistle. "That is the craziest thing I've ever heard." He immediately ducked his head. "Sorry. I didn't mean anything bad by that. It's just that I've never heard of a demon living inside a human like that."

"Actually you have. Did you know that vampires have demon parasites inside them?"

They stared at me with similar expressions of shock. Roland found his voice first. "Nikolas told you all this?"

"Yes."

"That must have been some conversation."

"You could say that."

He ran a hand through his hair, causing it to stick out in places. "I can't believe you've been carrying this around since last week. No wonder you seemed so out of it."

"I was afraid you guys would think I was some kind of freak. You have to admit it's pretty messed up."

Roland barked a laugh. "We turn into giant mutant wolves. You don't think there's anything strange about that?"

"You can't compare yourselves to demons." My voice rose. "Demons are evil. They come from a hell dimension."

His eyes widened, and his smile faded. "You think you're evil?"

"I don't know," I replied honestly. In my heart I didn't believe I was a bad person, but I had glimpsed my dark side before. I didn't know what I was capable of. What if I lost control of the demon inside me? What if I hurt someone even worse than I had hurt Scott?

"There is no way you're evil," Peter stated unwaveringly.

I wanted so much to believe him. "How can you be so sure?"

"I'm sure because I know you. You're a good person and you never hurt people – well, except for Scott but some exceptions are okay. You hate bullies, and you always watch out for Jeffrey at school. I seriously doubt an evil person would care about him. I know you love Nate, and it's easy to see how much you loved your father. I don't think an evil person can love like that. And you're so good with animals. Uncle Brendan says animals can sense when someone is bad, so there is no way they'd let you near them if you were evil."

Roland reached over to take my hand. "You can't possibly be evil, no matter what you are. I think evil is a choice, and you choose to be good. In fact, your demon is probably dormant because you're too good for it."

I sniffed. "You mean that?"

"Yes," Roland replied with conviction. "Do you think Nikolas is evil?"

"No." Evil was the last word I'd use to describe Nikolas. Hard and direct, maybe a little overbearing. But also strong and courageous. He had put his own life at risk to save mine, and he'd displayed kindness on the wharf.

"Me either," he said to my surprise. "The Mohiri are arrogant bastards and I don't like them, but they do kill vampires. That Mori demon might be bad news on its own, but they keep it under control and use it to make them better hunters." He pointed at himself and then at Peter. "We had to learn to control our wolf sides so they didn't take over. There's a reason for the scary werewolf stories. Not all weres are good, and sometimes even good ones lose control."

It felt like an enormous weight had been lifted off my chest, and I was able to take a deep breath for the first time in a week. I let out a shaky laugh. "When did you get all wise and philosophical?"

Roland gave me a lopsided grin. "Hey, I'm not just all good looks, you know."

I fell back in the grass, giddy with relief. "I can't believe how much I let this screw with my head."

"Maybe next time you'll come to us before you freak yourself out," Roland chided. "Don't ever be afraid to confide in us. No more secrets, okay?"

I didn't answer him. My Mohiri lineage was only one of my many secrets. What would my friends think of me if they learned that I'd peddled troll bile on the black market? How would they react to my healing power or my friendship with Remy? And what would they say if they knew why I really went to the Attic that night?

We were interrupted by a cell phone ringing. "Oh crap!" Roland muttered, reaching for his phone. "I forgot I was supposed to pick up Mom. She dropped her car off to get the brakes done."

We hurried to his truck and headed back to town. The mood on the return trip was a lot lighter. Roland and Peter compared werewolves and Mohiri, and they wondered if I'd be stronger or faster than them if I used my demon side. I told them to keep guessing because there was no way I was unleashing that thing.

Nate made beef stew for dinner, and I could smell it simmering in the slow cooker as soon as I entered the apartment. I set the table then spent an hour doing homework before he came out of his office.

"Smells great," I said as he popped some take-and-bake rolls into the oven.

He gave me a sideways look. "You seem to be in a better mood today."

I grinned. "I am, and I'm starving, too."

After dinner I cleaned the kitchen and finished my homework. I felt so light and happy that I sat down to draw for the first time in two weeks. I was almost done before I saw that I'd sketched Nikolas emerging from the shadows with sword drawn, his face hard and angry like an avenging angel. I stared at the face on the paper for a long moment, not sure why I'd drawn him. He'd saved my life, but he was also a reminder of everything that had gone wrong with my life lately. I closed the sketchbook and threw it on the desk. I didn't want to ruin my good mood by thinking about Nikolas or any of that negative stuff tonight.

I opened my laptop to check email before I went to bed. There was one from Roland with a funny cartoon of a werewolf at the dentist that made me laugh. I was still smiling when I logged into my regular message board.

Five minutes later my smile dissipated along with my good humor. A new thread had been started earlier today. LOOKING FOR FOY. A cold knot started to form in my stomach as I read the dozens of replies in the thread. Most of the replies were jokes and snarky comments telling the poster that they had a better chance of winning the lottery than finding FOY. Some users dismissed it as a legend with no merit. No one seemed to take it seriously.

Except me.

FOY is the little known acronym used for troll bile. It stands for "fountain of youth." No one mentioned New Hastings, me, or Malloy, but the posting gave me goose bumps. Someone was digging around.

Don't panic. Even if there was something to it, there was nothing to trace it back to me. In any case, there was nothing I could do about it tonight. I opened a new email and sent a quick message off to Malloy. He had just as much at stake as I did if someone was nosing around. And he had a lot more contacts than I did. He'd get to the bottom of it. I hoped.

I shut the laptop and rubbed my face. How had my life gotten so damn complicated so fast?

"If it's not one thing, it's something else," I groaned, turning out the light.

8

Gino's was a small family-owned pizza place two blocks from school that used to be popular with the kids before they rebuilt the food court and added a cinema at the mall. Now most of its customers were young couples and small families. Papa Gino, as everyone called him, made the sauce and crust himself, and this place was practically an institution in town. You couldn't pay me to give up Gino's for any of the large pizza chains.

I ate my slice of pepperoni pizza and watched the door from my booth. After five more minutes, I glanced at my watch. *Is that man ever on time?*

A minute later, the door opened and Malloy slunk in. He went to the counter and bought a slice of pizza and a beer before dropping into the seat across from me.

"Hello, kid."

"Malloy."

He took a swig of beer. "Ah, that's good after a busy day." Then he picked up his slice of pizza and bit into it.

I tapped a finger on the table. "Busy getting to the bottom of certain things I hope."

He sighed and laid down his pizza. "You won't even let a man have a bite, will you?" he complained, wiping his mouth with a paper napkin. "For your information, I've been on this ever since I got your email. You're not the only one with something to lose here."

It was good to know he was taking this seriously. "So do we have anything to worry about?"

Malloy shook his head. "Don't think so. I got an acquaintance – a computer guy – who did some tracking or tracing or whatever he called it on that account that posted the message. He says it came from a high school in New Jersey, and he thinks it's just a kid messing around."

I let out the breath I was holding. "You're sure?"

"I am. Listen, kid, I take my business very serious. Even if someone was nosing around for real, they couldn't trace it back to me. I hardly ever do business from this podunk little town for one, and I got some protections in place. That's all you need to know."

I took a sip of soda, ignoring his insult to my town. "You deal with me here."

"I make exceptions," he replied with his mousy little smile. "I can't have my top suppliers showing up at my place in the city where the competition can see them."

Was that what I was – a top supplier? I guessed it made sense considering what I'd sold him a few weeks ago. That explained why Malloy had agreed to meet me in person today. He'd said he could let me know what he found out by phone, but I wasn't taking any chances. I'd wanted to see his face to make sure he was being honest with me.

"That's good to hear," I said in a calm voice that belied the storm of emotions inside me. I had been a bundle of nerves ever since I saw that posting last night.

Malloy took another bite of pizza and washed it down with a gulp of beer. He leaned across the table toward me. "Since I'm here, I wanted to ask if you think you'll be needing my services again anytime soon. With your currency, I can get you anything you want."

I crumpled my napkin and threw it on top of my leftover pizza. "Probably not for a while. I'm kinda broke right now."

"Ah." He winked at me. "Well, if you come into more money, let me know."

"You'll be the first to know." The truth was this whole thing had scared the crap out of me and made me remember that this was not a game. It was a false alarm this time, but next time we might not be so lucky. I had to tell Remy we couldn't use bile again. It was just too dangerous.

Malloy finished his pizza. "You know this place ain't so bad. I'll have to remember it next time I'm in town." He guzzled the last of his beer and stood. "See ya around, kid."

"Sara?"

I almost jumped out of my seat at Roland's voice behind me. Cringing inwardly, I turned to look at him and noticed how his eyes swept suspiciously over Malloy. The last thing I needed was for my friends to find out about my illicit dealings. That would open up a whole other can of worms that I was not ready to deal with yet.

"Hey," I said, scrambling for an explanation about why I was eating with a strange man almost old enough to be my father.

Roland stepped closer. "Is this guy bothering you?"

I laughed, hoping I didn't sound as guilty as I felt. "Roland, this is Tom Malloy. He's... Greg's uncle."

"Greg's uncle? The biker uncle?" Roland's expression was dubious with good reason. I looked like more of a biker than Malloy.

Malloy laughed and waved his hands up and down his short frame. "Only bike I can fit on is one of them scooters, and that don't seem too manly, if you know what I mean." He adjusted his coat and tucked his hands in his front pockets. "Better be off. The missus is probably wondering where I am."

Roland frowned as I stood up. "I don't like the looks of him. He looks like a drug dealer or something. What did he want?"

"He didn't want anything. He just stopped to chat."

"What are you doing here by yourself anyway?"

I shrugged. "Craving some Gino's." That part was true anyway. "You, too?"

Roland grinned and held up a large pizza box. "Dinner. Mom's on night shift." Judith was a nurse over at St. Anne's nursing home, and her shifts rotated every two days. Not that Roland needed an excuse to eat pizza.

"Come on. I'll give you a ride home."

Walking to his truck, my eyes fell on a blond man sitting alone at a table outside the coffee shop across the street. Our eyes met briefly before he looked away, and I had the strangest feeling I knew him from somewhere. Doubtful. Even from here I could tell he was hot, and I would not forget someone that gorgeous...

"No way!"

"What's wrong?" Roland asked, but I was already crossing the street, striding toward the blond man who watched with mild interest as I approached.

"I thought I made it clear that I didn't want anything to do with you people."

He peered up at me with the most striking bottle-green eyes I'd ever seen. "Excuse me?"

"Please don't insult my intelligence," I scoffed at his innocent smile. "Chris, right?" His face barely betrayed his surprise. I'd only seen him for less than a minute that night at the Attic, but I have a good memory. And who would forget a face like his?

94

"Where is he?" I scanned the street. "Obviously, I wasn't clear enough, and we need to get a few things straight."

"Sara, who is this?" Roland asked from behind me.

"Probably one of my long lost cousins or something," I said hotly, my eyes never leaving the blond Mohiri. I saw the blond's lip curl slightly and heard Roland's sharp intake of breath, but I had bigger things to deal with than some ancient feud between werewolves and Mohiri.

"Miss Grey, there is no need to – "

"Don't 'Miss Grey' me. Is he even here, or did he send you to spy on me?" I crossed my arms and glared down at him. He probably didn't deserve my ire, but the person I was really mad at wasn't here to yell at. I'd just made it through one of the worst weeks of my life, and things were finally starting to look up again. No way was I letting these people come back and ruin things for me.

Chris smiled at me, showing two ridiculously cute dimples, and a few feet away a waitress dropped an empty cup she had cleared from a table. Blushing, she muttered an apology and hurried inside.

I scowled at him, refusing to be swayed by his charm.

"I see," he murmured, nodding slightly as if he had just solved a puzzle.

"See what?"

Ignoring my question, he pulled out a cell phone, hit a number, and held the phone out to me. I hesitated for a few seconds, then took the phone and put it to my ear.

"What's up, Chris?" said a familiar deep voice on the other end.

"Good question," I responded tersely.

"I told Chris you'd recognize him if he got too close." Was that amusement in his tone?

"Great. You won the bet. Buy him a beer or whatever." I glanced at Chris, saw that he looked amused now, too, and grew even more agitated. "I thought we had an understanding when you left here last week."

"And what understanding would that be?"

I gritted my teeth. "The one where you go your way and I go mine and we all live happily ever after."

"I don't recall that particular arrangement," he replied in his infuriatingly easy manner. "I believe I told you I'd be seeing you again."

I opened my mouth, but words would not come out. People say "I'll be seeing you" all the time when they say good-bye. It doesn't mean anything. It certainly doesn't mean they will send their friends to stalk you.

"Sara?"

"What do you want from me, Nikolas? I told you I just want to be left alone."

There was a brief silence then a quiet sigh on the other end. "We got word of increased activity in Portland, and we have reason to believe the vampire might be searching for you."

It felt like an icy breath touched the back of my neck. Eli's face flashed through my mind, and my knees wobbled.

Roland stepped closer to me. "What's wrong, Sara? What is he saying to you?"

I smiled weakly at Roland and put up a hand to let him know I'd fill him in when I got off the phone. "I don't know anyone in Portland, so there's no way he can trace me here, right?"

"There's more than one way to track someone." Nikolas's voice hardened. "Don't worry. We'll keep you safe. Chris will stay close by until we handle this situation."

Great, I was the "situation" again. "I don't need a babysitter. I'm not a child."

"No you're not," he replied gruffly, and warmth unfurled in my stomach. "But you are not a warrior either. It is our duty to protect you even if you don't want our protection."

I felt like stomping my feet like a two-year-old. Didn't I get any choice in this? My eyes fell on Chris as I spoke. "How close is he planning to stay? He's kind of conspicuous, and I can't have my uncle or anyone else asking questions."

Chris peered in confusion at his form-fitting blue jeans and black sweater as Nikolas said, "Conspicuous?"

I looked heavenward. "If you guys wanted to blend in, you shouldn't have sent Dimples here. The way some of the women are staring at him, I might end up having to protect him instead."

There was a cough on the other end, and Nikolas sounded like he was grinning when he said, "Ah, I'm sure Chris can take care of himself. He'll be in town in case we suspect any trouble is coming that way."

"Fine," I relented unhappily. "But as soon as this is cleared up you guys have to go so I can try to have a somewhat normal life again."

I didn't wait for his response before I shoved the phone at Chris. I turned to Roland. "Let's go. I'll explain it to you on the way."

Once we were in the truck, I told him what Nikolas had said. Roland's face grew grim when I said that Nikolas was afraid Eli was trying to track me.

"He would have to be the stupidest vamp alive to come into this area," Roland stated confidently. "This is werewolf territory, and vamps don't mess with us if they can avoid it, especially on our home turf. I'm surprised they're still in Portland with all the patrols we have out there now."

"So you think Nikolas is overreacting?"

"According to Maxwell, the Mohiri are very thorough and they like to take care of things themselves. They won't sit back and take our word that this area is safe."

"Well, I don't want them hanging around." I groaned in a bout of self-pity. "I'm trying to move past all this."

Roland pulled the truck in behind Nate's car. "Just ignore them," he said as I opened my door. "Besides what harm can it do to let them poke around for a few days?"

"Easy for you to say. You're not the one on a leash."

"Yeah, that's no fun, believe me." He made a howling sound, and we both burst out laughing. I was still wiping my eyes when I got out and walked around to his side of the truck.

"Hey, let's do something on Saturday," he said. "Let's go out and have some fun and forget about all of this."

"Okay, but no vampires this time."

"We won't even leave town." He put the truck in reverse. "I'll see what's happening on Saturday and let you know. Smile. It'll be a blast."

I climbed into Roland's truck and squeezed in between him and Peter. "So where are we headed?"

"We narrowed it down to two options, and we're going to let you pick," Roland said as we drove along the waterfront. "Party at Dell Madden's house or party up at the lighthouse with Dylan's band."

"So a party or a... party." I put my finger to my lips. "How will I ever decide?"

"Well, you said you wanted to have some fun."

"Okay, then let's do the lighthouse party." I knew Dylan better than Dell Madden. And an outdoor party would be less crowded.

The lighthouse's overgrown parking lot was already half full of vehicles when we pulled in. Dell Madden had picked the wrong night for his party because it looked like everyone was coming to Dylan's shindig instead.

Parked in front of the lighthouse was a white van belonging to one of Dylan's band mates. Two large speakers had been rigged up, and music was already blaring when we arrived. Someone had brought a bunch of solar lights and battery operated lanterns and strung them up around the lighthouse yard, and on the beach at the lower end of the bluff, a group of boys were starting a bonfire. Everywhere I looked there were coolers of ice.

Roland reached behind his seat and pulled out a six pack. I raised an eyebrow at him and, he smiled and tossed his keys to Peter. "Pete's designated driver tonight."

Peter pocketed the keys. "It's my turn," he explained glumly.

"Well, if Roland would teach me to drive, I'd get my license and I could be the designated driver next time." It wasn't like I drank often anyway.

"Great idea!" Peter hooted as he and Roland high-fived each other. I just shook my head and followed them over to the small group of people standing by the van.

Dylan gave me a goofy smile that made his hazel eyes twinkle. "Sara, this is the second time I've seen you in two weeks. I'm starting to think you have a crush on me."

I gave the ginger-haired boy an exaggerated sigh. "You know me, full of yearning and all that."

Everyone laughed, and Dylan introduced me to the rest of his band and two of the band members' girlfriends. Everyone seemed to know Roland and Peter pretty well. The drummer, who had long, wavy blond hair and surfer good looks, gave me a quiet smile as he shook my hand then offered me a beer. I shook my head and said maybe later.

"Didn't I see you at the Attic last time we played there?" Samson asked, popping open a beer for himself.

"Yes." I smiled even as my gut clenched at the mention of that night. Watching Samson do his solo was one of the last normal things I'd done before my world went to hell. Determined to put that night behind me, I said, "You guys were great. A lot better than the rap thing Dylan used to do."

"Hey, don't be a hater!" Dylan cried with mock outrage.

Samson laughed, and I saw that he had a great smile. "Not into rap?"

"Sara likes the old stuff, classic rock," Roland told him. "I bet she can name every one of Carly Simon's albums."

"Who's Carly Simon?" asked the tall raven-haired girl named Beth. All the boys snickered, and I struggled to keep a straight face as I told Beth who Carly Simon was.

Roland put his beers, except one, in Dylan's cooler. "Come on. Let's go see who all is here."

A lot of the kids who knew Roland and Peter were strangers to me. Dylan's band mates had all gone to another school, and most of the kids were from there. I did see some familiar faces from St. Patrick's, and most of them looked surprised to see me at a party. It's not like I was a hermit. I did go out and have fun, just not as often as everyone else.

Based on the number of girls who came up to us, Roland's popularity extended beyond our high school. A couple of girls flirted blatantly with him, and a few others – who had already dated him – attempted to act casual, hoping he'd notice them again. Sometimes their attempts to catch his eye seemed a bit ridiculous to me, and I wanted to tell them all to stop behaving like idiots. If I ever got this stupid over a guy, I hoped someone would slap some sense into me.

I did feel bad for one of the girls who gave Roland a forced smile when he said hello to her. Cassidy Downs was the last girl Roland dated just before school started, and she still had a "what did I do wrong?" look that made me want to sock my best friend. The tall brunette tossed her hair and tried to look unaffected when Roland flirted playfully with other girls, but I could see the hurt in her eyes. Cassidy and I were not friends, but I hated to see someone hurting, which is why I finally pulled Roland aside.

"Stop being a douche," I scolded him when we were out of earshot of everyone.

He looked genuinely surprised. "I'm being a douche?"

I shook my head and groaned. "Roland, I know you think girls are okay if you only date them once or twice, but not all girls are the same. Can't you see that Cassidy still has a thing for you?"

"She does?" He looked over my shoulder at the group of girls we had just left. "But we only saw each other twice, and that was weeks ago."

"I guess you made a bigger impression on her than you thought."

"What am I supposed to do? I can't help how she feels."

I had to stop myself from shaking him. Boys could be so dense sometimes. "I know that, and I'm not saying you have to stay away from other girls. Just try not hook up right in front of her face."

After that, Roland kept a polite distance between him and Cassidy. He continued to flirt with other girls but to his credit, he toned it down a bit. An hour later, I saw Cassidy laughing with one of her friends, and I was glad I'd decided to say something to Roland.

By ten o'clock the crowd had almost doubled and I recognized a lot more of the faces. At some point, I separated from Roland and Peter and made my way down to the beach where a dozen or so people sat around the fire drinking. I found a flat rock to sit on and enjoyed the warmth of the fire on my face and the sound of the waves in the darkness.

The sensation of being watched made me glance around at the other faces to see who was looking at me. One boy I didn't know smiled at me, but I knew that wasn't what I'd felt. My eyes travelled along the top of the bluff. It was more like...

Son of a bitch. My gaze landed on Jessie Clark and Marie White practically hanging on the tall blond man watching me. If this was Chris's idea of staying in the background, I'd hate to see what the alternative was like.

By the time I made it up the low embankment, Chris had detached himself from the two girls and met me at the top. The girls' crestfallen expressions changed to open glares when they saw who the object of their attention had left them for. Jessie and Marie were two of Faith's cronies, so I couldn't have cared less what they thought.

"What are you doing here?" I hissed at Chris. "What happened to keeping your distance?"

Unfazed by my anger, Chris checked to make sure no one was close enough to hear us. "There have been some developments. We are bringing more people into Portland to investigate, and we thought it would be best to keep a closer eye on things on this end."

A small chill ran down my back. "What kind of developments?"

"Nothing I can elaborate on at the moment."

"Well, since it obviously has to do with me, you'd better give me more than that," I whisper-yelled at him. Did they really expect me to accept their vague explanations just like that?

Chris gave me a patient smile, and I had the feeling that between him and Nikolas, he was the more temperate of the two. That was probably why I was dealing with him instead of Nikolas. I think he knew it, too.

"All I can say right now is that we believe the vampire who attacked you may be stepping up his attempts to find you." He scanned the partiers as if assessing them for threats. "It might be advisable for you to go home and stay there for the next few days."

I blinked at him. "Are you serious? I'm in the middle of werewolf territory with two of my *werewolf* friends. We haven't heard or seen anything out of place – except you – in two weeks. I think I'm safe enough here." No need to tell him that ever since I'd spoken to Nikolas on Tuesday, I'd taken to carrying the knife he gave me everywhere. It was tucked inside the inner pocket of my jacket tonight.

"Nikolas said – "

"That's another thing. Since when does he get to call the shots here? So I'm an orphan. That doesn't give him the right to run my life." I spun away from him. "And if I want to party, then I'll party."

I stomped away, looking for Roland and Peter. Seeing neither of them, I headed for the crowd standing around by the van. Samson intercepted me as soon as I got close.

"I thought you'd run off. You ready for that beer now?"

"Definitely."

"Alright." He flipped open the nearest cooler and pulled out two beers. He opened one and passed it to me, and I took a long swallow. I didn't care what kind it was. It was cold and wet, it tasted like rebellion, and I was thirsty.

Samson grinned at me. "Slow down there, chugger."

I let out a loud burp and slapped a hand over my mouth. "Oops, sorry."

He laughed good-naturedly. "That's what happens when you drink the first one too fast."

A laugh bubbled out of me. "I'm not exactly much of a drinker."

"That's funny coming from one of Roland's friends."

"He thinks so, too," I said as we moved away from the cooler to grab a couple of plastic chairs at the edge of the crowd. I noticed a few girls watching us, and their expressions told me they were not happy to see the drummer with me. *What is with girls and good looking guys?* A girl couldn't even talk to a guy without every other female baring their claws. Nate had no idea what he was talking about when he said he wanted me to be like normal girls.

Samson leaned toward me so I could hear him over the din. "I don't know any girls who are into the older music. What stuff do you like?"

"I don't know. Most of it, I guess. Not the real heavy stuff. I like Janis Joplin, the Eagles, Fleetwood Mac, Foreigner. Stuff like that."

"What, no Backstreet Boys or 'N Sync?"

I made a face. "Did you really just ask me that?"

We both laughed. Samson had the rocker look nailed, the hot drummer with groupies and all, but he was a lot more down to earth than I had expected. We talked a lot about music and the different bands he'd been in. He told me Delilah's Crush was the first band he'd started on his own, and he had great hopes for them. I was surprised when he told me he was also doing a couple of business classes at USM. He said you had to have a backup plan.

"So you haven't said much about yourself," Samson said when he returned from getting us another beer.

"Not a lot to say really," I replied, accepting the cold beer from him. I took a long drink. "I'm a senior at a Catholic school, so you know there's not much to say about that. I live with my uncle, and unlike you I have no idea what I want to do in college, even though my school counselor keeps telling me I have to start applying soon."

He raised his eyebrows suggestively. "Catholic school girl, huh?"

"Ha, don't believe the hype," I quipped, earning a laugh from him. I laughed with him, aware that I hadn't been this relaxed in a long time and never with a boy who wasn't Roland, Peter, or Greg. I always figured that if you talked to boys too long, they'd make something out of it. I wasn't the best at reading male signals, but Samson seemed to be genuinely interested in only talking. Maybe he was tired of girls clamoring for his attention all the time and just wanted some normal conversation.

Our laughter drew the curious stares of the people nearby. I caught Dylan's eye, and he winked at me. I couldn't tell if he was playing along with his earlier comment about me crushing on him or if he was insinuating there was something going on between me and his drummer.

I turned my attention back to Samson, and I found him watching me with a soft, almost wistful expression. As soon as our eyes met, he turned on his good-natured grin again, but it was too late. Uh-oh, there it was. I groaned inwardly. *Men need to come with a user manual.* One that said, "Don't push this button."

My first impulse was to start looking for a way to politely slip away from him. But then I thought, *Why?* I liked Samson, and he seemed like a great guy. We laughed a lot, and he hadn't tried anything inappropriate. He hadn't even pushed me to drink more like a lot of guys would have. And it wasn't like I had anything to be afraid of. I was here with Roland and Peter *and* a Mohiri bodyguard.

Samson must have seen the conflict in my eyes because he stood and said, "Come on, we can't sit over here by ourselves all night. People will call us wallflowers."

"Ha. Can't have that. It would totally ruin your image."

"Damn straight." He took my hand and pulled me to my feet. The world spun for a second, and I suddenly remembered why I didn't drink. Only two beers and I was tipsy.

Samson reached out to steady me. "Whoa. Lightweight."

My scowl only got a laugh from him. "You know what the best cure is for that?" he asked, and I shook my head. He tugged me toward a group of people dancing on the other side of the van. I tried to pull back because I wasn't much of a dancer, but he wasn't having any of it. I soon discovered that he wasn't much better than me, but that didn't stop him. Soon I was dancing with everyone else and really enjoying it. We danced two fast ones before it switched to a slower song. Samson stood back and gave me a questioning look. I shrugged. What the heck?

He was a lot taller than me so my head only came to his shoulder. It felt awkward at first, dancing so close to him, but he suddenly began dipping me and acting all goofy. I was flushed and laughing by the time the song ended. Could I really be enjoying myself at a party... with a boy? What had come over me?

A sudden annoying niggling sensation in my head told me a Mohiri was near, and my lips thinned as I scanned the area looking for Chris. What was his problem now? Was dancing with a boy some kind of security risk? When I found him I was going to let him know how creepy it was to have someone watching me all the time.

My watcher stood in front of the lighthouse, arms folded and a shuttered expression on his face. When I faced him, he moved slightly and I saw the set of his jaw and the stormy stare that I was starting to think he reserved just for me.

Lucky girl.

9

I pulled away from Samson and started walking in the opposite direction.
"Are you alright?" Samson asked behind me, and I slowed to let him catch up. It wasn't his fault I was being stalked by two overbearing demon warriors. The absurdity of that thought almost made me burst out laughing. I just smiled instead.

"I'm fine, just a little thirsty."

"You want another beer?" he asked, stopping by a large cooler.

"Water if you have one. Or a soft drink is fine."

He looked in the cooler. "None here. I think we have some in the van. Be right back."

I knew Nikolas was behind me, and I turned to confront him before he spoke. "What are you doing here?"

Nikolas's brooding eyes studied my flushed face for a moment before they moved to the van and back. "Obviously protecting you from yourself. Are you drunk?"

My spine stiffened. "No, I'm not drunk. And even if I was, it would be none of your business."

His expression did not flicker. "You are my business. Whether you like it or not, you are one of us and we protect our own."

Indignation flared in me. "First of all, I am nobody's *business*, and I don't belong to you or your people or anyone else. This bossy act might work on little kids, but it won't work on me, and if I want to party with my friends or drink or do *anything* else, I will."

I had no idea what made me go off on a tirade like that. I swear something about Nikolas pushed all my buttons. Maybe I resented him for being the one to turn my life upside down. Or maybe he reminded me how weak I really was out there in the world. Maybe it was me and not him at all.

I began to whirl away from him and stumbled, and his hand shot out to steady me. "You *are* drunk."

I was wrong. It was *all* him.

"Everything okay here?" Samson asked.

I tried to make my expression neutral when I faced him. "Peachy. My... cousin was worried that I might be drinking too much. He's a lot older than me and way too uptight."

Nikolas's eyebrows shot up, and Samson did not look convinced. "Cousin, huh?"

"Distant cousins, practically unrelated." Was that a challenge I heard in Nikolas's voice? God, all I needed was to end up in the middle of some stupid testosterone match.

Samson glanced from me to Nikolas. "Listen, if there is something going on between you two, I – "

My laugh came out as more of a snort. "Yeah, not in this lifetime." I looked at Samson, ignoring Nikolas altogether. "I think I'll go see what Roland is up to. Maybe I'll see you again later."

I hadn't stomped off like that since I was five. Nikolas made me feel like throwing a tantrum; how could one person be so damn aggravating? But then a couple hundred years is plenty of time to learn how to piss people off.

I spotted Roland with Dylan and a few other guys, but I found that I had no desire for company so I headed to the beach and grabbed a seat near the fire. Someone had brought a guitar and he was playing a Lifehouse tune while everyone else talked amongst themselves. I watched the fire, content to sit quietly and listen as the guitarist finished his song and started another one.

Why did he have to show up and spoil everything? I was enjoying myself, really enjoying myself for the first time in weeks before he came along, acting arrogant and superior and reminding me how messed up my life was. All I wanted was to put the last few weeks behind me, and for a short while with Samson I had been able to do that. If Nikolas and Chris had to follow me, couldn't they do it a little more subtly? It wasn't like either of them could go unnoticed in this crowd, or any crowd for that matter, and I wasn't blind to the attention I received from people when I was with either of them. I liked to stay in the background, and I hated being stared at. I hated all of this.

I heard footsteps behind me, but I didn't have to look up to know it wasn't one of my self-appointed protectors. The girls coming down the embankment scrambled and squealed like they were tumbling down a mountain.

"I don't get it. What is the deal with her?" whined Jessie Clark. "Did you see Samson practically drooling over her? Samson – who won't even look at a girl if she's not in college!"

"I know!" Marie cut in. "I tried to talk to that dark-haired hottie, but he was watching her like frigging hawk. I thought he and Samson were going to fight over her."

My ears burned, and I was relieved no one could see the flush creeping up my cheeks. I had no doubt they were talking about me.

"I don't think she even wears makeup," Jessie declared as if wearing no eyeliner was a capital offense. I was wearing mascara and lip gloss; didn't that count?

Faith snickered. "Well, what do you expect? She only hangs out with guys. Maybe they're getting something we don't know about."

"You think she's like that?" Marie asked eagerly.

"Who knows with her," Faith replied. "But if you ask me...?"

I didn't get to hear the rest of her comment because they walked past me without even realizing I was there. My hands clenched in my lap, and I was glad no one had noticed me overhearing the exchange between the three girls.

All the fun had left the party for me, and I felt like crawling under a bush where no one could bother me until it was time to leave. I stood and picked my way a dozen feet down the beach where I could be alone but still keep the fire in sight. The night was cooling off, and it was chilly away from the fire. I pulled my jacket closer around me and drew my knees up against my chest. Close to the water, the waves drowned out the voices and music and made me feel like I was completely alone here.

I picked up a stone and flung it out into the water. *This is their fault.* I couldn't even pretend to act like a normal teenager without the two of them messing it up.

I felt the brush against my mind, and I had to stop myself from crying out in frustration. Was it too much to ask for five minutes to myself?

"Please go away," I said without looking up. "I promise I won't have any fun or fall into the ocean in my drunken state if you'll leave me alone."

He sat down beside me, and I ignored the warm arm touching mine. Silence stretched between us. I didn't want to fight again, so I kept quiet and waited for him to speak.

"I've heard that some orphans take the transition to the Mohiri life well and others struggle to adapt. Eventually, they all come to love our way of life."

I stared at the black water. "Maybe that's because their life before wasn't that great. It's got to suck being a little kid with a demon wreaking havoc in your head. But I'm not like them."

"No you're not."

"Why?"

It took him a minute to reply. "You are very strong. I don't mean physically. Like I told you before, you have amazing control over your Mori; it's almost effortless."

"You don't seem to have any trouble with yours," I said.

Nikolas chuckled. "I've had many years to learn this much control, and it's still not as good as yours."

"Oh." I pondered that for a bit. "But you do control it, right? You're not going to go all Linda Blair on me, are you? Because I've had all the craziness I can handle for one year."

His laugh was rich and warm, and in spite of my dark mood, I felt a smile tugging at my own mouth. How was he able to infuriate me one minute and make me smile the next?

"I don't think you have anything to worry about," he said lightly.

I sighed and looked at him, but he was silhouetted against the fire so I couldn't see his face. "How long is this going to go on? I just want to go back to some semblance of a normal life."

"Sara – "

"I know what you're going to say. How normal can it be when I'm immortal and everyone else is not? Why can't I have it for now, at least until I have to leave?"

It was his turn to sigh. "That might have been possible before the vampire found you. You don't know what they're like; once they decide they want something, it's like a predator scenting their prey. And you are the one that got away."

I shivered at the image of being hunted like a deer. "The werewolves don't think the vampires will enter their territory."

"I hope they're right, and I wish I could tell you that this will all go away, but I won't lie to you. I believe you are in danger here, and I won't leave you unprotected as long as that danger exists."

And we were back to square one. I threw another stone at the water and got to my feet. "Just do me a favor and don't act like every person you see is out to get me. It is possible that some boys might actually like me."

"*Ya znayu*," he muttered softly as I walked past him.

I slowed my steps. "Did you say something?"

"I said I'm sure they do."

"Too bad the party got rained out," Roland lamented, leaning back and stretching out his legs as far as he could. "It was just getting good."

"At least you two got to have a few," Peter groused as he focused on the wet road ahead.

Roland poked me with his elbow. "That's right! Did I actually see you drinking?"

"I've had beer before. I'm not a saint or anything."

On either side of me I heard snickering, and Roland leaned toward me. "According to Samson, you're an angel. What did you say to that guy? He was like a lovesick puppy all night."

My face grew hot, and I shouldered Roland away. "I didn't say anything to him. I mean, we talked about music and whatever, but that's all."

"Must have been some *whatever*," Peter teased.

"Why? He didn't think I was coming on to him, did he?" I liked Samson, and I found him easier to talk to than most guys, but I hadn't intended to lead him on. I admit there might even have been some interest on my part, but flirting had been the last thing on my mind tonight.

Roland chuckled. "No, and that's probably what snared him. Samson's used to chicks throwing themselves at him. He said he's never met a girl who was 'so real.' His words."

"Oh God." I covered my face with my hands.

"Hey, look at the bright side. We'll get in free to all their shows now."

I elbowed Roland hard in the ribs. "Shut up!" I half shouted, half laughed at him.

"And just think, if he gets famous, you'll already have your own body-guards," Peter gibed, and my mood dampened at the mention of my Mohiri shadows. I wondered where they had gotten to. Chris had disappeared after Nikolas showed up, and I hadn't seen Nikolas much after our talk on the beach. But I knew he was there in the background even if he did give me space. There was no sign of a vehicle behind us, so hopefully he had finally realized I was safe here.

"Where are we going anyway?" I asked, noticing for the first time that we weren't headed to my place.

"Well," Roland answered, dragging out the word. "Since Dylan's bash was cut short, we thought we'd check out Dell's party. It's not that late and – "

The truck began to shudder violently, and the tail slid sideways on the wet pavement. Peter cursed and gripped the wheel as he reduced speed and eased over to the shoulder of the road.

"What was that?" I exclaimed breathlessly.

"Feels like a tire blew out." Roland jumped out into the rain, ran around the back of the truck, and climbed inside again. "Yep, rear tire is shredded." He groaned and waved at the rain hitting the hood like pellets. "Someone does not want us to party tonight."

"Do you have a spare?" I asked, and he nodded. "Maybe you should wait until the rain lets up a bit. You'll get drenched by the time you change the tire."

We waited ten minutes for the rain to lessen before Roland reached for the door. "Looks like it's not going to stop. Come on, Pete."

They hopped out of the truck. I slid over to follow Roland, but he put up a hand to stop me. "No need for us all to get wet."

Several minutes later he opened the passenger door again, frowning. "We found the spare but no lug wrench."

"You're kidding," I said as they climbed in, water dripping off them.

"We're on Fell Road, less than half a mile from the turnoff," Peter told me. "It'll take me no time to run to my house and grab my mom's car."

I looked at the dark road, which was obscured by a curtain of rain. "It's cold and you'll get soaked through. Can't we call someone?"

He shook his head. "Dad, Uncle Brendan, and Mom are in Portland, and Aunt Judith is working." He opened the door. "Don't worry. I'm already soaked, so getting a little wetter won't make a difference."

"Be careful," I called after him, and he gave me a thumbs up before he set off toward home. Within minutes the darkness had swallowed him up.

Roland reached over and flicked on the hazard lights just in case anyone happened along. I leaned back, and we sat quietly, listening to the rain drumming on the hood and roof.

Roland roused me from my doze. "It's been half an hour. Pete should have called or been back by now." He picked up his cell phone and hit a number, and Peter's phone vibrated on the seat between us. Roland swore.

"Maybe he got held up. Let's give him a few more minutes." Two weeks ago I might have been worried, but that was before I'd discovered what Peter was. I doubted there was anything out there that could harm a werewolf.

Five more minutes passed before Roland opened his door and bellowed Peter's name several times. We both got out of the truck and stood in the rain, which had lessened to a heavy drizzle. "Peter?" I called as loud as I could.

"Wait, did you hear that?" Roland said in a hushed voice. He held up a hand. "I think I hear something."

I listened hard, but all I heard was water dripping from the trees. Roland's werewolf hearing was a lot better than mine, so I waited for him to say something.

"There, down that way," he said, pointing the way Peter had gone. "Pete?" he called, running up the road with me close on his heels. The cold rain flattened my hair against my head and drenched my light coat, but all I could think about was finding Peter. Then I heard it, faint but unmistakable – Peter's voice calling from somewhere up ahead. "Help."

"Roland, I hear him," I cried. "Peter, where are you?" I shouted.

"Help!" Peter called again, closer this time, somewhere in the woods to the right of the road. What the hell was he doing out there? I plunged into the trees, too wet now to care about the cold droplets showering me from the branches overhead.

Beneath the tree canopy it was almost pitch black, so I pulled my cell phone from my pocket and opened it to give me a little light. It wasn't much, but it allowed me to see a foot or so ahead of me.

"Peter, where are you?" I called again, and when he answered it sounded like he was no more than a dozen yards ahead of me.

"Sara, wait!" Roland shouted frantically from behind me. "That's not – fuck!" he swore as he tripped and crashed through the trees. "Sara, stop!"

But I was almost there. Plunging forward, I broke through the trees into a wide clearing. I strained my eyes until I could barely make out the dark shape crumpled on the ground. "Peter!" I cried, starting toward him.

A strong hand grabbed my wrist and jerked me backward. "What the hell, Roland!" I cried angrily. "What are you doing? Peter is hurt."

"That's not Pete," he whispered urgently as he started pulling me back the way we had come. It took me a full five seconds to realize what he had said and to recognize the fear in his voice.

"Of – of course it's him," I stammered, trying to pull away from Roland. "I heard him."

"I did, too," he said hoarsely. "But it's not – "

I heard movement behind me, and I looked over my shoulder to see the figure unfurling from the ground. It rose up on four legs, large and dark and in no way resembling a teenage boy. I couldn't make out the creature's features, but I thought I saw two glowing eyes – predator's eyes – and coarse fur covering its body. My breath caught. Nothing prepared me for the horror that lanced through me when the creature opened its mouth. "Help me. Please help me," it said in Peter's voice, followed by a spine-chilling cackle that set my hair on end.

"What is...?" The words died on my lips as the woods at the other end of the clearing moved and a second shape emerged. I stood on frozen legs and watched in fascinated terror as the second creature faced us for several seconds, then said, "Peter, where are you?" in an eerily perfect imitation of my voice.

In the next instant, I found myself over Roland's shoulder, fending off the branches that slapped at me as he tore through the woods. "What was that?" I wanted to shout, but the only sound I could make was an occasional "Oof" as I banged against his hard shoulder. Peter, oh God, Peter! That thing knew his voice.

I could almost taste the fear rolling off Roland as he pounded toward the road in long strides. It filled my nostrils and buzzed through my head like a live wire as a new terrifying thought struck me. *What the hell frightens a werewolf?*

Behind us a high-pitched giggle pierced the air, followed by a second. From off to one side came an answering giggle and farther away, a fourth one, moving closer. Four of them!

Moving in.

Hunting us.

We reached the edge of the trees, and Roland practically threw me out onto the road. "Run, Sara! Get to the truck," he yelled as I stumbled from my landing.

"What about you?"

"I'm going to shift. I need you to get to the truck."

Branches snapped close by like a gunshot and spurred me into a run. I heard fabric ripping and an awful stretching, crushing sound, then a savage howl that almost stopped my heart. *It's just Roland*, I told myself as I skidded on the wet road toward the headlights that shone like a beacon a few hundred yards away.

The growling became a roar as two large bodies slammed together viciously, rolling over and over, snarling and barking in the underbrush. *Roland!* I agonized, powerless to do anything but run. He was outnumbered four to one, and I had no idea what was out there or how strong the creatures were. *Please be okay*, I begged as I swiped wildly at the tangle of wet hair obscuring my vision.

There was a thump behind me, followed by a loud scraping sound. I dared a glance over my shoulder and nearly tripped at the sight of the dark shape on the road, its claws clicking against the pavement as it slunk toward me like a lion zeroing in on its prey. I screamed, and my pursuer let out a laugh so human-like that my stomach dropped like a lead weight.

The headlights blinded me when I sped inside their range. The truck's dome light was on, and the driver's side door still hung open just as Roland had left it when he took off after Peter. I was so close now – less than twenty feet.

Fifteen feet. The monster snarled in outrage and increased its speed.

Ten feet. I could hear the creature's teeth gnashing as it closed the distance between us.

Five feet. I skidded past the headlights and grasped for the door, but I missed.

Spinning around, I got my first good look at the monster bearing down on me. I saw a large head with rounded ears and a wide grinning mouth, a thick, maned neck, a sloping back, and powerful legs with clawed feet. It reminded me of a hyena, but it was as big as a buffalo.

I scrambled for the door and threw myself into the truck. My arm hooked on the seat belt, and I lost precious seconds untangling it before I could grab for the door. Through the windshield I saw the hyena-thing leap at the truck a split second before I hooked the door handle and slammed the door shut. The creature bellowed in rage as it went flying past the door.

I barely had time to catch my breath before the truck shook violently and something landed on the hood in an ear-splitting screech of claws on metal. The hood buckled beneath the weight, and I saw jagged scars in the metal where the creature's six-inch claws had found purchase. *That could have been me*, I realized, fighting the terror that threatened to suffocate me. *Stop it*. I had to keep my head if I was going to get out of this alive.

The hyena-thing turned and looked at me through the rain-splattered windshield like someone studying an insect under glass. Leaning forward, its face touched the windshield and its hot breath fogged the glass, its black eyes never leaving my face. The mouth opened, and I gasped at the double rows of jagged teeth in a powerful jaw strong enough to shred flesh and bone. *If that thing gets in here, I'm dead.*

I looked around frantically, and my eyes fell on the keys dangling uselessly in the ignition. An hysterical giggle bubbled from me when I thought of all the times I could have asked Roland to teach me to drive and I had to wait until tonight to do it. Even with a busted tire I could have driven it as far as the Knolls for help.

Call 911, said the logical part of my brain. I scrambled to find my cell phone, then remembered in dismay that it was somewhere out there in the woods. "Give me a goddamn break!"

Then I spotted Peter's phone lying on the dashboard. I leaned forward but froze when the hyena-thing's eyes hungrily followed my movement as if it might break through the glass at the slightest provocation. Drool dripped from one enormous fang and splattered the windshield. *Don't move, don't move*, I chanted.

My gut twisted painfully. Roland and Peter were out there, fighting for their lives, and I was inches from a phone to call for help. They could be hurt or dying while I sat here like a coward. I couldn't live with that. The thought of losing either of them broke through my paralysis, and I reached for the phone.

The hyena-thing saw my intention, and it grinned at me again, its eyes sizing me up with eerie intelligence. Then it looked up at the roof of the truck... and jumped.

10

The creature hit the roof, and I watched in horror as four claws punched through the metal and began to move with deadly intent, opening the top like a pocketknife opening a can. My brain froze, refusing to function, and it felt like I was watching it all happen in slow motion. The creature moved slowly, deliberately, like it was sure of its kill. In seconds it would be able to reach in and...

Move! Some part of me screamed. I flattened my body against the seat and searched for something to use as a weapon to fight off the thing about to come through the roof. I wasn't going to die without a fight.

Something dug into my right side where it was pressed against the back of the seat. *The knife.* I shifted and reached inside my coat, feeling my fingers close around the leather sheath. A sob escaped me as I pulled the knife free and held it tightly, preparing to face the monster above. The polished silver blade gleamed wickedly, and I almost laughed at the absurdity of the situation. I'd told Nikolas I was not a warrior, and I was probably going to die with a warrior's weapon in my hand.

Metal screeched as the hole in the roof grew larger. A monstrous paw reached through the opening, razor-sharp claws aiming right at my chest like a cat batting at a mouse.

For a split second, fear seemed to short-circuit my brain. Then I felt something shifting, moving in me, and gathering strength. A wail issued from me as I slashed at the paw, the sharp blade slicing through fur and tissue with sickening ease. Revulsion filled me as hot blood splattered my face and hands, and I gagged as a coppery smell filled my nose.

The hyena-thing let out a human-like bellow of pain and withdrew its injured paw. There was no time to celebrate because the other paw came crashing through the hole. More blood sprayed me as I hacked at the limb, desperate to keep those claws from reaching me. Another agonizing scream split the air, and the paw retreated, a wisp of smoke curling behind it.

The silver burns them.

Strength surged through me, and I coiled defensively against the seat, waiting for another assault. Through the hole in the roof I saw the hyena-thing crouching, moaning, and glaring at me with pure hatred as it contemplated its next move. "Not so sure of yourself now, are you?" I yelled, meeting the black stare. The eyes narrowed as if it could understand me. I immediately wished I'd kept my mouth shut as the creature advanced again.

Something hit the passenger door with the force of a battering ram. The impact tossed me in the air, and my head struck the steering wheel on the way back down. It wasn't enough to knock me out, but I lost my grip on the knife. The impact also knocked the creature off balance, and it scrambled for purchase. I flipped onto my stomach and reached frantically for the knife, which had become lodged behind the brake pedal.

"Aarrgh!" The scream was ripped from my throat as fire burned across my back. Agonizing pain stole my breath and made my sight go dark for a few precious seconds.

I couldn't think past the pain, and it was like some deeper instinct took over, making me swing around and sink my blade deep into the paw that dripped with my blood. The creature roared and lunged again, and this time I felt unbearable pain shoot through my left arm. My right hand shook as I sliced at my attacker, making it pull back again. Weariness washed over me, and I realized blood loss must be robbing me of my strength. Soon I would not be able to wield the knife at all, and it would be over.

Movement drew my attention to a second hyena creature looming outside the passenger door. Long cracks webbed through the window, and my pain-dulled mind knew one more blow would shatter it. Both creatures let out victorious whoops.

A second later, something large collided with the creature outside the door. Above me another dark, blurred shape flew over the truck, taking my attacker with it. Sounds of fighting filled the air – ripping, gnashing, howling, screams of pain. Struggling to sit, I clenched the knife to my breast and stared through the rain at the two enormous werewolves locked in bloody battle with the hyena creatures.

They're alive! My heart swelled with hope and then fear for my friends who were fighting for their lives out there. The werewolves and the hyena creatures clung to each other, slashing and biting with claws and powerful jaws. Over and over they rolled across the road until it was impossible for me to tell one from the other.

The sound of bone snapping was followed by a sickening gurgling noise, and I knew a life had just ended. I almost collapsed in relief when one of the werewolves detached itself from its opponent and joined the other against the second hyena creature. It was two against one now.

Into the headlight beams stepped two more hyena-things. I cried out as the creatures bore down on my friends, who were completely unaware of the new threat.

Pale gold hair flashed in front of the truck as a new shape appeared out of nowhere to land between the truck and the creatures. Armed with a long thin sword, Chris advanced on the hyena-things. There was a glint of metal as his weapon moved, blurring through the air to cut into the shoulder of the nearest creature. Pulling the sword free, he slashed at the second creature, the blade opening the hyena-thing's neck in a nauseating spray of blood. The creature dropped and he turned back to finish off the other one.

"No," I sobbed as another two creatures ran out of the woods. "Behind you!" I cried weakly, and the Mohiri flung his body aside just in time to avoid the surprise attack. He recovered, and he and one of the creatures began to circle each other.

My warning had gained the attention of one of the new creatures, and it turned toward the truck, wearing the same laughing grin as its brethren. I steadied myself, gripped the knife tightly, and prayed that I had enough strength left to fight it off. The pain in my back and left arm and loss of blood had weakened me, and I tried to draw on the same strength that had filled me a few minutes ago.

It wasn't enough. My eyes were already growing heavy, and the sounds of fighting seemed farther and farther away. *Am I dying?* I wondered numbly as I watched the creature draw near.

The rumbling noise came out of nowhere, vibrating through the air seconds before a single headlight appeared around the bend ahead of us. Like a missile, the motorcycle roared down the wet road, sending up a spray of water in every direction. It slammed into the creature advancing on the truck with a grisly crunch of metal and bone. The rider leapt from the bike a second before impact, landing on his feet with sword drawn. He moved swiftly toward the fallen creature. With deadly force he brought his sword down, beheading the creature with a single powerful blow. Withdrawing his sword, he strode into the mass of flailing bodies and quickly dispatched a second creature. The werewolves immediately moved in and finished off the last one.

I saw him say something to the werewolves before they ran off into the trees. I wanted to yell at them to come back, but my voice no longer worked and I sagged against the seat as tears coursed through the splatters of the creature's blood on my face.

The crumpled driver's-side door creaked and groaned as someone ripped it from its hinges. "Easy, man. You'll frighten her," a male voice said as if from a long way off.

A warm hand lifted my chin, and my dazed eyes met raging gray ones. For a moment, I forgot the burning pain coursing through me, and all I could feel was the hypnotic pull of those eyes.

Nikolas's fingers snapped in front of my face, and I realized he was speaking to me. I came out of my stupor to hear him say, "Sara, can you hear me?"

"Yes," I replied hoarsely, my throat raw from screaming.

His hand left my face and enclosed my hand that still gripped the knife. "You're safe now, *moy malen'kiy voin*. Let the knife go," he said in an uncharacteristically gentle voice.

I opened my hand and let him take the bloody weapon that had saved my life. I knew with unwavering certainty that if he had not given it to me, I'd be dead right now.

Nikolas tossed the knife on the floor of the truck and took my hands in his. He looked at me then at the roof, and his jaw clenched when he saw the shredded metal. "You fought them off? By yourself?"

"J-just one."

His harsh chuckle seemed to fill the truck. "Just one? *Khristu!*" He shook his head at the blood splattered cab. "We need to get you out of this thing. Do you think you can stand?"

I nodded, wanting nothing more than to get away from the place where I'd almost died. I started to slide out of the seat, but cried out when searing pain shot through my back and arm.

"What is it? Did it hurt you?" There was concern and something else in his voice, something dark and violent.

I nodded and closed my eyes against the pain. "G-guess I'm not much of a fighter after all."

His hand left mine. "Stay here," he ordered tersely and disappeared into the rain. I heard movement and voices raised in argument, but I couldn't make out the words. A few minutes later, Chris appeared in the opening where the driver's-side door had been. In his hand was a small metal cylinder, and he unscrewed the top and scooped out something that looked like green putty. Holding the stuff to my lips, he said, "Eat this. It will help with the pain."

"Nikolas?" I murmured.

"He's still here. Now take this like a good little girl."

I obeyed, letting him place the putty in my mouth. Immediately, I tried to spit it out as a dry, bitter taste flooded every corner of my mouth.

"No, you don't," he said, forcing my mouth closed with his hand. "I know it tastes awful, but trust me, you'll thank me in a little while."

Glaring at him, I had no choice but to chew and swallow the stuff, certain that I would never get the horrid taste out of my mouth. Within minutes, blessed numbness began to spread across the throbbing muscles of my back and arm. I let out a soft sigh as the pain retreated and I was able to think clearly again.

"Better?" Chris asked, and I nodded. "Good. Now let's get you out of this death trap so we can check out your injuries." He reached around me with both arms and effortlessly lifted me out of the cab of the truck. My legs wobbled when he set me on my feet, and I clung to his arm until I could stand on my own. The light rain was a cooling balm against my heated skin, and I lifted my face to let the water wash away tears and the creature's blood.

Chris examined the scratches on my upper arm through the tear in my sleeve. "These don't look too bad. Their claws and teeth have venom in them, and it makes the cuts feel worse than they actually are. The gunna paste I gave you will prevent infection and will speed up the healing process." He moved around me and reached for the opening of my coat. "I'm going to look at your back."

I was too happy to be alive and not hurting anymore to be embarrassed by a strange man looking under my clothes. I let him slide the thin coat off my shoulders then felt him gently prodding the scratches on my back. The foul stuff he'd made me eat must have been pretty powerful because I didn't feel any pain when he touched my wounds.

"These are a little deeper but nothing life-threatening," he announced a little louder as if he was saying it to someone else. I looked up and saw Nikolas standing rigidly by his crumpled bike with his arms crossed, watching us. He didn't seem like the type to stay on the sidelines.

Chris saw where I was looking and must have read the question on my face. "I have a better bedside manner than my friend," he explained with a wry smile.

"He looks angry. Is he mad at me?"

"No. He's upset that we were too late to stop you from getting hurt. He's worked himself into a bit of a rage and he just needs a minute to calm down."

"A rage?"

"Yes, it happens when..." He stopped and glanced back at Nikolas. "It's a Mori thing. You'll learn about that stuff soon."

"Oh." It struck me then how quiet it was. Shouldn't Roland and Peter be back by now? "Where are my friends?"

"They are making sure there are no more crocotta hiding nearby." He looked around and let out a whistle. "Six of them. That is an unusually large pack. Someone is very serious about finding you."

I shivered. "Finding me?"

"The crocotta are trackers. Someone sent them after you, probably with orders to retrieve you."

"They... almost killed me."

Chris helped me back into my coat. "The thrill of the hunt got the better of them. Good thing they're not as good at killing as they are at tracking."

My teeth started to chatter as his words sank in. Nikolas's earlier words came back to me. *We believe the vampire is searching for you... There is more than one way to track someone.*

"I think I'm going to be sick," I moaned and ran to the other side of the road where I began to retch miserably. After a minute, I straightened shakily and wiped my mouth with my wet sleeve. I wrapped my arms around myself, shivering violently as I looked away from the two Mohiri, not wanting to see them witness my humiliation.

Cloth rustled and a leather jacket slid over my shoulders.

"I'll get blood all over it," I protested weakly.

Strong hands turned me as Nikolas wrapped the jacket around me. It was way too big for me, but it was soft and warm and smelled comfortingly of aged leather, soap, and a warm spicy scent.

"I think it can stand a little blood," he said gruffly, letting go of me.

"I... thank you."

"Are you still in pain?"

"I'm much better, thanks." Between the warm coat and that foul stuff Chris had made me take, I felt a hundred times better than I had ten minutes ago.

I looked around, seeing the carnage for the first time. Six hyena-things – crocotta, Chris had called them – lay dead on the road. Even in death the creatures were terrifying. I had never seen or heard of anything like them.

Ten feet from the truck lay Nikolas's black motorcycle on its side and looking like he would not be riding it out of here tonight. My gaze fell on

Roland's truck, and I sucked in a sharp breath. The hood was buckled and scarred by long deep scratches, and the mangled door lay on the ground. Metal stood up in jagged edges from the roof, making it look like someone had taken a machete to it. It was almost inconceivable that I had come out of *that* with nothing more than a few nasty scratches.

"Only someone with warrior blood could have survived that," Nikolas said as if he'd heard my thoughts.

"I'm not a warrior."

"So you keep telling me." He walked away before I could think of a reply. I watched him go to his motorcycle and lift it upright. When he started it up, I thought he was leaving, but he turned it off and put down the stand.

"Sara!" Roland yelled, running toward us and looking a lot better than I felt. He had scratches on his face and one of his sleeves looked torn and bloody, but otherwise he looked alright considering he had been engaged in mortal combat. I held up my hands to stop him from grabbing me in a hug, and concern flooded his face. "Are you hurt?"

"Yes, but I'll live." I tried to sound flippant but failed miserably.

He ran a hand through his wet hair and let out a ragged breath. "I nearly lost it when I saw it attacking you." He stared at the closest corpse. "I studied crocotta, but I never thought I'd see them around here. Fuck! They were strong." He looked at me then cast a sad glance at what was left of his truck. "You were incredible, fighting it off like that."

"I wouldn't have lasted much longer without you guys," I told him. "Where is Peter, by the way? There's no way I'm going out there looking for him again."

Roland laughed. "He went to find his clothes. There was no one home when he got there, so he grabbed a lug wrench and headed back. He was coming up the road when he saw us getting attacked."

I didn't want to think of what would have happened if Peter, Nikolas, and Chris hadn't shown up when they did. "How did you know?" I asked Nikolas.

"One of our men called to tell me a crocotta had been seen in the Portland area," Nikolas said. "I knew that they could track you, even if the vampires couldn't."

"But how did you know where we were?"

"I put a tracker on your friend's truck at the pizza place a few days ago," Chris replied smugly. At my look of disbelief he said, "You didn't think I was going run around town all week looking for you, did you?"

Peter showed up then, and his appearance distracted Roland from whatever angry remark he'd been about to make. "I think we got them all. No worries about one of them reporting back to whoever sent them." He stared at the mutilated truck. "Damn! What the hell happened to the truck?"

Nikolas dug through one of the compartments on his bike. "You three are like a disaster magnet." He stopped searching and came over to reach into his coat pocket and pull out a cell phone. "I'm going to call for a pickup," he said to Chris.

Somehow I didn't think he meant a pickup truck. "A pickup for what?"

He narrowed his eyes. "Not what, *who*. Look around. It's not safe here for you."

I moved closer to Roland. "I'm not going anywhere."

"Be reasonable, Sara. You need to be with people who can protect you."

Roland put an arm around me. "We can protect her."

"I can see that," Nikolas retorted. "Why is it that both times she's been attacked were when you've been 'protecting' her?"

"Listen I – "

"Are you implying something?" Roland shot back.

"Look around you."

"No one could have expected a large pack of crocotta to show up like that. And you couldn't have held off that many alone either."

"No, but if she was with her own people, she wouldn't have had to worry about that."

"I'm not – "

"Her people? We're her friends. We care for her more than a bunch of strangers."

"They wouldn't be strangers for long. And she can train to protect herself."

"Stop it," I yelled, finally getting their attention. "Stop talking about me like I'm not even here. I'm not leaving New Hastings, so drop it." Every part of me was tired, and I desperately wanted to sit down. But there was nowhere to sit except for the truck, and I really didn't want to go near it right now. I was eager to put as much distance as possible between me and this place.

"Sara, I think you should come home with us tonight," Roland suggested.

"But you guys got them all."

"Yes, but you're covered in blood and your clothes are all ripped up. You don't want Nate to see you like this."

I looked down at my wet, bloody jeans. My coat was hidden by Nikolas's, but I knew it had been shredded by the crocotta. First vampires and now a bunch of mutant hyenas. At this rate I wouldn't have any clothes left.

"You're right," I told him. "Nate can't see this."

Peter went to the truck and found his phone, which had miraculously survived the carnage. He hit a number and said, "Dad, you won't believe what just happened here." He walked away with the phone to his ear.

Nikolas looked displeased but resigned with my refusal to leave. "Is there anyone around here who can clean this up before the locals see it?" he asked Roland. "If not, we'll bring in someone."

"Yeah, I'll call someone." Roland produced his own phone and made a call. A few minutes later, he hung up. "My cousin Francis will be here in a few minutes with a crew to take care of this. We'll take Sara to my house."

"Chris and I will come with you to make sure there's no more trouble," Nikolas said.

"There's no need for that," Roland said. "She'll be safe in the Knolls."

There was a hard edge to Nikolas's jaw that I was beginning to recognize. "Forgive me if I have my doubts. We will accompany you."

I looked at Chris. Nikolas had ridden up on his bike, but Chris had arrived on foot. "How did you get here so fast?" I asked him.

"My bike is half a mile down the road. When I heard the crocottas' hunting calls I decided to come in on foot to surprise them." He slanted a wry look at Nikolas. "I had no idea some people would come roaring in, making enough noise to wake the dead."

I leaned against Roland for strength and gave Chris a tired smile. "Thank you."

Chris inclined his head. "And I thought small town life was boring."

Minutes later, headlights glowed around the bend up ahead and a silver Hyundai appeared followed by a large Ford pickup. Roland's cousin Francis jumped out of the car and stared in awe at the scene before him. Older than Roland by four years, Francis had the same dark hair but a slightly leaner build than his younger cousin. Watching his face, I couldn't tell if it was the six crocotta bodies, the mangled truck, or the presence of two Mohiri warriors that stunned him the most. "Fuck," was all he could say over and over as he walked to the nearest crocotta corpse and took in the sheer size of the creature.

Someone whistled behind him, and I saw two guys I didn't know in their mid-twenties. "You guys did this?" one of them asked Roland and Peter as if he could not believe what he was seeing.

"Yes, with help," Peter said, and I could hear a little swagger in his voice. Hell, he'd earned the right to brag after what he'd done tonight.

I saw Francis and the two other guys turn hostile stares on Nikolas and Chris. "What are they doing here?" one of the guys bit out.

"They helped us fight the crocotta," Peter replied, and I could tell that he was torn between gratitude to the Mohiri and the dislike that had been ingrained in him his whole life.

"If you guys don't mind," Nikolas cut in coldly. "Sara is hurt."

"You're hurt?" Francis asked as if seeing me there for the first time. "Do you need to go to the hospital?"

"No hospital," I stated firmly.

"Maybe you should get checked out," Roland suggested.

"She'll be okay," Chris said. "I gave her something to help with the pain and to speed up the healing." At Roland's look of doubt, he said, "Trust me. It's a very powerful medicine. The Mohiri have used it in battle for centuries. With her own accelerated healing, her injuries will go away in a few days."

"Her accelerated healing?" Francis asked, and Roland and I both answered at once. "It's a long story."

"Take my car," Francis said, handing his keys to Roland. "I'll stay here with the boys to take care of this. We'll need to call in a few more hands to get rid of all these."

"Come on." Roland helped me into the front seat of the car. Peter jumped in the back. I laid my head back against the headrest with a huge sigh, happy just to be off my feet and out of the rain. Roland handed me his cell phone to call Nate since I'd lost my own phone in the woods. His voice mail picked up, and I left a message that I was going to stay at Roland's tonight and I'd see him tomorrow. Nate would most likely be delighted that I was spending more time with Roland and Peter again.

The drive to Roland's house took less than five minutes. Roland went around turning on lights, and I sank onto the couch, careful not to hurt my back. But whatever Chris had given me had worked its magic, and I could feel no pain. I closed my eyes and wrapped Nikolas's jacket tighter around me. Then I kicked off my shoes and curled up against the cushions. Roland's old couch had never felt so comfortable.

I heard the front door open. In the kitchen, Roland and Peter talked in hushed voices with someone else, but I was too tired to care. Someone laid a quilt over me, and I mumbled a thank-you without opening my eyes.

I dozed restlessly and awoke in the middle of the night to a darkened room. Fearful, I tried to sit up, but my body was too tired and stiff to respond. I heard a faint rustle and looked across the room to see the outline of someone standing by the window.

"Nikolas?"

"Go back to sleep."

I lay back and closed my eyes again until I heard him shift position.

Suddenly, I was afraid he might go and leave me alone in the dark. "Don't go," I said in a small voice, too desperate to care how plaintive I sounded.

His tone was gentler when he answered. "I'm not going anywhere."

Relief and a profound feeling of peace filled me. Heaviness stole over me again, and I fell into a blissfully dreamless sleep.

11

The smell of coffee and bacon woke me the next morning. At first I was disoriented when I saw where I was, but the events of the night before soon came crashing back. I pushed back the quilt and got gingerly to my feet, aching all over but surprisingly well-rested considering the night I'd had.

I looked down at the large leather jacket I wore. It smelled like Nikolas, and warmth suffused me when I remembered him wrapping me in it. The scent also conjured a hazy memory of him here in the room with me last night. Was that real, or had I dreamed it?

"Oh, you're up." Judith walked into the living room and gave me an appraising look. "Well, you don't look too bad, considering. How do you feel?"

I winced. "Like I was attacked by a pack of giant mutant hyenas."

She laughed softly. "I'm glad you can joke about it. What a goings-on. I'm just relieved you three are okay, though I hear you got the worst of it."

"Yeah, lucky me."

"Here, let me have a look." She came over and reached for Nikolas's jacket, sliding it off me and laying it across the back of the couch. Then she helped me out of my own ravaged coat and inspected my arm.

"I can hardly believe it. These scratches look at least a few weeks old." She straightened and smiled at me. "Roland told us about your mother. I guess you inherited the Mohiri ability to heal."

Her remarks were so casual I had to know. "It doesn't bother you – what I am?"

"Of course not. Just because we don't associate with the Mohiri doesn't mean we think they are bad people. Some of the younger hotheads like to hold on to the old grudges, but they'll grow out of it. In any case, your parentage doesn't change who you are, just like finding out what we are didn't change how you feel about us."

"Never." I reached for my coat when an object on the coffee table caught my attention. It was the knife Nikolas had given me – or one just like it. I picked it up and ran my hands over the finely made sheath before I drew the knife and marveled over the small blade that had helped save my life. In the light of day, it was hard to believe all that had happened last night.

Judith stepped back when I flashed the silver blade. "Oh, I'm so sorry." I rushed to sheathe the knife. "I forgot that you guys can't touch silver."

She waved dismissively. "Don't worry about it. It burns, but we heal fast."

I tucked the knife into the pocket of the leather jacket. "I thought silver was deadly to werewolves."

"Only if the silver gets inside and we can't get it out, which is where the whole silver bullet legend came from. It poisons us, and we can't heal as long as it's there." She smiled. "Luckily, you don't see many pure silver bullets."

"There's still so much I don't know."

"I think you're doing pretty good." She waved a hand at my clothes. "Now let's get you cleaned up. I can't believe Roland let you sleep on that couch and in your wet clothes."

I grimaced at my badly wrinkled jeans and shirt. I didn't want to imagine what my hair must look like. I'd been so worn out last night that I didn't even realize I was wearing wet clothes when I'd lain down.

"My clothes are a bit big for you, but they'll do while I wash yours. I left some things on my bed for you. Breakfast will be ready by the time you're done."

I was suddenly ravenous, so I showered and changed as fast as I could. When I entered the kitchen, Judith was putting scrambled eggs, bacon, and toast on a plate. I sat at the table, and she laid the plate in front of me with a glass of orange juice. She disappeared for a minute, and I heard the washer start up. Then she came back and sat across from me with a mug of coffee. I dug in and polished off half my breakfast before I realized she was watching me with an amused expression.

"I forgot how good your appetite is. When you kids were younger, I used to make extra whenever you stayed for dinner. You and Roland were quite the pair."

I smiled at her sheepishly. "Where is he by the way?"

"He and Peter went with Max to show him where you were attacked. We're all shocked that something like this could happen so close to us."

"Shocked" was a polite way to say it. Werewolves are very territorial, and other predators rarely cross their boundaries. Even having the Mohiri here last night had raised a few hackles, despite the fact that Nikolas and Chris had helped to fend off our attackers. A pack of crocotta hunting in werewolf territory was probably unheard of.

"Did you guys find anything in Portland?"

Judith's smiled faded a little, and it looked like she was trying to decide how much to tell me. "We found no vampires, but there were signs that they were there for a week, maybe longer."

"By *signs* you mean the missing girls?" I suppressed a shudder. I was the same age as those girls, exactly Eli's type.

"You know about them?"

I nodded. "It's not hard to guess what happened to them."

Judith ran a finger along the rim of her mug. "You're handling all of this amazingly well."

"I'm coping." If you didn't count the nightmares. Strange that I didn't remember having one last night. I would have expected to wake up screaming about giant hyenas.

"I'm not sure many girls your age could cope as well."

"To be fair, it's not like I didn't already know this world existed. I just never realized how sheltered I was here." I made a face. "And most girls don't have their own bodyguards following them around."

She watched me pensively over the top of her mug. "And how do you feel about your new relations?"

I had to think about it before I answered. How *did* I feel? I was still coming to terms with the things I'd learned about myself. All my life I'd known that the dark thing in my head was bad and had to be repressed, but the idea that it was a demon still repulsed me. I had to keep telling myself that it did not change who I was. I didn't know why that was so hard for me. When I looked at Nikolas and Chris I saw men, not demons. Good men, if I was honest. If I wasn't so annoyed with them for following me everywhere, and if Nikolas would stop being so damn high-handed, I might actually like them. It didn't help that Nikolas's suspicions last night had been right on the mark and I would have been toast if he hadn't shown up to save my life... again. Was it possible to resent someone and feel grateful to them at the same time?

"Honestly, I have no idea what to think of them. If Nikolas had his way, I'd be having Thanksgiving with them... if they even celebrate Thanksgiving.

They just seem so focused on hunting, like that's all they do. I don't think I could live like that."

Judith nodded in understanding. The werewolves were hunters too, but I'd spent enough time with them to know that they lived a normal life otherwise. Their families were close, and they had regular jobs like anyone else – a far cry from the warrior lifestyle of the Mohiri.

"Judith, why do you think the vampires came to Portland in the first place with it being so close to you guys? Why would they risk it?"

"Our best guess is they were searching for someone or something. Not you," she added quickly. "I think you were just unlucky enough get their attention."

I pushed my eggs around with my fork. "Do you think... is it possible that my dad's murder had anything to do with my mother being a Mohiri? I mean, vampires hate the Mohiri, right? Maybe one of them came looking for her and found my dad instead."

Judith's hand went to her throat, and her expression told me I'd hit on something. "If you know anything, you have to tell me," I begged her.

"Sara, you need to leave this to Maxwell. I can see how you would want answers about your father's death, but he wouldn't want you getting hurt over this."

"I just want to know what you found. Please. I have a right to know."

She got up and poured herself another cup of coffee, then sat across from me again. "We've been in touch with some of our contacts around the country since Roland told us about your mother. The Mohiri are too closed off to tell us anything about her, but our network is very large and we did find some details. Not a whole lot but it's only been a few days."

"We know that your mother spent a lot of time in California, Texas, and New Mexico after she left you and your father. Then a week before your father was killed, we believe she was in Portland for a very short time. We have no idea why she went back or if she even saw your father while she was there."

Judith didn't say what both of us were thinking. It was too much of a coincidence that Madeline went back to Portland the same week that vampires showed up and killed her husband of all people. Madeline had led them to us – maybe not intentionally – but it was her fault they found us. First she abandoned us, and then she led those monsters right to our door.

"Is she still alive?" I asked, almost spitting out the words.

Judith hesitated then said, "Yes. We believe she is somewhere in South America now."

"My dad was murdered, and I might as well have been killed too for all she cared," I said with so much bitterness that I didn't recognize my own voice. "How could he have loved someone like her?"

"I'm sure she must have had some good qualities. And as for your father, people will overlook a lot when they are in love."

"What kind of person does something like that?" I said almost to myself. "Are all the Mohiri that unfeeling?"

Judith set down her cup. "I don't know much about the Mohiri so I can't speak for them, but don't judge them all by the actions of one. I will tell you that the man who gave you his coat and stood guard over you all night can't be all that bad. Maybe he's not as friendly or easygoing as the people you're used to, but he's certainly not unfeeling either."

So I hadn't dreamed it. Her revelation confused me even more. Nikolas was like two different people in one body: the cold, hard warrior and the kind protector. It was hard to know which one would appear when he showed up.

"He feels responsible for me since he was the one who found me. I don't think he even likes me because I don't fall in line like a good little orphan."

"I see."

I got up and carried my dishes to the sink. "The Mohiri have this thing about orphans," I explained as I rinsed my plate. "They find their orphans and raise them and train them to be warriors. Only I'm not like most orphans because I'm older. I can't be persuaded to join the Mohiri like little kids can, and now Nikolas feels like he has to watch over me until he can get me off his hands. I don't think he knows what to do with me."

Judith chuckled softly and came to rinse her cup. "I think you may be right about that." She nudged me away from the sink. "I'll clean up here. Go throw your clothes in the dryer."

I spent the rest of the morning helping Judith with housework, although she wouldn't let me do anything too heavy because I was still recovering from the attack. There was something comforting about doing mundane chores after such a crazy night. Laundry and vacuuming have a way of grounding you when your life seems like it's about to spin out of control.

By the time Roland showed up for lunch, the house was spic and span and I was learning how to make chicken rice casserole, which Judith guaranteed Nate would love. It was the kind of thing I should have learned from my own mother, if she'd cared enough to stick around. I hoped Judith saw how much it meant to me, because as usual I couldn't find the words to say it out loud.

After lunch, Roland borrowed his mother's car to make good on a promise he'd made to me. We drove down to the small Presbyterian Church in the Knolls, and he spent two hours teaching me to drive. Judith's car was a stick, and it took me most of the lesson to get the hang of the gear stick and all the pedals. By the end of the lesson, I'd managed to drive once around the parking lot without stalling or popping the clutch.

"Can't I learn on an automatic?" I whined after the car jerked forward for the hundredth time.

"Not if you want to learn anytime soon. Looks like the truck will be out of commission for a while – a long while."

I quit complaining after that. He had worked and saved for two years to buy that old thing, and now it was ruined because of me. When I tried to apologize, he dismissed it. Apparently, he and Peter were some kind of local heroes after last night, since few werewolves get the chance to tangle with a crocotta, especially a pack of them. I wasn't sure if that honor was worth losing his wheels, but Roland seemed to think so.

At three o'clock I decided I'd hidden out at Roland's long enough. Judith put my casserole in a carrier, and I rolled up Nikolas's jacket and stuck it in a plastic bag with my ruined coat so Nate would not see them. Roland drove me home in his mother's car, and I couldn't help but wonder more than once where Nikolas and Chris were today, if they were following us right now. After last night, I was torn about them hanging around. I definitely felt safer knowing they were nearby, but I couldn't spend my life being followed and watched all the time. There were things in my life, secrets that I couldn't share, and they would be hard to conceal if I was forever under surveillance. Hopefully, the vampires would give up soon and the Mohiri could leave and let things go back to normal. Judith told me that Maxwell had beefed up patrols in New Hastings today. The crocotta had struck too close to home, and the werewolves were worried about their own families. With the increased werewolf presence and the Mohiri warriors, New Hastings was probably safer right now than it had ever been.

Nate was at his computer when I got home. I stopped in front of his office door and held up the carrier. "Judith taught me how to make a casserole," I gushed like a kid who'd just learned to tie her shoelaces. "Chicken and rice."

"Really?" He eyed the carrier with anticipation. He didn't say it, but I could tell he was happy – not because of Judith's cooking, but because I was spending a lot more time with Roland and Peter. For once I agreed with him. Despite all the bad things that had happened in the last few weeks, I was happier than I'd felt in a long time.

Dinner was nice. Nate had two helpings of casserole, and we were both more relaxed than we'd been in a while. That didn't stop him from noticing that something was off with me. "Are you feeling okay? You look a bit pale."

"Just tired. We stayed up late last night, and I helped Judith around the house today."

"Cooking *and* housework?"

"Hey, I do housework," I protested, even though we both knew how much I disliked it. I'd rather gut fish down on the wharf than clean the bathroom.

Nate smiled like I'd said something funny, and I scowled at him.

"Why don't you ask Judith if you can stay with them while I'm at the conference next week?" he said. "That way you won't have to be here alone? Imagine what you could learn to cook in five days."

Nate had started going to an annual writer's conference in Boston two years ago, once he finally realized I was old enough to get along without him for a few days. Five whole days of total freedom. I loved Roland and Judith, but no way was I giving that up.

"Are you kidding? I'm going to order from Gino's every day and dust off the *Buffy* DVDs."

He grimaced. "Pizza and vampire slayers. What more could you want?"

"Hey, you should be glad I'll just be lounging around in pajamas," I said with a sly grin. "Although I could call up the cute drummer I met at the party last night and see if he wants to hang out."

His eyes widened in dismay. "A drummer?"

"Yeah, but don't worry. He's also taking college classes in case the band thing doesn't work out."

The look on Nate's face was priceless. "College? How old is this boy?"

"Um, twenty, I think." I had no idea how old Samson was, but I was having too much fun to stop. "So really he's more of a man than a boy when you think about it."

Nate's expression of horror was so funny I couldn't hold back my laughter any longer. "Breathe, Nate. I'm just messing with you. I mean, I did meet a very nice guy, but nothing happened. Of course, that might not be the case if I was a *normal* girl who was going out and dating and all."

He glowered at me. "How long have you been waiting to use that one?"

"A loooong time." My heart felt light as I wrapped up the leftover casserole and put it in the fridge. I couldn't remember the last time Nate and I had bantered this way. "When are you leaving?"

"Not until next Tuesday morning, and I'll be back on Sunday. You have my cell number, and I'll leave the hotel information on the fridge before I go." He sipped the strong black tea he liked to have after dinner. "That way you can get hold of me anytime."

"I'll be fine," I assured him. "Oh by the way, I need to get a new cell phone. I lost mine last night. It's probably water logged now after all the rain."

"How did you lose your phone?"

"Dropped it somewhere in the woods out in the Knolls," I replied vaguely.

He looked at me over his cup. "Do I want to know what you were doing in the woods in the middle of a storm?" He shook his head. "Never mind, forget I asked. I'll get you one tomorrow. I don't want you here alone without a cell phone."

Nate went back to his book, and I cleaned the dishes before I headed to my own computer. Judith had found information about Madeline so easily that I was hopeful I could learn more about her movements on my own. But I soon realized that Judith's network knew a lot more than anything I could find online.

I was in the second hour of my fruitless search when I got the email from NightWatcher. It showed up in the email box I'd set up for message board correspondence to keep my real identity safe. I stared at the unopened message for a good five minutes before I clicked on it. It was the first time I'd heard from him since we made the arrangement to meet at the Attic, and I wondered what he wanted and why he'd waited this long to finally contact me. For a second, I contemplated deleting it, but my curiosity won out. I wanted to know why he hadn't shown up that night. More than that, I wanted to know if he really knew anything about my father's murder.

> I'm sorry I didn't go to meet you at the Attic. I did intend to go in, but when I got there it didn't feel safe. I heard later that someone was attacked by a vampire that night. Portland is not a safe place these days. I left town that night, and I've been keeping a low profile ever since.
>
> If you still want to talk, I want to meet you. Just not in Portland. Let's pick a place away from there, where the vampires aren't likely to go. I'd prefer to meet during the day if we can. I think that would be safer for both of us.

I sat back in my chair, staring at the screen. I had expected to never hear from NightWatcher again, and his email stirred the same need that had sent me to the Attic in the first place. No matter what had happened, I still had to find out why my dad was killed. The sane part of me protested that I didn't know this guy from Adam and for all I knew, he could be luring me into some kind of trap. But a bigger part of me argued that I was never going to find the answers I sought, sitting in my bedroom searching Google.

I sent a quick email back, telling him I might have trouble getting away and asking if he could share what he knew online. His reply was almost immediate.

The things I know could mean my death if the wrong person learned of them. I need to meet you in person to be certain I can trust you. You will understand once we meet.

Hmmm, cryptic. I was more determined than ever to meet him now, but slipping away to meet him was going to be damn near impossible with my self-appointed bodyguards following me around, especially after the crocotta attack. There had to be a way to do this.

I still want to meet you. I just need to figure out some things. I'll think of a place we can meet that will work for both of us. Let me see what I can work out and I'll get back to you.

I clicked *send* and let out a long breath, wondering if I had done the right thing or made a huge mistake. The way things were going for me lately, I never knew what to expect when I set foot outside my door. But I couldn't let that keep me hiding out at home and afraid to ever take chances again. I loved my freedom. If fear stole that from me, what kind of life would I have?

Bad things could happen whether you left your house or not – a painful truth I'd learned with my father's death. And it wasn't just me I had to think of now, but Nate as well. What if the crocotta had followed my trail back here instead of finding me on the road last night? Nate would have been helpless against such creatures.

Remy would know how to keep Nate safe. I needed to go see him as soon as possible, because the least I could do was try to protect Nate.

My injured back and arm ached as I undressed for bed. The scratches were healing at an incredible rate, and Chris said they would be completely gone in a few days. I'd have to make sure I wore long sleeves until they faded, because there was no way I could explain away those scars.

I turned off the light and pulled back my comforter, but instead of getting into bed I was drawn to the window. Parting the curtains, I looked down at the dark waterfront and wondered if Nikolas or Chris was out there right now, standing guard over my place. Roland told me that Nikolas had refused to leave the house even after Maxwell and the others arrived, though some of the younger wolves were very unhappy to have a couple of Mohiri hanging around. I had to say one thing about him; he was pretty serious about this whole protection thing. I just wished I knew how long it was going to last. Didn't he have warrior business to take care of?

A movement in the shadows caught my eye, and I realized someone actually was out there, standing just outside the glow of the nearest street-light. As if they heard my thoughts, the shadows moved again and a tall figure stepped into the light. I couldn't see Nikolas's face, but I knew it was him. A feeling like contentment settled in my chest, and I stepped back from the window. *It's nothing. I just feel better knowing he's there... for Nate's sake.*

For the second night in a row, the nightmares stayed away.

Slipping away to see Remy or anyone else turned out to be a lot harder than I had anticipated with my two Mohiri bodyguards stepping up their watch after the attack. It wasn't like I could just jump on my bike and ride down to see my troll friend, and if I admitted it to myself, I wasn't too keen on going out into the woods alone right now. But it was frustrating as hell to have someone watching my comings and goings around the clock.

It wasn't until Wednesday afternoon that I finally saw an opportunity to steal away. I got home from school to find a note from Nate saying he was at one of his environmental meetings. Peering out the window, I saw that Chris was on duty, sitting casually on a bench as if he didn't have a care in the world. Didn't he get bored just sitting there? I thought warrior business was supposed to be a lot more exciting.

As I watched, two girls approached and sat on either side of him, engaging him in conversation. At that moment, I could have kissed Jessie and Marie. I felt no pity for Chris because he seemed more than capable of holding his own against two teenage girls, and this was the perfect diversion to keep him occupied long enough for me to make my escape. In minutes, I was pushing my bike through the back door and between two buildings to Market Street.

Remy was standing just off the road, waiting for me, when I arrived. It was uncanny how he always knew when I was coming to see him. I'd asked him about it more than once, and he'd only smiled and said it was a troll thing.

Today he was not smiling. He spent a full five minutes going off about the crocotta attack and how I'd almost been killed. I should have known he'd know all about it. There was no way something that big had happened close to troll territory without them being aware. "This what happens when you go to city. Bad things come from city," he ranted as we walked to the cliff.

"I know, I know. But I can't go back and change that now. I guess you probably know about my new bodyguards too, huh?"

He nodded seriously. "Warriors are strong. They protect you."

I told him about Nikolas coming to see me last week and his news that I was Mohiri. Remy didn't blink an eye. "Did you know what I was all this time?" The possibility that he had known sent a pang of hurt through me.

"No," he answered sincerely. "I knew you not normal human, but even trolls not know everything."

"You knew I wasn't normal?"

He smiled wickedly. "Everyone know that."

"Funny guy!" I retorted, hitting him in the shoulder.

We sat in the cave for an hour while I told him about Nikolas and how he wanted me to go live with the Mohiri. "I don't want to leave here. And I don't want to live forever. Everyone I know will get old and die and I'll still look like this."

"I live long time."

My eyes widened. "That's right!" There was nothing I could do to change my immortality, but for the first time, the long years stretching before me didn't seem quite as bleak.

"Do you think we will still be friends in a hundred years, Remy?" Just the thought of the two of us still being here after a century and looking like we did today was too much to imagine.

"We always be friends," he stated with conviction.

My joy dimmed when another thought hit me. "I'll have to go away for a long while, because if I stay here people will know I'm not aging. I won't be able to come back until they're all gone." I gave him a hopeful smile. "You could come with me if you want. I could find us a place out in the country somewhere, maybe up in the mountains."

He shook his head sadly. "Have to stay with family."

"Oh." I sighed heavily. Remy was adventurous for a troll, but he still had the deep sense of faith and family ingrained in all of his people. He was a steadfast friend, but his first loyalty would always be to his family. I understood it and respected it, even if the thought of leaving him for years saddened me.

I shook off my gloom; I would worry about leaving my friends behind when the time came to do it. Right now, I had more important things to take care of.

"Remy, I need to protect Nate in case a vampire or some other monster finds out where we live, maybe some spells to watch over him. You have warding spells, right?"

"I have strong ward for home, but it not help when uncle not at home. Troll magic not good for humans. But there some good spells you can use."

"I need something really strong. Nate's all the family I have."

He stared at the floor of the cave for a minute before he said, "Ptellon blood. It most powerful protection, but it only last one moon. Then you use again."

I made a face. "Blood! You want me to give Nate blood?"

His raspy laughter filled the cave. "Not real blood. Ptellon is special flower from mountain in the Asia land. It have red nectar like blood."

"Oh, okay. I just didn't want a repeat of the baktu – which was pretty gross by the way." I rubbed my arms against the chill coming off the ocean. "How do I use it, and what does it do?"

"Put it in drink or food. It make bad smell to demons and Peoples, and they not go near him."

"Won't he smell it?"

"No smell for humans and animals."

I gave him a wide smile. "That's brilliant! I'll see if Malloy can get it. How much will it cost?"

"It very strong. Maybe many human dollars."

Money meant little to Remy, so when he said many dollars I knew he meant way more than I could come up with. I chewed my lip as I tried to figure out how to get the Ptellon blood.

"Bile worth many human dollars," he offered, and I shook my head vigorously.

"We can't use your bile again or someone will find us." It was scary just thinking of the bile we had stashed in this cave; enough for someone to kill for.

Remy paced the cave a few more times then zipped to the mouth of the cave. "Wait here," he called before he disappeared up the side of the cliff.

"Where do you think I am going to go?" I shouted after him. There was no answer.

I sat near the opening with my back against the smooth wall. The wind moaned through the cave, reminding me how lonely this place was without Remy. I peered down at the ocean churning around the rocks like a great frothing mouth full of sharp teeth. I loved the sea, the wide openness of it, the smells and sounds. It always seemed to call to me when I was near it. One of the old fishermen told me once that he had saltwater in his veins and he would never be happy anywhere but on the ocean. At times like this, I knew exactly what he meant.

Remy reappeared after a few minutes, bearing a small sack of what looked like sticks. I looked at him in confusion before he laid the sack on the floor of the cave and flashed a wide grin at me as he held out his hand. On his palm lay a dozen or more large sparkling diamonds and one small ruby. He pointed to the ruby. "That buy Ptellon blood."

I peered at the ruby, which didn't look like it was more than half a carat. I didn't know much about gems, but I knew rubies weren't worth a whole lot.

"A ruby? Is it like magic or something?" I asked him tentatively, trying not to hurt his feelings.

He shook his head like I should know better. "It not ruby. It diamond."

A red diamond? "Oh. Are they expensive?" It looked like a ruby to me. But then what did I know?

"This enough to buy you plenty Ptellon blood for uncle."

"That little thing? Seriously?" It didn't look like much, but if Remy said it was valuable, I believed him. "Listen, if this is worth so much, are you sure you want to give it to me? Won't you get in trouble?"

He showed his teeth when he grinned. "Clan have many pretty baubles. You take all diamonds. Save others for when you need them."

I knew the trolls had great wealth, but it occurred to me that their riches were way beyond my comprehension. "It's like Smaug's treasure," I said, tucking the diamonds in the snug front pocket of my jeans. It wasn't the first time Remy had given me precious stones to use as currency, and I wasn't as dazzled by them as I used to be.

"Smaug?"

It took me several minutes to explain *The Hobbit* and the dragon sleeping on a mountain of treasure. Remy shook his head when I finished. "Dragons not care about baubles. They only like to eat."

"Good to know," I muttered, hoping I never had the opportunity to witness that for myself. I pointed to the sack on the floor. "So what's with the sticks?"

"This for warding house." He explained what all the items in the sack were and how to use them to create a ward. It took me a good thirty minutes to memorize the phrases he gave me to recite during the spell, and I figured I'd better do the ward as soon as I got home before I forgot something.

When it was time to go, Remy insisted on accompanying me back to town. He stuck to the woods as I rode my bike, and every now and then I caught a flash of him in the trees. If he'd wanted to he could have stayed invisible the whole time, but he let me see him so I'd know he was there.

The motorcycle came up behind me as I passed the city limit sign. I didn't turn around, and the Ducati purred behind me like a big hungry cat all the way downtown. I considered making a run for the door when I got home, but apparently Nikolas had anticipated that. When we hit the waterfront he went on ahead, and by the time I reached home he was standing by the corner of the building with his arms crossed and wearing a scowl that made me want to turn around and ride the other way. His moods changed so fast it was hard to keep up with them. The angry man waiting for me now did not resemble the person who had given me his coat and watched over me while I'd slept two nights ago.

"Did you not learn anything the other night?" he demanded, taking a step toward me. "Are you *trying* to get yourself killed?"

Swallowing dryly, I got off my bike and walked it toward him. "Of course not." There was no way I could tell him that I'd been quite safe with a troll who could handle any threat to me.

"No?" His eyes darkened. "Do you want to tell me where you had to sneak off to that was so important?"

"No," I replied, ignoring the command in his voice.

His jaw clenched and I knew he was furious, but I wasn't going to cower to him. I did not have to explain my every move to him.

"There is nothing but woods for miles south of town. What were you doing out there?"

Instead of answering his question, I asked, "How did you find me anyway? Did you put one of those trackers on my bike, too?"

"No, but maybe I should."

"No, you should not!" I sputtered. I couldn't tell if he was serious or not, but right now I would not put it past him. "I'm not helpless, you know, and I don't need you guys following me around twenty-four seven. I took care of myself pretty well before you came along."

Nikolas cocked his head, and one corner of his mouth lifted arrogantly. "Yes, I can see how well you do on your own," he drawled in an infuriatingly condescending tone. "I'm amazed you lived this long."

It hurt that he thought so little of me, but I refused to let him know that. More than that, it angered me that I should care about his opinion of me at all. "I'm sorry I'm such a *trial* to you, but no one is asking you to stick around here. You can go back to doing your warrior thing – hunting vampires or whatever you do – and forget all about me."

I moved past him, but he did that blurring thing again and I found my way blocked by a wide chest. A hand grabbed my handlebar when I tried to go around him, and it felt like my bike was cemented to the ground. He leaned down and spoke with deadly softness into my ear. "If I was a vampire, you'd be dead – or worse."

My breath hitched, and for several seconds I was back in the alley, pressed against the brick wall, unable to move. Shaking off the memory, I glared up at him, hating him for reminding me how weak and helpless I'd felt with Eli. Our eyes met inches apart, and the Mori in me shifted restlessly, sending a ripple of some foreign emotion through me. I tore my gaze from his, angry that he had the power to affect even a little part of me.

"Does it even matter?"

"What?"

"You said that day on the wharf that you can't save every orphan. What difference does one more make?"

Nikolas stiffened, and I realized I'd probably just insulted his warrior ego or something. I was tired of this overbearing, He-Man routine, and it felt good to know that he wasn't as invincible as he let on.

"Do you mind letting go of my bike?" I asked when he didn't respond to my question. "Nate will be home soon, and it's my turn to make dinner." And I needed to get away from him because he made me feel angry and safe and afraid at the same time and I didn't know why.

Instead of loosening his grip, he growled. "*Khristu!* Do you not understand the danger you're in? I know you want to believe you're safe here surrounded by your werewolf friends, but someone went to great lengths sending that pack of crocotta to find you. If it is that vampire, he won't give up."

His words made the back of my neck prickle, and I remembered the hunger in Eli's eyes when he had been forced to release me.

Nikolas saw me waver. "If you are honest with yourself, you'll admit I'm right." He let go of the handlebar and laid a warm hand over one of mine. "I can protect you if you'll let me."

I tried to ignore the small tremble that went through me. How was it possible to dislike someone and feel fluttery inside at the same time? His nearness suddenly made it hard to think straight. Pulling my hand away, I stammered, "I really need to go inside now."

This time he didn't try to stop me. He stepped aside, and I pushed my bike past him. I hurried around to the back door and stood the bike against the wall while I searched for my keys. I didn't realize he had followed me until he spoke.

"You can run away from me, but you can't run from the truth. The werewolves can't protect you forever, and eventually, you'll have to leave New Hastings. What will you do then?"

My hand stilled on the doorknob. "When that happens it'll be my problem, not yours," I replied without looking at him. I opened the door and pushed my bike inside. "I don't want you following me around anymore."

"And I don't want you to keep putting yourself in danger. Seems like neither of us will get what we want."

I didn't reply. I just let the heavy door close behind me.

12

I pulled the cloth sack Remy had given me from my backpack and dumped the contents on the storeroom floor. Looking over the two small bundles of ash and elder twigs, the paper packet, the stone bowl, and something that looked like a crude artist's brush, it was hard to believe that these simple items could ward off something like a vampire. But I trusted Remy and the trolls' magic. If he said this was the best way to protect Nate, then I believed him.

I arranged the twigs in a crisscross pattern in the bowl exactly as Remy had instructed, then sprinkled the contents of the packet over the twigs. "*Il vekk'it zuhh ymen,*" I whispered in a poor imitation of Remy's guttural troll tongue. It was close enough, because the twigs burst into flame just as Remy had said they would. The small fire burned quickly, the flames going from white to blue to green before collapsing in a pile of ashes that smelled of burnt sage and basil and charred wood.

Picking up the bowl and brush, I stood and went to the back door. I laid the bowl on the floor and dipped the brush in the ashes. Then I traced the outline of my left hand in the center of the door, softly reciting the words, "*Atal'al il, atal'ak.*" Loosely translated, it meant "protect me, protect mine." I stood back and waited. Seconds later the ash outline of my hand sank into the steel and vanished. There! As long as I called this building home, nothing or no one with harmful intent could come through this door.

Now I just needed to do the same with every door and window in the whole building.

The confrontation with Nikolas bothered me more than I wanted to admit. I hated how weak and vulnerable I felt when he had grabbed my bike, and I couldn't stand being followed and watched out of some misplaced sense of obligation. It didn't help that the stupid demon in me always knew when he was around, stirring restlessly every time his presence brushed against my mind. If this was how Mori demons connected, it must be absolute sensory overload living among Nikolas's people. How did the Mohiri live with it?

By the end of the week, I was ready to scream every time I spotted Nikolas or Chris. They were everywhere I went: outside the school, the grocery store, the library, the waterfront. They did not approach me, and I pretended to ignore them, but their constant presence meant I was no longer free to come and go as I pleased. I wracked my brain for days to come up with a way to meet with NightWatcher, but so far it looked impossible. The Mohiri were going to protect me into insanity.

I started hiding out at home when I wasn't at school, because it was the only place I could avoid them – or more specifically, avoid another run-in with Nikolas. The only problem with my self-imposed confinement was the fact that I was going stir crazy after a few days. The last time I hid at home it was because I was dealing with the trauma of the vampire attack and the discovery that I was not quite as mortal as I'd believed – valid reasons in anyone's book. This time it was pure cowardice, and I hated myself for it.

The only high point in my week was when Malloy sent me a message saying that he knew a guy who dealt mainly in exotic plants and he was working on getting the Ptellon blood for me as soon as possible. When I'd told Malloy how I would pay, he got almost as excited as he did about the troll bile. I immediately did an online search and discovered that red diamonds are one of the rarest gemstones in the world. I wished I'd known that before I took it from Remy and offered it up as payment. It could draw too much attention to me when I was trying to keep a low profile. I pushed my worries aside. I had to protect Nate first, then deal with the rest if anything came of it. Besides, it was unlikely that someone would make a connection between troll bile and diamonds, no matter how rare they were.

When my cell phone rang on Saturday afternoon, I assumed that it was Roland because he always called me on Saturdays and he was one of the few people who had my number. The number on the screen was unfamiliar, and I answered the call gingerly. "Hello?"

"Sara, hi. It's Samson Long. We met at the party last weekend."

"Um, hi," I replied, trying to hide my shock. *How on earth did he get my number?*

"I hope you don't mind. I got your number from Roland. He said it was cool."

Note to self: kill best friend. "No, it's fine."

Samson cleared his throat. "I know it's kind of short notice, but would you like to do something tonight?"

"Do something?" I repeated dumbly.

"Yes, like a movie or dinner... or whatever you like to do."

"I – " I stammered, not sure how to respond. Samson Long was asking me out on a date. Heat flooded my face. A boy was calling to ask me out for the first time in my life, and all I could do was stand there like an idiot.

"Or we could just go for coffee now if you want to do that," he offered quickly.

"Okay," I heard myself saying. I liked Samson, and I'd enjoyed talking to him at the party before Nikolas had shown up to ruin my mood. "Coffee sounds nice."

I heard the smile in his voice. "Great. How about I pick you up in half an hour?"

"Okay," I said again. I gave him my address and hung up in a daze. Shaking myself out of it, I went to change and do something with my hair. With a few minutes to spare, I sent Roland a text: **UR so dead.**

I expected Samson to be in the white van from the party, but he showed up in a yellow Jeep Wrangler that suited him somehow. He smiled broadly when I got in and said he was glad I'd said yes. I ducked my head so he couldn't see the heat in my face and occupied myself with buckling my seat belt. I was around boys all the time, but this was my first time alone with one who was not shy about letting me know he liked me.

As we drove away, I looked out my window and saw Chris sitting in his normal spot. He pulled out a cell phone and spoke to someone, and I had no doubt he was talking to Nikolas, probably passing me off like a baton in a relay race. I turned away, determined to have a good time today and not let them ruin this for me.

Samson said he was taking me to his favorite coffee place, and on the way we talked about the party and how it was too bad it had gotten rained out. "Next time, we'll have to hold it inside so rain doesn't drive everyone away," he said with quiet meaning.

The coffee shop was called The Hub. I had seen it in passing plenty of times, but today was my first time inside. It was more of a hangout for the college crowd, and I could see the appeal in the cozy ambience created by a large fireplace and comfortable couches. Samson bought us two mochas, and we weaved through the couches to a pair of big chairs near one of the windows. It was obvious how often he came here by the number of people who waved or said hello to him as we passed. It took me a few minutes to realize why it seemed so different than the places I normally went to. If I walked into one of those other places with Samson, all the kids there would have watched us and started whispering right away. Here, people looked up and went back to whatever they were doing. There was nothing out of the ordinary about the two of us, and I found it a refreshing change.

"I have a confession to make," he announced after we had settled into the comfy chairs. "I asked around about you this week."

"Oh." I took a sip of coffee to hide the blush creeping up my neck again. "What did you find out?"

His laugh was nice and easy, and I noticed that his eyes were a beautiful leaf green. "Not much. Everyone knows who you are, but no one seems to really *know* you except Roland and he said I'd have to ask you. You are a woman of mystery."

It was my turn to laugh. "Maybe they had nothing to say because there is nothing *to* say."

"I don't believe that. I think there's a lot more to you than you show people." He took a drink from his cup. "You said you live with your uncle. How did that happen, if you don't mind me asking?"

I had never talked to anyone except Roland and Peter about my dad and how I'd come to live with Nate. It felt strange telling another person now. I gave him a very abbreviated version of the story. "My dad died when I was eight. It was just the two of us, and his younger brother took guardianship of me. Nate's a writer, so it made it easy for him to stay home and take care of me."

"You and your father were very close, weren't you? I can hear it in your voice."

I nodded, expecting the tears to come, but to my surprise they stayed away. "My mother left when I was two, and my dad raised me alone." In my mind I saw Dad's face, and for a moment I was with him again. "He was... the kindest, funniest person I've ever known. And smart. He loved books and music, and he found pleasure in the simplest things – like having pancakes for dinner or listening to a thunderstorm. He always said you could learn a lot about a person by the things they valued. I didn't know what he meant then. I do now."

Samson smiled wistfully. "I think I would have liked your father. I grew up with both parents, but we aren't what you'd call close. My father owns an engineering company and works overseas a lot. My mother is a math teacher."

"Wow, an engineer and a teacher. I bet you weren't allowed to get less than an A in school."

He toyed with the plastic lid on his cup. "You could say that."

"Any brothers or sisters?"

"I have a younger brother in junior high and an older sister who lives in New York."

I swirled my coffee slowly. "Must be nice to have siblings. Roland's the closest I have to a brother."

"I gathered that you two were pretty close. When I talked to him he dropped a not too subtle hint that he takes your welfare and happiness to heart. I take it as a good sign that he gave me your number at all."

I couldn't suppress my grin. "He's been like that since we were little kids. I used to have to beat him up to get him to stop treating me like I was breakable." In hindsight, I must have looked so fragile to my werewolf friends back then.

Samson's eyes sparkled. "I bet you were a real tomboy."

"Totally. I could climb trees with the best of them."

"You said you like to draw, too. What do you draw?"

"Whatever comes to mind. It's just a hobby, not something I show people."

"Will you draw something for me?" he asked earnestly.

I shook my head. "I'm really not that good, and I have nothing to draw on anyway."

He was already standing. "One minute." He went to the counter and came back with a plain notepad and a wooden pencil, which he laid on the small table beside me. "No pressure. Draw anything you want."

I thought about it for a minute before I picked up the pencil and pad and began to draw. As I worked, Samson went to get us two more mochas, and we kept up a steady stream of conversation about school, hobbies, friends, and his band. He lived in Portland, and I asked him how he met up with Dylan and his friends here in New Hastings. He told me he grew up in New Hastings, and he still knew a lot of people here. A mutual friend, who knew that both Samson and Dylan wanted to start a band, got them together.

I finished my drawing and signed it with a flourish before turning the pad so he could see what I'd drawn. His eyes widened as he studied the sketch I'd drawn from memory of him playing his drums at the Attic. Without my good pencils it wasn't my best work, but I thought I'd captured him pretty well.

"This is incredible! How can you say you aren't any good?"

I flushed with pleasure from his praise. "Thanks. Maybe I should keep this one. One day when you're a famous rock star I can sell it on eBay for a lot of money."

"You should keep it." His eyes darkened to a moss green, and his voice warmed. "So you don't forget about me."

The meaning in his gaze was unmistakable, and I looked down at my hands nervously. I was in foreign waters, and I had no idea what to say or do next. I'd faced vampires and a pack of crocotta, but put me in front of a cute boy and I had no idea what to do.

Samson laughed softly. "You have no idea how adorable you look right now."

I turned my heated face away from him to look out the window. "That's not exactly the look I was going for – "

The words stuck in my throat when I felt the all-too familiar fluttering in my mind. It wasn't like I hadn't known one of them would be following us, but for a little while I'd put it out of my mind and I was just a normal girl out having coffee with a nice boy.

I scanned the street, looking for my tail. There was no sign of them, but my senses told me that either Nikolas or Chris was here. Seriously, what did they think was going to happen to me in a coffee shop in the middle of the day? Caffeine overdose? Hot coffee burn?

Well, they were nowhere in sight unless... I turned my searching gaze on the room behind me. *They wouldn't. Please tell me they did not follow me in here.* The thought of being chaperoned by Nikolas or Chris as I fumbled through my date was beyond mortifying. Chris, I could almost stand. He was more amiable than judgmental. Nikolas was another story with his moody temperament and his overbearing attitude. If it had to be one of them, please let it be Chris.

My stomach dropped when I found him sitting alone at the far side of the shop, his eyes so dark they were almost black as they glowered at my date. His gaze shifted, and I met it defiantly, lifting my chin to let him know how I felt about this invasion of my personal space. His eyes softened, and he arched an eyebrow at me.

"That's the guy from the party," Samson said, reminding me that I was ignoring him. I cast another look at Nikolas and then looked at Samson, who stared at Nikolas with narrowed eyes. "Is he following you?"

I let out a sigh and made a note to thank Nikolas once again for complicating my life. "I told you my mother left when I was very young. Nikolas is from her side of the family, and he found me recently." *True.* "My mother's family wants me to come live with them and get to know them, and Nikolas has appointed himself as a kind of chaperone." *Also true.*

"A chaperone? He's what – twenty?"

I lifted my shoulders then picked up my mocha. It had cooled off, but I needed the fortification. "Try to ignore him. I do."

Samson glanced over at Nikolas again. "He doesn't look at you like a relative. If anything, he looks jealous."

I sputtered and coughed as coffee went down the wrong pipe. "Trust me," I wheezed when I could speak. "You don't know Nikolas. I'm a family obligation to him, nothing more."

"Seeing his expression right now, I find that hard to believe," Samson replied. Before I could refute it, he smiled and said, "But if you can ignore him, I can too."

"Good." Samson was handling Nikolas's presence a lot better than most guys would in the same situation.

We stayed at the Hub for another thirty minutes, and then Samson drove me home. When he put the Jeep in park, neither of us spoke for a long moment and I was suddenly nervous he was going to try to kiss me. Was that normal after a coffee date? How would I know if he did want to kiss? Did I want him to try? For the first time in my life I regretted not having girlfriends I could talk to about this stuff.

He looked over at me. "I had a great time today."

"Me, too."

There was another moment of silence before he laughed and ran his hand through his blond hair. "Sorry, I'm not usually like this. I don't know what it is about you, but I feel like an eighth grader on his first date."

"Is that a good or a bad thing?" I asked, and he laughed again.

"Bad for a guy who's trying to look cool and ask a girl out again."

"Oh," I breathed, blushing to the roots of my hair. I looked away from him, across the waterfront, to see Chris walking toward his favorite bench again. My smile fell away as I was hit with an unpleasant realization. As much as I enjoyed Samson's company, I couldn't date him. I couldn't date anyone. My life was so messed up right now; how could I start a relationship with anyone, knowing I would eventually have to leave them? I was immortal; I could never have a life with a human. Hell, maybe that was why Madeline had taken off and deserted my dad. I could never do that to someone I cared about, and I had a feeling Samson was someone I could come to care about a lot.

"I really like you, Samson, but I'm not ready to date anyone right now. I have some stuff going on in my life and I need to figure it out before I do anything else."

"Your mother's family?" he asked without pushing.

"That's part of it." I made myself look at him. "I'm sorry."

He smiled sweetly, but he couldn't quite hide the disappointment in his voice. "So it's a 'not right now' instead of a 'not ever' thing."

"Kind of." I hated lying to him, hated my life fervently in that moment. I got out of the Jeep and walked around to his side. "I did have a nice time."

"Same here," he replied. I started to turn away, and he said, "Oh wait, don't forget this." He held up the sketch I'd done of him. "So you don't forget me."

I smiled sadly at the sketch as I took it from him. "I won't."

Nate was in the kitchen making muffins when I got home. "Out with Roland?" he asked as I hung up my coat in the hall closet.

"No, I had a coffee date."

There was a loud clatter as the muffin pan bounced off the tile floor. "A date? With a boy?" Nate gaped at me as I retrieved the pan for him.

"No, with Father Glenn." I wasn't sure whether to be insulted or amused by his look of disbelief. "Of course it was with a boy. I do know some, you know."

"So, was it someone from school?" He tried to sound nonchalant, but I could tell he was very curious.

"No, he's a friend of Roland's." That's all I was going to say since nothing would come of it anyway. "I'm going upstairs to work on an English paper. You need any help here?"

"No, go on," Nate replied absently, and I wondered if he was finally realizing what it meant to have a teenage girl under his roof.

Roland texted me as I was pulling my books out of my backpack, but I didn't want to talk to anyone. Part of me reveled in the afterglow of my first date, and the rest of me mourned the fact that it was likely my last date with Samson – or anyone else. I'd never thought much about dating and relationships until the possibility of having them was gone. I wasn't the type of person who could casually date someone while knowing there was absolutely no chance of more between us. I guess deep down I'd always believed that someday I'd meet "the one" and we'd live happily ever after. *Ever after* held a whole new meaning for me now, and it wasn't a happy one.

I reached across the desk and picked up my sketch pad to tuck Samson's drawing inside. I flipped open the pad to the picture I'd done of Nikolas the night we met. Laying both sketches side by side, I realized I'd drawn the two of them as I'd seen them on the very same night. Samson was laidback and smiling in his picture, enjoying himself as he played to the crowd. Nikolas was fierce, almost predatory as he brandished the sword. They were as different as two men could be – one golden and warm, and the other dark and furious. One wanted to be part of my life, and the other wanted to run my life. One was sweet and easy to be with, and the other caused a maelstrom of conflicting emotions to twist my stomach in knots.

I slammed the sketchbook shut and threw it on the desk. "Ugh! Why do guys have to be so complicated?"

Oscar rubbed against my legs, and I bent down to pick him up. "I wasn't talking about you," I crooned, stroking his fur. He purred and butted his head against my chin, then curled up in my lap and went to sleep without a care in the world. It was the first time I was ever jealous of a cat.

I spent Sunday morning working on my English paper and trying to keep Oscar away from the attic and his growing unhealthy fascination with imps. "Trust me, you don't want to mess with those little monsters," I warned as I chased him away from the crack beneath the attic door for what seemed like the hundredth time.

By some stroke of luck he finally managed to corner one in the bathroom, and the angry chattering tore me from my work. I shooed Oscar away from the bathroom and looked at the tiny demon. Six inches tall, pasty white, and bald, the little fiend stood on the toilet tank with one hand on his hip and the other waving a fist at the cat. I felt something brush against my leg and knew Oscar had not heeded my warning to stay away. The imp began to jump up and down, emitting little furious shrieks at the sight of the cat, his loincloth fluttering around him.

"Oh stop it," I scolded him. "The last thing I need to see is your nasty little demon parts."

The imp halted immediately and looked down at the bit of cloth covering him. They liked to pretend they couldn't understand humans, but I'd suspected all along they were faking. "Got you!" I said with a smirk before I bent down to pick up Oscar and carry him over to the bed. "You stay there if you don't want to get bitten. I don't think imp bites will go over too well with the vet."

At noon my phone rang, and I scrambled to answer it, ready for a distraction. "Hey, Roland."

"Finally. I thought you were ignoring me. I texted you like four times yesterday."

I sat on the bed and fell back until I was staring at the ceiling. "I *was* ignoring you."

He gave a nervous laugh. "I take it Samson called? Before you say anything, he's a great guy and I thought you two hit it off last weekend."

I let out a loud sigh. "I do like him. But you know I can't get... involved with anyone, especially with my life as crazy as it is right now." I didn't mention the whole immortal thing. Roland and I hadn't talked about the fact that we wouldn't age together. I'd already tried to imagine him at forty when I still looked like a teenager, but the thought had freaked me out, so I'd shoved it away where I didn't have to deal with it.

"I just thought you could use some fun in your life. Now that Greg's gone you can expect more guys to ask you out."

Wait. What? "What are you talking about?"

He laughed, and I could picture him shaking his head. "Sara, Greg let every guy in school know that he'd take it personally if anyone hurt you or broke your heart. They were all too scared of him to go near you after that."

"You'd better be kidding me." My face burned. I couldn't believe Greg had done something like that. Actually, yes I could, which was why I was mortified.

"Greg was a badass, but he had a soft spot for you. Probably because you were the only one in school besides his friends who wasn't afraid of him."

"Because I knew there were a lot scarier things out there." I groaned into my hand. "God, I can't believe he did that." Wait until I sent him another email. He was going to hear it from me.

Roland's tone grew serious. "Listen, I actually called because Pete and I want to talk to you about something. You want to go get something to eat?"

"Can you give me a hint?"

"No."

"Cryptic. Okay, see you in a bit."

They picked me up twenty minutes later in Peter's mother's car, and after a quick discussion, we headed for the mall. A lot of the stores were closed on Sundays, but the food court was open and the boys loved the burgers and milkshakes from Benny's. We got our food and grabbed a table away from everyone else. I let them take a few bites before I asked them what they wanted to talk about that couldn't be said over the phone.

They shared a look, and Peter said, "I overheard Dad and Uncle Brendan talking last night – about you and your parents."

My hand stopped halfway to my mouth. "What?"

"Dad said they lost Madeline's – your mom's – trail, and they were trying to piece together what happened to your father. He said Aunt Judith told him you thought it might have something to do with your mom being Mohiri." Peter took a deep breath. "He said Aunt Judith was afraid you were too involved in this and might do something careless. What did he mean by that?"

"I..."

Roland's eyebrows drew together as he laid down his burger. "You talked to my mom about this, but you can't talk to us?"

"It's not like that. I only talked to your mom because she told me they were going back and tracing Madeline's movements from the time she left us." I twisted my paper napkin until it tore. "I think vampires followed Madeline to my dad. I don't know why she was in Portland when he died or why they went after him. I just know it's all related."

"You've been trying to find the truth yourself?" Roland said in an accusing tone.

I nodded, not meeting their stares. They weren't going to like what I said next, and I didn't want to see their faces when they heard it. "I wanted to look for years, but I didn't really start until I heard about the missing girls in Portland. A guy I know online, who knows a lot about this stuff, said he thought it was vampires. He said he heard there were vampire sightings in Portland when my dad was killed."

"What guy? Who is he?" Roland demanded. "Please tell me you aren't talking to some kook online."

I glared at him defensively. "He's not a kook, and he does know a lot. I only know his screen name, just like he only knows mine. And before you say anything, we've been talking for three years, and he's never tried to meet me or anything. He tracks vampire activity and reports it online. These guys are very serious about this stuff."

"Guys? There's more than one?" Peter asked.

I took a sip of my drink before answering. "Yeah, there's a whole online community. And I... um... I met a new one online last month. He says he knows something. We were supposed to meet in person, but something happened and he was scared away."

Roland's face grew red. "You were going to meet a total stranger alone... in person? Are you out of your mind?"

"I wasn't alone," I said slowly. "You guys were there."

"Wha – ?" Peter started.

"No fucking way!" Roland swore a little too loud, drawing the disapproving stares of some people across the food court. "The Attic? You were going to meet him at the Attic – the same night a vampire just *happened* to attack you? You don't think that was a bit *too* coincidental?"

Peter paled, and his freckles stood out even more. "Holy shit, Sara."

"It wasn't a setup," I argued, knowing that it looked suspiciously like one. "He told me later that he didn't show because he got wind of some vampires there. He is seriously scared of them. He won't try to meet again unless it's broad daylight and somewhere public."

I probably shouldn't have said that last part. Roland's eyes nearly bugged out of his head, and he made a sound deep in his chest. "You are not going to meet this guy."

"If he can tell me what happened to my dad, then I *will* meet him." I hated arguing with my friends, but I would not back down from this now that I was so close.

"You have to let Dad take care of this," Peter pleaded. "Please."

I looked from Peter to Roland. "What would you do if you were in my shoes? What if it had been one of your parents? You can't tell me you wouldn't do everything to get to the bottom of it."

"Yes but – "

"No buts, Peter. You wouldn't sit back and let someone else handle it, and neither can I."

Roland shredded the top of his hamburger bun. "So you only went to the Attic with us to meet someone."

The betrayal in his voice made me want to say no, but I couldn't lie to him anymore, not about this. "I asked him to meet me there after you asked me to go."

Roland let out a breath, and I could tell he was hurt and thinking that I'd only gone with them to meet someone else. "I'm sorry," I said softly.

The silence at the table hung over us like a shroud, and I felt a small tear appear in the trust we'd always had between us. My deceit hurt them, and now they were wondering what else I'd lied about.

"I swear it was the only time I ever did anything like that."

"Why didn't you tell us or ask us for help?" Roland demanded. "Don't you trust us?"

"Why didn't you tell me what you were?" I countered.

He shifted on his chair. "That's different. We thought you were human. We were protecting you."

"I thought you were human, too. I didn't want to drag you into this." It wasn't enough to ease their hurt feelings, but it was the truth.

We sat there quietly for several long minutes, each of us toying with our food and waiting for someone to say something to break the uncomfortable silence. I didn't know what to say to fix things between us.

The quiet was shattered by a small group of girls who clamored around a table nearby. Glancing their way, I saw Faith, Jessie, and Marie along with two other girls from school. The five of them chatted and giggled loudly, making enough noise to draw annoyed stares from the other customers.

It didn't take Faith long to spot us, and her smile fell away as she glared at me. The other girls followed her stare, and their laughter died as they looked at me with narrowed eyes. Their lame attempt at intimidation was so comical I almost burst out laughing. If they had seen half the things I'd seen in the last month alone, they'd be at home cowering under their beds. Sometimes I wondered if I should be doing that myself. I returned their stares until one by one the girls turned away to whisper amongst each other.

"We should go." My appetite was long gone.

We picked up our trays and carried them to the nearest trashcan. I pointed at the restroom. "I'll meet you over by the entrance."

"Okay," Peter said. Roland only nodded.

The restroom was empty, and I washed my hands then leaned against the counter with my back to the mirror. I'd never hurt my friends before, had never seen them look at me with doubt. I swallowed the lump that started to form in my throat. *What did you think would happen when they found out you lied to them?*

I had to find a way to fix this. Maybe it was time to come clean about all my secrets. Now that I knew they weren't human, there was no reason to hide anything from them anymore. Remy had warned me in the beginning that the wrong people would try to use my power for their own needs so I had to keep it hidden. But my friends would never hurt me that way. I knew their secret; they should know mine. In fact, I wanted them to know. I needed to think of the best way to tell them, to show them. Not today, but very soon.

I felt lighter when I emerged from the restroom. I saw Roland and Peter waiting for me by the large glass doors, and a smile crept across my face as I imagined their expressions when I revealed my power to them. What would they say when they heard about Remy or when I told them about the visit from Aine? After I told them everything, my friends would never doubt my trust in them again.

My happy thoughts were cut short by the shock of icy liquid splashing across my shoulder and down my left arm. I gasped at the orange stain spreading over my light blue jacket before I looked up at Faith's smug face and the empty smoothie cup in her hand.

"Oh, I'm so sorry!" Faith exclaimed without a hint of sincerity. "You ran right into me. You really should watch where you're going, you know."

The monster in my head came roaring to life, crying out for swift retaliation. I clenched my teeth so hard it hurt, and it was only extreme willpower

KAREN LYNCH

that kept me from slugging that smirk right off her face. Images of Scott's bloody face still haunted me, and I would not let the demon use me like that again. As much as I detested Faith, she was human, and I had to be careful not to hurt her.

Faith glanced at the mall cop watching us from the entrance, and her lips twitched with glee, assuming he was the reason for my lack of action. Behind her, the other girls twittered and enjoyed the show.

I brushed past her to get some napkins from the closest concession. The blond boy behind the counter gave me a sympathetic smile and shoved a stack of paper napkins toward me. I grabbed a handful and started mopping up the slushy liquid running down my arm.

"What? No witty comeback this time?" Faith's voice dripped acid behind me.

I took some more napkins to wipe smoothie off my jeans. "I have nothing to say to you, Faith."

"Figures. You're such a loser." She held up the empty smoothie cup. "Think I'll get another. That first one went down so good."

I let my eyes fall to her waist. "You might want to lay off those for a while. That stuff is full of empty calories."

Faith's mouth fell open like a fish gasping for air. The boy behind the counter made a snorting sound, and she shot him a scorching look. She whirled angrily, her long blond hair whipping my face as she stalked off.

"What the heck is her problem?" the boy asked.

"Don't mind her. She's still pissed about her boyfriend."

He leaned on the counter, his eyes sparkling. "You went out with her boyfriend?"

"Yeah, not likely." I crumpled the pile of wet napkins and handed them to him to throw away. "I broke his nose."

I looked down at my stained, wet clothes and grimaced. There wasn't much I could do about it until I got home. I joined Roland and Peter, who had witnessed everything and were holding back grins. "Not a word," I warned them as we walked through the automatic doors.

It came as no surprise to find Nikolas leaning against his motorcycle across from the mall entrance. At least this time he had stayed outside. We walked right by him on the way to the car, and his eyebrows rose when he saw the orange stain down one side of me. I thought I saw the corner of his mouth twitch, and I knew right then and there that I was going to haul off and deck him if he started laughing.

"What? You think vampires are messy?" I scoffed as I passed him. "Try tangling with the homecoming queen."

154

13

Nate left for his conference on Tuesday morning, and Malloy contacted me later that day to let me know his guy had come through with the Ptellon blood. The timing sucked, but I figured Nate should be safe in Boston and if anything bad came, it would come here. Not a comforting thought, but better than the alternative. I could slip the blood to him when he got back.

My immediate problem was how to meet up with Malloy to make the exchange without one of the Mohiri tailing me and interrupting us. I didn't think Malloy would appreciate Nikolas or Chris crashing his business, and I could only imagine what Nikolas would say about my extracurricular activities.

The Mohiri were not my only obstacle. Since I'd confessed about trying to meet NightWatcher, Roland and Peter had been watching me more closely, too. They sat with me at lunch, followed me to the school library – the last place Roland liked to hang out – and offered to give me rides home from school. If they were still upset over my admission, they didn't show it. I appreciated their concern, but right now they were seriously cramping my style. How the hell was I going to outsmart two werewolves and two Mohiri warriors at the same time?

Jed's was out of the question because I was still spooked by the unknown person asking about troll bile. I did not want to take the chance that someone would see me there with Malloy again and connect the dots. The fact that Malloy didn't argue when I rejected that location told me I wasn't the only one thinking about it. After much back and forth, we settled on a place, and I started planning how to sneak away to complete the deal.

When the final bell rang on Wednesday, I stuffed my backpack into my locker. Instead of heading for the exit where I knew my friends were waiting for me again, I surreptitiously made my way to the faculty entrance near the teacher's lounge. There was no one around to see me when I opened the door and slipped outside to the back parking lot the school shared with the church next door. Hidden from the street and conveniently located next to the cemetery, this spot was perfect for my getaway. I sprinted across the half-empty lot, past the church, and hopped over the waist-high iron fence surrounding the cemetery. Ducking down, I swiftly navigated between the headstones and exited by the small gate on the far side. It was so easy I almost laughed out loud. I couldn't believe I hadn't thought of it until now.

I knew it would not take long for my watchers to figure out that I'd given them the slip, so I set out at a fast walk, trying not to run and draw attention to myself. I skirted the waterfront, and took a slightly longer route to my destination. Last night, Malloy and I had agreed to do our business on a boat belonging to an acquaintance of his. The boat, named Mary's Hope, was docked in a slip at the Bayside Marina, and Malloy said it was highly unlikely that anyone would connect it to either of us. I had a feeling it was just one of many places where Malloy handled his business.

As I approached the marina, I couldn't help but feel rather pleased with myself. I'd managed to evade my growing posse of protectors, and in a short while I'd have the means to keep Nate safe if more monsters came to call. It was the least I could do for attracting them to us in the first place.

"Going for a spin on your sailboat, are you?"

I whirled to face Roland. "How...?"

He jogged toward me on silent feet, his expression serious. "You didn't really think you could give us the slip, did you?" He stopped in front of me. "I knew you were up to something as soon as I saw you this morning."

I looked behind him, expecting to see Peter and one of the Mohiri appear any second.

"It's just me. Pete and I split up; he took the front door, and I got the back. The blond fellow is probably just realizing you're no longer at school."

Poor Chris. He didn't seem like a bad sort, and he was going to develop a complex if he kept losing me.

"You're going to meet that guy, aren't you?" Roland said in an accusing tone.

For a second I thought he knew about Malloy, but then it hit me that he was talking about NightWatcher. "No. This has nothing to do with that. I swear."

He gave me look that said he didn't believe me. The loss of trust sent a small stab of hurt through me, but I had only myself to blame.

"So what is so important that you had to sneak away like this?"

"It's just something I have to take care of, and I'm tired of having someone watching my every move, okay?"

"Maybe I can help you," he pushed.

I sighed loudly. I planned to tell him everything – just not yet. "Roland, there are some things I keep to myself, just like I don't know what werewolves do half the time."

His mouth formed a stubborn line. "Werewolves can protect themselves if they go off alone. And none of us are being hunted by an obsessed vampire." He crossed his arms. "Go ahead and do what you have to, but I'm coming with you."

Damn it. I *had* to meet with Malloy, and I was pretty certain it would be a hell of a lot harder to get away after my stunt today. Too much was riding on this to turn back now.

"You can come with me, but you have to do what I tell you to." His eyes narrowed, and I said, "I'll explain if you promise to do what I say."

"I promise to do it *if* I don't think you are in any danger."

I chewed the inside of my lip as I wondered how much to tell him without actually saying who I was going to see. Rule number one in this business was to never reveal your contacts, and Malloy held that rule close to his vest. He might never do business with me again if he thought he couldn't trust my discretion. Troll bile and diamonds meant nothing to him if he got killed acquiring them.

"I'm going to buy something to keep Nate safe in case something tries to hurt him because of me."

Roland's eyes widened, and I could tell that whatever he'd been expecting, it wasn't that. "Keep him safe? How?"

"Have you ever heard of the Ptellon flower?" He shook his head, so I explained where it came from and how it could be used to repel vampires and other creatures. "I warded our building, but that won't help Nate when he's away from home. The Ptellon nectar is all I need now."

He looked at me like I'd sprouted a third eye. "You warded the whole building by yourself? How do you know how to do that? And how do you know all this protection stuff?"

There was so much I wanted to tell him, but this was neither the time nor the place. "There are some things about me you don't know, and I promise I'll tell you soon – just not now. All I can say is that I have this friend Remy who taught me, and he knows more about this stuff than anyone I know. I have a guy who can get things, and I'm going to get the Ptellon from him."

"Have I met this Remy guy before?" he asked as we began walking toward the marina entrance.

"Not likely. He doesn't, um, hang out with werewolves."

"And what about the guy we're going to meet?"

I stopped walking. "You're not going to meet him. When we get there, I'll go in and you'll wait outside." Roland opened his mouth to argue, and I held up a hand. "This guy won't deal with me any other way. And we'll be on a boat tied to the dock with you right outside. I'll be fine."

He made a grumbling sound. "I don't like this."

"You're going to have to trust me on this. I know what I'm doing." I looked down at my watch. "I have to meet him in five minutes. Come on."

We entered the marina parking lot and passed between the office and the clubhouse to the main pier. Beyond the pier, a wooden dock extended into the water in a large L-shape, and along the dock were four narrow docks with six slips on each side. Most of the slips had a boat secured to them. Anchored at the end of the main dock was the biggest yacht I'd ever seen. Most of the boats in the marina were cabin cruisers, sailboats, and powerboats, and occasionally we got some small yachts in the summer. Nothing as big as that yacht though.

I caught Roland gaping at the boat, and I laughed. "Yeah, in your dreams."

There was a lot of activity on the pier as marina workers rushed around with ropes and tarps. I stopped one as he hurried by and asked him what was going on.

"Storm coming," he said as if I should already know that. He lifted a coil of heavy rope to his shoulder. "We have to secure the boats so they don't get banged around too much."

I looked at the partly overcast sky and the calm water of the bay. "Really?"

"Yep. If you guys had any plans to go out, you'll have to cancel them. Harbormaster sent out a weather warning."

"Okay, thanks," I said as he started to hurry away.

"Hey," Roland called after him. "Who owns the monster yacht out there?"

The man shrugged. "Some oil guy from what I heard. They put in here because of the storm." He hoisted his rope again. "Gotta go."

I grabbed Roland's arm. "We'd better hurry up. They'll shut this place down soon if it's a bad storm."

The Mary's Hope was a forty-foot cabin cruiser moored at slip twenty-eight, and there was no sign of activity onboard when we reached it. I hoped

Malloy was already here because he might not show if he arrived and saw Roland.

More dock hands passed us, and I saw them head for the massive yacht where a tall olive-skinned man with black hair and a hawkish appearance directed them to their tasks. I wondered if he was the same oil guy Nate's group was trying to keep from drilling in the area. The thought made me glare at the man before I turned back to the business at hand.

"Okay, I'm going in." I hopped onto the deck. "I should only be a few minutes if he's here."

Roland nodded, and I hurried down the two steps to the cabin that housed a small table, a tiny kitchenette, a bathroom, and a small sleeping area. Tinted windows obscured the interior from the outside.

Malloy sat at the table waiting for me.

"Look at you on time for once," I quipped, making him scowl. I sat across from him even though I was in a hurry. Malloy liked to keep up the appearance of a formal sales transaction. His quirks didn't bother me as long as he came through for me.

"Payment first as usual," he said, watching me closely as if I was about to pull off a David Blaine act. I reached into the front pocket of my jeans and rooted around until my finger hooked the diamond.

"I don't know what the big deal is with these, but whatever." I held out my hand with the red gemstone lying on my palm, and Malloy twitched with anticipation. My other hand stretched toward him. "Your turn."

He didn't take his eyes off the diamond as he produced a tiny black vial and handed it to me. As soon as I had it in my possession, I extended my open hand to him and he picked up the red diamond almost reverently. I stuffed the precious vial in my front jeans pocket as he examined the gem.

"Perfect," he gushed, holding the stone up to the light. "I almost didn't believe it when you said you had one. But I figured someone who could get their hands on troll bile could get almost anything." He stuck the diamond in his jeans pocket like I had and gave me a satisfied smile. "Listen, I know there's no way a kid your age can get this stuff on your own. Whoever you work for is bloody brilliant to have a nice, normal-looking girl like you running their goods for them. You let them know that I'm their man for whatever they need from now on."

"As long as you keep coming through for them, they'll keep doing business with you." If he wanted to believe there was a boss man in the background, I had no problem with that. In fact, I liked the idea.

"Good to hear. I'm sure we – "

Malloy jumped to his feet as a thump sounded above us followed by footsteps and a body running down the steps. Roland burst into the cabin. "We gotta get out of here! Someone's coming, and they look like trouble."

"Who the hell are you?" Malloy demanded, his eyes darting around for other intruders.

"This is my... lookout," I replied, saying the first thing that came to mind. "You didn't think my boss would send me to these meetings alone, did you?"

"Hey, I know you," Roland said to Malloy, and I saw a disaster in the making.

I got between them and faced Roland. "Forget him. Who's coming?"

Alarm flashed in his eyes, and he grabbed my hand, pulling me toward the steps. "I don't know, but they look like they mean business. Probably some of his friends."

"Not that way!" Malloy hissed at us. I turned to see him halfway up a ladder propped against a window open to the bow of the boat. Leave it to him to have an escape route in case things went south.

Roland lifted me and practically threw me up the ladder. Malloy had already disappeared through the window, and by the time I scrambled out onto the bow he had jumped to the next boat and vanished from sight. For a small guy he was pretty damn fast on his feet. I turned to see Roland coming through the window behind me just as footsteps pounded on the dock. Peering around the wheelhouse I saw three large, muscled men who looked like they should be guarding some foreign diplomat. The one in the lead was well over six feet with short, spiked blond hair. Behind him were two darker-complexioned men with short black hair. The looks of determination on their faces as they approached the boat scared the crap out of me. What the hell had Malloy gotten me into?

"What are you doing?" Roland whispered hoarsely as soon as he was out. "We need to get to the other boat like he did."

The men were a boat-length away. "It's too late. They'll see us." I looked around and quickly saw there was only one avenue of escape. Roland wasn't going to like it.

"Come on." I grabbed the rail at the end of the boat and lowered myself over the side, gasping as freezing water lapped at my legs.

Roland's eyes widened, and he latched onto my hand before I could let go of the rail. "You're going in the water?"

"Yes," I whispered urgently. "Now get your ass down here before they find us!"

He let me go, and I sank up to my neck in the frigid seawater. The cold punched the air from my lungs, and I took in a mouthful of water before I got my balance. The tide was out, but the water was still over my head and I had to thread my feet to keep from going under.

Roland hoisted himself over the rail. "Oh man, I knew I should have switched places with Pete," he moaned as he joined me with a small splash. "Fuck, this is cold!"

"Shhh," I whispered. The men were at the Mary's Hope, and the boat rocked as they climbed aboard. We were tucked out of sight beneath the front of the boat, but it wouldn't take them long to figure out where we'd gone. Voices and footsteps came toward the bow. If we didn't move in the next thirty seconds, we'd be caught.

"Follow me," I mouthed through chattering teeth. Roland nodded miserably, and I quickly but quietly moved toward the dock. The pilings were slimy, and I lost my grip on them several times before I managed to pull my body between them. Roland did not hesitate this time, and he was right behind me when I turned to look back for him. I put my finger to my lips and pulled us into the deeper shadows beneath the dock.

"They couldn't have gone far," said a deep voice in halting English. He sounded German.

"He will not be pleased if they get away, Gerhard." The voice was clipped and cold with a Middle Eastern accent. "I told you to grab the little man as soon as he arrived."

I knew it – they were after Malloy. I gritted my teeth. If we got out of this alive, he was going to hear it from me.

"Split up and check every boat," ordered the Middle Eastern man. "And have Cesar watch the entrance."

"Why don't we have the witch find them for us?" the German man named Gerhard asked.

His companion's laugh was colder than the water lapping at my chin. "He's already doing his thing. They better pray we find them before he does."

Roland and I stared at each other with frightened eyes, and he mouthed, "Witch?" I shrugged. What kind of mess was Malloy in? Whatever it was, we were not going to stick around to find out. I had enough to deal with without adding witches and a bunch of thugs to the mix.

I waited until I heard the men move to search the surrounding boats then I pointed to the long tunnel of darkness beneath the dock that led to the cement pier. Roland nodded and followed me as I moved through the water with agonizing slowness. My hands grabbed at the cross beams under the dock to pull myself along, but my fingers were too cold to hang on. If we didn't get out of this water soon, the men pounding on the dock above us would not be our biggest problem.

Roland stayed so close behind me I could feel his reassuring bulk every step of the way. It seemed to take hours to travel a few yards, even though I knew it was only minutes. We did not speak, but I feared my thumping heart or chattering teeth would give us away any second. Every now and then, footsteps moved over our heads and we froze in place, expecting a shout and a muscled arm to reach underneath the dock for us. Then they moved on, and we started breathing again.

When my feet hit bottom, I knew we finally were making progress. It was hard walking through the water but a lot easier than trying to keep afloat. Soon I felt rocks under my feet and I saw the slope of rocks that marked the end of the dock. Once we reached it, the tricky part began, because there would be no more dock to hide beneath and the only way to shore was across the pier or circling it. We might be able to keep low enough to avoid detection, especially if the men were still busy with the boats. We'd just have to deal with that when we got there.

Roland put a hand on my shoulder as I started to climb the rocks. "Wait. Do you hear that?"

I turned my head to listen, and my ears picked up scraping sounds ahead followed by a series of squeaks. "Rats. They live under the pier."

He shuddered. "Rats!"

"You live in the country, and you're strong enough to rip a vampire apart. How can you be afraid of rats?"

He drew himself up taller. "I didn't say I was afraid. I just hate the little bastards."

I hid my smile. "Just ignore them. They're more afraid of you than you are of them."

"I'm not afraid – " His eyes bugged, and he looked like he was gasping for air. "Uh, Sara…"

I followed his horrified stare to the rocks above me where a squirming mass of fur and teeth suddenly streamed from beneath the pier. Hundreds of brown and gray bodies formed a moving barrier between us and the pier, while hundreds of pairs of black button eyes watched us with eerie intelligence.

"Jesus Christ!" Roland muttered close to my ear. "This isn't normal, is it?"

"No."

"Maybe they can feel the storm coming. Would that freak them out?"

I shook my head, not taking my eyes off the pack of rats. I shifted my position slightly, and a couple of rats bared their sharp incisors at me. I'd been around plenty of rodents and had healed more than one rat over the years, and I had never seen this kind of behavior. Most animals were at ease around me, and never threatening toward me. What if they were sick? My power was strong enough to heal some of them, but not hundreds.

I opened myself and let a trickle of power flow from me, directing it to the closest rodent. The big brown rat's nose twitched when it sensed the warm energy permeating the cold air around its body, and then it reacted to my power in a way no animal had ever done – it recoiled. I swallowed my gasp of surprise. Animals loved my power. It calmed them and made them feel safe and unafraid. Something was very off with this rat.

A little mental push was all it took to send a stronger stream of power at the squirming rodent. It was almost enough to put him to sleep, but I had to get past his fear and figure out what was wrong with him. I could barely believe my eyes as the brown body twisted and jerked and tried to scramble over the other rats to get away from me. *What the hell?*

The pack shifted, tossing the fleeing rat around until it lost its footing and tumbled down the mass of bodies to the rocks. Its feet scrambled for purchase on the slimy rocks before it slipped and flew straight at me and Roland.

Roland made a "Gak" sound as my hands shot out instinctively to catch the rat before it hit the water. My fingers closed around the long furry body just as I remembered that the rat had hissed at me a minute ago and would likely sink its not so small teeth into my flesh any second. I let power pour from my hands and into the animal's body. My power was always stronger with direct contact, and if there was something wrong with this rat, I would know soon what it was.

"What are you doing?" Roland asked in a horrified whisper, his hand clenching my shoulder in a death grip.

I couldn't answer. My tongue was silenced by the shock of my power colliding with another presence inside the rat's mind. It was intelligent and strong, and it felt like I touched the outside of an angry hornet's nest when my energy made contact. I had never encountered anything like it, and it frightened and amazed me at the same time. I felt the rat's heart race and sensed its terror as it cowered from the thing invading its body. If this same alien presence had infected the whole pack, it was no wonder they were so hostile. What could do something like this, and why?

Roland shook me from behind. "Are you fucking insane? Drop that thing before it gives you rabies or something."

"Be quiet or those men will hear us," I warned him hoarsely, securing my hold on the rodent so it could not try to bite me. "There's something wrong with these rats. Stay still so you don't frighten them."

"Frighten *them*?"

I shrugged out of his hold. "Shhh."

"Listen, I know you have this weird way with animals, but these are not cats or dogs, Sara. These are rats – huge, crazy rats that look like they are about to eat us. And in case you've forgotten, we already have enough to deal with."

"Just give me a minute, will you?" Roland didn't know what I knew. As soon as I felt the sinister consciousness in the rat's mind, I knew it was not going to let us pass. I also knew I could not leave these poor tortured animals without trying to help them.

I let power pool in my hands as if I was going to do a healing. My energy worked on sickness and injuries, but I had no idea how to use it against another power. Except for that one time that I had pushed back on Nikolas when he entered my mind, I'd never used my power offensively, and I had no idea if I could do it again. Time to find out.

My palms grew hot, and the rat began to squirm. "Easy there," I crooned, caressing its back with my thumbs as I let the power flow into him. The instant I came up against the unnatural presence, it shifted and pulsed like a cold, slimy maggot, and the rat began to squeak and twist frantically. Bile rose in my throat at the feel of the foul thing burrowed in the animal's mind, and my power flexed unconsciously, pushing at it, surrounding it like it was an infection to be burned from the body. The invader pushed back, and I turned up the heat until I felt the thing shrink away, twisting in pain. I latched on and sent a blast of white-hot energy into it, and I felt the explosion of power in my own mind like a scream. The rat stopped struggling as a healing current swept away the last traces of the sickness and replaced it with a warm sense of safety and wellbeing.

"What the hell...? What did you do?"

"I..." I struggled for the words to explain what I had done. I'd already decided to tell Roland and Peter about my power, but I thought I'd have more time to think of a way to show them. But this – I wasn't sure what I'd just done. How could I explain it to him?

"Look." He pointed ahead, and I looked up to see rats disappearing between the narrow slats beneath the pier. I reached out to lay the rat on one of the rocks, and he scampered after his pack without a backward glance.

I resumed my climb over the rocks. "Let's get out of here," I whispered. There was no guarantee that what had infected the pack would not return, and we had to make our escape while we could. I sensed that Roland was brimming with questions, but he followed me quietly, as eager to get away from there as I was.

We made it over the rocks without further incident and came to the end of the dock and our only cover. We listened for our pursuers, and I heard them still searching the boats. The whole encounter with the rats had only lasted a few minutes, although it had felt longer, and I'd half expected to find the men right on top of us. I allowed myself a small sigh of relief. One man still watched the entrance, but there was more than one way out of the marina if you didn't mind getting dirty. And we were already wet and filthy.

Roland followed me as I let myself slide back into the water, clinging to the slats and ropes along the side of the pier. My body hung flush against the pier as I moved sideways, pulling myself along as fast as I dared with my head just above the water. The sun had disappeared while we were under the dock, and a steady wind tossed the water, camouflaging the ripples caused by our progress. *Guess that storm is on its way.*

My feet touched bottom again, and I trudged the last few yards to shore where I sank wearily on the narrow strip of rocky beach beneath the club-house's deck. Using my power on the rats had not drained me as much as I would have expected, and I just needed a few seconds to catch my breath. At least I wasn't freezing anymore; that was one good side effect of my power. I hoped Roland was okay. I knew werewolves could withstand extreme temperatures, but I didn't know if that applied to their human form.

Roland risked a peek round the building and pulled back quickly, shaking his head. He held up a finger and pointed to tell me he'd seen one man standing by the clubhouse door. The parking lot was less than twenty feet away, but there was no way to get to it without being seen.

I saw the worry on his face and gave him what I hoped was a reassuring smile as I examined our situation. The only way out from our current location was if we followed the beach for about fifty yards then cut across the parking lot of the nearby seafood restaurant. There was a good chance of being seen by the men on the docks, and I wasn't sure if it would give us enough headway to lose them if they gave pursuit. It was getting darker by the minute because of the approaching storm, so our best option was to wait until the light faded enough to obscure us and hope the men searching the marina did not think to look down here for us.

I whispered my plan to Roland, and he nodded grimly and settled down beside me to wait. Above the rising wind and the lapping waves, we heard the sounds of activity from the marina as the workers hurried to finish their preparation for the storm. I couldn't hear our pursuers, but I knew they were still there. I didn't know what beef they had with Malloy, but with his business it could be anything, and I didn't want me or Roland dragged into it. The men had not mentioned either of us by name, so hopefully they had no idea who we were or how to find us.

Thirty minutes later, we stood shivering while Roland checked the parking lot again. His mouth formed a thin line as he faced me again. These guys did not give up easily.

We could not afford to wait around here any longer. It was dark enough to risk the beach escape route, so I motioned for Roland to follow me since I knew the area better. Picking our way along the rocks in the near dark was hard going, but we were too glad to be getting out of there to care. Thankfully, both of us had worn dark clothes today, and we managed to blend in well with the beach. Before long, we reached the restaurant and scurried like mice across the parking lot to the street where we set out for my place at a run.

When the lights from the waterfront came into view, we slowed and caught our breath. The wind had really picked up, and I felt cold raindrops against my face. We were already soaked from head to toe, so rain was the least of our worries. Still, I couldn't wait to get home, peel off my stinking wet clothes, and sink into a tub of hot water. Normally I was a shower person, but I made exceptions for special occasions, and this certainly qualified as one.

"I'm sorry I got you involved in that – whatever it was," I said when it felt safe enough to talk. "I swear nothing like that has ever happened before."

"It's not your fault. I insisted on going, remember? And I'm glad you weren't alone, though you handled it all better than I did." He grew quiet for a minute. "What happened with those rats? You did something to them. Is it some Mohiri thing?" he probed. "I don't know what you did, but I know you made those rats back off."

We had just spent a harrowing hour jumping off a boat, hiding under a dock in freezing salt water, and running from a group of men who wanted God only knew what, and the one thing Roland zeroed in on was something I was not ready to talk about.

"I did do something. There are things I need to tell you about me, and I promise I will soon... just not right now. Can you wait a few days?"

"Why can't you tell me now?"

"I just need a few days, and then I swear I'll tell you and Peter everything. Besides, we've had enough excitement today, don't you think?"

"Alright," he conceded reluctantly. "But we are going to have a serious talk very soon. You have to stop keeping stuff to yourself like you did about your dad. You know you can tell me anything."

"I know."

"And no more running off like this. It's just too dangerous."

I didn't reply at first, and his tone grew more serious. "Sara?"

"I promise I'll be more careful."

He made a sound like he didn't believe me. Then he surprised me by chuckling. "And as for having enough excitement today, I think you forgot one thing."

I shot him a sideways glance. "What?"

Roland smirked as he looked straight ahead. "Him."

14

I felt the Mohiri presence brush against my mind a second before I looked down the street to see Nikolas stalking toward us, his expression darker than the sky. Sucking up my courage, I braced myself for a lecture as we walked toward him. Whatever his honorable intentions, this was still my life. Eventually, he would have to get that through his head – I hoped.

Whatever Nikolas planned to say was forgotten when he got close enough to take in our wet clothes and salty, fishy odor. "What the hell happened this time?"

"We – "

"Nothing," I said before Roland could answer.

Nikolas muttered something in another language that sounded like swearing. He shook his head then looked at Roland. "I'll take her from here."

"I don't think so," I sputtered and filled with dread at his look of determination.

Roland stepped forward. "I'm not sure that's such a good – "

"Sara and I need to talk – just talk," Nikolas told him, ignoring my protest. "And judging by the look on your face, I think you agree with me."

I turned in disbelief to my friend. "Roland?"

Roland's eyes were troubled when they met mine. "You won't listen to me. Maybe it will be good for someone else to…"

"Traitor," I accused, walking past them both. I couldn't believe it; my best friend was siding with Nikolas – a werewolf siding with a Mohiri. If I wasn't so upset, I would have laughed at the absurdity of it all.

"Sara, wait..."

I ignored Roland's plea. The rain began in earnest, and the wind picked up as if the storm was tethered to my mood. I was drenched all over again by the time I reached my building.

Peter was there in his mother's car waiting for us. "What happened?" he called.

"I'm sure Roland will tell you all about it," I replied sourly, heading straight for the stairs.

I contemplated locking the door behind me as I flicked on the light in the hallway, but I had a feeling that a deadbolt would be no deterrence to Nikolas in his present mood. For a moment, I held onto the faint hope that the troll ward would keep him out, but that hope was dashed when the door opened as I was kicking off my ruined Vans. I dropped my coat to the floor with a loud plop and moved to the stairs without bothering to look at him. "Make yourself at home," I said in a voice that was anything but welcoming.

Upstairs, the storm was louder as the wind groaned around the eaves and rain battered the windows. I cracked a window and whistled for Harper who sometimes liked to ride out bad weather inside. There was no sign of the crow, and I soon had to close the window to keep the rain out.

I heard shuffling and turned as Daisy hopped over the top of the stairs. Storms didn't bother her, but she always turned to me for company when Nate was gone. I rubbed her head, and she trailed after me when I went to the bathroom to start water running in the tub. Nikolas's talk would have to wait until after I had that nice hot bath I'd promised myself. If he wanted to chat he'd just have to cool his heels downstairs until I was ready.

I wriggled out of my wet jeans and reached into the front pocket for the vial of Ptellon blood, cupping it in my hand reverently. Everything that had gone down at the marina was worth it to secure Nate's safety. We might not be as close as either of us would have wanted, but I'd do almost anything to protect him from the danger I had brought into our lives. I opened the bottom drawer in my bathroom vanity and stuck the vial in the very back to keep it safe until Nate got home. I only had to slip three drops of the blood-red liquid into his food or drink every month, and the vial held enough to last for at least a year. Between the wards and the Ptellon, Nate should be safe from almost anything supernatural. The Ptellon blood did not repel humans, but it wasn't humans I was worried about.

A happy moan escaped me when I sank into the hot water. I laid my head against the bath pillow and closed my eyes as the steaming soapy water soaked the grit and stench from my pores. My mind raced from what had happened at the marina. The men chasing us had been frightening, but it was the encounter with the rats that really shook me. I'd never felt anything like that thing in the rat's mind, and I shivered in spite of the hot water. How was I able to push it out of the rat and then have the strength to affect a whole pack of rats at once? Was my power getting stronger? Nikolas had said that Mohiri powers grew as they reached maturity. Maybe that's what was happening to me. There was so much about my power that was still a mystery to me, and I wished I had someone to explain it.

I made myself relax and pushed the confusing thoughts aside. The constant drum of rain on the roof lulled me into a pleasant doze, and I stayed there until the water began to cool. I let the water out and stood to wash my hair under the shower. Despite the last few hours and the unwelcome guest downstairs, I felt considerably lighter when I wrapped a large towel around me and walked into my bedroom.

"Hey! What do you think you're doing?" I shrieked at Nikolas who sat on my couch with my traitorous cat curled up beside him. My sketch pad laid open on his lap as he studied one of the drawings. My drawings were like my journal, and there was something disturbingly intimate about him sitting in my private space, looking at them. "Get out of my room and keep your hands off my things."

He ignored my outburst, his gaze dark and unfathomable as he looked at me. "You took so long I thought you'd tried to run off again."

I pulled the towel tighter around me and tried to ignore the heat infusing my face. "Well, as you can see, I am still here. Now do you mind leaving my room so I can get dressed?"

An infuriating smile played around the corners of his mouth, and the room suddenly felt too warm. "Of course." He laid the sketchbook on the couch and stood. "Your drawings are quite good. Has anyone ever told you that?"

"I don't show them to anyone. They're *private*," I said pointedly to remind him again that he was violating my personal space. Inside I felt a small flare of pleasure at the praise, but I would never let him know that.

He looked entirely unapologetic for the intrusion as he walked unhurriedly to the stairs. "I'll see you downstairs shortly."

Fuming, I went to the couch to close the sketchbook and stopped just short of reaching for it when I saw Nikolas's face looking up at me. I felt the familiar stab of fear I experienced every time I remembered that night in Portland. I didn't write down my feelings in a journal. I drew them, and for some reason this image was the one that stood out most in my memory from that night. Maybe because it was the moment I knew I was not alone. It made me feel open and vulnerable having someone else look at it, especially Nikolas.

I took my time getting dressed, and I planned to take overly long to dry my hair to avoid facing him for as long as possible. The storm had other ideas, however, and the power went out just as I picked up my hair dryer. "Great!" I muttered, groping for a flashlight. I grabbed a towel to dry my hair as best I could and then, unable to delay any longer, made my way downstairs with Daisy close at my heels.

I found Nikolas in the kitchen, making sandwiches by candlelight with his sleeves pulled up and his leather jacket thrown over the back of a chair. The casual, domestic picture was such a contrast to the image of the warrior I was used to that I stopped short, and Daisy ran into the back of my legs.

"What are you doing?"

"Dinner. I would have ordered in, but it looks like power is out all over town. So sandwiches it is." He slid a plate across the counter toward me. "Hope you like roast beef."

"Um, thanks... I do." I mumbled, trying to figure out what he was up to. One minute he was furious, and the next he was making me dinner. If he thought he could throw me off guard by being nice to me all of a sudden, he was right. I had no idea how to respond to this new side of him. To hide my discomfort I grabbed a bag of potato chips from the pantry and a bottle of dill pickles from the fridge, laying them both on the table with two glasses of soda.

Nikolas carried our sandwiches to the table and placed the pillar candle in the center. I chewed my bottom lip and tucked my damp hair nervously behind my ear when it struck me what a cozy picture we made, eating by candlelight while a storm howled outside. I peeked at Nikolas who seemed quite at ease, piling chips on his plate as if we ate together like this every day. His hair was still damp from the rain and his features were relaxed, almost like he was enjoying himself. He looked up, and his eyes were like liquid smoke in the candlelight when they met mine. My stomach did a little leap, and I immediately found my own sandwich fascinating.

The sandwich was just how I liked it: roast beef, cheese, and horseradish sauce on rye. I almost asked him how he knew what my favorite was, but I refrained. I wasn't sure I wanted to know how much he knew about me.

We ate in silence for a minute before he asked the question I knew was coming. "You want to tell me where you disappeared to today and why you came back smelling like you went for a swim in the bay?"

I stopped nibbling a chip to say, "It was personal business I had to take care of... and I did go for a swim in the bay. Satisfied?"

"Not even close."

There was more silence as I picked up my sandwich and bit into it, refusing to expand upon my story. I felt Nikolas's gaze, but I ignored him. It was going to take a lot more than a candlelight dinner to make me spill.

It took me a few minutes to realize the scolding I was expecting was not coming, and I glanced at Nikolas to find him enjoying his meal. Where was the man who had practically shot daggers at me out on the waterfront less than an hour ago?

"Aren't you going to yell at me or something?"

He shrugged without looking up from his sandwich. "Will it make you tell me what you were doing today?"

"No."

"Then why don't we just have a pleasant meal instead?"

I scowled at him, not sure what to make of his answer. Was he trying to trick me into telling him the truth? He shows up looking like he's about to bring the wrath of God down on me and then he makes me dinner and wants to exchange pleasantries. Did I just step into a *Twilight Zone* episode?

His next words surprised me even more. "You remind me of someone I knew a long time ago. She was stubborn to a fault, too."

"If you say it was Madeline, I'm going to throw my pickle at you." There was no way I was anything like the woman who had given birth to me. She was my biological mother, but that was where the connection ended.

Nikolas smiled, and his eyes had an almost faraway look. "Not Madeline, no. Her name was Elena, and she was actually Madeline's aunt, though she died before Madeline was born."

"Was she your girlfriend or something?" I asked, surprised by the fondness in his voice. Before tonight, I'd thought of Nikolas only as a warrior, all business and no time for a personal life. But I guess he had to have some kind of life outside of hunting vampires. My Mori stirred, and an alien feeling twisted my gut. Was that jealousy? I gave a mental shake to let the demon know that we didn't give a fig about Nikolas's romantic involvements.

"No, Elena was like a sister to me. She was beautiful, but willful and very spoiled."

"Are you calling me spoiled?" Typical male. A strong man was just fine, but let a woman show some free will and she was spoiled.

He laughed and took a drink from his glass without answering. I glared at him, and his grin grew. "Okay, maybe not spoiled but definitely obstinate."

"Pot, meet kettle." I picked up my own glass. "What happened to her?"

His expression darkened. "She ignored the rules that were there to protect her and went off by herself alone. She was killed by vampires."

I sucked in a sharp breath. "Oh, I'm sorry." That might explain his over-protective ways toward me. His friend had died at the hands of a vampire, and here I was being pursued by one.

"It was a long time ago."

"So does Madeline's have any family left?" I asked in an effort to change the topic.

It was the first time I'd expressed any interest in possible Mohiri relations, and Nikolas smiled in response. "She still has some living relatives; her sire for one."

"Sire? That sounds so... impersonal." I thought of my dad, the way he would catch me up in a big hug and read to me before bed. I could not imagine thinking of him as my sire.

Nikolas laid his napkin across his plate and leaned back in his chair. "It's just a title. Mohiri families are as close as human families, maybe more so since we do not grow old and die naturally."

"So you and your parents all look the same age? Don't you find that weird?"

He shook his head. "We don't think of age the same way mortals do. Humans see it as a way to mark one's passage through life. Physically, we don't age once we reach maturity."

He might find it normal, but I found it hard to imagine being the same age as my grandparents. Ugh. "So, my grand... Madeline's father is still alive. Does he know about me?" It was a bit of a shock to learn I had a living grand-parent I'd never met. My dad's mother died when I was ten, and I never really knew her that well.

"Yes, and he is looking forward to meeting you." My hesitation must have shown on my face because Nikolas caught my gaze and held it. "He will wait until you're ready to meet him."

"A patient Mohiri, who would have thought it?" I got up and carried our plates to the sink to hide my suddenly conflicted feelings. I had no intention of going to the Mohiri any time soon, but the knowledge that I had a grandfa-ther – even if he was Madeline's father – out there who wanted to see me caused emotions I did not want to think about.

"A Mohiri has all the patience in the world when something is worth waiting for," he replied, and I got the feeling we were no longer talking about my grandfather.

I started running hot water over the plates. "I guess it helps that you guys are immortal, huh?"

"So are you," he said close to my ear, and I almost dropped the plate in my hand.

"Don't do that!" I choked, and he laughed softly. He took the plate from me and began to dry it with a dish towel. *Does he have to stand so close?* I griped as I rinsed the other plate and handed it to him. Something in his manner told me he was doing it just to irk me, and he was enjoying himself immensely. I found myself wishing the old Nikolas was here. I knew what to expect from him; this new Nikolas was too confusing by far.

Wind rattled the kitchen window, and I rubbed my arms, wishing I'd thought to bring down a sweater or hoodie. Without the power, there was no heat, and this close to the bay, the air was growing cold fast. I reached for the flashlight to go upstairs and get something heavy to wear.

"The temperature is going to drop a lot tonight. Does that fireplace in the living room work?"

"Yes, it's gas."

He walked past me to the dark living room. "Go put on something warm, and I'll start the fire."

I spoke to his back. "So what, we're going to sit by the fire and roast marshmallows now?"

"You have anything better to do?" he called back without turning around.

I had no answer for that, so I went upstairs and dug out one of my dad's old sweaters. It was my favorite because I could still remember him in it, though sadly it had lost his scent a long time ago. I pulled on a pair of fuzzy moccasin slippers Judith had given me last Christmas and sat on my bed thinking of the irony of the situation. Nate had left me alone here knowing there was no way I'd have a boy over, and his first night away there was a guy here making dinner for me. My uncle would probably have heart palpitations if he walked in the door right now. Just one look at Nikolas and he'd never believe this whole thing was innocent. I couldn't help smiling at the hilarity of it all as I made my way downstairs again.

"Where did you find marshmallows?" I asked in surprise when I saw the open bag on the coffee table. I'd been joking about roasting them, but now it looked like the best idea ever.

Nikolas looked up from his seat on the floor as he threaded one on a long metal skewer and held it over the fire. "Top shelf in the pantry. Want one?"

"Yes!" I sat in the chair closest to the fireplace and sighed as the heat surrounded me. Daisy came into the room and stretched out in front of my chair.

"Here." He handed me the skewer. I blew on the blackened marshmallow as he started another one for himself. For a few minutes, there was no sound but the hissing of the fire and the storm battering the building. I found myself strangely at ease. After my close call at the marina, I was surprised I wasn't jumping at the slightest noise. But this was actually nice.

"Have you always done this – hunting vampires? Do all Mohiri become warriors?"

He sat with his back to the couch and his long legs stretched out across the rug. "Most do, though we have some scholars and artisans. Being a warrior is in our blood, what we are born to do. I have never wanted to do anything else."

I absorbed that for a minute. "What's it like growing up there? Do you live in houses or on some kind of military base? Do you go to school or start training when you're little?" Since I'd first learned about the Mohiri, I imagined them living like soldiers, sleeping in barracks and training to fight every day. It all seemed so cold and militant, and it did not reconcile with the way he spoke about family.

He smiled and skewered another marshmallow. "We live in fortified compounds all over the world. The larger compounds look like private campuses, and the smaller ones are basically well-fortified estates. It is not safe for a Mohiri family to live outside a compound because they would be vulnerable to vampire attacks. Families live together, and the living quarters are large and comfortable. Children attend school until they are sixteen, and physical training begins when they reach puberty." He leaned forward, and the fire played across his handsome face. "It's a good life. There is a deep sense of belonging among the Mohiri, and everyone who comes to live among us is happier than they were living among humans."

I stared at the flames. His meaning was clear, and I did not want to break our moment of peace by replaying the old argument. Maybe the Mohiri were not as cold and impersonal as I'd thought, but I could not imagine being any happier there. My dad would still be gone, and I wouldn't even have Nate or Roland and Peter.

The ringing of the kitchen phone cut through the silence, and I jumped up to answer it. It was Nate, calling from his hotel in Boston, his voice full of worry.

"Hey, I hear you guys are getting hit by a hard nor'easter. Everything okay there?"

"I'm perfectly fine, Nate. You know how I love a good storm."

His relief was audible. "Well if the power goes, there are extra flashlights and a battery operated lantern in the hall closet."

"Don't worry. I have it all under control. How is the conference?"

He told me about his day and that he'd be at his hotel for the rest of the night if I needed to call him. I laughed and told him he sounded like Judith when she got all over Roland about something. That was enough to get him to say good night with a promise to call and check on me tomorrow.

As soon as I hung up from Nate, the phone rang again. "Jeeze, what now?" This time it was Roland.

"Well, you answered the phone so I assume you're not bound and gagged," he quipped.

"No thanks to you."

"Ah, don't be mad. I was kind of freaked out after what happened, and I thought maybe someone else should talk to you."

"I don't want to talk about that now." I was still a little hurt by his defection, and I was in no mood to assuage his guilt tonight.

"Mom said the power's out all over town. Are you alright there? Because I can come get you if you want."

I let out a sigh. It was impossible to stay mad at Roland when he was sweet like this. "I'm fine. We have the fireplace going and lots of candles."

"*We?* Is he there with you now?"

"Yes."

Roland's voice raised a notch. "I thought he kept guard outside or whatever. I'm not sure he should be in there with you with Nate gone."

"You should have thought of that before you left." I couldn't resist the dig. "Did you think we would talk outside in the middle of a storm?"

"I... um..." he stammered.

"I have to go. I'll see you tomorrow." I did not want to continue this conversation with Nikolas within earshot.

"Oh, okay," Roland said reluctantly. "See you tomorrow."

I hung up and went back to the living room to reclaim my seat by the fire. "Everyone's checking up on me."

"The werewolf cares for you."

I glared at him. "He's my best friend, and he has a name, you know."

His shoulders lifted indifferently. "We don't make a habit of being on a first name basis with weres, and I'm sure you know they feel the same about us. It's just how it is."

"Well, I am Mohiri and I have loads of werewolf friends, so you'll just have to get over it." His mouth curved as if I'd said something funny, and I snapped, "What?"

"That's the first time you've admitted what you are."

My hand smoothed the fabric on the arm of my chair. "It doesn't change anything." I had accepted my heritage weeks ago, because denying it didn't make it go away. That didn't mean I was happy about it.

"It's a start." He put his arms behind his head and gave me a devastating smile that I bet had bewitched more than one female. I felt the urge to throw a cushion at the smug bastard, but the challenge I saw creep into his eyes stayed my hand.

"What else would you like to know about the Mohiri?" he asked when I stayed silent. I didn't want to satisfy him by showing any more interest in his people, but there were more than a few things I was curious about since I could find absolutely nothing about the Mohiri online.

"Who is in charge of everything? Do you have a president or a king or something?"

"Not exactly," he said with a laugh. "We have the Council of Seven who make up the ruling body, and the most important decisions come from them." He went on to explain that the seven seats represented the seven continents and the members convened once a month, always in a different location. I asked how they were chosen to be on the council, and he told me that if someone left the council or died, the remaining members selected someone to fill the empty chair. It wasn't something that happened often. The last new member had been appointed to the Seven three hundred years ago.

"Do you want to join the council someday?"

He scowled and shook his head. "Never. I have no time for bureaucracy and not enough patience to endure the long meetings. I am a warrior, and that is all I aspire to be."

I tilted my head sideways. "Didn't you just say you guys have lots of patience?"

"When something is worth waiting for," he qualified. "I care very little for political matters."

His statement did not come as a surprise. I could not picture Nikolas adhering well to rules or attempting diplomacy to please anyone. "Something tells me that sentiment doesn't make you popular with the folks in charge."

His eyes gleamed. "They are good at their job, and they know that I'm good at mine. We differ in opinion sometimes, but we all work to the same end."

"What do they think about you hanging around some town no one's ever heard of, wasting time with an orphan instead of out doing your warrior business?" I couldn't see how one orphan's safety was more important than all the evils out there that needed to be dealt with.

"You think you're a waste of our time?" His voice, though low, had taken on an edge I recognized.

"I didn't say I'm a waste of time, but there must be other orphans who need rescuing more than I do. And since I won't change my mind about leaving, it doesn't make sense to stick around."

"There is an immediate threat here. We were tracking vampire activity in the area before we found you; it was what brought us to Portland that night." His tone did not soften, and I knew my comment had really bugged him. I didn't bother trying to figure it out because I doubted I would ever understand Nikolas.

That reminded me of something else I had wondered about. "Where are you from? You have this faint accent I can't place and sometimes I think you're speaking another language."

"I was born in Saint Petersburg, and I lived there for the first sixteen years of my life until my family moved to England and then America." One corner of his mouth lifted. "My accent is usually noticeable now only when I'm aggravated."

I wanted to say that wasn't true, that I had picked up on it since the first time he spoke to me, but instead I moved to another subject. "And what's Chris's story? Is he your partner?"

"I normally work alone, but we sometimes work as a team. Christian and I have known each other for many years."

"Christian," I repeated the name. "It suits him better than Chris."

"I'm sure he'll be pleased to hear that," Nikolas said dryly.

"Well, I aim to please," I replied just as tartly, relieved we were moving back onto familiar ground. Arrogant, sarcastic Nikolas I could handle.

He actually snorted. I had to suppress a smile because we both knew I'd done everything to thwart his plans since we'd met. I still had no intention of letting him dictate my life, but it seemed like we had reached a truce of sorts tonight.

"Listen, I know you'd rather be off hunting monsters even if you guys feel like you need to be here. And I know you think I'm a pain sometimes, but – "

"Sometimes?"

"What I'm *trying* to say," I continued, ignoring his interruption, "is that even though you are way too bossy and you can be an arrogant ass sometimes, I guess you're not all bad."

His eyebrows rose. "I think that's the most backhanded compliment I've ever gotten. And I will say that you are without a doubt the biggest pain in the butt I've ever met."

I couldn't hold back my smirk. "The biggest pain, really?"

He grinned back. "Yes, but I do like a challenge." The gleam in his eyes unnerved me, and I knew he would not give up easily. I was loath to shatter our fragile truce, but backing down from my own position was not an option.

"I don't want to fight with you anymore." The words were out before I knew what I was going to say. I didn't know who was more surprised by my statement. At that moment a gale of wind made the walls creak and the fire dance as if the elements themselves were in agreement.

"I'm glad to hear that."

"I haven't changed my mind or anything," I rushed to add before he mistook my olive branch for surrender. "I just don't want us to be at each other's throats all the time."

"You want to be friends?" His voice held a note of amusement.

I made a face. "Let's not get carried away. How about we agree to disagree and take it from there?"

"A truce then?"

"Yes – or a cease-fire." I had my doubts either would hold up long between the two of us.

He studied me for a few seconds before he leaned forward with a hand extended. "Okay. A cease-fire it is."

I tentatively reached out my own hand, and he grasped it in his larger one. His grip was warm and strong, and a tingle ran up my arm at the contact. When he made no move to let go, I yanked my hand away and buried it beneath my thigh. If he noticed my quick withdrawal, he made no mention of it.

A yawn rose inside me, and I wondered why I was sleepy before I remembered my freezing dunk in the ocean and the power I'd used on the rats. I almost cringed when I remembered the foulness that had infected those poor animals.

"You look tired." Nikolas stood, and I had to crane my neck as he towered over me. "Go to bed. I'll let myself out."

The windows rattled again, and I thought of him standing out there in the storm all night just to watch over me. "You can stay in here tonight – if you want to."

His eyes reflected his surprise at the unexpected offer, and I suddenly felt self-conscious. It wasn't like I invited guys over as houseguests every other day. Hoping my blush wasn't visible in the dim light, I said, "You're already here, and it makes no sense for you to be out in that weather when you could have the couch. I'll get you some blankets."

I almost tripped over myself to get to the linen closet where Nate kept the spare quilts. When I returned with a quilt and a pillow, Nikolas was standing where I'd left him, his face hidden in shadow. He took the quilt and pillow from me with a quiet "thank you."

"Um, okay, good night." I didn't wait for his reply before I turned to the doorway. I heard the creak of the couch when he sat on it.

"Sara?" His voice was deep and warm, and my heart sped up a little as I stopped in the hallway to look over my shoulder.

"Yes?"

"You're still the biggest pain in the ass I've ever met."

I grinned all the way to bed.

15

I awoke the next morning to the heavy silence that follows a big storm. Snuggling under my covers with Oscar sprawled across my pillow and Daisy on my feet, I wanted nothing more than to go back to sleep. That is until I remembered everything from the night before and the unexpected houseguest who'd spent the night on the couch. I slipped out of bed, pulled on a hoodie and my moccasin slippers, and padded quietly downstairs. In the living room I found the quilt folded up neatly on the couch and no sign of Nikolas. I was not surprised that he had already left. Knowing him, he'd probably had his coffee and dispatched a couple of monsters before the sun came up.

I poured some Cheerios and mulled over the strange turn our relationship had taken last night. I still found it hard to believe that the easygoing man who had laughed and roasted marshmallows was the same mercurial person I'd known up until now. I had come downstairs last night expecting a roaring fight with one Nikolas and ended up spending an almost pleasant and somewhat confusing evening with his alter ego. And then I'd offered him a truce… and invited him to stay. I groaned over my spoon. What the hell had come over me last night?

The power was back so that meant school was open. I ran upstairs to get ready, then booted up the laptop to check email. *Funny*, I thought as I waited for the login screen. Any other night I would have missed my internet, but I hadn't even noticed it was gone last night.

The email from NightWatcher took me by surprise. I hadn't talked to him in a week and a half – since the night after the crocotta attack. His message was short. He was leaving Maine for his own safety, and if I still wanted to meet him, I had until Saturday. He said he was sorry but things were getting too scary for him to stick around. He felt like we had to meet before he took off. I cursed the timing because it was going to be damn near impossible to get away to see him now, but I replied that I would get back to him that night with an answer.

I worried about it all the way to school, and by the time I reached the schoolyard, I'd finally decided that the only way to make it happen was to include Roland and Peter. They were waiting for me on the steps with expectant expressions, but I brushed them off and told them to meet me in the library for study period. They had said they wanted to help, and now I was going to find out if they were good to their word.

When third period came around I hurried to the library to get a table as far from the front desk as possible. My mind was completely preoccupied with replaying everything that happened yesterday and last night as I followed my usual path through the stacks. That explained why I did not see the boy crossing in front of me before I plowed into him and knocked us both sideways.

"Sorry," I breathed as I grabbed a shelf to keep myself from falling on my butt.

"Don't worry about – "

I spun and faced the boy as recognition hit us at the same time. I hadn't seen much of Scott in the last few weeks, and I noticed that his face had healed completely from our fight. That did little to alleviate the guilt I still carried for what I'd done to him, especially after learning what lived inside me and how much worse I could have hurt him if I had not restrained myself.

We stared at each other for several seconds, and I waited for one of his typical scathing comments. What I did not expect was the sad, wounded look that suddenly flashed across his face. In a blink it was gone, replaced by the haughty expression I knew well. He pushed past me to walk the other way as if nothing had happened.

I continued to my table and laid my backpack thoughtfully on it as I mused over Scott's strange reaction. I didn't think it had anything to do with the fight; if anything, he still resented me for that. There was no love lost between us, for sure. Chances were I'd just caught him in an off moment that had nothing to do with me at all.

But I could not help but compare the hurt I'd glimpsed on his face to his expression that day in the school yard when I yelled at him and told him I didn't want to be his friend. I'd been too full of childish anger over the injured crow to see that I'd hurt Scott. It made me wonder, as I pulled out my biology book, if Scott and I would still be friends if I hadn't caught him hurting Harper. Would either of us be the people we were now if our friendship had survived?

I shook my head to clear my mind. It was useless wondering about it after so many years, and I had bigger things to worry about right now.

"Talking to yourself now? That's not a good sign." Roland sat next to me with a searching look.

Peter took the chair across from me and leaned forward to whisper, "Roland told me what happened. That was some crazy shit!" His eyes glowed with excitement. "I can't believe you know people like that Malloy fellow."

"Yeah, Greg's uncle my ass," Roland added with some indignation over the lie I'd told him when he had run into me and Malloy at Gino's.

I took a breath. "Listen, I'm sorry about that. I really am. But men like Malloy don't like a lot of people knowing their business. After yesterday, I think you can see why."

Roland's mouth tightened. "No freaking kidding."

"So what happened last night?" Peter asked. "How pissed was the Mohiri when he found out what you were up to?"

I gave him a disbelieving look. "Are you nuts? There's no way I'm telling him about that." I had very little doubt that last night would have gone a lot differently if Nikolas had discovered the truth.

Mrs. Cope the librarian walked by, giving us a stern look, and we all quieted until she was gone.

Roland was the first to speak. "Didn't he ask where you went?"

"Yes, but I wasn't stupid enough to tell him."

"I bet he was mad," Peter said.

I shook my head. "He was...weird. He kind of let it go and told me about the Mohiri." How could I explain the change in Nikolas last night when I didn't understand it myself? "You won't believe this. I have a grandfather who wants to meet me, and he doesn't look much older than me. How messed up is that?"

"Are you going to meet him?" Roland's eyes were worried, and I wondered if he was afraid I would be drawn to the Mohiri now that I knew I had family there.

"I don't know. Someday," I said honestly. "It's a bit much to take in, but it doesn't change how I feel about going to live with them."

Peter let his breath out noisily. "Jeeze, I thought *our* lives were complicated. I don't know how you can look so calm with all the craziness in your life."

Seeing the opening I had been waiting for, I pursed my lips and motioned for them to come closer. "There *is* one thing I need to do," I whispered. "Someone else I need to meet."

"No!" Roland hissed as loud as he dared. "It's too dangerous, Sara."

"Shhh. Listen to me before you go off," I said quietly. "I only have two more days to see this guy before he's gone for good, and I may never get another chance to find out what he knows about my dad. He wants to meet in the daytime, and he said I can pick the place as long as it's public. And he didn't say I couldn't have a friend close by."

"But – "

"No buts, Roland. You guys said you wanted me to stop hiding stuff from you and to ask you for help, and that's what I'm doing. I'm doing this with or without your help, but I'd rather it was with you."

"You really think you'll be able to ditch your bodyguards after your last stunt?" Roland asked in a tone that held zero confidence.

"You really think the three of us can't outsmart a couple of Mohiri – on our home turf?" I watched them straighten their shoulders at my well-placed dig. I'd learned two things about my werewolf friends: they did not like being compared to the Mohiri, and they really took the whole "this is our territory" thing to heart.

"What's the plan?" Roland asked with a new gleam in his eyes.

"I'm not sure yet. I was hoping you guys could help me come up with one."

We put our heads together – literally – and began tossing around ideas. Each one we came up with was quickly discarded because I'd given Nikolas and Chris the slip one too many times for them to fall for another of my ruses. Whatever we went with had to be a little more intricate, something that required strategy and planning. Only problem was I had run out of ideas and my friends were not doing much better.

Our brainstorm session was interrupted when Dylan walked up to our table. I hadn't talked to him since the party, and I felt self-conscious around him now after the thing with Samson. Did guys talk about that stuff the way girls did? I almost squirmed on my seat praying the answer to that question was a resounding no.

Dylan gave me his trademark lopsided smile, and I immediately relaxed. Either Samson hadn't said anything or Dylan was playing the gentleman. He sat on the corner of our table. "Just who I was looking for. I wanted to give you a personal invite to the party of the semester."

Roland grinned. "Oh, yeah? Anything like the July Fourth bash? Man, it took me two days to recover from that one."

"A two-day hangover? How appealing," I commented drolly, wondering how much you had to drink to be hung over that long.

"Better. The folks are going to Miami tomorrow, so I've got the place to myself all weekend. They said no parties in the house, but the boathouse is not off limits. Some of the guys are coming around noon on Saturday to jam, and we figured why not make a day of it. Spend the day on the lake and fire up the grill for dinner. Then party all night." He furrowed his brow. "Oh, and it's invitation only. The parental units will disown me if the whole school district shows up like last time."

I'd never been to Dylan's house on Clear Lake, but Roland and Peter had raved about the boathouse and boats and jet skis on more than one occasion. I could tell by my friends' expressions that this promised to be one of those "I was there when it happened" parties they lived for.

Roland gave Dylan a high five. "Hell, yeah!"

Dylan looked at me. "That invitation includes you too, Sara."

"Thanks. I... might have something else going on this Saturday, but I'll try to make it if my thing doesn't take too long." I had to meet NightWatcher somehow, but even if I pulled that off, I'd feel uncomfortable spending the day at the same party as Samson. I really did like him, and I would have dated him if I'd met him before my life had been turned upside down. He'd made his attraction to me more than clear. What if he got the wrong signal if I showed up at his party? Maybe most girls would not be bothered by it, but I wasn't other girls.

Roland and Peter looked like I had just told them they were extending the school week to Saturday. "Oh, yeah," Roland said glumly. "We promised to give Sara a lift somewhere, so we might miss out on the afternoon. But we'll definitely make it for the after party."

Dylan nodded good-naturedly. "No problem. I hope you all can make it. Some of the guys in the band won't be there, so I need my best drinking buds there." He spoke to Roland and Peter but his eyes were on me, making sure I got the message that a certain blond drummer would not be in attendance.

I smiled at him. If I didn't have to worry about an awkward encounter with Samson then I wouldn't mind spending a day at the lake. Clear Lake was huge. I imagined taking a boat out and anchoring somewhere in the middle where I didn't have to deal with boys or the growing list of other things I didn't want to think about. And best of all – no Mohiri. Nikolas and Chris might be good, but I was pretty sure they couldn't walk on water.

My smile grew as an idea started to form. "Hey, Dylan, do you have wetsuits for those jet skis?"

"I haven't seen you at Dylan's parties before."

I looked at the striking brunette standing a few feet from me on the dock. Her heart-shaped face was tilted to one side, and her blue eyes watched me with a mixture of curiosity and jealousy. Bethany Chase was gorgeous, popular, and rich, and I couldn't think of a single reason for her to be jealous of me.

"Roland made it sound like too much fun to pass up."

She moved closer. "Can I ask you something?"

"Sure," I replied absently, toying with the zipper of my borrowed wetsuit while I watched Roland and Peter whipping across the lake toward us on jet skis. I couldn't wait for my turn.

"Is that blond guy up by the boathouse a friend of yours?"

I didn't need to turn around to know she was talking about Chris, who'd arrived an hour ago. How he'd finagled his way into Dylan's private, invite-only party was beyond me since everyone else here appeared to know each other. I'd spent a good five minutes asking him to leave, but he only smiled and said to ignore him. Ignore him? He stuck out like a steak on a vegetarian buffet for Christ's sake.

"Chris is like a cousin to me." Hell, for all I knew he could be one of my cousins.

She giggled. "I thought he might be your boyfriend after I saw you with him. He keeps looking over here at you."

I glanced over my shoulder at the Mohiri, and an evil plan began to brew. "Nope, Chris is a free man." I gave her a meaningful look. "And I'm pretty sure he's not looking at me."

"Oh!" Bethany's face lit up like the sun coming from behind a cloud, and she turned her head to watch Chris hungrily. *Sorry, Chris*, I thought, hiding my smile of satisfaction. *But all's fair in love and war, right?*

"Maybe I'll go say hi to him."

"Good idea."

The jet skis pulled up beside the dock, and Peter grinned up at me. "You ready to lose to me, too?"

"Ha! In your dreams buddy!" I hitched a thumb at Roland. "My turn."

Roland grinned as he nudged his jet ski alongside the dock and climbed off, but his face grew serious as I switched places with him. "Be careful and call me if there's any trouble," he whispered.

"We'll be back before you know it." I sat on the seat and murmured, "I'm more worried about you having to deal with the fallout on this end."

"I can handle them."

"I know. That's why you're staying instead of Peter." Well, that and the fact that Nikolas and Chris were more suspicious of Roland after our little escapade. I was pretty sure that my cease-fire with Nikolas was going to come to a fiery end after this. But it wasn't like I had promised never to run off again. In fact, I assumed that was just a foregone conclusion by now.

I pushed away from the dock and followed Peter a short ways onto the lake. We lined up side by side and waited for Roland to play his part.

"Okay, guys, to the other side and back," Roland shouted at us. "Kick his ass, Sara," he added for good measure.

We shot forward like we were in a real race. Opening our throttles, we sailed across the wide expanse of water with water spraying up around us. I still remembered my icy dip in the harbor, making me doubly glad for the sun and the layer of neoprene protecting my body from the cold lake water.

According to my research, the lake was a mile across at this point and fourteen miles from Dylan's to the opposite side of the lake if you followed the shoreline. I hoped that was enough distance to allow us to get away before Chris realized what we were up to. The Mohiri were super fast, so I'd had to come up with a plan to outsmart them since I couldn't outrun them.

I slowed my jet ski as I neared the far shore and eased into a small shady cove with an old dock. Nudging the jet ski against the dock, I clipped it to one of the posts and leaped off, knowing that Peter was right behind me. Our feet pounded the boards as we ran up the short dock to the shed at the edge of the property and found Peter's backpack right where he had stashed it last night. *So far, so good*, I thought as we peeled off our wetsuits and dressed in the clothes Peter pulled out of the backpack.

We had picked this particular spot for several reasons. First, it was a summer cottage, and like many of the houses on this side of the lake, it was closed up now for the fall. Second, it was strategically located directly across from Dylan's. And third, it wasn't far from the home of an old friend of mine – more like one of Greg's old buddies, but I knew him well enough. I hadn't seen Phil since Greg had gone away, but Greg told me before he left that if I ever needed anything, to call Phil. It turned out Phil was more than happy to help me out today.

"I feel like Ethan Hunt," Peter said with a silly grin as we rolled up our wetsuits and hid them with the backpack.

"Who?"

"From Mission Impossible. We're like spies on a covert mission."

I rolled my eyes at him. "I hope not. Doesn't he get shot at a lot?"

Less than five minutes after reaching the dock, we ran across the yard and emerged on the street. I wondered if Chris had figured out that something was up yet and decided I didn't want to wait around to find out.

"This way," I said, setting off down the road with Peter beside me.

"Are you sure this guy is okay?" he asked cautiously. "He's not like that guy Malloy, is he?"

I let out a laugh. "Phil is a teddy bear. I told you he's one of Greg's friends."

"Yeah, because those guys were all angels," Peter said with a snort.

It took us five minutes to reach Phil's little white bungalow. A few years older than Greg, Phil worked at a dockyard in Portland and lived alone in the house inherited from his grandmother.

He threw open the door as soon as I rang the bell. "Little Grey!" boomed the hefty redhead before he grabbed me in a beefy hug. He smelled of sweat and beer, and his arms were covered in tattoos. "You've grown up since the last time I saw you."

I grinned as I stepped back. "It's only been four months."

"Really? Seems longer than that," he said, leading us inside. "Not the same here since the boys went away. I remember when you were younger and you used to have the biggest crush on Greg." He let out a whoop. "Ha! I bet the tables will be turned next time he comes home and gets a load of the beauty you grew into. Not that I'm surprised, mind you."

I couldn't help the blush that crept up my cheeks when I thought of the crush I'd had on Greg in eighth grade. "Ugh, don't remind me about that."

Phil laughed again. "I gotta say I was surprised to hear from you last night, but I'm glad you called me. I promised Greg I'd check in on you, and to be honest, I've done a piss poor job of that. So you two need a ride somewhere?"

"Phil, this is my friend Peter. And yes, we need to get to the rest stop up by exit 75. You know where that is?"

They shook hands, and Phil frowned. "You guys aren't running away, are you?"

"No, we're meeting someone there. It's kind of hard to explain, but I promise we're not running away." I pulled out my cell phone, which I'd snuck inside my wetsuit and looked at the time. If Chris was looking for us, it probably wouldn't take him long to start searching this area. "And we need to go now if that's possible."

"Okay, no problem." He grabbed a set of keys off the kitchen counter. "Let's go."

Phil drove a black Pontiac Trans-Am just like the one Burt Reynolds drove in Smoky and the Bandit, except Phil's was rusted in places and in desperate need of a paint job. But it ran well, which was all we needed. We left the lake area and headed toward the nearest on ramp to the interstate. Once we were safely away, I sent Roland a smiley face text to let him know things were going as planned. He replied with a thumbs down to let me know Chris was onto us. I bit the inside of my cheek. That meant Nikolas knew and they were both looking for us right now. I hoped I had enough time before they managed to track us down.

"This is a strange place to meet a friend," Phil said, pulling up to the rest stop diner.

I laid my hand on the door handle. "He's passing through and doesn't have time to go into town."

"Alright then. You call me when you're done, and I'll come get you."

"I will thanks." I got out then lifted the seat forward for Peter to climb out. We waited for Phil to pull away before we turned to look at each other. I glanced at my watch and saw that I had ten minutes before I was supposed to meet NightWatcher. I told Peter we should split up now.

Peter's eyes were anxious. "You sure you don't want me to come in with you?"

"I promised to meet him alone. It's a busy place in the middle of the day, so I'm sure it's safe." He didn't look convinced, so I squeezed his hand. "There's not a cloud in the sky, so you know we won't run into anyone with UV allergies. Besides, you'll be right outside. I'll try to get a table by the window so you can see me."

He nodded reluctantly, and I turned and went into the diner. The waitress told me to grab any table I wanted, so I took a booth near the window in the back where Peter could see me and I could see anyone entering the diner. After a few minutes, the waitress brought me a menu and I ordered a milkshake, then settled back to wait. My phone rang and Roland's name came up. **Hope u get back here before he finds u.** I didn't need to ask who *he* was.

I was sipping my milkshake when the door opened and in walked the last person I'd expect to run into here. I shook my head in annoyance. Lots of locals stopped here driving to and from Portland, but what were the chances of seeing Scott Foley here today of all days?

Scott spotted me around the same time I saw him. He stared at me in surprise, and I think he started to come over but changed his mind. I let out a small sigh of relief when I saw him pay for a milkshake and leave. It was one thing having Peter outside. I didn't think NightWatcher would approach me if I was arguing with Scott when he showed up. I'd worked too hard to set up this meeting to have someone screw it up now.

At two o'clock on the dot, the door opened and a young Japanese man with short, spiked hair came in. He stopped and looked around until his eyes landed on me, then he walked purposefully toward my booth.

"You're a lot younger than I expected," he said in a low voice as he slid onto the vinyl seat across from me.

I didn't bother to hide my surprise. "How did you know it was me?"

He smiled, showing off perfect white teeth. "Aside from the fact that you're obviously not a trucker and you had your boyfriend wait outside for you? Let's just say I have a way of knowing things about people just by looking at them."

I looked more closely at his face and spotted a faint gold ring inside his brown irises. "You're an Emote!" I breathed, and he nodded. Emotes were people who could read auras – and not like those fake psychics you saw at carnivals. Their perception was so good that an experienced Emote could tell what you were feeling, if you were lying, or if you were hiding something just by seeing your aura. A vampire couldn't get within twenty feet of an Emote without being detected, which explained why NightWatcher hadn't entered the Attic that night. It also explained why he'd insisted we meet in person. He wanted to read me.

I knew something else about Emotes. They could tell small lies but big deceptions were very difficult for them, which meant I could probably trust what this man had to say.

"What does my aura tell you about me?"

His dark brown eyes studied me. "I can see that you mean me no harm and you desperately hope I have the answers you've been looking for. I also see that you are running from someone – but you are not afraid of them. Curious."

"Impressive." I'd met one other Emote a few years ago, and she could only tell if someone was lying. Being able to read beyond that takes a lot of skill. "I guess we should introduce ourselves. I'm Sara, but you know me as PixieGirl."

"David, aka NightWatcher." He gave me a small smile as he extended a slender hand. "I have to tell you that I was very curious about you as soon as I heard you were asking questions about Daniel Grey. It's been a long time since I heard that name. Before I say anything else, I want to know why someone as young as you is interested in a man who has been dead for ten years."

I met his gaze without blinking. "Daniel Grey was my father."

David's eyes widened, and his mouth made an O. "So you're Madeline's daughter."

"Yes," I said bitterly. "You knew her?"

"My father knew her." He quieted because the waitress came over to take his order. He ordered a coffee and waited until she walked away before he spoke again. "Ten years ago, Madeline Croix called my father to tell him she was in a lot of trouble and needed his help. I was fourteen, and I remember he was not happy to hear from her. I could see his fear, though he tried to hide it from me. A few days later, Madeline came to our house. They talked for about an hour, and he gave her a leather pouch that he'd apparently been keeping for her. It was full of cash and some papers. She said she had to disappear."

"Did she say why?"

He glanced around nervously, and his voice dropped so low that I had to lean forward to hear him. "Madeline told my father that she had discovered the identity of a Master."

Goose flesh spread across my arms, and an unpleasant tingle ran down my spine. Everything I knew about vampire masters I'd learned from Remy, and that was just enough to scare the bejesus out of me. Masters were old and powerful with powers far beyond any normal vampire. You couldn't just stake a Master. Beheading was the only way to kill one. The most frightening thing about them wasn't their physical strength but their mental prowess. Only a Master could command other vampires, and they literally created a small army of vampires to serve them and make them nearly invincible. Because of that, Masters used to live as openly as other vampires, but fear of them drove hunters to start killing them off one by one a few hundred years ago. The Masters who survived went into hiding, and now it was rare to even hear of one. A Master's identity was their most closely guarded secret.

The waitress returned with David's coffee. As soon as she left he said, "I see you know what that means. If Madeline somehow found out the identity or location of a Master, he would stop at nothing to find her, especially considering what she is."

"You know what she is?"

He nodded gravely. "I wasn't supposed to hear any of this, but I knew something big was going down because my father did not scare easily. I hid upstairs while Madeline was there. Before she left, she said she was going to see Daniel – your father – to warn him. I saw in her aura that Daniel had no idea what she was."

I felt a stab of pain in my chest at the mention of my dad. "What happened next?"

"After Madeline left, my father panicked and sent me to my grandparents' house for a week. I never saw Madeline again, and two days later your father was killed."

My throat tightened, and I swallowed dryly. "What about your father?" I asked hoarsely. "Did you ever ask him about what you overheard?"

Pain darkened his eyes. "My father was murdered on the same day as yours."

A heavy silence fell over the table as we shared each other's sorrow and pain. All these years I'd carried my grief alone because I knew no one could understand what I had been through. Now I sat across from someone who had suffered as much as I had.

"We used to own a laundromat. One of the employees found him, and it was... pretty bad. They wouldn't let me see him, and my grandparents had him cremated." He took a shaky breath. "My mom died when I was little, so I lived with my grandparents after my father died. I never told anyone about Madeline. I was afraid *they* would find out and come after me, too."

I found my voice at last. "I'm sorry. I know how hard it must have been for you."

"You do know, don't you?" he said sadly. "What about you? You were so young when it happened. Where did you end up?"

"An uncle took me in." I was still reluctant to give up my personal information, but it was no use lying to an Emote as good as David.

"I bet that was rough. My grandparents are good people, but it was hard after..."

I nodded. "I was pretty messed up after my dad died, and it took me a long time to learn to deal with it. I don't think it would have mattered where I went because nothing could have changed what I went through."

"True." David sipped his coffee and made a face. "I see you didn't pick this place for the coffee."

"The milkshakes are good." I toyed with my cup lid. "Thanks for telling me all this. I see why you were so spooked at the Attic. You have even more reason than I do to be scared of vampires."

"I doubt that." He added more sugar to his cup and stirred it thoughtfully. "I heard the police found you with the... with your father's body. Is that true?"

"I found him."

"Jesus," he rasped.

I made sure no one was close enough to hear us. "I've always known what killed my dad, but I never understood why they went after him. I guess I know why now."

David nodded and stared out the window for a minute before his eyes returned to me. "Are you like Madeline?"

"I'm nothing like her."

He held up his hands. "No, that's not what I meant. I meant, are you

Mohiri? I heard my father call her that. I tried to find out what I could about them, but they are very secretive. All I've been able to learn is they are some kind of warrior race and very deadly."

"I know about them," I admitted. "But I am no warrior, trust me." He nodded in acceptance, and I remembered that my aura would tell him if I lied.

"Madeline left us when I was two, so I wouldn't even know her if she walked up to me." A vague memory surfaced of a beautiful blond woman in a worn picture in my dad's wallet.

"You don't look like her. I never would have guessed you were her daughter. Her hair was so blond it almost looked white, and she was tall with blue eyes."

"That's something, I guess," I muttered.

The corner of his mouth lifted. "Back then I was terrified that they'd realize my father had a kid and track me down. I used to wonder what happened to Daniel Grey's daughter, and I hoped they didn't come back for you."

"What would vampires want with a kid?" A shiver ran through me at the thought of facing something like Eli when I was eight.

"They're monsters," was his reply. I rubbed my arms to ward off the chill.

"You have nothing to worry about now, though. No one who saw you would ever think you're related to Madeline. If they ever did come back, they'd look for someone blond and – "

He stared at me so hard that I grew alarmed. "What? What's wrong?"

"How old are you? Sixteen? Seventeen?"

"Seventeen, why?"

"The missing girls in Portland – they were all your age."

"I know. It was in the news."

"They were all blond."

The meaning in his words hit me, and I recoiled as if I'd been slapped. "No. You're wrong." The idea that four innocent girls were hurt or killed because of me was too much to bear. "There has to be hundreds of blond teenage girls in Portland. Do you honestly think vampires are going to randomly pick girls on the chance they'd find Madeline's daughter? And why now after all this time?"

"I don't know," he admitted. "But I don't think those missing girls were random either. As soon as the third girl disappeared, I started looking for a connection between them."

"Looking for a connection how?"

"I'm really good with computers."

For some reason, that did not surprise me. "What did you find?"

"Nothing at first. Not until the last two girls went missing. I had a bunch of searches running, cross-referencing school records, social websites, and some other not-so-public records when I came up with something all four girls had in common. They were all adopted."

"What?"

He nodded slowly. "What are the odds of vampires taking four blond, adopted girls of the same age in Portland? It's no coincidence."

"My God." I felt the color drain from my face.

"I don't know how you stayed under their radar, but keep doing it. My guess is that they want to use Madeline's daughter as bait to draw her out."

"I don't understand. Vampires must have a lot of resources. It should have taken them no time to track down my uncle and find me."

David shook his head. "I can find anyone if there's a paper trail, and I couldn't find you. It looked like you went into the foster care system and then just disappeared. Someone obviously went through a lot of trouble to hide you. I didn't even know there was an uncle until you mentioned him."

Someone hid me – and Nate? They must be really good to hide the fact that my dad had a brother. But who would do that and why? The werewolves had a large network, but Maxwell had said he only suspected vampires had killed my father. Surely if he or someone he knew had covered my trail, he would have told me after everything that had happened in the last month. And it wasn't the Mohiri because they didn't even know I existed before a month ago.

"Whoever did it was very thorough, and you owe them a big thank you if you ever find them, because they probably saved your life. Just keep your head down and don't do anything to draw the vampires' attention to you, and you should be okay."

I gulped soundlessly. *Too late.*

"From what I've heard, the vampires are keeping a very low profile in Portland now. That scares me even more. I'm a freelance programmer, and I can do that from anywhere. I'm leaving for a while, heading south to stay with some friends." He gave me a small smile. "That's why I agreed to come here today. Something told me I had to meet you before I left."

"David, you don't know what this meant to me, to learn anything about what happened to my dad. I still have questions, but I feel like I'm closer to understanding it all now." The aching hole in my heart felt a tiny bit smaller after meeting the one person who shared my painful history. I'd never find real closure as long as my dad's murderer was alive and free to kill again. But I always knew this was as close as I would get. It had to be enough.

David pulled out his wallet and laid some bills on the table. "Listen, I have to go. Keep your head down, kid, until this mess blows over. You know where to reach me online if you want to talk." He fixed me with a hard stare. "I understand how badly you want answers, because I've spent years trying to find my own, but it's not worth risking your life. Be careful who you talk to online and especially who you meet." He smiled. "I know that's weird advice from a guy you met online, but the next one might not be as nice as me."

I stayed in the booth and watched David walk out to a white Ford Focus and drive away. When I had planned this meeting, I never really knew what to expect or what I hoped to get out of it. Meeting David and learning how he had suffered because of his father's association with Madeline made me despise my mother even more. My dad, David's dad, and those girls – how many more people would be hurt because of her?

One thing was clear; this was way bigger than me and David and our fathers' murders. If Madeline was still out there, and she knew the identity of a Master. The Mohiri needed to know about it. With their resources, they could track her down and find out what she knew, and if anyone had the fire-power to go up against a Master, it was Nikolas's people.

I glanced at my watch. It was two-thirty, which meant we'd been gone from Dylan's for over an hour. I grimaced as I slid out of the booth. Maybe my news about the Master would deflect some of Nikolas's anger. Not likely, but a girl could hope.

I left the diner and joined Peter, who stood by the old phone booth. He wore a relieved smile as I approached him. "Well, how'd it go?" he asked impatiently.

"He knew a lot more than I expected. His father and Madeline knew each other."

"Seriously? Tell me what he said."

I rubbed at the beginning of a headache. "Can we talk about this later with Roland? I just want to call Phil and go back to Dylan's before Nikolas finds us."

His face fell, but he didn't push it. "Okay. You call Phil, and I'm going to run in and get a milkshake. I'll be back in a few minutes."

I pointed to the picnic tables partially hidden by a semi on the other side of the parking lot. "I'll be over there." The tables had a good view of the inter-state so we could see Phil's car when he arrived. I sat on the hard wooden seat and pulled out my phone.

"Date ran off and left you, did he?" a male voice jeered from behind me before I could make my call.

Am I being punished for some horrible crime in a former life? I groaned inwardly, turning on the seat to face Scott. "Go away, Scott. I'm so not in the mood."

"Free country. If you don't like me here, you can always leave."

I started to make a retort then decided it wasn't worth it. Fighting with Scott seemed so petty after the things I'd learned today. "Suit yourself," I muttered, turning my back to him again.

His footsteps moved away, and I couldn't help but think I needed to try this tactic the next time I wanted to get rid of unwanted company. I had just finished congratulating myself when he walked in front of me to sit on the next picnic table.

"Are you broken down here or something?" he asked, scanning the vehicles in the parking lot. His voice held curiosity instead of scorn, and I wondered why he even bothered to ask.

"Why? You offering a lift?"

It was meant as a joke, and I was surprised when it seemed to take him off guard. He looked off to the side and back at me. "I... no."

"So what do you want?"

"What makes you think I want anything from you?" he asked defensively.

I waved a hand at him. "Oh, I don't know. You're hanging around a highway rest stop on a Saturday, talking to me of all people. You couldn't find anyone else to fight with?"

His brow furrowed in a scowl, but whatever he said to me went unheard. My full attention was drawn to a man standing beside a black Escalade on the other side of the rest stop. His profile seemed familiar, and I strained to make out his face. At this distance, I could only tell he had dark hair and a dark, olive complexion, but something made me think I knew him from somewhere.

The man shifted position, and I saw thick eyebrows, a square jaw, and an unsmiling mouth. A jolt of recognition went through me, and I ducked my head. He was one of the men from the marina.

He didn't get a good look at me that night, I thought frantically, trying to slow my racing heart. I had to calm down and act normal. The man was alone, and he had no idea who I was. It was nothing more than a coincidence that he was here now. Still, I really wished Peter would hurry up. Ignoring Scott's puzzled look, I raised my head enough to peek at the man again. My breath caught.

The man looked right at me and smiled.

16

My gut clenched. This was very, very bad.

I scrambled away from the picnic table and stood like a cornered rabbit with my heart thumping in my chest before my mind began to quickly evaluate my options. The Escalade was on the far side of the parking lot. The diner was blocked from view by the semi, but I knew it was closer than the SUV. Even if the man was fast, I could make it to the diner and Peter and hope the man did not want to risk a public commotion.

The man must have realized it, too, because he started walking briskly toward us. Any hope that he did not recognize me drained away.

Scott stood. "What's wrong?"

Movement to my right brought me up short. A dark figure stepped into view around the rear of the semi. Tall and thin, he was dressed in a black robe covered in strange symbols that shimmered in the sun like white gold. A black hood covered his head and hid his face from me, but I could feel something, some kind of power emanating from him. He halted and reached up to push back the hood, and my mouth opened in a silent gasp. The man – if he was a man – was as black as ebony with a small black goatee and a bald head. His face and head were covered in a strange pattern of red and white markings that appeared to be gouged into his skin. But it was his eyes that sent fear racing along my spine. Two white orbs glowed in the black face, and when they turned on me I felt like a deer staring into two headlights coming out of the dark.

"What the fuck is that?"

Scott's bewildered voice pulled me from my own paralysis. "Run!" I yelled and whirled away to bolt in the only direction available, toward the interstate.

Hands grabbed my arms roughly from behind, and I cried out. I twisted and kicked at the person restraining me, but he held me in an iron grip. "It is no use to struggle," he said in a clipped Middle Eastern voice. "You are coming with me."

"Help!" I screamed as I was spun toward the SUV. I saw Scott on the ground looking dazed, and I realized my attacker must have hit him. "Scott," I yelled at him. "Please help me!"

"What the hell?" he moaned, teetering to his feet. "Someone hit me."

The man began pulling me backward, effortlessly dragging me away from the picnic tables. "Do something!" I shouted at Scott.

At first I thought he was going to stand there and watch me get hauled away. It took him a minute to comprehend what was happening, and then he started toward us. "Hey, what do you think you're doing? L-Let her go..."

He stammered to a stop, and his expression went blank. I watched in confusion while he stood swaying in a trancelike state. My eyes went to the tattooed man and found him watching Scott with a small smile on his face.

"Leave him alone! He's got nothing to do with this."

"Come with me and your boyfriend will be okay," the man holding me barked.

"No!" I struggled and screamed Peter's name.

Dragged backward, I stumbled and almost felt. The man jerked me up, and I used the momentum to bring my head up and slam him hard under the chin. I heard his jaw crack at the same time pain shot through my skull. He staggered, and his grip loosened enough for me to tear free. I spun to face him and kicked out, landing a hard blow to the side of his knee. Off balance, he fell to the ground swearing. I could tell he would not be down for long.

I heard running feet as Peter tore around the front of the semi and took in the scene before him. "Sara!" he bellowed and tossed his milkshake aside, racing toward me. He reached me just as my attacker gained his footing again.

"Watch out!" I yelled to Peter.

Peter turned as a hard fist flew at his face. Moving faster than I'd ever seen him go, he leaned to one side and brought his own fist up, slamming it into the man's stomach. The man parried with a shot aimed at Peter's chest, but he only managed a hit to the shoulder. Peter recovered fast and delivered a second punch to his opponent's gut. I had never seen Peter fight, and the force and speed of his blows surprised me. It also answered my question about whether or not werewolves were strong in their human form. It was clear that my friend was more than a match for the larger, more muscled man.

I was so engrossed in the fight it took me several seconds to register the gentle pressure on my mind, touching, prodding like fingers testing a piece of fruit. My mental walls flew up, and I sensed a flare of surprise from the one trying to invade my head. In the next moment, it surged forward with a force that left me gasping. Horrified recognition filled me as the thing buzzed inside my head like a live wire. My walls faltered at the shock of encountering the same awful presence that had infected the rat at the marina, and my hesitation was all the alien force needed to shove its way around my defenses.

I screamed and grabbed my head as the thing invaded me. It reached into the recesses of my mind, and wherever it touched, it left a path of filth like the slime trail of a slug. In the back of my mind I felt the Mori recoil as my whole being shuddered at the violation, the slow rape of my mind.

"*Sleeeep*," a chilling voice hissed in my head. "*All is welll.*"

"No..." I protested weakly. A cool numbing fog began to steal over me until I no longer felt the ugliness in my head, or much else.

"*You will sleeeep now.*"

"Can't..." I mumbled as my eyes grew heavy.

My walls fell. I was vaguely aware of something cold and slimy burrowing inside me like a parasite. The Mori shrieked in agony. Choking, dying, the Mori was dying. I'd always hated the dark thing that had been a part of me my whole life. I should be happy now that the beast would be no more. Instead, sadness bloomed in my chest and tears of grief welled in my eyes.

Coldness reached down, inching toward the center of my being. It came up against my last defense, the gate that held back the wellspring of my power. "*Let meee innn*," it commanded as icy fingers pulled at the barrier in vain. I did as it asked, and I felt its triumph as it punched through and touched the essence of me.

Someone began to scream.

I was on fire. No, I *was* the fire. Roaring, raging, I was an angry volcano spewing molten rock up from deep within the earth. The lava scorched everything in its path with a cleansing fire that burned away the coldness and filth and bore down on the ugly thing pulsing in my mind. I felt a flash of terror that was not my own, and then the pressure in my head was gone.

My eyes opened to see the witch – I knew what he was now – stagger and fall to his knees. His eyes no longer glowed white, and his face had paled to a dark gray. "What... are you?" he choked, his black eyes full of shock and fear.

Instead of answering him, I stood and turned my attention to Peter who still fought my assailant. They traded blows like it was a heavyweight match, and I wondered how either of them was still standing. Across the parking lot, several men stood near their cars watching the fight, but no one moved to break it up. Anger rose in me. What was wrong with these people? They were going to just stand there while teenagers were attacked in broad daylight?

Peter appeared to be gaining ground, and I watched breathlessly as he forced the older man backward with each blow. I glanced behind me nervously at the witch, expecting him to recover and try that mind magic on me again. But he was still on his knees with both hands on the ground like he was about to pass out. *Good, serves you right.*

"Argh!"

At Peter's cry of pain, I whirled back to the fight to find him clutching his belly and blood running between his fingers. The dark-haired man advanced on him again, brandishing a bloody knife and wearing a sneer that left no doubt about his deadly intentions.

A howl of rage escaped me as I threw myself at the man's back, wrapping my legs around his waist and my arms around his throat in a stranglehold that might have broken the neck of a smaller person. My would-be kidnapper dropped his weapon and clawed at my arms as I clung to him, squeezing his windpipe with strength I did not know I had and screaming like a banshee. The fear, the pain, the endless attacks for the last month had finally made me snap, and I poured all my pent up anger and fear into choking the life from the man who was trying to kill my friend.

We tumbled to the ground as the man's legs went out from underneath him, and the impact jolted me from my murderous rage. Beneath me, the man was no longer moving, but I felt his chest rise and fall so I knew he was still alive. I loosened my chokehold and looked around for Peter, emitting a squeak when I found him lying on the ground a few feet away.

"Peter?" I disentangled my arms and legs from the prone man and crawled across the grass to my friend. Peter's normally pale face was so white that even his freckles looked washed out. His eyes opened when I leaned over him, and I saw they were glazed with pain.

"Oh, Peter!" Gut wounds were always the worst, and I had no idea if his accelerated werewolf healing worked in human form. I pressed my hand over his stomach to staunch the flow of blood.

He tried to smile and failed miserably. "A knife is nothing compared to a crocotta claw."

I fumbled for my cell phone with my free hand. "I'll call nine-one-one. Don't worry; you'll be okay."

"More are coming."

The deep African voice drew my eyes from Peter to the witch, who was sitting back on his heels watching me.

"What?"

"Tarek." He pointed to the unconscious man behind me. "He called for backup as soon as we found you. They will be here very soon."

His meaning was clear. If I waited for the police or an ambulance, Tarek's reinforcements would get to us first. "Why are you telling me this?"

The witch shrugged. I had no reason to trust the person who had just tried to violate my mind, but then he could have kept his mouth shut and let me be ambushed.

"How did you find us? Were you following me?"

He let out a deep laugh. "You are not such easy prey. I merely sensed your mind as we passed by. But the others know you're here now."

I looked at Peter. "We can't stay here. We have to go."

He grimaced. "I know."

"Can you stand?" My hands slipped behind his shoulders and helped him into a sitting position. Between the both of us, we managed to get him to his feet.

"Come on." I wrapped an arm around him, and together we walked slowly toward the diner. I wanted to urge him to go faster, but his haggard breaths told me how much pain he was in. I felt him weakening with every step.

As we neared the diner, it looked less and less like the refuge I thought it would be. These men had no qualms about attacking me in the middle of the afternoon alongside a busy interstate. People like that would think nothing of barging inside the restaurant and taking us. I looked around frantically. We couldn't stay here, and we couldn't call Phil and wait for him to show up. We needed to get out of here now.

At that moment I saw Scott shuffling like a zombie toward his shiny red Mustang parked in front of the diner. Jesus, I had forgotten about him.

"Scott," I called as we hurried after him as fast as Peter could move. We caught up to Scott as he stopped beside the driver's-side door, swaying slightly, and one look at his slack-jawed face told me he was in no shape to drive out of here. The way Peter hung heavily on me, I knew he was about to pass out. "Damn it! Why does this shit keep happening?"

I leaned Peter against the car and searched Scott's pockets until I found his keys. Gently nudging Scott aside, I unlocked the driver's-side door and levered the seat forward so I could get Peter into the back. He stretched out across the seat with a moan, then promptly went out cold. My breath caught painfully in my chest, and I scrambled to check his breathing and pulse to make sure he was still alive. "I'm so sorry, Peter," I whispered hoarsely. "I'll get us out of this, I promise."

I got out and propelled Scott around to the passenger side and into the seat, fear causing me to slam the door with more force than was necessary. Then I ran back to the driver side and climbed in. Only then did it hit me what I was about to do, and I stared around me in confusion. The Mustang was so different from Judith's car, and I'd only had one lesson so far. How was I ever going to figure this out?

Okay, first things first. I reached down until my fingers found the seat adjuster mechanism and moved the seat forward until my feet could touch the pedals. *Gas on the right, brake in the middle, and clutch thingy on the left. No problem.*

I pressed down on the brake. Grabbing the gear stick, I jiggled it into neutral and turned the key in the ignition. Nothing. *Don't panic. Think about what Roland told you.*

I lost precious seconds recalling my lesson before I remembered. The clutch! I pressed the pedal to the floor and tried the key again. The Mustang rumbled to life.

Scott made a moaning sound, but there was no time to check on him. The one time I needed him and he was completely out of it. *Figures.* I looked around me again. Scott loved his Mustang. I wondered how he'd feel if he knew who was about to drive his precious car.

Movement in the side mirror caught my eye, and I saw Tarek stirring on the ground. I must have really done a job on him because he was having trouble lifting himself to his hands and knees. He scanned the parking lot, and his eyes zeroed in on the Mustang. Even from here I felt the rage radiating off him. He was not happy to be taken down by a pair of teenagers, and his expression told me payback was coming if he caught up with us.

I took a deep breath and moved the stick into what I hoped was Reverse. *God, don't let me kill us all*, I prayed as I took my foot from the brake and pressed gently on the gas while letting up on the clutch.

The car shuddered to a stop.

"No, no, no, please don't do this to me." I pressed the clutch and brake, put the car in neutral, and started it again. This time after I put it in reverse, I eased up on the clutch more slowly as I pressed the gas. The car shot backward a few feet before my right foot found the brake again and brought it to a screeching stop. My heart pounded. Damn, this was a lot harder than people made it look!

I gripped the wheel and pressed the gas gingerly as I let off the clutch.

The car rolled backward until I tapped the brake. *Now to turn this thing around.*

Something banged on the back of the car, and I jerked my head around to find Tarek leaning over the trunk. The tendons stood out on his neck, and his eyes burned into me through the rear window. *Christ! How did he get to us so fast?* I gulped and reached frantically for the gear shift.

I got it into first gear, but my feet got all tangled up trying to find the right pedals. I turned the wheel as I released the clutch and pressed the gas, and the car moved forward in short jerky movements. I was too afraid to look to see where Tarak was, so I kept my eyes straight ahead.

The car narrowly missed hitting two parked pickups, but the Escalade wasn't so lucky. I winced as metal grinded against metal, but I didn't dare stop. A few scratches on the Mustang's paint job were the least of our worries, and I couldn't care less about the SUV.

I straightened out the wheel, and the car lurched forward. Shouting reached my ears, and I glanced furtively over my shoulder at the furious man limping after us. *Just keep going. Don't let him catch you.*

The exit loomed before me, and I hit the brake suddenly, making Scott fall forward. My arm shot out just in time to keep him from hitting the dashboard. *I can't do this. I'm going to get us all killed.* I glanced back at Peter to make sure he was okay. He was still laid out across the seat, totally oblivious to what was going on around him.

Scott mumbled incoherently, and I prayed the witch had not screwed up his mind. Another injury he could lay at my door. At this rate Scott would be lucky to get through senior year intact.

I stole a look in the side mirror and sucked in a sharp breath when I spotted Tarek going for the Escalade. I gritted my teeth and pulled out into the merge lane. The car shook every time a vehicle sped past and my heart pounded in my ears, but there was no going back now. Risking a glance in the rearview mirror, I spotted a black SUV pulling out of the truck stop, and my foot stomped on the gas, making the car shoot forward. I saw a gap in traffic and swung sharply into the next lane, just barely correcting the Mustang before it careened into the middle lane. I hit the gas again, and the engine started to whine. Terrified to take my eyes off the road, I fumbled with the pedals and gear stick until the car stopped sounding like it was about to strain something.

My heart felt ready to burst through my ribs, and I swallowed dryly, suddenly very thirsty. I gripped the wheel and focused on my bigger problem. We couldn't stay on the highway. I could barely keep the Mustang in my lane; there was no way I could outrun them. Our only hope was to take the next exit and try to lose them in town.

The closest exit was four miles away, and those were the four longest miles of my life. Every second I expected the Escalade to catch us and run us right off the road. I checked my mirror whenever I dared take my eyes off the road. There was no sign of the SUV, but I knew it was behind us somewhere. I wasn't foolish enough to think a man like that would give up easily.

I hit the off ramp going a little too fast and almost stalled the car at the bottom, which did nothing to help my confidence. The road I merged onto did not look familiar at all, and I let out a nervous groan. I had no idea where I was, and I had no business being behind the wheel of a car. Not to mention Scott was blubbering like an idiot next to me, I had no clue where my attackers were, and Peter was probably bleeding to death behind me.

Don't think about that!

I got off the road as soon as I could, taking a series of turns until I was hopelessly lost. A few times I thought I spied a black SUV on a parallel road, so I just kept driving, afraid to stop for even a minute. My phone rang several times, but my hands clenched the steering wheel too tightly to answer it. It was probably Roland, wondering why we weren't back yet.

Despair of ever finding my way home was settling over me when a large building I recognized came into view. My heart quickened. I had never been so happy to see the mall. Following this street I would reach the high school in ten minutes. I couldn't go home. There was a strong possibility those men knew where I lived. They might not be able to get past my wards, but I couldn't take that chance with Peter and Scott incapacitated as they were.

"Thank you, God!" I sobbed when I spotted the steeple of St. Patrick's church. I pulled into the church parking lot and drove around to the back. My hands shook as I turned off the car and immediately checked on Peter, afraid of what I'd find. "Peter?"

"Hmmm?" he murmured without moving.

"How are you doing?" I probed anxiously.

"Better than I expected. You know, your driving really sucks."

I laughed and cried at the same time. Falling back into my seat, I pulled out my phone. My strength almost failed me when I heard Roland's voice. "Roland... we need your help."

"What happened? Where are you guys?" he demanded with a desperate edge to his voice.

"We're behind St. Patrick's. Just hurry. Peter's hurt."

There was a short pause. "Sit tight. I'm on the way."

I laid my head back against the headrest, but my body was too tense to relax. Scott moved, turning his face toward me, and his eyes tried to focus on my face. "Why do you hate me?" His voice was small and vulnerable like a little boy's, and I was too shocked to respond. It took me a long moment to remember that his mind was messed up, and he probably had no idea who he was talking to. "I wish you didn't hate me," he mumbled sadly.

"I don't hate you, Scott." It was the truth. I didn't like him, but I didn't hate him either.

"I'm glad." His head lolled to the other side, and he pointed at the empty parking lot. "What a funny looking camel," he said before his eyes closed again. *Definitely messed up.* I bit my lip. Scott and I might not get along, but I didn't want to see him hurt.

I was still puzzled by Scott's strange behavior earlier and why he had hung around the rest stop in the first place. It was almost like he had been waiting for me to come out of the diner. But that couldn't be right. The last person Scott Foley would willingly spend time with was me.

A few minutes later, Judith's car raced into view. I sagged in relief. "It's Roland," I told Peter, who lifted a hand in acknowledgement then let it fall back to his side.

Roland ran over and tried to open the door. I hit the unlock button, and he yanked the door open. He stared open-mouthed at Scott before his eyes moved to me sitting behind the wheel and then to Peter on the back seat. "What the hell happened to you guys?"

I let out a shaky laugh. "It's a long story. Can you look at Peter first? He's been stabbed."

Roland helped me out of the car because my arms and legs felt a little like wet noodles. Then he pushed the seat forward and leaned in to look at Peter. He withdrew, gave me an encouraging nod, and spoke low so Scott couldn't hear him. "He's okay. It takes us a bit longer to heal when we're not in wolf form. As soon as we get him somewhere private, he can shift and heal that in a few minutes."

"Oh, thank God!" I sat on the driver's seat again and rested my forehead against the wheel. At least I hadn't gotten one of my best friends killed. I wasn't a total screwup.

"We heard the police were called for a commotion out on the highway an hour ago. They said a crazy girl choked a guy at the rest stop and tore out of there in a red Mustang, banging up cars and being chased by a black SUV. I guess I don't need to ask if you know anything about that."

"I only hit one car, and that man deserved to be choked for stabbing Peter."

Before he could reply, a motorcycle roared around the corner of the church.

"You called him," I said accusingly.

"I didn't have to. He's been all over my ass since you disappeared from Dylan's. He probably put one of those damn trackers on the car before I took off to look for you."

The motorcycle stopped a few feet from us. Nikolas leapt off and strode straight for the Mustang. His hand closed around my arm, and he unceremoniously hauled me from the car. "Do you have a death wish?" he shouted.

"Hey!" I protested, but my mouth clamped shut at the thunderous look on his face. He pulled me closer until I could feel the heat radiating from him. Oh crap, was he in one of those rages Chris had mentioned?

I struggled futilely. "Let me go."

"Forget it. You're coming with me since it's obvious you can't be trusted to take care of yourself."

"Now wait a minute," Roland protested, coming around the car as I tried to pull away from Nikolas.

If Nikolas had hackles I swear they would have been raised at that moment. "I'll do whatever is necessary to protect her, even if it's from herself."

My own outrage boiled over. "The hell you will! You don't own me."

Surprisingly it was Peter who stepped in – figuratively from the back seat – to play referee. "Hey, this is not helping anyone. Before you all go off half-cocked, why don't you let us tell you what happened?"

Nikolas nodded stiffly and released my arm, but did not move away from me. Ignoring his towering form, I explained to Roland how I had met with David as planned and I was about to call Phil to pick us up when the man named Tarek showed up. I heard Nikolas's sharp intake of breath beside me, but I refused to look at him. When I got to the part about the witch, I saw comprehension dawn in Roland's eyes and I knew his thoughts mirrored mine. Why were the men from the marina after me? I had been in such a panic to get away from the rest stop that I didn't think to ask the witch that question.

Nikolas cut in. "You're sure about him, what he looked like?"

"I don't think I'll ever forget that face after what he did," I said, unable to keep the quiver out of my voice. Thinking about the way he had touched my mind made me feel violated all over again.

"What did he do?" Nikolas's voice took on a dangerous note I'd never heard before. I paused, afraid to tell him what had happened next.

"Sara, did he hurt you?"

"No, not really. He tried to do something to my mind. It felt like something… awful got inside my head and took control of me. I couldn't move or say anything." I shuddered at the memory. "It was the most horrible feeling, like I'd never be clean again."

Roland blanched. "Fuck! How did you get away?"

"I don't know. One second there was a creepy voice in my head telling me to go to sleep, and the next thing I knew the tattooed guy was screaming." I wrapped my arms around myself and stared past them at the hulking shape of the high school next door, allowing my mind to dwell on what I had refused to think about since the witch's attack. My mind probed at the silent part of me where the demon was, like a tongue touching the gap where a tooth used to be. "I think… I think my Mori is dead. I felt it dying," I said hoarsely, filled with an inexplicable sadness. Evil or not, its voice had lived inside my head my whole life, and it felt like a part of me had been extinguished.

A warm hand touched my back, sending a small flare of heat through me. "It's been hurt, but it's still alive," Nikolas said in a gentler voice.

"How do you know?" I asked without looking at him.

"Trust me. I would know if it was gone." My breath caught at the rough edge in his voice, and I wondered if his demon felt pain or anguish if another Mori died.

"What kind of witch can hurt a demon like that?" Roland asked, awed.

"A Hale witch." Nikolas spat out the words as if they were poison. "A desert witch from Africa. They get their power from the spirit world."

"Like a shaman or witch doctor?" I asked. I'd thought shamans were all about healing and helping people.

"Hale witches only deal in dark magic, and their power is much greater than a shaman's. A Hale witch can cripple a person with a single thought, and their compulsion is even stronger than a vampire's, almost unbreakable." Nikolas paused, and I looked up to meet his searching gaze. "Not even the Mohiri are immune to their power. I've seen warriors brought to madness after a single encounter with a Hale witch."

I had no answer for the question in his eyes.

"Hale witches abhor demons, and they do not work with vampires," Nikolas informed us. "And they usually stick close to their tribal region of the desert. It would take something big to get one of them to come all the way to America." He fixed me with a hard stare. "You aren't telling us everything. Who else is after you?"

"No one," I declared and saw the doubt on both of their faces. "I swear, I have no idea why they attacked me." It was true. As far as I knew, they were after Malloy, not me.

"What happened after you got away from the witch?" Roland asked.

I told them how Peter fought Tarek and then the man had pulled a knife on him and slashed him. "I kinda lost it when I saw him cut Peter. I just jumped him and squeezed his throat until he went down. Then we took off."

Roland pointed at Scott, who still sat quietly in the car. "Where does he come into this?"

"He was there at the rest stop when those guys showed up. He got blasted by the witch when he tried to stop Tarak from taking me."

Nikolas's anger was still evident when he spoke again. "What were you thinking going off to meet a total stranger in the first place with everything else that's going on?"

"I had to go," I said defensively. "You don't know how long I've waited to find answers about my dad. I've been trying to meet with David for weeks."

"How do you know he didn't lead those men right to you?" he demanded.

I remembered the anguish and the pain in David's eyes, and I knew his story was real and his motives had been good. "He's an Emote, and I believe he was telling the truth. He knew things... things about Madeline." I felt Nikolas stiffen beside me. "Ten years ago Madeline went to see David's father to tell him she was in trouble. They were friends or something, and David's father gave her a lot of money to leave the country. She said vampires were after her and before she left she had to warn – " My voice broke, and it was a moment before I could continue. "She had to warn my dad. A few days later, my dad was killed."

"Jesus, Sara," Roland breathed.

"David wanted to meet with me because he lost someone, too. The vampires killed his father the same day they killed mine. David's afraid the vampires will come after him because of what he knows. He was hiding upstairs while Madeline was there, and he heard something he wasn't supposed to. He thinks it's why his father was killed."

"Did he tell you what it was?" Nikolas asked tightly.

"Madeline told David's father that she knew the identity of a Master."

Before I could blink, I found myself beside the Ducati with a helmet shoved down over my head. "Stop," I sputtered, pushing the helmet away. "What are you doing?"

"I'm getting you out of here," Nikolas ground out. "I can't protect you from a Master by myself. The only place you'll be safe now is at a Mohiri stronghold."

"That happened ten years ago. There is no Master after me."

He barked a laugh and tightened his hold on my arm. "To you ten years is a long time, but to a vampire who has lived hundreds of years, it's nothing.

And what of this witch and the man who grabbed you? Either way, someone is looking for you and we need to get you out of this town."

I shoved against him, but he was like a marble pillar. "I'm not going anywhere with you."

"I'm not asking."

"So, that's it? You're going to force me to go against my will?" I cried in helpless anger. "You're no different than them."

"Sara, maybe he's right," Roland cut in. "I don't want you to go, but I don't want you to get hurt either." He spoke to Nikolas. "But maybe we should talk to Uncle Max first to see what he thinks."

I blasted them both with an icy stare. "I see. So everyone gets a say about my life but me?"

Nikolas grabbed my shoulders and forced me to face him. "If you stay here, you or someone you care about is going to end up hurt or killed," he said mercilessly. "Someone is trying very hard to get to you, and they obviously won't think twice about going through your friends to do it." I thought about Peter's stab wound and winced. "Next time it could be worse. They could go after your uncle. Is that what you want?"

"Of course not!" I wouldn't let anyone hurt Nate. If I had to leave New Hastings to draw the people pursuing me away from him, I would, but it would be on my own terms. My mind immediately began to formulate a plan. Remy would hide me somewhere in troll territory where no one, especially vampires, would dare to look for me. I just needed to find a way to get to him.

Nate would be home tomorrow. I had to talk to him, try to explain things to him before I up and disappeared. He was not going to understand and he would struggle with the things I was going to tell him, but he deserved to know the truth. After everything he'd done for me, I owed him that much at least. I felt a pang of regret that we had never been as close as my dad would have wanted. I always thought there would be time to fix it somehow.

"Talk to Maxwell all you want," I conceded. "But I am not going *anywhere* until Nate gets home tomorrow. And if you make me go, I'll run away the first chance I get."

"Fine. You'll stay with me and Chris until then," Nikolas stated firmly.

"I don't think so." There was no way I'd be able to contact Remy from some Mohiri safe house or wherever they were holding up. "I'm going home, and you are free to follow me if you want."

Nikolas shook his head. "That location is not secure."

It was my turn to laugh. "Trust me. The devil himself couldn't get into that building."

"Um, guys, can we just figure out where we're going?" Peter called from the car. "Bleeding here."

Nikolas raised an eyebrow at me as he pulled out his phone and called Chris to tell him to meet us at my apartment. I turned toward Judith's car and saw the Mustang. "What are we going to do about Scott? We can't leave him here like this."

"Don't worry about him," Nikolas said, following close behind me. "Once we get you safely to your fortress of an apartment, we will take care of your friend."

"Those guys are looking for a red Mustang. We can't take a chance of them finding Scott before you come back. Besides I think he needs a doctor."

Nikolas went to the Mustang and looked at Scott, peering into his eyes and checking his vitals. He pulled out some of the same nasty green stuff Chris had given me after the crocotta attack and forced Scott to eat some.

"I think he'll be okay in a few hours," he told us. "If he'd been permanently damaged, he'd be catatonic. I gave him something to speed healing. By tomorrow he won't remember any of it and he'll feel like he has a bad hangover."

And banged up his car, I thought guiltily looking at the dented right fender and smashed headlight.

"How will he get home?" I had to make sure Scott was okay before I left. I was leaving no casualties from this mess.

Nikolas called Chris again then held out the phone. "Chris is on his way here. If one of you can tell him where your friend lives, Chris will drive him home."

Roland took the phone and gave the other Mohiri directions. I walked to the Honda to wait for him without a backward glance at Nikolas. I didn't need to look behind us to know he was right on our tail for the short drive to my place.

Roland parked in Nate's spot, and the two of us helped Peter up the stairs and into the apartment. I refused Nikolas's offer of help, and he followed us with a stony expression, bolting the door behind us. Instead of putting Peter on the couch, we carried him up to my room where he would have enough space and privacy to shift and heal. I wanted to stay with him until Roland reminded me that Peter would have to disrobe to change. That sent me down the stairs pretty fast.

I found Nikolas going around the apartment, checking the windows and doors as if a vampire was going to burst through them any minute.

"I told you this place is safe. I warded it myself." I grabbed the orange juice from the fridge. "Anyone thirsty?"

Nikolas stood by Nate's office doorway. "*You* warded it?"

"Don't look so shocked." I poured juice into a tall glass and took a long gulp. "I told you before I'm not helpless. And I got away from those guys, didn't I?"

Roland came into the kitchen, and I handed him the juice carton. "I'd believe her if I was you," he said to Nikolas. "Sara knows things, and if she says we're safe here, then we – "

"Argh!" he yelped a second before the carton hit the kitchen floor and orange juice sprayed up my legs. He jumped in front of me and pushed me back against the refrigerator. I heard Nikolas shout something and fear rose in my throat.

"Sara, stay behind me," Roland shouted as I struggled to push his weight away so I could see what was happening. Had something gotten past the ward? No. It was just not possible.

"Keep her there," Nikolas barked. "I'll take care of it. Damn it, I knew this place wasn't safe."

"Take care of what?" I cried, afraid for my friends. With a mighty shove I squeezed out from behind Roland to face the new threat.

It stood in the hallway outside the kitchen, teeth bared menacingly and glaring between Nikolas and Roland, ready to pounce at the slightest provocation. A more frightening snarl I had never seen.

Nikolas reached inside his jacket and pulled out a long gleaming blade.

"No!" I screamed and ran to throw myself in front of the creature that could rip everyone in the room to shreds.

17

"Sara, are you insane? Do you know what that is?" Roland yelled, running toward me.

"He's my friend!" I shouted at them. I threw up my hands to let Roland and Nikolas know I was okay. "His name is Remy."

Roland skidded to a stop and stared at me in stunned silence. His eyes moved warily from me to Remy and back again as if he could not believe his eyes. "*That* is Remy?"

"Yes. Now back off, both of you." I turned to Remy and took his hand in mine. "Are you okay?" Something really bad must have happened to make him come here and reveal himself to other people. I'd never seen him look this distraught.

"Is *he* okay?" Roland asked in disbelief. "I nearly had a heart attack and she's worried about a troll. A goddamn troll!"

"Roland, shut up," I said more harshly than I'd ever spoken to him. "Remy, what's wrong? Please tell me."

Remy's large eyes finally met mine, and I saw something I'd never expected to see in a troll's eyes: fear.

"Minka gone. Creah and Sinah, too."

"Gone? What do you mean gone?"

He gripped my hand painfully, but I didn't cry out. "Humans take them," he said, bringing one of my worst fears to life. Ever since we'd sold that troll bile I'd worried that someone might track it back to my friends. The thought of sweet little Minka in the hands of someone like that made my blood run cold.

"We'll find them," I promised him fiercely. "We'll get them back."

Nikolas spoke for the first time. "Does your uncle have any alcohol here?"

I shot him a puzzled look. "How will that help us?"

"It won't. I need a drink."

"I'll help you look," Roland added weakly.

"You guys are not helping the situation," I told them irritably. "Remy's little cousins are in a lot of danger, and we have to find them."

Nikolas leaned against a wall, looking at a loss for the first time since I met him. "We have enough problems to deal with without going out looking for missing trolls. Have you forgotten your own considerable troubles?"

"But this is my fault," I said. "I have to help them."

"Is *our* fault," Remy corrected me. "Sara warn me it dangerous but I not believe it. I need medicine for boggie."

"What on earth is he talking about?" Roland asked me.

I bit my lip as I gathered my courage. "Remy has this boggie friend who was sick, and they needed a special medicine that you can't get here. It only comes from Africa, and it's very hard to find – and really expensive. I found someone to get it for us, but we needed it as soon as possible so Remy gave me something to trade for it... something very hard to find."

Nikolas straightened, and his eyes widened in disbelief. "Please tell me you're joking."

I shook my head slowly, and he let out a string of Russian curses that made my ears burn even though I couldn't understand them.

"What? What am I missing?" Roland asked, looking between us.

"*Iisus Khristos!*" Nikolas began pacing the hallway. "You used troll bile to buy the medicine? What the hell were you thinking?"

Roland shot me a horrified look. "Oh, Sara, you didn't."

"I was careful," I protested. "I went through a guy I used a few times before for other things, and he's always careful. He said he went through a middle man with an overseas buyer and there was no way to trace it back to me. But a few weeks later I found out that someone was posting on some of the message boards, asking about troll bile, and I got worried." I rubbed my eyes miserably. "I never believed they would find us, let alone be brave enough to do something like this."

"Not brave, incredibly stupid," Nikolas said wearily. He looked at Remy. "How long do we have?"

"Elders meet now. I come find Sara to see if we find little ones before."

"Before what?" Roland asked just as it dawned on me what Nikolas and

Remy were talking about. I gasped as the full seriousness of the situation hit me.

"A rampage," I whispered. "The elders are going to rampage."

"That does not sound good," Roland said weakly.

There was no humor in Nikolas's laugh. "There is a reason why no one – not even a vampire – tangles with trolls. If you mess with one troll, you get the whole clan, and if you harm one of their young, you die. And if a young troll goes missing, the clan rises up to find them – or who took them. Trolls are even better trackers than crocotta, and once they are worked up into a rage, they will kill anyone who has come into contact with their missing children. And during a rampage, trolls do not distinguish between the innocent and the guilty."

Roland blanched.

The doorbell rang, making me and Roland jump. Nikolas opened the door to admit Chris whose good-natured smile did not falter even when he saw our grim faces. Then he saw Remy. I didn't think I had ever seen someone's eyes go that round before. Roland shoved a glass of Nate's whiskey into Chris's hand while Nikolas brought him up to speed on all he had missed.

The kitchen was getting crowded, so we moved into the living room. I took the chair by the fireplace, and Remy sat on the ottoman beside me. Roland and Chris sat on either end of the sofa. Nikolas stood by the window looking like a sentry.

"Your little orphan is just full of surprises," Chris quipped to Nikolas. "Never a dull moment."

I bristled at Chris's words. "I'm nobody's little orphan."

Chris ignored my denial. "So, what's the plan?"

There was no question in my mind about what had to be done. "We've got to find them." No one said anything so I said, "They're only babies. God knows what those people will do to them."

Roland pointed at Remy. "Can't he track them?"

Remy shook his head unhappily. "Only elders know tracking. If I close, I find them."

I pulled out my phone. "I'm calling Malloy. If anyone has heard about this, it's him."

"Who is Malloy?" Nikolas asked suspiciously.

"Buyer," Roland offered as I dialed the number. Nikolas shot him a questioning look, and Roland grimaced, no doubt remembering his last encounter with Malloy. "Don't ask."

Malloy picked up right away, and I cut right to the chase about the missing trolls. "If you've heard anything at all, tell me now. If we don't find them, their parents are going to come looking, and you really don't want that, especially after what I sold you."

"You got to be crazy to mess with them trolls," he uttered in a frightened voice. "Don't I always tell you that?" There was a short pause, and then he said, "Give me half an hour and if there is anything to find out, I'll know it."

I hung up. "He's checking into it."

I saw that Nikolas had pulled out his own phone and was speaking in a low voice to someone. He hung up and looked at Chris. "I called in Erik's team. It has to be a big player to risk the trolls' wrath. I guess we know who sent the witch, too. It had to be someone with a lot of power and influence to get one of them."

His words sank in, and the pieces began to slam into place like bullets sliding into a gun chamber. A big player who was able to employ a desert witch who lived in a tribal region of Africa. The man on the yacht. Tarek with his Middle Eastern accent. Malloy's wealthy overseas buyer.

Oh God, what have I done?

The weight of my actions threatened to suffocate me. I'd been so caught up in all the drama in my life the last few weeks that I did not see this new threat until it was right on top of us. I'd thought I was helping Remy by getting the Baktu, but all I'd done was put his family in danger. If the trolls went on a rampage, a lot of people were going to die and that would all be on my head. "This is all my fault. I'm so sorry, Remy."

He laid his slender hand over mine on the arm of the chair. "It my fault, too."

I leaned toward him and gave him a quick hug. "I promise we'll get them back."

We pulled apart, and I saw three pairs of eyes watching us with open curiosity. It occurred to me how strange it must look – a teenage girl with a troll friend – but I was in no mood to offer explanations. There would be time for that after Remy's little cousins were safe.

"Am I delirious, or do I really see a troll over there?" Peter stood in the doorway, his eyes nearly bugging out of his head. Except for the mussed hair and bloody T-shirt, I never would have believed he'd been stabbed an hour ago.

Roland gave him the condensed version of the story. Peter listened open-mouthed, his eyes never leaving me and Remy, and when Roland finished, Peter sat on the floor with his back against the archway, not saying a word.

Malloy called me back ten minutes later. "Now you did not hear this from me, understand?" he said as soon as I picked up. "I got nothing about those trolls specifically, but supposedly there are some very rare goods being shipped out of Portland tomorrow morning on a private jet. More security than anyone's seen around here. Word is that it's living cargo."

My pulse quickened. "That's it. It has to be. Do you know where the shipment is now?"

The others watched me expectantly when I hung up. I related what Malloy had told me and jumped to my feet. "Come on, we have to go before it's too late."

"Chris and I will go," Nikolas said. "I think we can handle whatever kind of security they have in place."

"I'm coming, too. I got them into this nightmare, and I'll get them out."

Nikolas crossed his arms. "Forget it. It's not going to happen."

I matched his stance. "Stop telling me what to do. I'm going whether you like it or not." The trolls were my friends and my responsibility. How dare he try to stop me from helping them?

A tic started at the corner of his jaw, and he took a step toward me. "Like hell. I'll tie your little ass to that chair over there if I have to."

"You can kiss my – "

Chris jumped between us, facing Nikolas. "I don't think this little debate is getting us anywhere." He turned sideways, and his eyebrow rose when he looked at me. "As entertaining as it promises to be."

"There is no debate. She stays here," Nikolas stated unwaveringly.

It was time for another tactic. "Alright Mr. I-Know-Better-Than-Everyone-Else, what will you do when you find them? I bet they didn't teach you in warrior school how to handle a bunch of frightened troll kids."

"Your troll friend will come with us."

"And who will stay here with me while you guys are on your rescue mission?"

"The werewolves should be able to keep you safe here for a few hours," he replied as if that settled everything.

"Really? And what happens if that witch finds us again? Wouldn't I be safer with a bunch of warriors, two werewolves, *and* a troll?"

"Sara come. I keep her safe," Remy vowed firmly, and I saw Roland shiver at my troll friend's fierce face. No one in the room could argue that there was a better bodyguard in the world.

Nikolas glowered at me for a good ten seconds. "You do not leave his side." His tone brooked no argument, and for once I conceded without a fight.

I grabbed my coat from the hall closet and felt the comforting shape of the Mohiri knife in the inside pocket. I really hoped I did not have to use the knife tonight, but lady luck appeared to have deserted me lately and I'd hate to be caught out without a weapon.

Peter called shotgun, and I glared at him when I was forced to share the back seat with Nikolas. Remy refused to go anywhere near the car and said he would follow us on foot.

I looked around for Chris, and Nikolas said, "Chris will follow us."

A tense silence fell over the car as we headed for the interstate. I looked out my window, intending to ignore Nikolas the whole way to Portland. So much for the olive branch I'd offered him the night of the storm. The whole damn tree was going up in smoke now.

Peter lasted a whole ten minutes before he turned in his seat to fix me with a "don't you think you have something to tell us?" look.

"What?"

He shook his head. "Really? That's all you have to say about the *troll* who was just sitting in your living room?"

I felt Nikolas's eyes on me, and I saw Roland darting glances at me in the rearview mirror. "I met Remy not long after I moved here to live with Nate, before I met you guys. I used to go exploring down by the old lumber mill, and one day he saw me and just decided to show himself to me. He was only a year older than me and pretty adventurous for a troll." What I did not tell them was that Remy had spied on me healing a squirrel with a broken leg and he was so curious that he'd watched me for a few weeks before he finally decided to introduce himself.

"Weren't you scared?" Roland asked. "I would have wet my pants if a troll walked up to me in the woods when I was that age."

Peter snickered. "You still would."

A smile broke over my face as I remembered that day. "I was scared at first. Even back then Remy looked pretty fierce. But he knew some broken English, so we were able to talk and I found out he was as nervous as me. It was a... pretty hard time for me. I'd just lost my dad and moved to a strange place, and I was lonely. Remy was my first friend here." My chest tightened. It was the first time I'd ever talked to anyone about those dark days when I first came to New Hastings.

"But trolls don't like anyone, especially humans," Peter protested. "They kill anyone who gets near their young. Weren't you afraid of the adult trolls?"

I laughed. "I didn't know any better at first and Remy didn't tell me. He was a lot of fun to be with. I taught him English, and he taught me all about the real world. He was the one who told me that vampires really did exist and most likely killed my dad. By the time he took me to meet his family, I didn't know I was supposed to be afraid of them. They weren't happy, but they didn't threaten me either. Maybe it's because I was a little kid or maybe they knew all along I wasn't human – I don't know. Anyway, I don't see them very often. Usually, it's just me and Remy."

"Okay, you are officially the most badass girl I've ever met," Peter declared. "To think we were worried you'd be afraid of us when you found out what we are."

After that, Roland and Peter peppered me with questions until I threw up my hands and said no more. Nikolas remained silent throughout the entire conversation, but I felt his gaze on me the whole time. It took a lot of effort not to sneak a glance at him to see what he was thinking. He was probably wondering what the hell he had gotten himself into.

I hadn't been to Portland since that night at the Attic and I thought it would bother me, but I was too worried about Remy's cousins to feel anything but worry for them. My hands clenched painfully in my lap while Roland drove around looking for the address Malloy had given me, and there were fingernail impressions in my palms by the time we found the gated estate. We drove by once to check it out then parked the car in a new development a street away to avoid detection.

Remy ran up to me as soon as I climbed out of the car. "Little ones close!"

"I thought you couldn't track them," Roland said.

"Not unless they close," Remy explained. He touched his chest. "Feel them here."

A spark of hope lit in my chest. "Malloy was right."

Chris joined us a few minutes later after he did a bit more surveillance. He described what he'd seen to Nikolas. "The place is heavily guarded but nothing we haven't dealt with before. I'd say a dozen or so armed men on the perimeter with more inside the house."

Nikolas turned to us, his eyes on me as he spoke. "Chris and I will go in and neutralize their defenses. Once it's safe and we have located the young trolls, we'll come back for you."

"You expect us to stay here?" Roland asked, waving around at the empty lot. The look on his face told me he had been looking forward to getting in on the action. But now that I knew we were close to Minka and the others, I was happy to let Nikolas and Chris handle the threat. I'd never admit it to Nikolas but I was still shaken from the attack earlier, and the thought of facing more dangerous men scared me more than a little. And werewolves or not, I wanted my friends here with me out of harm's way. I had seen Nikolas fight vampires and crocotta, so I was confident he could handle a bunch of armed men.

"You can shift and be okay, unless those men are packing silver ammo, but what about Sara?" Nikolas said to Roland. "Are you willing to put her in that kind of danger?"

Roland started to say something then shook his head. "No."

Satisfied, Nikolas said, "There will be several layers of security. Whoever orchestrated this will not take chances with so valuable an asset and will expect trouble. If you hear gunshots or other commotion, stay here out of sight with your heads down. We can handle this. Is everyone clear on that?"

"Yes," I said for all of us. Nikolas nodded, and he and Chris began to arm themselves with weapons from the bag on Chris's motorcycle. When they were ready, Nikolas looked like the warrior who had walked out of the shadows in the alley. The churning in my gut eased a little because I knew that if anyone could make this right, it was him. *I trust him.* The acknowledgement took me by surprise because trusting people did not come easily for me. But then I thought about all the things he had done to earn my trust even though I had fought him at every turn, and how time and time again he jumped into dangerous situations just like this because of me.

"Be careful," I told them, but I was looking at Nikolas when I said it. He smiled confidently, like he was heading off to a rugby match instead of going into battle.

Chris smirked at me as he turned to leave. "Careful, Sara, or people might think you care."

Left alone, the four of us were subdued as we waited for Nikolas and Chris to return. Roland and Peter paced the lot, stopping often to listen for sounds of fighting. I sat on a stack of plywood with Remy, clutching his hand.

"What will happen after we get Minka and the others back? Will the Elders still be angry?"

Remy hung his head. "I tell them about bile and they very angry. I think they will say we no longer friends."

"No!" Remy was one of my dearest friends. He was going to be there when everyone else I knew grew old and died. I couldn't lose him. I couldn't.

"Maybe not forever but for long time," he said sadly. "Elders not forget easy."

I swallowed back my tears. I had messed up so many things, but I never imagined destroying my friendships. What else would I ruin before all of this was over?

"Where are they?" Peter fretted after ten minutes. "Shouldn't we have heard something by now?"

"I don't know." Roland's voice was uncertain. "We'll give them a few more minutes and – "

Remy shot to his feet, nearly knocking me over, his eyes wide and luminous in the darkness. "Little ones very frightened! Something bad happen."

Roland and Peter came running over to us. "What is it?" Roland asked.

"Remy said something's wrong with his cousins." I refused to think what that could mean. "We have to go in."

Peter rubbed the back of his neck. "What about the Mohiri? Shouldn't we wait for them?"

"There's no time. The trolls need us." I strained to make out their faces. "Remy and I are going."

"Okay, hold on for a minute," Roland said. "It'll be better if we shift first."

He and Peter disappeared behind the structure and two large dark shapes returned in their place. I'd forgotten how ferocious they looked in wolf form, and my breath caught when they walked up to flank me. Standing on their hind legs they towered over me, making me feel very small and insignificant next to their powerful bodies.

"Don't crowd me," I chided, shoving at them until they gave me a bit more breathing room.

We left the lot, moving stealthily through the quiet neighborhood until we were within sight of the gated entrance to the estate. I studied the locked ten-foot tall gate and wondered how on earth we were going to get past it.

Roland tugged at my arm, leading me away from the gate and into the woods around the estate. I pulled out my knife and followed him with Remy at my side and Peter taking up the rear. The woods and grass were wet from an earlier rain, but I was too worried about not making any noise to care about the dampness seeping into my jeans and sneakers.

Halfway around the estate, we found a small gardener's gate hanging slightly ajar, and I knew this was where Nikolas and Chris had gone in. That became even more evident when we slipped inside and saw two men unconscious on the ground. At least I assumed they were unconscious; I wasn't about to check. I didn't believe in senseless killing, but I had no sympathy for people who would steal or hurt children.

We crouched behind a shed and surveyed the broad expanse of lawn dotted with large trees and carefully tended flower gardens. There was no sign of movement between us, and the well-lit house so we set off across the grounds, running from one tree to the next for cover. Adrenaline coursed through me, and my heart pounded so loud that I thought anyone within ten feet of me would hear it.

Remy stopped abruptly and let out a low growl that set my hair on end, and in front of us, Roland made a similar sound. Remy pushed me up against a tree with a finger to his lips and took up a protective stance in front of me as my two werewolf friends dashed off into the darkness. The night was suddenly filled with snarls and the sounds of violent fighting. My palms scraped against the rough bark of the tree as I imagined horrible things happening to my friends.

Remy's head swung toward our left, and he made a rumbling sound deep in his chest. Before I could speak, he disappeared in a blur, leaving me alone and trembling beside the tree. Somewhere in the darkness I heard hissing and more sounds of combat, and my heart felt like it was about to explode from my chest.

"Thump, thump goes the little rabbit's heart," drawled a cold inhuman voice.

I let out a muffled scream when the vampire appeared in front of me. Tall with ebony skin and short spiky dreadlocks, his white fangs almost glowed when he smiled at me. "Hello, little rabbit."

Before I could react, a breath of wind heralded the appearance of a second vampire with upswept blond hair and a hungry leer.

Vampires here, working with humans? Impossible.

Brandishing the knife, I shrank against the tree. "Stay back!"

The black vampire's soft laugh was like ice water on my skin. "Such a big weapon for a little girl."

"Haism did not tell us snacks would be provided," said his companion, drifting closer.

The first one advanced. "Just remember, I saw her fir – "

There was a blur of gray followed by a horrible gurgling sound, and I felt warmth spray across my face and in my eyes. Something hit my legs as the black vampire slumped to the ground. I stared in shock at the corpse and then at the severed head near my feet and felt my gorge rise.

My eyes met the blond vampire's stare as his own shock turned to fear then rage. In my mind, a voice I'd thought dead, whispered, *Move now.* Fear blocked out all but the Mori's instincts, and I felt my body shift sideways with a speed that left me dizzy. The air beside me swirled as the vampire rushed at the spot where I had stood a split second ago.

Wield the blade, the demon said calmly, and I raised the knife just as the vampire came at me again. We both gasped in surprise as the blade sank into his chest. It missed his heart, but the silver burned and he shrieked in agony as smoke poured from the hole in his chest. His clawed hand reached for me. Desperately, I pulled the knife out and drew back to plunge it in again.

The vampire suddenly fell away from me, his snarling mouth going slack as he flailed against the pair of slender gray hands around his throat. My eyes found Remy's, and he nodded with grim intent. Moving forward, I grabbed the knife in both hands and shoved it into the unprotected area above the vampire's heart.

There was no death scream, no bursting into flames. The vampire gasped and shuddered, then folded to the ground like an empty suit. I stared at the knife in my hands, christened with the blood of my first vampire kill and felt a surge of exhilaration unlike anything I'd ever felt before. The Mori gave a sated sigh.

"Come," Remy urged, taking my hand and pulling me away from the two dead vampires.

"What about Roland and Peter?" I whispered hoarsely, trying to look behind me for them.

"Wolves strong. Little ones need us."

I let him lead me toward the house, using my sleeve to wipe most of the vampire blood from my face. My friends were vampire hunters, trained for this; I had to trust they could take care of themselves. And I was as safe with Remy as with anyone else at this point. I still could not believe humans and vampires were working together in this. What could the humans have promised them in exchange for their help and risking a war with the trolls?

Remy did not speak, and I followed him with something akin to awe. In all the time I'd known him, he had been the gentle friend who used his knowledge to help other creatures. I knew trolls were deadly fighters, but I could never imagine him that way until now. He was my age and he'd taken out that vampire without blinking. I shuddered to imagine what an adult troll could do. It made it even more urgent to find his cousins and return them to the clan before the elders came looking for them.

We stopped at the pool area where there was no more cover. The pool deck was bathed in light, and I saw that a glass door at the back of the house was open. I wondered if Nikolas and Chris had gone in this way. Or were they still out here on the grounds fighting vampires? *Or maybe they didn't make it.* I shook off that horrible notion as soon as it popped into my head. I refused to believe that vampires would get the better of the two warriors, especially Nikolas.

No one tried to intercept us as we ran around the pool, and I saw why when we came across three unconscious men. Through the door I saw two more crumpled shapes, which turned out to be more dead vampires. Jesus, the place was crawling with bloodsuckers! I shivered, never so happy to have Remy close by. A knife protruded from the chest of one of the vampires, and I smiled in grim relief when I recognized the handle. Nikolas's calling card no doubt. At least I knew they'd made it this far.

We passed through the door and emerged in a large entrance with marble tiles, and the highest ceilings I'd ever seen hung with a row of glittering chandeliers. An elegant staircase curved up to a second floor landing where a large window overlooked the grounds. Past the staircase there was a hallway with several doors.

"Where to?" I asked Remy, relying on his unfailing senses to lead us to his cousins.

"There." He pointed down the hallway. "That way."

The house was as quiet as a tomb as we moved swiftly down the hall, and the silence scared me more than anything else. As heavily guarded as this place was, there should be some noise, some sign of the inhabitants. Where was everyone? Where were Nikolas and Chris?

We reached the first closed door and pushed it open to find an empty library. The next door opened to reveal a game room with a massive pool table. *Third time's the charm,* I thought as I cracked open the third door. A cool breeze touched my face. The cellar.

"Down there," Remy whispered behind me. It was all the confirmation I needed, and I started down the stairs with him close behind me. At the bottom, we found ourselves in a rectangular room with stone walls and floor and an arched doorway on either end. I listened for guards, but more silence greeted us. *This is too easy,* I thought nervously. If Remy's cousins were down here, this cellar should be crawling with security.

I turned to the doorway on my right but stopped when I heard clicking sounds from the other direction. I shot Remy a fearful look as the clicking grew louder and faster, mixed with strange snuffling noises. The first thought that came to my mind was crocotta, and I froze at the terror those images created.

Remy yanked me toward him as two massive black bodies burst into the room, snarling. My troll friend bared his own teeth and let out a growl that brought the beasts skidding to a stop. I had never seen dogs like this. Their bodies were muscled and stocky, and I might have thought they were Rottweilers if they weren't the size of small horses with frightening red eyes. Their snouts were longer and wider than a normal dog's, and I could see long top and bottom fangs protruding from their snapping jaws. Their coats were coarse and black, and I couldn't help but think they were beautiful in a monstrous kind of way. I would have appreciated them more if they weren't looking at me like I was on the menu.

"What are they?" I whispered to Remy as the huge dogs paced back and forth, looking for an opening to get past the equally menacing creature in their way.

"Fell beasts," he replied calmly, his eyes never leaving them. One of the dogs tilted its head eerily as if it understood Remy's words.

"What?" I croaked. "You mean hellhounds!" Vampires and now hellhounds? Who on earth were we dealing with here?

I looked at the bloody knife in my hands and wondered if silver even worked on hellhounds. I took a deep breath. I had never harmed an animal in my life, but the pair of hellhounds looked ready to rip us to shreds. They stood between us and the trolls, and I'd fight them if I had to.

"No," Remy said softly, laying his hand over mine that held the knife as if he'd read my mind. "You talk to them."

"Are you crazy?" I asked out of one side of my mouth, afraid to take my eyes off the beasts. "These are hellhounds, Remy. You know – beasts from *hell*."

A small shrug was his only reply.

Great. I was in the bowels of a mansion crawling with vampires and God only knew what else. I had no idea if my friends were okay, and I was facing down two of hell's own. And all Remy could say was "talk to them?"

"Okay, but if we get eaten, don't blame me."

I eased down to a cross-legged position on the cold floor with my back against the wall and my knife on the floor beside me. The hounds watched me intently, but neither of them made a move for me. I was pretty sure that had more to do with their uncertainty about Remy than anything else.

"I guess you guys are wondering what I'm doing, huh?" I said in my calmest tone, not looking either of them directly in the eye. Words didn't mean anything to animals; it was your voice and your movements they responded to. I really hoped that applied to hellhounds.

The closest hound lowered his head and let out a long, low growl.

"Alright, so you're a little pissed that we invaded your turf. I get that. But is all this snarling and foaming at the mouth really necessary?"

Both dogs bared their glistening fangs. This was going about as well as I'd expected.

Reaching inside, I unlocked my power, letting its golden warmth flow through me. I opened my wall and let a stream of energy seep into the air around me.

One of the hounds stopped growling to sniff the air, then took a step back, his hackles up. I let more power escape. The second hound made a small whining sound then resumed growling.

"I've never met a hellhound before," I continued softly as a gentle flow of power moved outward from me in waves. "I gotta say, you've got the scary image down, but I don't think you're as bad as everyone says. And if you give me a chance, you'll see that I'm actually a nice person." *And I don't taste good at all.*

The growling petered out as one dog then the other lay on the floor, whining and still watching me warily.

"I always wanted a dog, a big one like a Great Dane or German Shepherd. I never imagined one as big as you, though." I let myself imagine one of these beasts living in our apartment and laughed softly. "I'd like to see Nate's face if I brought home something like you."

One of the great black bodies shuffled forward a few inches. I looked down at my lap, pretending to ignore them. I focused my power, and it filled my voice. "I wish you understood that we only want to find our little friends and take them home. I know you're just doing what you were taught to do, but you don't have to hurt anyone anymore."

Nails scraped on stone as the closest hound moved. I held my breath as a heavy black head laid itself in my lap. Biting my lip, I raised a tentative hand and touched the creature's wide forehead. The hair was thick but softer than I'd imagined, and I pushed my fingers through it, amazed by the texture. "What a beautiful beast you are," I said as my fear gave way to wonder.

The hound let out a shuddering sigh as my hands rubbed its powerful jaw and thick neck. Whimpering nearby made me look up at the second dog that had ventured closer, but hadn't yet decided whether or not to trust me.

"It's okay," I crooned. "I know exactly how you feel. I have trouble trusting people, too."

The second hound inched forward until his nose rested on my ankle. I continued to pet the huge head on my lap while directing more calming power at his brother.

"A most interesting picture," said a heavily accented voice I'd hoped to never hear again. "A tamer of trolls and the devil's beasts. So many gifts you have, young one. Such a curiosity. It is no wonder so many seek to possess you."

The Hale witch stood in the doorway to the room we were headed for before the hounds arrived. The white around his dark pupils stood out in sharp contrast to his dark skin, and his white tattoos seemed to shift in the dimly lit cellar. He looked well recovered from our last encounter, but he did not instill the same fear in me this time.

"Are you as curious as you were a few hours ago?" I challenged, and I saw in his eyes the remembered pain of our earlier showdown. The head in my lap lifted at the edge in my voice, and I scratched it soothingly. Remy stood silently beside me.

The witch's lips twisted into a small smile. "Curious, yes. Foolhardy, no. I see now that there is much more to you than I was given to understand."

"Pretty words, but forgive me if I don't believe you." I scoffed. I was suddenly grateful for the two hulking beasts between me and him.

He stepped into the room, and the hound at my feet growled. "See? Who am I to provoke one who commands the devil's own?"

"I don't command anything." I ran a hand through the thick fur of the dog's neck, and he gave a rumbling sigh. "They've never known kindness before. I just showed them how it feels." I realized I had stopped using my power the moment the witch arrived. The hellhounds were under no one's influence but their own.

The Hale witch stared at me with open fascination. "Compassion and kindness are powers unto themselves if wielded correctly. Look at these beasts – they will serve no other master now. Yusri al-Hawwash will not be happy to lose two valuable servants along with his cargo."

Remy made a threatening sound at hearing his little cousins referred to as cargo. I reached over to pat his leg, and he laid a hand on my shoulder.

Our interaction didn't go unnoticed by the witch. "And did you show the troll kindness as well to gain its allegiance?"

"No. *His* kindness gained *mine*."

Muffled thuds upstairs and faraway sounds of shouting made us all look at the ceiling. It was the first sounds of other people since Remy and I had entered the house, and it reminded me that we had no time to dawdle down here. I had no idea if it was the Mohiri or my werewolf friends fighting up there or what could come down those stairs at any moment.

I gently pushed the heavy head off my lap and got to my feet with my knife in hand. The hounds stayed on the floor, looking up at me expectantly.

"We know the trolls are down here, and we're going to get them now," I said.

The witch put up his tattooed hands. "I will not stop you. I came here to fulfill a debt, and it has been repaid. My part in this is done."

"I heard that your people never work with vampires, that you hate demons. Why are you helping them?"

He scowled. "I do not work with demons. I had to honor my debt. But as I said, my debt has been paid."

"So you won't try to stop us?"

"Were you alone, I might try," he answered honestly. "You are a mystery to me. Your power runs deep and mostly untouched, and yet you have no desire to explore it. I would like to see how deep it really is, but I think that will have to wait for another day."

To prove it, he stepped aside and waved us toward the room behind him. I took Remy's hand, and we backed along the wall to the doorway. The dogs watched us, and I put out my hand and said, "Stay." I had no idea if they could understand the command, but they did not move.

At the doorway, I said, "You said others want to possess me. What did you mean by that?"

He laughed, and the sound echoed chillingly off the cellar walls. "That I cannot say. I am still bound by an oath of silence. But I will tell you what I know that they do not, what my far sight shows me. Those who hunt you will ultimately give you the power to become the thing they fear the most."

I scowled at his cryptic words. "That tells me nothing."

"Then I have not broken my oath."

"Well, maybe you can answer another question for me." He raised his eyebrows, and I asked a question that had been niggling at me for a few days. "You set those rats on us at the marina so you had to know where we were. Why didn't you tell your friends we were under the dock?"

His white teeth showed when he smiled. "You intrigued me when you pushed me out of the rodent's mind. I had never met someone who could best me, and I wanted to take you on myself, to see if you were as worthy an opponent as you seemed to be. It felt... disrespectful to let you be taken by brute force after such a display."

His answer surprised me, but this was neither the time nor the place to ponder it. Maybe when all of this was over, I would speculate about why I was able to challenge the witch's power when Nikolas said that even a seasoned Mohiri warrior was no match for a Hale witch. Right now though, my little troll friends needed me.

Remy went under the arch, and I followed him, colliding with his back when he stopped abruptly. I peered around him and gasped.

We were in a wine cellar with empty wooden racks covering the walls and a small shaded light in the center of the ceiling. In the middle of the room on a raised glass platform sat a glass cage that measured about three feet by four feet. The glass bars appeared to ripple as currents of red light moved through them like electricity. The hairs rose up on my arms as if the air in the room was charged, and I felt the power in the cage from where I stood.

Three tiny bodies huddled together as far from the sides of the cage as possible, and their frightened whimpers tore at my heart.

"Minka?" I called, and the little trolls lifted their heads to stare at us. One of them moved too far, and I heard a painful screech as red sparks flew from one side of the cage. Fresh sobbing filled the room.

Outrage swelled in me. What kind of monster did this to children? I rushed forward until the blazing power running through the cage would let me go no farther. "We're here," I called, backing away from the cage. "We'll get you out of there."

I turned to Remy to see him staring at the cage in fear. "Remy, come on. We have to get them out."

"Yusri al-Hawwash spared no expense on this endeavor," said the Hale witch, and I spun to face him. "Trolls do not have many weaknesses, and the sheik knew he would need a way to control his bounty." He swept a hand toward the cage. "Demon fire. A legion of trolls could descend upon this place and not one of them could touch this cage. Only a demon can touch it."

It hit me then why the house had been so quiet, the cellar unguarded except for the hell hounds and the witch. The people behind this knew the cage was all the security they needed. It also explained why they were working with vampires. Protected by their demon side, vampires could freely handle the cage and move it when it was time for transport. It was brilliant really, sick but brilliant.

From somewhere in the house above us I heard what sounded like gunfire before a blood-curdling howl rent the air. My heart leapt into my throat. My friends were up there fighting for their lives. I had to do something and fast. I searched the room for something I could use even as my heart told me there was nothing here to help me. What I needed was a demon. I let out a desperate laugh. Where were all the vampires when I actually needed one?

"Sara." Remy's voice was filled with despair. "Help them... please."

"I don't know what to do," I cried. I'd barely gotten within two feet of the cage before the demon fire had driven me back. I was as helpless as Remy.

Remy's tortured eyes met mine, and he placed a hand over my chest. "Demon in here."

I shook my head and backed away from him. "No! I can't do that. I-I don't even know how." All my life I'd struggled to control that side of me. Before I ever knew what it was, I knew it was dark and ugly, something to be kept locked away. The thought of releasing my hold on it now terrified me. What if I couldn't restrain it again? What it if took over and I went insane like those other orphans Nikolas had told me about? What if I hurt one of my friends?

"Sara!" cried a small plaintive voice from the cage.

Tears spilled down my cheeks. The trolls were in danger because of me. If I didn't save them, I could never live with myself. "I'm coming, Minka."

I heard noise on the stairs and growling in the other room, and I knew our time was running out. God only knew what was going to come through that door.

Come on, I told the Mori hovering in the shadows of my mind. *I need you*. I had no idea how to do this so I just dropped the wall that held back the demon. At the same time, I closed off the well of power at the center of my being. The demon was afraid of my power, and it would not emerge unless I promised it safe passage.

The demon shifted and stretched and inched forward hesitantly as if it could not believe the barrier around it was gone. Like a moth emerging from its cocoon it pulsed and spread its wings joyfully. My body shuddered as a new consciousness invaded my mind, rapidly spreading until my head felt like it would explode from the pressure inside.

I cried out and fell to my knees, holding my head in my hands. "Stop!" I screamed as the demon moved through me, filling me, boiling beneath my skin. I tried to push it back, but it was too late. I could no longer tell where I ended and the Mori began. It was strong, so much stronger than I ever realized. It was consuming me, and I was powerless to stop it.

My legs moved and I found myself on my feet, walking toward the cage. Dimly I waited for the blast of scorching heat. It never came, and I knew the demon owned this body now. I watched as hands that looked like mine grasped the glass bars and ripped them apart like they were toothpicks. Through a haze, I saw the smallest troll throw her arms around the neck of the demon that looked like me, felt it lower her impassively to the stone floor and turn away as the two remaining trolls jumped from their glass prison.

"Sara?"

The voice came from a long way off. The demon whirled to face the man filling the doorway, and my shrinking consciousness gasped at the powerful primal connection that stretched between the two of them like an elastic band pulled too taut. The band began to shrink, drawing the man and demon toward each other.

"What happened to her?" the man demanded of the troll as he strode toward us. The troll said something, but I did not hear it. The man stopped in front of us and took the demon's face in his hands with gentle firmness. "Look at me," he commanded. The demon sighed at his touch, and we looked into the man's stormy gaze. I felt a tug at my dwindling consciousness, but no name came forth.

"Sara, it's time to come back now. Your friends need you. Roland needs you."

Those names meant nothing to us. The demon blinked and stood with its arms at its side. I took one last look at those demanding gray eyes and began to slip away into the endless cavern of the demon's mind. I sensed rather than felt the slap against the demon's cheek and its head snapping back as the man shook the demon.

"Goddamnit! You will not do this. Do you hear me?" The words were faint, but the furious tone stirred a glimmer of recognition. I felt the demon twist violently as it struggled to break free of the arms that encircled it like bands of steel. I heard its roar of frustration when a voice began to speak incessantly into its ear. The words reached me like echoes in a vast room, and there was nowhere I could turn to avoid them.

"You were right, Sara; you are not weak. In fact you are one of the strongest, most infuriating people I have ever met. You fight monsters, you befriend trolls and beasts, and you face horrors that would break a lesser person. And you walk headfirst into danger to protect the ones you care about. You are loyal, stubborn, and foolhardy and, though you don't believe it, you are a warrior."

The demon stopped moving, and I floated closer to the man's voice. A name floated just out of reach and I knew it belonged to the man whispering in our ear. Nikolas.

"Few Mohiri could have done what you did tonight, giving up yourself to save those trolls," Nikolas said with quiet conviction. "You did what you had to do, and now you have to come back to us. To Roland."

The name conjured an image of a smiling face with warm blue eyes. "Roland?" I was not sure if it was me or the demon who spoke.

"That's right. Your friend, Roland. He needs you now."

Memories burst across my mind – my life, my friends, Nate – it all came rushing back. Roland needed me? I struggled against the demon, but it was too strong. The Mori settled back, enjoying its new freedom and the feel of the strong young body it possessed.

Desperation filled me. I reached for the power I had closed off when I released the demon. The Mori knew what I was going to do, and it fought me, trying to force me into the same place where it had been contained all these years. But I was gaining strength, enough to nudge open the gate. The Mori was strong, but it was no match for the tide of power that swept upward, pushing it back and forcing it into its previous state of sullen watchfulness. *No fair*, it whined as the barrier shot back up.

Sounds filled my ears: people talking and shouting, someone crying. My eyes focused, and I found myself looking at Nikolas's worried face. For a moment, I was disoriented until it all came back to me slowly. Then I remembered Nikolas's words, and the world slammed back into focus.

"What happened to Roland?"

18

"Where is he?" I cried as I raced through the main foyer of the house, skirting around fallen bodies of men and vampires without sparing them a glance. I burst through the front doors to find two men I did not know standing guard on the steps, their warrior garb identifying them as Mohiri. They stared at me curiously and one of them who looked Indian said, "Who?"

"My friend, Roland. Nikolas said he was shot."

"Oh, the werewolf," his Korean companion replied dismissively. "He took a round of silver to the chest. His pack came and took him away a little while ago. Didn't look good."

His words, spoken with such indifference, were like a knife in my heart. "No!" I darted past them down the steps to the driveway. My breath came in short gasps, and it felt like my chest was in a vise. I couldn't lose Roland. I turned back toward the house as Nikolas came through the door. "I have to go to him. Please. He needs me."

He came down the steps, sympathy written on his face. "Roland is with his people. If anyone can help him, they can." He stopped in front of me. "The men had silver ammo, most likely to protect themselves from the vampires they were working with."

I shook my head and backed away. "No, no, you don't understand. I can help him."

Nikolas put his hands on my shoulders. "He took a direct hit in the chest,

Sara. The pack will do what they can for him, but this type of injury is almost always fatal to werewolves. I'm sorry."

"No! I won't let that happen!" I pulled away from him and swiped at the tears running unchecked down my cheeks. I raised my eyes to his. I would beg him if I had to. I would do anything to reach Roland. "I know I've been nothing but trouble to you and you have no reason to do this for me, but I have no one else. Please help me, Nikolas."

Nikolas turned away, and I closed my eyes as my heart broke.

"Erik, I need your bike."

My eyes flew open as the Korean man who had so casually written Roland off as dead tossed a set of keys. Nikolas caught them and led me to two black motorcycles, handing me a helmet before he started one of the bikes. I jumped on behind him, and we took off. He slowed down at the gate, and I saw a tangle of bodies lying on the cobbled driveway. So much death. I closed my eyes and pressed my helmet against Nikolas's back to block out the sight. I would not let my best friend become another casualty of this bloodshed. *Please, God... let us get there in time.*

Nikolas did not try to talk to me as we sped back to New Hastings. I wrapped my arms around his body and clung to him as I tortured myself with images of Roland dying before I reached him. My visor was wet with tears by the time we hit the Knolls.

Brendan's farm had always been the hub of activity for the family, so I knew that was where we would find Roland. The house was lit up and the driveway packed with vehicles when we got there. What if we were too late?

Nikolas drove the motorcycle along the edge of the driveway, taking me right to the front door where a dozen or so people milled around the step. Roland's cousin Francis was there along with the two men who had shown up after the crocotta attack. I leapt off the bike and tossed the helmet aside as I ran up to them.

"Haven't you done enough?" Francis demanded angrily, blocking my way to the door. "You are not welcome here."

I had no defense because he was right. This was my fault. But Roland was my best friend and I would be damned if I'd let anyone keep me from him, especially now.

"I have to see him." I started to push my way through, but one of the other men held me back with one hand. I twisted, trying to break his grip. "Let me go!"

"Take your hand off her," said a voice so frigid that the air around us seemed to drop several degrees. Nikolas walked up behind me, and the man's hand fell from my arm but he did not move out of my way. The tension on the porch was palpable as the werewolves faced the Mohiri warrior.

The door opened and Brendan appeared holding a tobacco pipe. "What's going on here?" he growled, and everyone on the porch fell silent.

"Brendan." I used the distraction to slip between Francis and the man who had stopped me. "Please, I need to see Roland!"

He laid a large hand gently on my shoulder and shook his head. "I know how much you care about him, but you can't go in there right now. It's not safe."

"Not safe?"

"The silver went in too deep. It's too close to his heart, and we can't get to it. He's half mad with the pain, and he doesn't know anyone right now. He'd tear you apart."

At that moment, an agonized howl split the air, and I gasped at the pain I heard in it.

"He can't heal," Brendan explained gruffly. He coughed, and his eyes glistened. "A couple of hours at the most."

"No!" I pushed past him, and he did not try to stop me. "Roland is not going to die!"

The house was full of people, most of whom I recognized from my time spent out in the Knolls with Roland and Peter. Some looked at me in confusion as I barreled past them, and others sent me openly hostile stares. I ignored them all and shoved my way through them until I saw Judith step out of a room at the end of the hall. She carried herself with strength, but her face was lined with grief.

I went to her, expecting her to throw me out of the house. Not that I wouldn't deserve it. But I was willing to risk her rejection if there was the smallest chance I could help Roland.

"Sara, you shouldn't be here," she said in a choked voice. "Roland wouldn't want you to see him like this."

"I have to see him, Judith. I can help him."

"Oh, honey." She pulled me into a tight hug and I let her, sensing that she needed it. "I know it's hard to accept, but there's nothing we can do for him now."

"But I can. I really can. Just let me try," I begged.

"This is no place for you, Sara," Maxwell said from behind me, and I could hear censure mingled with sorrow in his voice. "There is nothing you can do in there but cause yourself more grief. You should leave."

I spun to face him. "No, goddamnit!" My voice rose above the din and people started to turn our way. It was the first time I'd ever raised my voice to

Maxwell, but right now I didn't care if he was the damn alpha of a werewolf pack. "I'm not going anywhere until I see Roland!"

I grabbed Judith's hand and stared into her reddened eyes, willing her to believe me. "We can't give up on him without doing everything we can. I can help him."

"Sara – "

From inside the room a werewolf let out a long painful cry. I laid my hand on the door and felt the agonizing waves of pain on the other side. "Please," I begged Judith.

Judith looked at Maxwell then nodded at me. I reached for the doorknob.

"What's going on?" someone asked behind us. "What is she doing?"

I opened the door. "Whatever it takes."

I walked into the room and let out a strangled cry when I saw the creature foaming at the mouth and thrashing wildly in the corner. The room had been hastily stripped of its bed, and there was only a mattress on the floor. Thick chains ran from loops embedded in the floor to manacles on the werewolf's wrists and ankles. I shuddered to think that they had a room already set up to deal with something like this.

The wolf's fur was matted in places and still wet with blood, and there was blood on the walls, mattress, and floor. It was impossible to believe that this savage creature was my best friend.

"Roland?" I called softly, and the wolf began to snarl and strain at the chains. Someone yanked me out of the room, and I turned to see Nikolas.

I held up my hand. "It's alright. I just tamed two hellhounds, remember?"

Whispers started in the crowd behind us. Nikolas reluctantly let me go, and I went into the room again. I sat on the floor like I had in the cellar earlier tonight and opened myself to let the warm energy fill the room. I forced myself to relax, and then I began to talk to him in the same soothing tone I'd used on the hellhounds. I had doubted myself when I first tried to tame the dogs, but now I knew what I could do. A crazed werewolf could not be much different than a pair of monstrous hellhounds.

"Roland, do you know who I am?"

The werewolf bared his impressive fangs and answered me with a low threatening growl.

"I see. Well, that won't do at all. I know you're in a lot of pain, and we're going to deal with that soon, but first I think we need to have a talk. Or I'll talk and you can listen. How does that sound?"

Another growl filled the room.

"I know I said that Remy was my first friend here, but you were always my best friend. The best times of my life have been with you and Peter.

Remember when we used to have slumber parties and Brendan let us camp out in the hayloft that one time? We told ghost stories until we were all too scared to sleep, and we ended up sneaking back into the house after everyone else went to bed. Or the time you nipped some of Brendan's whiskey, and we got drunk for the first time. I never touched that stuff again."

I talked for half an hour, reliving the happiest memories I had of him and reminding him of the things we hadn't done yet, the plans we'd made. My power filled the small room, and slowly the wolf eased its thrashing and stared at me with tortured eyes. I stopped talking and noticed the silence in the room. It took me a few seconds to realize that the whole house was quiet; everyone was listening to me.

"Roland?"

The wolf let out a short mournful whine, his yellow eyes never leaving mine.

"You were pretty shocked to learn about Remy, weren't you? But he's not my only secret. Remember the other day after the marina when I said there were things I had to tell you about me? Do you want to know what it is – what I can do?"

He blinked and made a small whimpering sound.

I got to my knees and began to inch slowly toward him until Nikolas grabbed my arm to hold me back. "What are you doing? That's an injured werewolf. He'll rip you apart."

"No, he won't," I said without taking my eyes off the wolf. "You always ask me to trust you. Now it's time for you to trust me."

He held on for a long moment before he slowly released me. I continued toward Roland, stopping at the edge of the mattress to let a stronger wave of power flow over him. "I know it hurts a lot, but I'm going to make the pain go away now. You know I would never hurt you, don't you?"

The werewolf eyed me warily as I reached out one hand. It felt like the entire house held its breath as my hand touched a hairy paw. As soon as I made contact I sent the power pooled in my hand pouring into him. The effect was slower than I was used to, but none of my other patients had been a four hundred pound werewolf.

"There you are," I said when the yellow eyes finally softened in recognition. "You had me worried there."

The wolf opened his jaws and made an inhuman sound like he was trying to talk to me before he sagged against the mattress and let out a shuddering sigh. My heart broke at seeing my friend in so much pain.

"Shhh," I whispered to him, laying my other hand on his chest so my power could search for his injuries. It did not take long to find the source of his pain, a silver pellet embedded in one of the muscles around his heart. I needed to remove it if he was going to live. I had never used my power to remove a foreign object, but I imagined it wasn't that different from forcing an infection from the body. I hoped that was the case, because Roland's life depended on it.

I laid both hands over his heart and focused my healing on the piece of silver, trying to shrink it like I would an infection. I felt it twitch, but it refused to be removed from the muscle.

The wolf looked up at me with trusting eyes, and I gave him a reassuring smile. "I think this is going to require a bit more contact."

I lowered my body to the mattress amid gasps from the people crowding the doorway, and wrapped my arms around the huge furry body. He did not resist when I pulled him to me and released a torrent of energy into him, directing it to the piece of silver that was slowly killing him. I held on tight as the heat built up in my chest where it touched him, and my hands began to glow like pieces of iron in a forge. The werewolf twitched violently when the fire surrounded the silver pellet, slowly melting it and incinerating it into oblivion. The healing fire receded enough to fix the damaged tissue and smother the deadly fever that had started to spread through his body. When I could feel no more injury or sickness, I pulled the power back inside me.

My arms loosened their hold, and I sagged against the wolf, more drained than I had ever been after a healing. "Now you know my secret," I mumbled happily.

After several minutes, I felt the body next to me begin to shrink and lose hair. From somewhere close by I heard shouts and Brendan's booming voice say, "Holy Mary, Mother of God!"

Arms lifted me and held me against a warm hard chest. "I think she's just exhausted," Nikolas said, his voice a mixture of worry and reverence. "Hopefully, all she needs is some sleep."

So I slept.

A shaft of sunlight across my face woke me up. I raised a hand over my eyes and stared at the vaguely familiar lace curtains and striped wallpaper for a minute before I shifted to look around the room. My eyes fell on the shape of someone sitting on a chair in the corner.

"How are you feeling?"

I rubbed my blurry eyes, feeling like the one time I'd had a hangover. "I've been better. Where am I?"

"At the farm. You weren't in any shape to go anywhere last night."

The farm? Last night came flooding back to me. "Roland!"

"He's fine. He's down the hall." The chair scraped and Nikolas sat beside the bed blocking the sunlight. His expression was hard to read. I couldn't tell if he was going to take my hand or yell at me.

"Is this normal after you do that?" he asked quietly. "Passing out?"

"After a healing? It doesn't usually knock me out like that, but I've never healed a werewolf before." I stifled a yawn. "Usually I'm okay if I rest for an hour or so."

"You do this a lot?"

I gave him a tired smile. "More times than I can remember. I've been doing it since I was six."

He looked thoughtful for a moment. "That day on the wharf, you asked me if Mohiri had other powers. You wanted to know if we could heal others."

"Yes."

He ran a hand through his hair, and I noticed he was wearing the same clothes he had on yesterday. "I don't know of any Mohiri who can do what you did last night. Is that what you did with those two monsters in that cellar?"

I nodded. "I've used it before to calm animals, but I had no idea it would actually work on hellhounds." I thought about the two hounds with a touch of awe. "What happened to them? You didn't – ?"

"They tried to follow you, so Chris and Erik had them restrained. They'll be transported to one of our facilities until we figure out what to do with them." He smiled for the first time since I woke up. "We couldn't have a pair of hellhounds running amok around Portland."

"What kind of facility? I don't want them hurt." I could only imagine the tortures those hounds had suffered already in their lives.

"No one will harm them." Nikolas shook his head and let out a short laugh. "They are yours now. Once a fell beast imprints on a new master, they are incredibly loyal. They will only answer to you."

"That's what the witch said." He raised an eyebrow, and I told him the Hale witch had been in the cellar but didn't try to stop me.

He rubbed his hand over his jaw, and I saw that he needed a shave. I felt the craziest urge to reach out and touch his face, but I stopped myself just in time. That healing must have really messed me up.

"A lot happened in that cellar last night. Do you want to talk about it?"

"No." I turned my face away so he couldn't see the horror and revulsion in my eyes. I'd let that *thing* take over my body. All my life I'd kept the demon subdued in a corner of my mind, never knowing what it was or understanding its real strength – until last night. I suppressed a shudder at the memory of how quickly the demon had grown, filling my skin and occupying my mind until I almost forgot I still existed. It was locked behind its walls again, but I would never forget how close it had come to imprisoning me. I would never let it have that kind of power over me again.

"Every Mohiri struggles with their Mori at some point in their lives. For most it happens when they are younger and lack the training to manage the demon impulses. You have such control over your Mori that it must have been very frightening to let your guard down the way you did. But don't let your fear make you forget why you did it. You saved those trolls."

I pressed my lips together tightly and fought the tears that burned behind my eyelids. After Nikolas had wrestled me from the demon, the first thing I saw was Remy kneeling in a corner with his three little cousins in his arms. The gratitude in his eyes and the happy cries of the little ones should have made it all feel worthwhile. I was happy Minka and the others were home safe again and we had prevented a bloody troll rampage, but coming so close to losing myself to the demon had changed something in me. I would still give my life to protect the people I loved, but I did not think I could ever give up my mind that way again... for anyone.

"You are stronger than the demon," Nikolas said as if he could see into my head and read my fears. "I knew that when I met you. But hearing how you fought off the Hale witch and then last night, watching you with the were-wolf, I realized you have power I can't comprehend. You saved more than one life last night. People here are calling you a hero."

I shifted and stared at the ceiling, remembering how Roland had looked when I walked into that room. "Some hero," I choked out. "Roland wouldn't have needed healing if I hadn't almost gotten him killed in the first place."

"What happened last night wasn't your fault, Sara. We found out who was behind all this. His name is Yusri al-Hawwash, and he is a billionaire oil sheik who found out two years ago he has Alzheimer's. He's been searching every-where for a cure, and he was looking for trolls long before you sold that bile. He's a desperate man with unlimited resources."

"But he would have looked somewhere else if I had been more careful."

"That still does not make you responsible for his actions." He moved closer. "Look at me."

I turned my head to meet his insistent gaze. "Yes, you have made mistakes, but you are not to blame for the greed and actions of another. Your fault lies in taking too much on yourself. You have to learn to trust people and stop trying to take on the world alone."

I sighed heavily. "My life was a lot less complicated a month ago. Maybe now things will start to settle down again."

It was Nikolas's turn to sigh. "I wish that were true, but after what I saw last night, I think you might be in more danger than we first thought."

I sat up with my back against the pillows. "What do you mean? We haven't seen any sign of vampires except those working for the sheik – which I totally don't get by the way. And the sheik's witch only tried to grab me to get to the trolls."

"Think about it, Sara. The young trolls were taken around the same time you were attacked at the rest stop, which means the sheik didn't need you to find the trolls. So why did they come after you when they had what they wanted?"

The implication of his words hit me just as he spoke again. "You want to know why vampires would risk helping humans kidnap trolls? What if the vampires wanted something and they made an agreement with the sheik – a trade of some kind? You for the trolls."

"No, the two vamps I ran into tried to kill me, not capture me." I realized I'd said the wrong thing when his nostrils flared. "Remy and I took care of them," I added quickly.

"You killed a vampire?" There was disbelief in his voice.

"With Remy's help. He's scary good."

Nikolas looked like he was about to say something but changed his mind. "Even if you are right about the vampires, there is one thing you're overlooking. You have an incredible ability. If word of it gets out, the sheik will be coming after you, and he won't be the only one."

"It won't do him any good. I can't heal humans," I said, earning a dubious look. "My uncle is in a wheelchair. If I could heal humans, don't you think he'd be the first one I'd heal?"

"But no one else would know that," he pointed out. "Last night was just a taste of what could happen. They will keep coming and people will get hurt. And don't forget, we still have a Master to worry about. He could come after you just to use you against Madeline."

My stomach tightened. "Don't hold back. I'm not quite paralyzed with fear yet."

"You need to hear these things, Sara."

"You're trying to scare me, to get me to go with you," I accused him.

His eyes held mine. "Yes, I am. But that doesn't make them any less true."

My heart sank because he was right. This was no longer about my freedom or what I wanted. If I stayed in New Hastings, I would put everyone I cared about in real danger. I might not be able to heal the next one who got hurt. What if they came after Nate? I would never forgive myself. I didn't want to go to the Mohiri. But for now, it looked like my only option.

I looked away so he couldn't see the tears threatening again. "I-I need to tell Nate, to explain it to him. It's going to be hard for him to understand all this." I had no idea how I was going to even start telling Nate about everything. But I couldn't just take off.

"We have some things to wrap up in Portland that will take a few days, and it should give you the time you need with your uncle. I know this is hard for you, but you're doing the right thing." He got up and carried the chair back to the corner then opened the door. "I swear to you that I will keep you safe."

He closed the door quietly behind him, and I slid down to bury my face in the blankets. Part of me wanted to cry out my misery, and another part wanted to scream about the unfairness of it all. I didn't want to give up everything and everyone I knew and slink away into hiding. I wanted things to go back to the way they were.

Pushing back the blankets, I stood and looked around for my sneakers. I slipped them on and ran my fingers through my tangled hair, wondering where I'd lost my scrunchie last night. I twisted my hair into a loose knot until I could find a hair tie then opened the door. I needed to see Roland before I did anything else.

I knocked on the other three doors upstairs, but Roland wasn't in any of them. Voices carried up the stairs, and I thought I heard his laugh. If he was well enough to be up, that was a good sign. I set my shoulders and descended the stairs.

The house had cleared out considerably since last night. In the living room I found Brendan, Judith, Roland, Peter, and Francis. It wasn't hard to figure out they were waiting for me. When I appeared, all talking stopped and everyone looked at me. Francis's glare told me he hadn't forgiven me for getting Roland hurt, no matter what I had done after. The others' expressions were a little harder to read, and I stopped nervously in the doorway, not sure what to say to them.

"Good morning, Sara. How are you feeling?" Judith asked.

"Good... thanks."

She jumped up and swept me into a tight hug. "Thank you," she whispered thickly into my ear. Sniffling, she let me go and hurried into the kitchen. I stood there feeling even more self-conscious.

Roland patted the spot next to him. "Are you alright?"

"I think I'm supposed to ask you that." I studied his face to see for myself that he was okay. He looked a little paler than usual but, other than that, no signs of illness.

His smile was tired, but his blue eyes twinkled. "*That* was the secret you were going to tell us? You don't like to do anything small, do you?"

Brendan cleared his throat. "What you did last night was... incredible. We've never met anyone with your ability so you can imagine we're all very curious. Can you tell us about it? Have you always been able to do that?"

"I found out I could heal animals when I was six." I told them how I started out healing animals and learned later I could heal nonhumans. I tried to describe how it felt when I used the power, but it was like them trying to tell me how it felt to shift. I explained that it always made me tired and how much depended on the extent of the healing. They had a lot of questions, and I tried to answer them all.

"So you've done a lot of these healings?" Brendan asked.

"More than I can count."

Roland sat up straighter and stared at me with new understanding. "That time Uncle Brendan's mare hurt her leg and everyone thought they'd have to put her down, no one could believe it when the vet said the leg was sound. That was you, wasn't it?"

I nodded. I would never forget that day three years ago when we showed up at the farm to find it in an uproar because one of the horses had lamed itself. I'd run straight for the barn and waited until everyone left before I fixed the fractured bone. Roland had found me asleep by the barn door and teased me about it all night.

"There were other times too, now that I think of it," Brendan said almost to himself. "My old Lab that got shot out in the woods, *and* that sickly litter of kittens the cat abandoned. I never could understand how any of those animals survived. Now that I remember it, you were here every time."

"How did you manage to keep this from us all this time?" Roland wanted to know. "How is that no one ever figured out what you could do?"

I lifted my shoulders. "I had to work to hide it. You don't know how hard it was. Remember when I started volunteering at the animal shelter and you guys couldn't understand why I quit after a few weeks when I loved it so much? Whenever they brought in a sick dog or cat, I had to heal it. I couldn't help myself. But then someone noticed all the animals suddenly improving. I had to leave to protect my secret. It's bothered me ever since, because there were so many animals I could have helped."

Peter had been quiet since I came downstairs, and I could tell he was still pretty shaken up by last night. He looked at me with a kind of reverence that made me uncomfortable. "So the biggest thing you've ever healed is a horse?"

"Yes, but that was nothing compared to a werewolf."

He grinned. "Well, you turned out to be a good one to have around in a fight. We're lucky you were here last night."

"Lucky?" Francis snorted angrily. "If she wasn't messing with trolls and dragging you guys into her mess, Roland wouldn't have been hurt in the first place."

"Francis..." Brendan began.

"I'm part of this pack, and I get to say my piece." Francis looked ready to jump out of his seat at any second. I thought about the animosity that had always existed between us and knew this just added to his reasons to dislike me. The hard part was that he was right. Roland and Peter had both been hurt yesterday because of me. What if Peter hadn't been able to heal himself? What if Roland had died on the spot or I hadn't gotten to him in time?

"Last night proved what I've been saying for years – we need to stick with our own kind and leave everyone else to their own business. Now we have crocotta coming onto our land, something they have never done before. We have Mohiri hanging around like they own the place and we've been dragged into a fight with vampires and goddamn witch doctors over trolls who would rather tear your heart out than look at you. And it's all because of her." He pointed at me, and I met his contemptuous stare quietly. "You all have always been soft on her because she's the poor little orphan girl. But she's not so little anymore *and* she's not even human. She's one of them for Christ's sake, so she should be with them. Since when do we welcome Mohiri into our homes?"

"Francis, that's enough!" Judith admonished sharply from the doorway.

"He's right," I said loudly, and everyone stared at me. "Everything he said is true – except about the trolls. Remy's always been a good friend to me. I should have known better about the bile, and I should have said no when he asked me to use it. Just because he's a troll doesn't mean he understands people or how dangerous they can be." I took in a shaky breath. "I understand if you hate me, but none of this is his fault."

Roland laid his hand over mine after I finished my impassioned speech. "Sara, no one here hates you. Don't mind Francis. You know how he is."

Francis sneered at him. "Of course you stand up for her, Roland. You've had a thing for her since you met her."

What? I turned to Roland, and a flush crept up his neck. "Maybe back when we were younger... but not for a long time." He gave me a sideways look. "Oh, come on. All the boys liked you when you started school with us. Pete did, too."

The look on Peter's face told me he wanted to pound Roland for pulling him into this. "Yeah, but after a while we decided that we didn't want to fight about it."

I made a choked sound. Judith coughed and disappeared into the kitchen again, and I was sure I heard muffled laughter from the other room. I sank farther into the couch, wishing it would swallow me up.

"See, that's what I mean. You guys were always biased when it came to her. I'm not saying Sara is a bad person. But she's not good for the pack." Francis leaned forward in his chair. "And I'm not the only one who thinks that."

"It's not your place to say that," Brendan said sternly, and I thought I heard a growl beneath the words. "Max and I discussed this last night, and we will decide what is good for this pack, not you or anyone else."

"Fine," Francis said sullenly. He stood and stomped to the door. "But if Maxwell agrees with you, why isn't he here right now?" He slammed the door hard behind him.

No one spoke for a long, cruel moment, during which terrible doubts assailed me. Was it true? Did Maxwell share Francis's sentiment? Maxwell could be a hard person sometimes – almost the opposite of his brother and sister – and his gruffness often made me feel like a little kid waiting for a scolding. I understood him a little better since learning he was the leader of a werewolf pack, but it didn't make me any less worried about his displeasure. If he was as angry as Francis implied, would he order Roland and Peter to stay away from me? As alpha his commands had to be obeyed no matter what my friends wanted. My heart squeezed painfully at the thought of losing them after everything we'd been through. My dad was gone, I'd lost Remy, and in a few days I had to leave Nate and my friends and everything I knew. I didn't think I could survive another loss.

Brendan let out a long, deep sigh, and my fear grew at the grim set of his jaw as he looked at me. Brendan was the kind-hearted one, the peacemaker, and they'd decided that he should be the one to tell me I was no longer welcome here. I braced myself for the blow and saying good-bye to the people who had been like a family to me.

"Max and I are not pleased with what's been going on here lately, especially how reckless and foolish you youngsters have been. Last night, you never should have gone off like that without alerting the pack to what was going on. Because of that, we almost lost a pack member, and that is inexcusable." Beside me, Roland tensed and hung his head as Brendan continued. "You two are young men now and should know not to go off alone, which means something is obviously missing in your training. That will be remedied soon enough, I promise you."

He turned his attention back to me, and I shrank away from the disapproval in his eyes. "We made some allowances for you, considering your past and everything going on in your life lately. It's a lot to deal with for someone your age. But you've shown a lack of good judgment and a reckless disregard for your safety that we never would have expected from you."

"I'm sorry," was all I could say past the lump in my throat.

"For all your mistakes you are a good person, Sara, and no one doubts your loyalty and courage. What you did here last night was nothing short of miraculous. You saved one of ours, and the pack does not forget something like that. So where does that leave us?"

"I... don't know."

Brendan's expression did not falter. "Max thinks you three need to be separated because you encourage each other's bad behavior."

"What?" Peter cried and Roland shouted, "No!" I didn't say anything because I was not surprised. The ache in my chest grew, and cold settled in my stomach.

Brendan held up a hand. "We talked it over, and we decided that breaking up your friendship would be cruel, *but* there will be some new rules if you want to keep it. To start, for the next three months, the only place you will see each other is at school. Every spare minute you boys have will go to extra training, and trust me you'll be too tired to get into trouble. There will be no more adventures like last night. You three pull something like that again and that's it. Understood?"

All I could do was nod. I was so relieved that Maxwell hadn't ordered me to stay away from the pack that I was afraid I'd start to cry if I spoke. Roland shifted like he was about to argue, and I squeezed his hand hard to stop him. This was the harshest I'd ever seen Brendan, which said a lot about how serious he was. I didn't want to push the matter.

Brendan was not finished. "There is one other thing. Sara, you need to tell your uncle what is going on in your life. We aren't going to try to force you to do it, but it's not fair to him for you to be running around putting your life and maybe his in danger and keeping him in the dark about it. He deserves better than that. You've been on your own for far too long without supervision. I'm not saying that Nate is a bad parent, just that he is not informed enough to guide you properly and set restrictions when needed."

"I'm going to tell him today when he gets home."

"Good." Brendan slapped his hands against his knees and stood. "The three of you have to work to earn back the trust you lost, starting now. Maxwell is coming over soon to talk to you boys, and I promise it will not be pleasant. The Mohiri is outside waiting to give Sara a ride home."

Roland tightened his grip on my hand. "Already? Can't she stay a little while longer?"

"No, I need to go," I said, already dreading the task ahead of me. "I should get home before Nate does."

Peter made a feeble attempt at a smile. "It's only three months, right?"

His words brought on a pang of anguish. I had to tell them I was leaving, and it hit me just how hard it was going to be to say good-bye to them. We'd stay in touch somehow, but it would never be the same as what we had here. It hurt to think of not finishing our senior year together, not sitting together at graduation or looking at colleges together.

"I... made a decision," I said, unable to look at them. "I'm going to stay with the Mohiri for a while."

"What?" Roland cried in disbelief.

"Nikolas doesn't think it's over with the vampires, and I-I think he might be right." I told them about the sheik and Nikolas's theory that vampires were working with the humans to try to get to me. And that the sheik might come after me if he thought I could heal his disease. "No one is safe as long as I'm here."

"We can take care of ourselves," Peter argued.

"You can, but what about Nate? He'd be defenseless if they came after him to get to me. Nikolas said I'll be safe with the Mohiri, especially if there is a Master in the picture." I looked at each of them, my eyes pleading with them to understand. "I don't want to go, but I don't think there's any other way to keep Nate safe."

"What about the trolls?" Roland asked hopefully. "They're your friends, right? Won't they help if you ask them?"

I shook my head. "Remy says the elders know about us selling the bile and they will forbid him from seeing me. If we're lucky, it won't be a forever thing, but I don't think I can count on any help there." I hadn't even begun to process the pain of losing Remy's friendship. I pushed it to the back of my mind because if I had to deal with one more loss right now, I would break.

"Damn! Even trolls get grounded," Peter said with a whistle.

We fell quiet for a few minutes until Roland finally said, "So, you're going to tell Nate everything and then leave. I don't think he's going to handle this well."

I groaned. "He's not going to take it well either way. And you know him – he won't believe anything without proof."

"I could come over and shift for him," Peter offered, and I let out a humorless laugh.

"Yes and give him a heart attack. I think seeing a werewolf up close and personal will be too much for him, even if it is you."

"Hmm, you're probably right."

"I'll figure something out. Maybe I can show him an imp. Our place is full of them."

"Probably not a good idea to tell him he has a demon infestation," Roland pointed out dryly. "Especially with you leaving."

This was going to be even harder than I'd thought. There was not going to be an easy way to break any of this to Nate, but I needed to show him something or he'd never believe me. "I need a way to show him proof without scaring the hell out of him."

"Okay, so no close encounters," Roland thought out loud. "Maybe a picture of something... or a video."

"You mean like a video of an imp?" Unless you got close enough to see their very sharp teeth, they looked pretty harmless. "How will he know it's not a fake? It has to be something he can't refute."

Peter's face lit up. "I have an idea. Give me your phone."

19

"Please say something."

Nate stared blankly at his hands clasped in front of him on the kitchen table. He had been sitting like that for the last five minutes.

My chest tightened. All day I had tried to prepare myself to talk to him while dreading his reaction. My worst fears had come to pass. He wouldn't even look at me.

His face lifted, and his troubled eyes met mine. "What do you want me to say? When you said you had to talk to me, I was worried you'd been suspended or something. Instead, you tell me this crazy story. If I didn't know you better, I'd ask if you were on something."

"I know it's a lot to take in."

He let out a strangled laugh. "Just a bit."

I wanted to reach across the table and take his hand, but I was afraid of his reaction. Anxiety and fear twisted my gut in knots. Nate was the only family I had; I couldn't bear it if he pulled away from me now.

There had been no easy way to come clean to him so I'd just dived in head first, fumbling my way through the story that grew more fantastic by the minute. How did you tell someone you loved that nothing in their world was as it seemed and that they were surrounded by a whole other world of magic and people and creatures that should not exist?

Nate had listened quietly while I told him I'd always believed there was more to my dad's death than the authorities had said. His eyes had grown wide when I explained how I had learned I could heal animals when I was little. When I'd begun describing how I met Remy and discovered that every mythical creature I'd ever heard of was real, his face had become a mask of disbelief.

Then the real hard part came. Using as little detail as possible, I told him about Eli, Nikolas, and the werewolves and what had been happening for the past month. His tight-lipped expression made my heart ache as I revealed what I'd learned about Madeline and the truth about my dad's murder. I stopped there because I couldn't go any further without hearing him say something, anything.

Nate let out a deep breath. "I'd think this was all a big prank if not for... You'd never make up stories about your father."

"No, I wouldn't."

"I-I don't know what to think. You have to understand that this would be hard for anyone to believe."

I nodded, grateful that he was still here talking to me. That was something at least.

He leaned back heavily, and his wheelchair creaked. "You're not telling me everything," he said, studying my face.

I swallowed. "I didn't want to lay too much on you at once."

"You wanted to see how I'd react?"

"Yes."

He rubbed his brow and fixed me with the look of a person waiting to hear something they knew would not make them happy. "Tell me."

I told him about meeting David and everything that happened at the rest stop. He made a sound when I recounted our close escape, but I kept talking, afraid that if I stopped I wouldn't be able to continue. I told him about Remy and the missing trolls, our trip to Portland, and the rescue. I glossed over the worst of it because I didn't think he could handle hearing the gory details, especially what I'd done to get the trolls out of the cage. It was asking enough of him to accept what I'd told him already. I finished by telling him about Roland being hurt and how I'd healed him.

He was quiet and still for a long moment, and I feared I'd told him too much, that he was in shock. Finally, he ran a hand through his already disheveled hair. "Jesus! I... Jesus..."

"Are you alright?"

"I don't know. I don't know what to think. I-I need some time to process this."

I let out a deflated sigh. It wasn't like I had expected him to be okay with everything right away, but I'd hoped... well, I don't know what I'd hoped for. It killed me to see how much I was hurting him. If I had been honest with him all along, he would not be looking at me right now like I was a stranger.

"I have something for you." I pushed my phone across the table to him. "Peter thought it might help you."

He stared at the phone without reaching for it. I stood and left the kitchen, almost running upstairs to my room. I stood at the top of the stairs and listened when he played the video Peter had made for him. Then I sat on my bed and waited for him to call me back down to talk about it.

When darkness fell, I climbed into bed and stared numbly at the ceiling until I could no longer keep my eyes open. I didn't even bother to undress.

I didn't get up for school the next day, and Nate did not call for me to get up. It was ten o'clock when I finally dragged myself downstairs, bleary-eyed and feeling like my heart was encased in lead. In all the years I'd lived with Nate, we'd had our share of arguments, but he had never let us start a new day without trying to sort things out.

His silence told me just how much I'd hurt him this time – not because of what I'd revealed to him – but because I'd been lying to him for years. Last night, lying in bed, it hit me just how much pain my confession had brought him. All this time, I'd carried the knowledge that there was more to my dad's death and all I could think about was how I needed to know the truth for me, for my own closure. Not once had I ever considered Nate's loss or grief or that he deserved to know the truth about his brother. I had to make things right. There was no way I could leave with things so messed up between us.

I walked into the kitchen, but my stomach was tied in too many knots to even think about eating. Disappointment swept over me when I looked out the window and saw that Nate's car was gone. I was hoping we could talk this morning, but it looked like he needed more time to sort through things first.

To while away the hours until he returned, I cleaned the apartment from top to bottom. Around eleven the school called, and I let the machine pick up. I paused wiping down the refrigerator when it hit me that I was actually dropping out of school – and in my senior year. I should be thinking about college applications, prom, and graduation – normal things. But nothing in my life would ever be normal again.

My cell phone rang a little while later. It was Nikolas letting me know he and Chris were still in Portland with some of the other Mohiri, cleaning up after Saturday night and hunting down any vampires that got away. The werewolves, he told me, had offered to beef up their patrols in town today to watch over me and Nate until Nikolas got back. He said he would be back in New Hastings tonight so we could leave tomorrow morning. I listened and said "yes" and "no" where I was supposed to. I figured I should wait until he got here to explain that I could not leave town tomorrow, not until I made things right between me and Nate.

At two o'clock, restlessness drove me outside. I sat on the top of the stairs listening to the familiar sounds of the waterfront while I waited for Nate to return. But soon a cold, damp fog crept in off the bay and sent me back into the warmth of the apartment. Gazing out through the living room window at the gray-shrouded waterfront, I felt more alone than I had ever felt before. All I wanted was for Nate to come home so I could ask him to please forgive me and tell me I hadn't destroyed our relationship, that there was still a chance for us to be a family.

Half an hour later, when I couldn't take another minute of waiting, I heard a sound at the front door. I raced from the living room to greet Nate and to beg him to please talk to me. Halfway to the door I stopped short, my stocking feet skidding on the hardwood floor when I realized I hadn't heard his car drive up or his wheelchair on the ramp.

The doorknob jiggled, and my heart began to hammer against my ribs. Did I lock the door?

The answer was a soft click. The door creaked open a fraction of an inch, and I stood frozen as whoever or whatever was on the other side prepared to come in.

I jumped as a low keening suddenly came from the door, and it took me a few panicked seconds to realize that the sound came from the door itself and not from whoever was on the other side. The noise grew, rapidly rising in pitch and volume until I had to clap my hands over my ears to block out the piercing sound. Around the door the frame glowed red, throwing off sparks like the embers in a fireplace. In the center of the door the shape of an ashy hand appeared.

Screeching and the nauseating stench of scorched flesh filled the air as someone or something thrashed violently on the other side of the door. Seconds later the door slammed shut followed by the sound of someone stumbling down the stairs.

Freed from my paralysis, I scrambled to pull the deadbolt and ran to the kitchen window. But all I could see was the swirling fog that obscured anything more than a few feet from the building. My whole body shook, and I gripped the counter with numb fingers. Something was out there, something that meant me harm, and if it wasn't for the troll warding, they would be in here now. The chill creeping along my spine told me it was still out there, hiding in the mist and waiting to try again.

I didn't have to wait long. A minute later I heard a high-pitched whine downstairs followed by an inhuman howl of pain. I almost knocked over a chair as I bolted from the kitchen like a frightened rabbit. Whatever was out there was determined to get inside. The troll magic was very powerful and it would protect me as long as I stayed inside, but it could do nothing to stop the fear knotting my stomach.

You're safe. Don't panic. Nikolas would be here in a few hours. Nothing would hurt me or Nate once he was here.

Nate! What if he came home while that person *or thing* was outside? He wouldn't stand a chance.

I tore around the living room, searching for my cell phone. My hands shook while I found the number Nikolas had put in my phone yesterday and listened to it ringing on the other end.

He knew something was wrong before I spoke. "Sara, what is it?"

"Something outside," I wheezed before I regained my voice. "They're trying to get in. The ward is holding, but Nate's not here. If he comes home and..."

My voice broke, and I heard him swear then shout harshly at someone. "We're coming. Stay right where you are, and do not hang up. I'm going to stay on the phone until we get there. Do you hear me?"

"Maybe I should call Maxwell," I told him, thinking the Knolls were a lot closer than Portland.

"No, stay on the phone with me," Nikolas ordered. "Chris is calling them now."

I heard a muffled sound then an engine starting. Nikolas's voice sounded a little hollow when he spoke again, and I realized he was using an earpiece inside his helmet. "I'm on my way."

"Okay," I said hoarsely, sinking down to sit against the wall farthest from the living room window. I pulled my knees toward me and laid my forehead against them as I prayed silently. *Please, please let him get here before Nate does.*

The phone in the kitchen rang, and I jerked upright. "What was that?" Nikolas asked.

"The house phone. Maybe it's Nate," I said hopefully, scrambling to my feet. I rushed into the kitchen and snatched up the cordless phone with my free hand. *Please let it be him.*

"Sara Grey?" asked a thickly-accented male voice.

"Yes?"

"I have your uncle."

My legs started to fold, and I leaned heavily against the cupboard as the cell phone in my other hand clattered loudly to the counter. I could hear Nikolas, shouting but my whole body was riveted to the phone in my hand.

"I will make a trade – him for you," the man continued in a businesslike manner. "If you care about him, you will do this because I have no qualms about ending his life if I don't get what I want."

"I'll do it," I cried, gripping the phone so hard my knuckles turned white. "How do I know I can trust you to let him go?"

He laughed coldly. "You do not, but he *will* die if you do not come to me. I will give you ten minutes. After that his life is forfeit."

"No! I'll come."

"Good girl. Go outside now. Someone is waiting to bring you to me."

The click on the other end was like a cell door slamming shut. I was trapped. If I didn't go, Nate would die. If I tried to stall until help got here, Nate would die. If I went, Nate might still die.

No. That is not going to happen, I swore as I laid the phone on the counter. Because I would die before I let anyone hurt him.

"Goddamnit, Sara, answer me!" yelled a furious Nikolas.

My hand was oddly steady when I put the cell phone to my ear again. "I'm sorry, Nikolas. I have to go," I told him flatly, guessing that he had heard enough of my conversation to know what I was going to do.

"Do not leave that apartment," he said in a tone that few people would disobey. "I'll be there in thirty minutes. Whatever it is, we can take care of it."

"It'll be too late." I was already running upstairs to change. "They have Nate, and they're going to kill him if I'm not there in ten minutes. I've made a lot of mistakes, but I will not let Nate die because of them."

"Sara, think about this. They are not going to just let your uncle go once they have you. If you do this, you could die."

"He'll die for sure if I don't go. I'm not going to hide here and do nothing while he's killed. I couldn't live with that." I picked up my coat and knife and went back to the kitchen. "You were right. All I do is put the people I love in danger. It has to stop now."

He started to say something, but I hung up. I pulled on my coat and tucked the knife in the inside pocket. My cell phone rang, and I knew it was Nikolas without looking at the number. I turned off the phone and stuck it in my back pocket before I let myself out and locked the door behind me.

I wasn't sure what to expect when I stepped outside, but it wasn't the eerie quiet that greeted me. There was no sign of whatever had tried to get past my wards, except for a few black drops on the landing that looked like burnt blood. I turned away from it, shuddering violently.

The fog was still thick but already starting to lift, allowing me to see a black Escalade with a dented bumper in front of our building. At the bottom of the stairs I took a deep breath to calm my racing heart before I approached the SUV. As I drew near, the door opened and the muscled blond man from the marina got out. He did not speak as he opened the rear door for me. I noticed bloody bandages on his hands, and I held back a smug grin. *Is that your blood on my doorstep? I hope it hurts like hell.*

I slid into the cool interior, and he returned to the passenger seat up front. I felt someone watching me, and I looked up to see a pair of angry, dark eyes in the rearview mirror. The driver turned his head toward me, and I sucked in a sharp breath when I recognized the man who had attacked me yesterday at the rest stop. Tarek's face bore the bruises from his fight with Peter, and his eyes told me he was itching for payback. Instead of speaking to me, he muttered something in Arabic to his companion, and they both laughed. I wrapped my arms tightly around me and stared blindly out the window. Part of me wanted to take one last look around, to drink in the picture of the place I had called home for most of my life, but a bigger part did not want to accept that this was the last time I might ever see it. I was willing to trade my life for Nate's, but that did not mean I was giving up yet. I'd survived too much these last few weeks to go down without a fight now.

It took us less than five minutes to reach our destination, and I was surprised to find us outside an empty three-storey building with a "For Rent" sign in the window only two streets away from mine. The Escalade parked on the busy street, and the blond man turned to me before he opened his door.

"Do not make a scene if you value your uncle's life," he said in halting English.

I nodded, and we got out. He led the way into the building where I had to strain to see through the dimness. Before my eyes could adjust, he took my arm. "Haism is waiting for you," he said, leading me toward a lit doorway at the back of the building.

"Nate!" I cried as soon as I saw him in his wheelchair beside a large metal desk. I broke away from the blond man and ran to kneel in front of Nate. "Are you okay? Did they hurt you?"

"I'm okay." He held me away from him and gave me a searching look. "Sara, what is going on? How do you know Mr. Bakr?" he asked in a lowered voice.

"Mr. Bakr?"

"Haism Bakr," said a familiar voice with a crisp Middle Eastern accent. I straightened and faced the hawk-nosed man I'd seen on the monstrous yacht at the marina. He was sitting behind the desk with his hands clasped in front of him and a scowl on his face. His dark eyes glittered with rancor as they swept over me. "My employer is very displeased with you, Miss Grey."

"You work for that sheik." I could not keep the disgust out of my voice.

His scowl deepened. "You have robbed him of something he went through great trouble to obtain," he growled.

My hackles rose. "That *something* was little children."

"Those creatures are not children," Haism spat. "The sheik is a powerful and important man. What are the lives of those things compared to his?"

"Will someone please tell me what the hell is going on?" Nate exclaimed. He turned to Haism. "What does my niece have to do with you and your employer, and why are you holding us here like this?"

"Remember what I told you about the man who took the trolls? Haism works for him." My mouth twisted in disgust. "You used that whole oil exploration thing as a cover to snoop around here, didn't you?"

Haism shrugged. "It made our presence here more believable. I do whatever is necessary for my employer."

I bit my lip to keep from saying what I thought of his employer. I wasn't going to help Nate by antagonizing this man. "I came as you asked. Please let my uncle go now."

Nate jerked forward in his chair. "What are you talking about?"

Haism's smile did not reach his eyes. "Do you really think you are in a position to negotiate, little girl? You have caused me nothing but headache, and because of you I have to go back to my employer empty-handed." He stood and came toward me. "In my country, a female is beaten for interfering in the business of men."

I heard Nate's sharp intake of breath as his hand gripped mine. Drawing strength from his touch I replied, "In my country, a man who does not keep his word has no honor."

Haism scowled darkly but stopped his advance on me. "I serve my employer. That is where my honor lies, so do not talk – "

A cell phone rang, and he pulled his from the front pocket of his pants. Something like fear flashed across his face when he looked at the screen. His eyes met mine as he put the phone to his ear.

"It's done."

The caller said something to which Haism replied, "Not so fast. My employer made a contract with you, but I am not so foolish as to trust you. I will tell you where to pick her up after my people and I are safely away."

My heart plummeted to my stomach. Her? He meant me. I thought he was taking me to his employer because they'd learned I could heal, but he was going to hand me off to someone else.

Haism let out a short laugh. "You have waited this long, vampire. A few more hours will not matter. I will call you and tell you where you can find her."

He hung up and tapped his chin with the phone. "For one so young you have drawn a lot of attention from some powerful... people. I do not know what you have done to bring this upon yourself, but what is done is done."

I barely heard his taunt because of the fear gripping me. Black spots floated before my eyes, and I gripped Nate's hand so hard he grunted in pain. After everything I'd been through, all the escapes and being watched around the clock, I was going to end up in Eli's clutches after all.

Nate pulled me closer to him. "What kind of people are you?" he demanded fearfully. "She's just a child."

Haism looked like he was going to answer, but then he turned away. He said something in Arabic to the two men flanking the door, and they nodded then took up positions just outside the door. Then he began to walk out of the room without a backward glance.

He's going to let them have Nate, too. The realization almost sent me to my knees. *No, I won't let that happen.*

The idea came to me out of sheer desperation, and I clutched it like a lifeline. "I want to make another trade," I called after Haism.

"You have nothing of value to me," he replied dismissively without looking back.

"How about the sheik's life?"

Haism stopped mid-stride and spun to look at me with narrowed eyes. "What did you say?"

"You heard me. How much is your beloved sheik's life worth to you?"

He stared at me, and I said, "I know he has Alzheimer's. It must be terrifying for such a powerful man to know he's going to slowly lose his memory, his mind before he dies."

He strode back to me, stopping inches away, his face contorted in fury. "Do not speak of him!"

I laughed coldly. "Or what – you'll kill me? Get in line. But that won't save your employer."

He studied me, trying to see if I was lying or trying to stall him. I stared back confidently, and he blinked first. "What do you have?" He could not disguise the hope in his voice, and I hid my triumph.

"Not more trolls if that's what you think," I said, reading the question in his eyes. "But I have the next best thing."

He stared at me blankly until realization finally dawned. "You have troll bile."

"Three whole ounces. Enough to keep your evil boss alive and kicking for many, many years."

There was no mistaking the hunger on his face at the prospect of redeeming himself in the eyes of his beloved sheik. "Where is it?" he hissed.

"Yeah, not so fast," I scoffed, determined to make this work. "First, we make a deal."

"Name it," he replied way too easily. Like I was going to trust him a second time.

"First, you let Nate go. One of your goons takes him home, and once he is safely inside he calls me to let me know he's there." There was no way Haism's men could get past my wards; their mauled hands were proof of that. The only way to assure Nate's safety was to get him inside our building.

Nate pulled me closer to him, his eyes wide with fear. "Sara, I'm not leaving you here alone with these people."

I squeezed his hand. "I'll be fine. Once I know you're safe, I'll take them to the bile and they'll let me go. That's all they want." It was probably the last lie I would ever tell him, so I might as well make it count.

"How do I know I can trust you to do this once I safely deliver your uncle home?" Haism asked.

"You don't," I replied, and his mouth tightened as his earlier words came back to him. "But can you afford not to?"

He glared at me, his eyes inky pools of hate. Haism was a man used to getting what he wanted, and he wanted what I had. He was also a very proud man, and I could see it rankled him a lot to not have the upper hand. However, it did not take long for his need to please his employer to overpower his pride. "We have a deal." He called to the blond man. "Gerhard, you will return Mr. Grey to his home. When it is done, I will tell you where to meet us. Tarek, you will come with me."

He looked at me again. "If you think to stall here until your friends find us, you are mistaken. We will take a ride until your uncle calls. Then you will take us to the bile."

Nate clung to my hand. "No. I'm not letting you do this, Sara."

I kneeled in front of his chair again and took both his hands in mine. "I know what I'm doing, and I'll be okay." I had no illusions about Haism willingly letting me go once I brought him to the bile, but this was the only way. I had a better chance of escaping Haism on my own if I didn't have to worry about Nate's safety.

A tap on my shoulder made me look up into Gerhard's unsmiling face. I stood and gave Nate a quick hug before the big blond man started to push the wheelchair out of the room. I fell in behind them with Haism and Tarak following us. Nate didn't say much until we reached the exit where he tried again to talk me out of it. Nothing I said to him convinced him I would be alright, and his face was drawn and fearful when Gerhard lifted him into the Escalade. My chest ached at the thought that this might be the last time I ever saw him, and I wanted to run to him and hug him one last time. But Haism kept a firm hold on my arm and I could only smile reassuringly at Nate as they drove away.

Haism led me to a white Cadillac sedan and told me to get in the back seat. He climbed in beside me, and Tarak got behind the wheel. He said a few words in Arabic to Tarak who started the car and began driving with no apparent destination in mind. Haism did not try to talk to me, and I was happy not to talk to him.

I thought about Nate and the vial of Ptellon blood still hidden in my room. If only I had given it to him yesterday, none of this might have happened. *It wouldn't have helped*, I told myself. Ptellon did not work against humans. I'd thought to protect Nate from monsters, but I forgot they came in human form, too.

It felt like an eternity had passed before Haism's phone rang, and I held my breath as he answered it then handed it to me. I saw my home number and exhaled deeply.

"Nate?"

"I'm fine. I'm home, and that man is gone."

"Good." My throat closed up in relief, and I could barely manage that one syllable.

Nate's voice shook. "Sara, he tried to come inside and he couldn't. Why?"

I shot Haism a glare. I'd suspected Gerhard had been ordered to deal with Nate once I thought he was safe. Getting what he wanted wasn't enough for a man like Haism. He needed to control everything. Not this time.

"I'll explain it when I get home," I replied, proud of myself for keeping the tears at bay.

I hung up and practically threw the phone at Haism. *I won't cry.* I would not let this man see me break down.

"My part of the deal is done," said Haism, his eyes glittering with anticipation. "Now you will do your part."

Nodding, I gave Tarak directions, and he immediately turned the car and headed south of town. It usually took me twenty minutes by bike to get to where we were going. It took five in the car. We turned off on the narrow dirt road that led to the abandoned mine, and branches whipped at the car as we passed. Soon we reached the spot where I usually hid my bike, and I told him to stop. "We have to walk from here."

Haism stared around suspiciously then fixed me with a hard look. "We're in the middle of nowhere. I pray for your sake you are not trying to deceive me."

"You think I'd hide troll bile at my house, or maybe in my school locker?"

He did not respond to that. We stayed in the back of the car until Tarak got out and came around to my side. They were obviously not taking any chances with me making a run for it.

"Check her," Haism said harshly, and I gasped as Tarak pulled me from the car and started to pat me down. My mouth went dry when his hands felt the weapon concealed inside my coat. He yanked open my coat and pulled out the silver knife to show Haism.

Stars exploded before my eyes and pain shot through the left side of my face as a fist came out of nowhere. My ears rang, and I staggered backward and would have fallen if Tarak had not caught me. Blood dribbled down my lips from my nose, and I dabbed it away with my sleeve.

"*Sharmoota!*" Haism shouted, his spittle spraying my face. "You think you can trick me?" He reached for me again, and I flinched, waiting for the next strike. Instead he pulled a plastic cable tie from his pocket. He wrenched my arms painfully and tied my hands behind my back. When that was done, he bent down and pulled off my sneakers and threw them into the woods.

"There. Try to run away now," he jeered. He took the knife from Tarak and flung it after the sneakers, then barked an order at the black-haired man. Tarak nodded and took up a lookout position near the car.

Haism grabbed my arm and pushed me so hard I stumbled and almost fell again. Jerking me upright, he shoved me forward. "Which way? And do not try anything. I will think nothing of breaking your neck and leaving you here for the animals to feed on."

I nodded in the direction we needed to go. "That way."

Walking over uneven terrain with my hands tied behind my back was difficult. Doing it with no shoes was excruciating. Within five minutes, my socks were bloody from the rocks and sharp sticks jabbing me mercilessly. The left side of my face had gone numb, and my eye had swollen and half closed up, making it harder to see where I was going. Haism yanked me forward viciously every time I faltered, and I pressed my lips together to keep from crying out. I would not give him the satisfaction.

"I am curious," he said as he waited for me to step over a fallen tree. "These trolls are savage creatures, even vampires fear them. You must be quite valuable to the vampires for them to willingly risk themselves to capture the young trolls."

"Is that a question or a statement?"

He scowled at me. "How is it that a human girl is able to befriend such beasts? How did you get your hands on the bile and live to speak of it?"

"You would never understand." In truth, there were very few people who could comprehend my relationship with Remy. I certainly wasn't about to explain it to the person who would terrorize children and who was about to hand me over to a vampire.

"Then perhaps you will tell me why that vampire wants you so badly. He is most determined to have you."

Just the mention of Eli made me stumble, and bile rose in my throat. "He tried to kill me and I got away. I guess he doesn't like it when that happens."

Haism barked a laugh. "All of that for a meal? I think not. He has worked too hard to possess you to end it that quickly."

My stomach churned. How could he talk about my death so casually? He had to know what Eli would do to me. Terror rose up, threatening to suffocate me, and I bit the inside of my cheek so hard I tasted blood. The sharp pain sliced through the dizzying fear so I could think a little clearer.

I'd known from the beginning that Haism had no intention of letting me go after I gave him what he wanted. His sheik had a deal with Eli, and Haism was going to deliver me as promised. His tone told me he actually enjoyed the idea of the horrors that awaited me. Even with a demon inside me, I was more human than the monster walking next to me.

The woods were somber and quiet, except for the occasional birdcall. Walking like a prisoner to my execution, it was hard to believe I'd spent so many happy hours in this place. There would be no Remy now to scold me or little Minka sneaking up to ambush me in a fit of giggles. The trolls could be watching me right now, and none of them would come to my rescue. It didn't matter that I had saved the little ones last night; to the elders I had only been righting the wrong I had done to them. I might have stopped a rampage, but I wasn't even close to earning their forgiveness. I was truly alone now. No one was coming to save me this time.

It was time to help myself. I took stock of my situation. I was shoeless, weaponless, and bound; there was no way I was running away from Haism like this. But we were headed for the cliffs, and I knew them better than almost anyone. And Haism would have to untie me to retrieve the bile. There had to be a way to escape him at the cliffs – because there was no way I'd let him turn me over to Eli. I swallowed hard as I made my decision. If I could not escape my captor, there was another way out and one leap was all it would take. One leap, a few seconds of fear, and then nothing. I would die on my own terms before I let Eli touch me.

As soon as I made my resolve, a sense of calm acceptance settled over me.

It was soon followed by sadness over the things I might never see or do and regrets for the unfinished things I was leaving behind. My biggest regret was Nate and all the time I'd lost that I could have spent building a relationship with him. He didn't deserve what I'd put him through, and if I didn't come back he would have to carry that with him for the rest of his life. My only comfort was that I'd been able to save him at least. I had made so many mistakes, and people I cared deeply about had been hurt because of me. Saving the trolls and Roland's life might have redeemed me if I hadn't put them in danger in the first place. Scott, too. He was a jerk, but I'd never wanted him to get hurt. He was just one more victim I'd left in my wake.

A phone rang. Haism pulled out his cell and rushed to answer it. He spoke in Arabic, and something in his submissive tone and posture told me it was the sheik. Haism appeared to explain something to him. Then his voice took on an apologetic, almost groveling tone. It was clear the sheik was not happy. I could hear his voice as he shouted at Haism, and I watched my captor's face grow pale and slack from the verbal lashing.

Haism slanted a look at me as if he realized for the first time that I was witnessing his castigation. His mouth twisted, and he pushed me roughly to the ground. I cried out as I landed in a heap with my arms twisted painfully beneath me. With great effort I scuttled backward until I was half-sitting with my back against a tree. The rough bark cut into my hands, and a low branch snagged my hair, making tears spring to my eyes. I was a mass of scrapes, cuts, and bruises, and I hadn't even been turned over to my real tormentor yet.

"Stay," Haism commanded sharply like he was talking to a dog. His frigid gaze swept over me before he walked a small distance away, now pleading with the man on the other end of the line.

To distract myself from my discomfort, I thought about Nate, Remy, Roland, and Peter and tried to remember a happy time with each of them. It surprised me to find myself thinking about Nikolas too, though in a way it made sense to think of him now. For the last month, almost everywhere I went he was there, jumping in to save me, stalking me, protecting me, scolding me. I remembered his teasing laughter that night at my place and the look in his eyes whenever he was furious with me. We were like two magnets constantly pushing at each other, and as much as he aggravated me, I had grown used to having him around.

I could almost hear him saying "I told you so" at the mess I'd landed in this time, and I could only imagine how angry he was at this moment because I hadn't listened to him – once again. Was he at my place now, trying to figure out where I was? He was pretty serious about this protection thing. How long would he search before he admitted I was lost this time?

A pang of sorrow stabbed me at the thought of Nikolas giving up on me and moving on with his life after everything we'd been through. My Mori stirred and gave a mournful sigh. *I know,* I consoled the demon. *He kind of grows on you.*

Consumed by my sorrow, I barely noticed the fleeting movement against my hand. It came again, and I held my breath as something warm touched my skin for a second. A mouse maybe. Animals were not afraid of me; it wasn't unusual for one to come up to me.

Another touch came, but this time it was not warm. This time something cold caressed the back of my hand. I sucked air in sharply as I heard a snip.

The cable binding my hands fell away.

Not daring to move, I shot a glance at Haism to see if he noticed anything. But he was still talking agitatedly into his phone and barely looking my way. Slowly I turned my head to look over my shoulder.

Whatever I was expecting, it wasn't a pair of owlish eyes in a small brown face partly hidden by a mass of untamed yellow hair. I almost fell over at the sight of the surly little creature I'd healed weeks ago. "Nog?" I whispered.

The goblin did not speak as he bent down to press something in my hand. I recognized the shape of a knife, *my* knife. My heart swelled with the knowledge that I wasn't alone out here after all. I raised my eyes to his again. He stared at me solemnly, and I wanted to say something, to thank him.

I blinked, and he disappeared.

The knife was still there, and I wrapped my fingers possessively around the handle that fit my palm like it was made for me. *Made for a warrior.*

I looked at Haism, who had his back to me now, speaking fervently in low tones – as if I could understand a word of it either way. He was distracted, gesturing with his free hand and pacing.

I might never get another chance. I flexed my aching arms and got soundlessly to my feet.

Then I ran.

20

I did not make it far before shouts rang out behind me, followed by the sounds of Haism crashing through the woods after me. I didn't look back to see where he was or if he was gaining on me. I ran as fast as my abused and bloody feet would go. Haism was strong and fast, and even with the knife, I would be no match for him if he caught me.

He might hold the advantage physically, but I knew these woods better than anyone. We weren't that far from the cliffs, and if I could reach them, I could shimmy down to my cave. It took a lot of nerve and agility to climb that cliff face, and I doubted that even Haism or his men could do it without a rope. I still had my cell phone because Tarek had stopped searching me after he found the knife, so I could call Nikolas and hole up in the cave until he came. I had a plan; now I just had to execute it.

A stream loomed ahead, and I scrambled across a dead tree I always used as a bridge. Seconds later I heard my pursuer hit the stream running, followed by a splash and a string of curses. I kept going.

I smelled the salt air a minute before the woods thinned, and I saw the break in trees ahead. So close. I put on an extra burst of speed, and Haism fell farther behind. Suddenly the trees were behind me, and I was hobbling across a small grassy meadow. The rumble of waves told me how close I was, and I stuck the knife inside my coat to free my hands for the climb of my life.

My feet touched bare rock, and I veered to the left, making for the lone stunted pine tree above the cave. Over the wind and the roar of the surf, I heard Haism shout something unintelligible at me, but he was too far away to matter now. I reached the tree and peered down at the rocks below. The ocean's show of power here never failed to take my breath away, but I'd always had Remy to carry me down and keep me safe. I didn't anticipate the climb, but I would rather face a hundred cliffs than the fate waiting for me.

There was no time to steel myself, to work up the courage. Haism was coming, I had to go now. Taking a deep breath, I turned to start the climb.

"Hello, little flower."

"No!"

Dark blue eyes straight from my nightmares gleamed as they locked with mine. Full lips curved in pleasure, sending my stomach plummeting. The last time I saw that mouth it was fanged and snarling at me as the monster behind it vowed to have me.

No, no, no, no, no! my mind screamed. I took an involuntary step backward and lost my footing.

Eli's hand shot out as I teetered on the edge. He pulled me against him and ran a finger down my face. I shuddered, and he smiled like we were reunited lovers. "Don't worry. I won't let you fall this time. I've waited too long to feel you in my arms again to lose you now." His finger lingered on my bruised cheek. "I am not happy about this, however. I shall have to talk to Haism about the terms of our contract."

"Eli," said a male voice, and I looked past him. My blood froze when I saw at least a dozen other vampires gathered nearby. The speaker, a black vampire who could have passed for one of my classmates, tilted his head toward the man standing frozen at the edge of the woods.

Even from here I could see the terror creep across Haism's face as he stared at the scene before him. On the phone with Eli he had been cocky because he knew he would not meet the vampire face-to-face. Now he faced a dozen of them, alone and armed with nothing but a cell phone. I think we both realized at the same time that my life wasn't the only one forfeited here today. I should have felt pity for him. I might have if he hadn't threatened Nate and planned to turn us both over to Eli.

"Haism, we meet after all," Eli called, turning us both to face my ex-captor. Eli's arms were like steel bands around my waist, holding me back against him. Revulsion, fear, and a dozen other emotions warred inside me, and it was all I could do to not scream or pass out.

"Yes... a change of plans, I see," Haism stammered. "But you have what you came for, just as promised." I saw him take a step backward. Did he really think he could flee?

Eli reached up to lift my hair away from my face. "Not exactly as promised. She is damaged. I cannot imagine what would have happened to her if we had not followed you."

Haism's jaw fell. He took another step toward the woods.

"My deal with your employer was that I deliver the trolls and you deliver the girl, whole and untouched. I believe this renders our contract null and void." Sadistic amusement laced Eli's honeyed voice. "Juan, Rose, please conclude our business with Mr. Bakr."

"Noooooo!" Haism got that one word out before the black vampire and a blond female appeared beside him. I tore my horrified eyes away, but I could not block out the screams. They seemed to go on forever before ending in a sickening gurgle that turned my legs to jelly and made my stomach revolt.

Eli lowered his head until his mouth was against my ear. "Calm yourself, my sweet. You belong to me, and no one else will touch you."

The promise in his softly spoken words turned my blood to ice. It would not be long before I would wish I had died along with Haism. There was only one way out of this for me now. Either way I was going to die. I had to make sure it was on my terms because the alternative was unthinkable.

"Why?" I asked hoarsely. "Why me?"

Eli sighed. "You don't even know how lovely you are, do you? Such a mix of fire and innocence, I saw it that night before we even met, and I knew I had to have you. Imagine my delight when I discovered what you are and then to find out that you were what brought me to Portland in the first place."

I thought of David's theory about the missing girls, and I had to know. Swallowing my fear, I said, "You took those girls in Portland because you were looking for me. Why did you pick them?"

"They were chosen because they were the right age and they all had certain *characteristics* in common. It did not take me long to discern that none of them was the one I sought."

Something in me shriveled and died. Those girls were dead because of me, and their families would never know what happened to them. "All of this to catch Madeline Croix?"

Eli laughed softly, his chest rumbling against my back. "Ah, Madeline. There was a beauty. I almost had her once, but she has evaded me all these years. My Master has not been happy about that." His arms squeezed me lightly. "But you are the greater prize, I think."

"Are-are you going to take me to your Master?" I didn't know what prospect frightened me more – being at the mercy of Eli or his master.

"Eli, we should go," said one of the other vampires. "This town is swarming with wolves and hunters. And the sky will start to clear soon."

"We leave when I am ready," Eli barked. He spun me to face him, and I placed my hands against his chest as a small barrier between us. "You are mine. My Master promised you to me if I found you."

I stared at his chest to avoid the hunger in his eyes as I pressed him for answers. "Why is Madeline so important to your Master? I don't even know my mother. If you think I can help you find her, you're mistaken."

"The *why* is between my Master and Madeline. And our search for Madeline revealed a few things about her life that were of great interest to my Master."

"I don't understand. What is so special about her being a Mohiri, except for the fact that you all hate each other?"

He laughed. "You are right. There is nothing special about her, but her daughter is an entirely different story. Do you know it wasn't until a few months ago that we learned Madeline had a daughter? That little tidbit she and your dearly-departed father kept hidden from us. By the time we learned of your existence, you were nowhere to be found. It was like you had disappeared into thin air."

I felt the blood drain from my face. "My father?"

He lifted my chin, forcing me to look up at him. "Oh yes, I was well acquainted with Daniel Grey – well, as acquainted as you can be with anyone on the last day of their life."

The world faded around us. I couldn't feel the wind or hear the ocean or see the vampires surrounding me. In that moment, there was only me and Eli.

"You... you killed him."

His cruel, beautiful eyes gleamed as he watched my face closely. "I was following Madeline, and her trail led me to him. He said he didn't know where she was. Of course, I had to make sure he was telling the truth." He sighed as if he was reliving a happy memory. "I believe he was."

I couldn't breathe as the image of my dad's mutilated body swam before my eyes. For ten years I'd carried that gruesome memory while trying to accept that I would never find his killer. Yet, here he stood. All the nightmares, the grief, and the loneliness I had suffered were because of the monster smiling at me right now.

"He actually held out longer than most – "

Heat blossomed in my chest. My body trembled as electricity danced through me and rippled across my skin like heat waves off pavement. Static crackled and my scalp tingled as some of my hair lifted into the air.

Eli's eyes widened, and he dropped his hands from my shoulders as if he had been shocked. I sensed the others moving closer, forming a half circle around us.

The strange electricity surging through me fizzled like a used match. I reached for it, but it was gone before I could grasp it and figure out how to use it to destroy Eli. Impotent rage flooded me.

Eli laughed once he recovered from his surprise. "A charming little display but hardly enough to hurt me. You have no idea what that is, do you? What you are?"

"Does it matter?" I asked, glad for the fury that swallowed some of my fear.

"Not to me," he replied, smiling. "I think we have dallied here long enough. We'll have plenty of time later to get to know each other."

My heart thudded painfully as his words sank in. This was it. If he took me away from here I was dead – or I'd soon wish I was. I felt the wind at my back. The edge of the cliff was less than two feet away; one jump and this would all be over. It was the only way out for me now. If there really was a God, then this wasn't the end and I'd be with my dad again. If there wasn't a God... well, I'd never know. But nothingness was better than the fate awaiting me with Eli.

Watching my face, Eli suddenly grabbed one of my wrists, his eyes flashing. "You would not be thinking about robbing me of our time together, would you my sweet?"

My heart sank. "No, I was just – "

Something brushed against my mind.

A vampire gasped. Another let out a small cry. Eli's eyes widened – with fear.

My breath caught. I whirled around, and there he was, standing like a vengeful angel between us and the woods. His leather jacket was gone, and in its place was his warrior harness. His hands gripped the hilts of two long, slender swords.

Our eyes met, and the look in his took my breath away. I'd seen Nikolas angry plenty of times, but that was nothing compared to the unbridled fury I saw in him now. I knew Nikolas the man, but it was the demon warrior who stood before me, and the demon was raging.

"He is only one," Eli growled after his initial shock had passed. "Risa, Heath, Lorne – take care of this."

"No!" I cried, but the three vampires reached Nikolas before the word even left my lips. My stomach clenched, and a sour taste flooded my mouth as I watched the vampires circle their quarry like lions surrounding a gazelle. *He's a warrior. This is what he does.* I tried to find comfort in those thoughts, but it was three against one. Nikolas was as fast as them, but how could he fight all of them at once? He'd always been so strong, so invincible that the idea of him falling now was unthinkable.

He can't die. I was too afraid for him to try to think about why the possibility of him losing sucked all the warmth from my body.

The red-headed male in front of Nikolas darted toward him. Nikolas brought his swords up, but the vampire whirled away out of reach at the last second. The feint distracted Nikolas, and I choked back a cry as the blond male on his left struck with the speed of a snake, his clawed hand aiming for Nikolas's throat.

Someone screamed. The air turned crimson around them, and the blond vampire drew back, staring at the stump where his hand used to be. Metal flashed again. The vampire gaped in horror at Nikolas for an endless second – before his head toppled off his neck and rolled a few feet away from him.

The female behind Nikolas let out an enraged wail and launched herself at him, her long black hair flying out wildly behind her. At the same time, the other male attacked from the front, going for Nikolas's chest. Moving almost too fast to see, Nikolas leapt into the air and flipped backward over the female's back, landing deftly behind her. She shrieked in rage and barely missed colliding with her brethren, but she was not fast enough to avoid his claws. Long, bloody gashes marred her pale pretty face by the time she stopped her forward rush and spun back to the fight.

Thrown off guard by his contact with the female, the red-haired vampire was unable to stop his own advance in time. The sound of steel against muscle and bone sickened me even as I rejoiced in the sight of the blade slicing through the vampire's chest. Nikolas withdrew and slashed again. The vampire went down, his stomach spilling out onto the grass.

My stomach roiled from the violence and gore, but I couldn't look away from Nikolas, who fought with the swift grace of a dancer, his movements controlled and effortless. The savage beauty in his face stole my breath as he pulled his blade from the vampire on the ground and pivoted to meet the female's second attack. Half demon or not, at that moment he was the most glorious thing I had ever seen.

The female, raging with grief over the loss of what had obviously been her mate, came at Nikolas head-on. It took him only seconds to bring both blades up and then down in crisscross strokes across her torso. She stumbled, and he drove a sword straight through her heart. In a single motion, he turned and slashed out to behead the red-haired male on the ground. He straightened and faced us again, looking like he was barely winded and not surrounded by bloody vampire parts.

Silence fell over everyone. Even the wind seemed to stall in anticipation of what would happen next. Eli's confident smile faded, and there was no mistaking the fear in his voice when he spoke. "All of you!" he ordered sharply. "Finish him."

None of the other vampires looked eager to follow that order, but they all turned to face Nikolas, preparing to rush him all at once.

Eli moved closer to me. "Coward!" I yelled at him for standing back out of harm's way while his friends did the dirty work.

A few seconds later, my attention was drawn away from Eli by movement in the trees. I watched open-mouthed as Chris stepped into the open followed by two, four – five massive werewolves. After everything that had happened with Roland, the pack had come. My heart swelled until it hurt.

As one, the vampires backed up a step.

"Let her go and we will let you live... for today." Nikolas's commanding voice rang across the short distance between us and sent tendrils of warmth through my frozen limbs. He was here. He'd asked me to trust him and swore to keep me safe, and he had come for me. No matter what happened now, I knew my trust had not been misplaced, and I felt a small flare of happiness in spite of my dire situation.

Eli pulled me back against his chest, his claws at my throat, and memories of that night in the alley rose up like bile, threatening to choke me.

"I think not." He took a step toward the edge of the cliff, pulling me with him. "We both know I could rip her throat out and jump before you reached us."

Nikolas's expression did not change. "But then nothing would prevent me from hunting you down, and this time I will not stop."

Eli's voice was steady, belying the tremble I felt go through him. "I think sweet little Sara is important to you and you won't do anything to jeopardize her life."

Nikolas's eyes blazed.

"Nothing to say?" Emboldened by Nikolas's silence, Eli let out an ugly laugh, and his other hand touched my cheek, the claws skimming lightly over my skin. "Will you still have nothing to say when I taste her?"

This time there was no mistaking the rage seething beneath Nikolas's calm exterior. I remembered how I had felt when I'd let the demon possess my body, the heady power and violence that had boiled through my veins, and I knew Nikolas was close to unleashing his own demon.

Eli saw it, too. "Stay back, Mohiri," he ordered, a note of desperation creeping into in his voice. "You *might* kill me, but not before I end her."

"Let her go and you'll have a chance of getting out of this alive. Is she worth your life – all your lives?"

"Do it, Eli!" the vampire named Juan whispered fervently, never taking his eyes off Nikolas. "Give him the bitch." The other vampires murmured in agreement.

"She is mine, and I will not give her up," Eli hissed back. "You heard the Master. Kill her or take her, but the girl is not to be left behind."

Eli's declaration was like a bucket of icy water thrown in my face. No matter what Nikolas did, Eli would not let me live. My jaw clenched painfully. At least it would be quick and I'd die knowing my friends had come for me.

"Kill me then." My words startled the vampires, and I was proud of how calm I sounded despite the storm of emotions inside me. "All I ever wanted was to find the one who killed my father, and here you are. Knowing that my friends will rip you to shreds – all of you – after I'm dead is enough for me." My voice grew stronger as I spoke, powered by my conviction that Nikolas and the werewolves would do exactly that.

A wave of panic rippled through the vampires surrounding us. My life was the only thing between them and certain death, and my willingness to die had just drastically decreased their chances of survival. Some of them looked poised to flee. They weren't stupid. The Mohiri and the wolves wanted me, and my friends would follow whoever had me.

"Stand firm!" Eli growled. "You would dare disobey the Master's orders?"

Apparently, the Master's wrath was even more terrifying than dying because the vampires moved to take up defensive positions around me and Eli. With the cliff at our backs and the line of vampires between us and his enemy, Eli's confidence lifted.

"Such a pretty speech," he rasped into my ear. "But you see I'm not ready for either of us to die yet." His lips touched my earlobe, and I suppressed a shudder. "I have such plans for us, sweet Sara. Before this night is out, I will own you, body and soul."

"I'll die before I let you have me."

His voice hitched as he fed on my terror and his own anticipation. "Fight me all you want. It only makes you more desirable."

I tried to block out the images his words conjured. "You're a monster."

Eli chuckled. "I've had many, many women, and all of them begged me for it... well, up until I made them scream, of course. Your daddy screamed, too, at the end, and so will you."

Pain shot through my chest. "I'll kill you!" I choked, struggling against him, making him laugh again.

I grunted as something sharp dug into my hip. *The knife.* An absurd urge to laugh flooded me as I remembered how I had tried to refuse the weapon when Nikolas gave it to me and how many times it had helped save my life since that day. Through it all, the knife always seemed to find its way back to me as if it was daring me to deny my heritage.

My right hand snaked inside my coat and touched the handle. At the same time, my eyes sought Nikolas's, and I drew strength from his unwavering gaze. No matter how this ended, I was not leaving this place with Eli. It was obvious that one of us was going to die here, and if it had to be me, I would go like the warrior Nikolas believed me to be. I owed him that much.

"Father and daughter and someday I'll have the mother, too," Eli gloated, oblivious to the resolve burning in my eyes. He pulled me against him again, and if it weren't for my newfound strength, I would have buckled under the vicious promise in his dark eyes. "Maybe I'll keep you until I find dear Madeline. I've never had a mother and daughter at one time."

"You sick bastard!" My fingers closed around the handle of the knife and slowly slid it free. "I'm going to enjoy watching you die, Eli." My whole life I had fought to save the lives of others, but today I would gladly try to take one, even if it meant my own death.

He smiled, but there was no humor in it. "You're brave enough to say that now, but soon you will beg to die. I will use you and drink from you over and over until I have had my fill. And when there is nothing left, I will send you to be with your dear father."

A lifetime of grief, loneliness, and fear powered the thrust that sent the knife into Eli's chest, up between his ribs and into his demon heart. My eyes met his as they flew wide in disbelief while his hands clawed at the hilt protruding from his body. I watched impassively as realization dawned on his face, as his dark, soulless eyes stared at the last person he would ever hurt. Inside me, the Mori reveled in the kill, but all I could think of in that moment was my dad. Killing his murderer did not ease the pain of losing him or bring me any joy, yet it felt right that I was the one to do it. I couldn't save him, but I could give him this.

Eli crumpled to the ground, and all hell broke loose.

Nikolas sped toward us followed by Chris, and they were met by six of the vampires. Swords and bodies flew so fast I could not follow the fight. Behind them the wolves began to race toward the rest of us on the cliff. Around me, the remaining three vampires quailed when they spotted the approaching threat, and they turned to jump into the ocean.

It took me a moment to realize I was free. I ran toward the wolves only to be snatched off my feet and thrown over a shoulder like a sack of potatoes. "For the Master," growled the vampire who'd grabbed me.

I screamed and struggled to break free as I was carried back toward the cliff. Behind me the wolves roared, and over the din I heard Nikolas yell my name.

We went down in a tumbling heap, and I rolled away to see a silver coated arrow sticking out of the vampire's chest just before he toppled over the edge of the cliff. Scrambling to my feet, I spotted Chris fitting another arrow into his bow.

"Sara, run!" shouted Nikolas as he ran his sword through one of the vampires he was battling. I needed no more encouragement, and I started forward.

I didn't feel the pain at first, just a cold numbness in the center of my chest. When the throbbing pain came, I looked down in confusion at the patch of red blossoming across the front of my shirt. By the time my dulled mind recognized the hilt of my knife sticking from my chest, scalding pain began to shoot through me.

"No!" someone bellowed above the roaring in my ears. I tried to move toward the voice, but my feet would not obey me and I tripped backward instead. My hands flailed as my feet tried to find purchase, but there was nothing but air as I toppled over the edge of the cliff.

I'm dying. The thought hit me at the same moment I collided with the little tree clinging precariously to the face of the cliff. My hands grabbed the thin branches, barely feeling the needles that tore at them as I clung to the tree with my rapidly fading strength.

Dangling over the boiling surf, I could barely hear the shouts and roars from the battle raging above me. I tried to call out to them, to let them know I was here, but when I opened my mouth, warm frothy blood was all that came out, running down my chin to drip into the sea.

Strange. I always thought I'd feel scared when death came for me – not this peace that slowly spread through my body. There was sadness too – for Nate who would be alone now, for never seeing Roland's playful smirk again, and for Nikolas whose handsome face swam before my eyes, his eyes sad instead of their usual stormy gray. He had tried so hard to save me, and I knew he would blame himself. I wished I could tell him that it wasn't his fault. More than that, I wished I could let him know that somehow through all of this, he had become an important part of my life.

My hands opened.

The last time I'd fallen, Nikolas had caught me in his arms, though I had no memory of it. This time it was the ocean that wrapped me in her cold embrace. I sighed as the pain vanished, the world went dark, and the waves closed over my head.

21

"Look, Daddy! I can go all the way around without falling now."

"That's great, honey!" Daddy watched as I skated in a wide circle around him. I made my way over to him on wobbly legs, and he caught me just before I fell. "Whoa, slow down there, Gretzky."

"I'm cold. Can we go get hot chocolate now?" I asked him hopefully, and he grinned down at me.

"Of course! When have we ever not gotten our hot chocolate?"

We sat on the bench, and Daddy blew on my drink for me. "There you go, honey." I took a long sip, and he smiled. "Be careful, or you'll burn your tongue."

But the chocolate did not burn me, and I drained the cup. I held the empty cup out to him. "Can I have some more?"

"More? Don't you want to skate again?"

I shook my head, shivering in spite of my warm coat and mittens. "Please, Daddy, I'm so cold."

"How does she fare?"

"She is alive, and she is a fighter. That is all I can say."

"She looks so human, so fragile."

"Aye, but she is stronger than she looks." A cool touch to the forehead. "Rest now and get well, little one."

. . .

"I don't feel so good."

Daddy's hand felt cool against my face. "Hmm, you are a bit warm. Where does it hurt?"

I coughed and winced. "My throat hurts, and it hurts here," I rasped, touching my chest.

He tucked the blankets around me and left my room, returning with a glass of water and some pills. I took the pills obediently and greedily drank the glass of water. "More," I gasped. I was thirsty, so thirsty.

"Why does her body resist the healing?"

"It is the demon blood. It is poisoning her."

"But the demon is part of her. How can it harm her?"

"No, it is the other demon's blood that was on the weapon. Her body must choose to accept it or reject it."

"What will it do to her if it does not kill her?"

"I cannot say. She is not like any other we have healed."

"Can we do something to help her?"

A sigh. "It is up to her now."

"Am I dead?"

"What an odd thing to ask, honey." The corners of my dad's warm green eyes crinkled when he smiled. He patted the sofa beside him, and I curled up happily in the crook of his arm. "I can't believe it. My little girl is all grown up."

My brow furrowed. "I don't understand. Where have you been all this time?"

He sighed and gave my shoulders a squeeze. "I never left. I've been with you every day."

"But I couldn't find you. I was alone and scared, and you were gone."

"You were never alone, Sara. You had Nate and your friends. You still do."

Tears burned my eyes. "I messed up so bad, Daddy. I lied to everyone, and I hurt Nate and my friends. They probably all hate me now. Everything I do hurts someone. Even Nikolas. He tried to help me, and I let him down, too. It's no wonder I died."

"No one hates you, honey, and you're not dead."

I shook my head. "You died, and the only way I can be talking to you is if I died, too."

He kissed the top of my head. "My sweet girl, you can talk to me anytime you want to."

I closed my eyes and laid my head against his shoulder. "I miss you, Dad."

. . .

Soft tinkling sounds like glass wind chimes pulled me up from the warm cocoon of darkness wrapped around me. My eyes felt heavy as if I'd slept for a long time, and when I opened them, it took them a minute to focus. When I could finally see my surroundings, I knew I must still be dreaming.

I lay in the middle of a large canopy bed, covered by white sheets made of soft linen and a comforter of the lightest down. The walls of the room were entirely covered in sweet-smelling flowering vines, and the domed ceiling was made of stained glass depicting the night sky. There was no window and no door that I could see, and when I leaned over to look at the floor I saw what looked like hard-pressed earth. On a glass-topped table beside the bed, a small oil lamp flickered softly.

I fell back onto the soft pillows. *I am so not in Kansas anymore.*

The vines parted, and a pretty red-haired girl appeared. She wore a pale green shift with a fine silver gauze overlay, and her delicate face had an almost ethereal quality to it. At first glance I guessed her to be around ten years old, but as she approached the bed I saw that she was closer to my age, maybe a little older.

"Welcome back, little sister," she said in a soft musical voice that was oddly familiar.

"Where am I?" My throat was dry and my voice raspy.

She moved her hand, and out of nowhere she seemed to pull a glass of what looked like water. Pressing the glass into my hands she said, "Drink."

I took the glass and put it to my lips, too parched to question what it was or how it had appeared from thin air. When I took my first drink I discovered the clearest, most refreshing water I had ever tasted. With my second drink, flavors exploded across my tongue like the smell of grass and flowers and rain and sunshine. It reminded me of standing in a meadow after a spring shower. I drank it all then looked forlornly at the glass, wishing for more. Like magic, the glass filled again, and I drank that down, too, before my thirst was quenched.

"Am I sick?"

She smiled sweetly, and her emerald green eyes sparkled. "You were very ill. I am delighted to see you have recovered."

I studied her face. I'd never seen her before; that much I knew. So why did I feel like we'd met before? "Do I know you?"

Her laugh was airy, musical, and something stirred at the edge of my memory. "We have met once, but I have been watching you for many years now."

"Who are you?"

The air around her began to shimmer, and a small breeze tossed the leaves covering the walls. Before my eyes, the girl faded and morphed into a small spinning column of air. "I told you we would meet again," said a whispery voice I would know anywhere.

My hand flew to my mouth. "Aine?"

The air shifted, and the smiling girl stood before me again. "It is good to see you again, Sara."

"I don't understand. Why are you here, and why have you been watching me?"

She laid her pale slender hand over mine where it lay on the comforter. "We always watch over our own."

Their own? I shook my head, thinking I knew exactly how Alice had felt down in the rabbit hole. "I'm not a sylph. I'm Mohiri."

"You are correct. You are not of the air, and you did inherit your mother's demon side." Aine nimbly hopped up to sit cross-legged on the bed beside me. "But you inherited something from your father as well. I know you have always wanted to know where you got your power to heal. That comes from your great, great, great, great grandmother."

"Are you saying that my dad wasn't human?" I refused to believe that. Nate was very human, and my dad had been, too.

"Oh, he was human. Your ancestor's gifts can pass only to females of her line." Aine's eyes danced. "Do you know you are her first female descendant? As you can imagine, we were very excited when you were born."

I struggled to keep up with her. "What are you saying?"

"Forgive me. In my eagerness I have confused you. Let me explain." She took one of my hands in her smaller one, and I felt a peaceful calm flow into me. My power surged in response, and a soft gasp escaped me when I sensed energy coming from Aine that was so similar to my own. It was like finding a piece of myself that I did not know was missing.

"Your great, great, great, great grandmother was named Sahine, and she was of the water and one of my dearest sisters. One day, Sahine fell in love with a human male and she chose to leave this life for a mortal one. It happens sometimes." Aine smiled wistfully. "We were sad when she left us, but she was so happy for the rest of her days. I was glad for her."

I rubbed my eyes and felt my forehead to see if I was feverish. But my face was cool to the touch. *Maybe I'm drugged.* What else could explain the things I was hearing?

"So I'm like a mermaid or something? Because if you tell me I'm going to start growing a tail, I'm going to freaking lose it." I moved my feet under the covers to make sure they were still there.

Aine gave another tinkling laugh. "You are undine. And I don't think our cousins would appreciate your sentiment."

"Undine?" I tried to remember what I knew about undines. Water elementals, always female with beautiful singing voices. Obviously not all of their talents were passed on. All elementals could heal, which explained my power. Undines were supposedly born without souls and marrying a human was one way to get a soul. I felt a moment of fear. I was already half demon. Did this mean I had no soul either?

Aine's brow furrowed. "I thought you would be happy, but you look troubled."

"Do I... do I have a soul?"

"Only those born in the water are full undine and have no souls. You were not born to the water, so you are not full undine."

I had a soul – that was something at least. But what did this make me? God, a month ago I was just another human, or so I thought. Now I was what – one-third human?

An ache started behind my eyes. This was too much to process. One minute I'm falling off a cliff, and the next I'm in a strange room with a sylph telling me I'm part elemental. If this was someone's idea of the afterlife, it was pretty messed up.

Aine slid off the bed. "I am sorry. You are weak from your illness, and I am upsetting you." She touched my forehead with her cool palm. "Go to sleep. I will be here when you wake up."

My eyes immediately began to droop, and I fought to keep them open. "Wait, I have more questions, and you didn't tell me where I am."

"You are in Seelie. Your injuries were grave, and this was the only place that could heal you."

Seelie! I thought before sleep claimed me.

When I woke again, I felt well rested and surprisingly serene, considering everything Aine had told me. True to her word, the sylph reappeared as soon as I opened my eyes. She brought me a pale yellow dress similar to her green one, and I marveled at the fine fabric as I slipped it over my head. Barefoot, I followed her through an archway behind the vines to a courtyard overlooking a glassy lake. We sat at a small glass table set with food and drink that made my stomach growl, and I reached for a pastry, wondering how long it had been since I'd last eaten.

My hand stopped halfway to the plate when I remembered where I was. Rule number one in Faerie: don't eat or drink.

"You are not mortal, little sister. The food is safe for you."

That was all I needed to hear. My appetite had always been good, but I'd never tasted food like this: pastries that melted on my tongue, fruit so sweet I licked the juice from my fingers, and cold, frothy milk flavored with mint. It was like pure bliss, and I sampled it all – twice – before I finally leaned back in my chair, sated.

After my meal, Aine took me for a stroll around the lake. Everything here was incredibly lush and vibrant, from the thick green grass to the sky so blue it almost hurt my eyes to look at it. The air was the sweetest I had ever smelled, and brightly colored birds sang to us from the trees. A few times I spotted tiny faces peering out from the underbrush and heard what sounded like giggles. When I asked Aine about them, she smiled and said the sprites were curious about their new cousin but they were too shy to come forward. I shook my head in wonder. The more I saw of this place, the more unreal it seemed and the harder it was for me to believe that part of me belonged to this world. I still was not entirely sure I wasn't dreaming.

We reached the far side of the lake, and I looked back expecting to see a building, but all I saw was the small courtyard nestled among the trees. I didn't need Aine to explain that it was Faerie magic at work.

We made our way back to the courtyard and walked through the hanging vines into a sunny room with comfortable couches and a low table set with a pitcher of juice and two glasses. Aine poured me a glass of juice, and I took a sip, savoring sweetness the likes of which could never be found in the human world. I leaned back on the soft cushions with a contented sigh. There was something about this place, a sense of tranquility that seemed to soak into every pore and lift every worry and fear from my mind. For the first time since my world had shattered ten years ago, I felt no fear or loneliness, just a deep sense of belonging.

I wasn't sure how long we sat there talking. Aine told me how a pair of selkies had rescued me from the ocean and called for her when they recognized me as one of their cousins. I told her I vaguely remembered hearing voices while I was unconscious, and she said the faeries had tended to me because nothing but their magic could have saved me. I had been stabbed with the same knife I used to kill Eli. To a Mohiri, vampire blood was just blood, but to a Fae, demon blood could be lethal. Aine said the faeries believed it was my own demon side that allowed me to finally absorb Eli's blood harmlessly into my body.

I asked many questions, and she answered them all. She told me about undines and how rare it was to find a female descendent of an undine/human mating. Because undines were female, only their female descendents inherited any of their powers. I *was* relieved to learn I would not get the sudden urge to take up residence in the nearest pond.

"Was it my undine power that let me control my Mori all these years without training?"

"Yes. Demons fear earth magic not only because of its strength but because of its purity. For that reason demonkind has hated us since time began. But you may be the first of your kind, half-Fae, half-demon, and your power is not like any other. It seems almost impossible for you to exist, but here you are. You are still so young. Only time will tell us what that means for you. You are something of a curiosity, even to us."

"Why would you or any Faerie help me? Aren't you afraid of my demon blood?"

Aine smiled, and her red curls bobbed when she shook her head. "Your Fae blood is stronger than your demon blood, or you never would have been able to hold back the demon in you. You are more one of us than them."

I didn't like talking about my demon half, so I asked her to tell me more about undines. She was happy to comply. She told me that all elementals had certain abilities in common and some unique to their element. Elementals lived forever unless they chose to give up their immortality. They had the gift of healing and could draw on the magic in the earth itself. They were the only beings in existence that demons truly feared. Undines could also manipulate water and create or control storms. Being only half undine, there was no way to know exactly what elemental abilities I had inherited until they manifested – if they did at all. She did say that if my healing power was any indication, there could be others and she would help guide me when the time came.

In addition to their elemental powers and angelic singing voices, undines – pure undines, not half-breeds like me – possessed an unearthly beauty that had a dramatic effect on humans. Females felt threatened and an instant dislike for undines, whereas males could be driven almost insane with desire. Such intense emotions affected males in one of two ways: they either became completely enamored and protective or they were driven to darker impulses that resulted in violence.

At my look of dismay she assured me that only a full-blooded undine could affect males to that extent and my mixed heritage diminished the attraction considerably. That made me feel only slightly better. It did explain, though, why I had no female friends. It also made me analyze every relationship I had ever had with males, and what I found did not make me happy. Both Roland and Peter had confessed to having crushes on me at one point, and they'd let me know that *all* the boys at school liked me that way when I first moved there. Scott was one of those boys, and his feelings toward me had definitely turned dark after I rejected his friendship. Then there was Greg, who for some reason chose to befriend me and who, according to Roland, had threatened every boy in school, effectively keeping them away from me. And I could not forget Francis, who despised me for no other reason than my existence. Was it actually my undine nature that made him feel such animosity for me?

And finally there was Eli who had been so obsessed with me after one brief conversation that he had died trying to claim me. I shivered even though I knew he was dead and could never threaten me again. I asked Aine if vampires could be affected, and she nodded delicately.

"Vampires were once human, so they are susceptible as well, but they can feel no love, only a dark desire to possess and inflict pain, not that they could act upon those desires with an undine."

Great where did that leave me? "Can a vampire tell I'm half undine? Eli said something about me having no idea what I was."

"If he tasted your skin or your blood – yes. A vampire would not face a full elemental, but you are very young and weak compared to one of us." Her smile faded. "Even though they fear us, our blood is like a drug to most demons, causing heightened infatuation."

"What?" I almost jumped out of my chair. "You're telling me my blood is a frigging aphrodisiac to demons?" Could this get any worse?

"In a manner of speaking," she answered bluntly.

"What about other half demons like the Mohiri? Please don't tell me I'm going to have to fight them off, too?" I thought about Nikolas and how overly protective he was for a guy who was just doing his job. I hated to think that it might be nothing more than my Faerie DNA driving him.

"No, the Mohiri were created to be the perfect warriors and are immune to most forms of compulsion and weakness."

"Good," I breathed, settling back onto the couch.

Thinking about Nikolas made me remember how I'd felt when he fought all those vampires and demanded my release. I remembered his rage and him shouting my name when I fell. After this, he'd probably try to lock me in my room forever, and I wouldn't be surprised if Nate helped him. My lips curved into a small smile. They could try.

Oh God, Nate has no idea where I am! I couldn't believe I had spent the entire day hanging out here with no thought about what my uncle must be going through.

I jumped to my feet. "Aine, I need to go home."

"This is your home now, if you want it to be," she replied. "Don't you like it here?"

"I love it. But my real home is with my uncle back in the human world. He's all alone, and he needs me."

Her happy smile faded a little. "But there is so much evil in that place. Why would you want to return to that?"

"The world isn't evil, even if there are bad things in it. I have friends and family there, and I couldn't imagine leaving them. Plus, out there I can help animals and the People. No one needs my help here."

She studied me as if still trying to understand why I would prefer that world over this perfect one. Her smile was sad when she finally nodded. "For you to wish to leave here this much means you really do not belong here yet. No one who truly belonged to Faerie could ever call another place home." She stood and held out her hand. "Come. I will take you to your human home."

I hugged her happily then took her hand. In seconds, the air around us began to shimmer and grow warm and the room started to fade. There was a terrifying moment of blackness where I could feel and hear and see nothing, and it felt like I was alone in a void between the worlds. But before panic could set in, the light returned and I found myself standing at my front door and looking down at Nate's car.

Aine let go of my hand and wrapped me in a gentle hug. "Good-bye for now, little sister. It made me happy to get to know you. You will always have a home with us if you ever choose to return."

Tears welled in my eyes as I hugged her back. I'd never been so happy to see my front door, but I'd only just discovered my new family and it felt like I'd lose that part of me when Aine left. "I'm glad I got to know you, too. Thank you for everything you did for me."

She pulled back, and her expression grew serious. "Sara, do not forget what I told you about demons and our kind. I fear there are many who will not be happy to learn of your existence. I have done what I could over the years to keep you safe, hiding you from those who sought you. Go to your Mohiri family, because you will not be safe on your own. I will find you and visit you no matter where you go."

Her words made me remember what David had said about how someone had wiped out all documents and trails that would lead to me and Nate, making it impossible to find me. All this time, Aine had been watching out for me and I had no idea.

"Stay safe, little sister."

"I will. Thank you, Aine, for everything."

Aine's only reply was a small smile before she quickly faded from sight. I found myself alone, barefoot, and shivering in a thin dress meant for the perfect warm, sunny days in Faerie. It was colder here than I remembered, but despite my discomfort I took a long moment to look around at the place I never thought I'd see again when I drove away from here a few days ago. I was home.

22

I dabbed at my eyes and reached for the doorknob, barely able to control my excitement. I couldn't wait to see Nate again. Between my revelations, his kidnapping, and then me going missing, the last few days had to have been pretty awful for him. I had miraculously been given a second chance, and I was going to use that to make things right with him. Starting now.

I tried the door, but it was locked of course and my keys were probably at the bottom of the ocean. *So much for a grand entrance.* Wearing a sheepish smile, I rang the doorbell.

It took a minute for Nate to reach the door. I heard the deadbolt move, and my stomach fluttered nervously as the door opened.

"You're early. I wasn't expecting you until – "

Nate's mouth fell open and his hand flew to his chest as he stared up at me like I was an apparition. It occurred to me that dressed as I was, barefoot in this flimsy dress, I probably looked like one.

"Sara?" he whispered hoarsely.

The words I had planned to say could not get past the lump in my throat, and I threw myself at him, almost knocking him out of his chair. His body was stiff, and I wasn't sure if it was because he was shocked to see me or because I was actually hugging him. But then his arms went around me and he held me so tightly I thought my ribs would crack.

After the longest hug of my life, he held me away from him so he could look at me, and I saw that his face was haggard. Wonder shone in his eyes. "Jesus – it's really you!"

I nodded and gave him a teary smile.

His hands dropped to his lap. "I-I can't believe it."

"Nate, I'm so sorry," I blurted before he could say anything else. "For the lies and keeping everything from you – and for what happened to you." I knelt in front of his chair and searched his face for some sign he might be willing to forgive me. "I know I screwed up, but I promise no more secrets. And I have so much to tell you."

"Sara, where the hell have you been?" he demanded, and the anguish in his voice spoke of the hell I'd put him through.

God, how did I tell him exactly where I'd been? I tried to start slowly. "I was hurt, and someone took me home with them to help me get better. I know you've probably been worried sick the last few days and I swear I would have let you know where I was, but I was pretty out of it."

"The last few days?" Nate echoed incredulously. "You've been gone three damn weeks."

"What?" I said dumbly.

"We thought you were dead. They searched the water for days, and they couldn't find your..." His voice broke, and I saw the pain and grief he had suffered. "We–we had a memorial service last week."

It was a good thing I was already on my knees because my legs wouldn't have been able to support me at that moment. Three weeks – how was that possible? Was I unconscious that whole time, or was it true that time moved differently in Faerie?

And all that time Nate thought I was dead.

"Oh God, Nate, I didn't know, I swear." My eyes pleaded with him to believe me. "I've made a horrible mess of everything, but I would never hurt you that way."

He closed his eyes and let out a long, shaky breath. "I'm afraid that I'll open my eyes and find out you're not really here."

I took both his hands in mine. "I'm here, Nate."

His eyes brimmed with tears when he opened them again. "Jesus, I need a drink. And then you are going to tell me everything."

I got up to shut the door and followed him into the kitchen. It was strange how everything seemed so familiar yet so different at the same time. The kitchen looked exactly as it had the last time I stood in it. I glanced at the phone and remembered pleading with Haism to not hurt Nate. So much had happened since that call, but it was not our home that had changed, it was me. I was not the same person who walked out of here that day. That girl had spent her life afraid and haunted by her past, unable to move past it and pushing everyone away, afraid of being hurt again. The girl who had returned in her place was no longer chained to the pain in her past. She was uncertain about her future, but she was also braver, stronger, and she would never let anything come between her and those she loved again.

Nate reached into a bottom cabinet and pulled out a bottle of Johnnie Walker. He laid the bottle in his lap then grabbed two small glasses from the rack on the counter and rolled to the table. "Sit," he ordered, pouring scotch into both glasses.

I took the chair across from him, and he slid one of the glasses toward me. "You're giving me a drink?"

He shrugged and took a long drink from his glass then refilled it. I'd never seen him consume more than one drink at a time.

Never one to drink much myself, I picked up my glass and took a cautious sip. I sputtered as the liquor burned my tongue and seared a trail down my throat. It hit my stomach and a warm, pleasant feeling spread through me. I took another sip for courage then laid the glass on the table.

"How much do you know about what happened that day?"

Nate set his own glass down, and I saw the bleakness on his face again as he remembered. "I know that man Haism took you down to the cliffs to turn you over to the vampires and they killed him. Then your Mohiri friends and the werewolves showed up and there was a fight. They told me you killed a vampire. Then one of the other vampires threw a knife at you and you fell off the cliff. Nikolas went into the water after you, but you were nowhere to be found."

It was surreal to hear Nate talking so easily about vampires, werewolves, and Mohiri. The last time I saw him he was still in shock from the things I'd revealed to him. It looked like I wasn't the only one who had changed.

"You met Nikolas?"

"He showed up here minutes after that man brought me home. I told him what I knew, and he took off looking for you. He's come by a few times since you... disappeared. He was sure you were still alive, and he refused to go to the service. I asked how he knew, but he wouldn't say. I'll say one thing; he doesn't give up easily." Nate gave me a questioning look. "Were you and he...?"

I choked as scotch went down the wrong way. "No. That's just how he is. He's pretty intense."

Nate did not look convinced, but he didn't push it. "So what happened? Where were you?"

I told him everything that went down from the moment we parted on the street in front of the empty building. I had intended to spare him some of the harsher details, but I found myself pouring it all out to him as if I'd opened a dam that couldn't be closed. When I got to the part about my dad, I choked, but I forced myself to keep talking. Nate's eyes reflected my own horror when he heard how Eli had revealed that he had killed my dad and meant to take me as well.

"I killed him." The fierceness in my voice startled Nate. He didn't speak, but his hand crept across the table to cover one of mine. I went on to tell him about falling into the water and dreaming of my dad, then waking up in the room with Aine. His face registered his shock when I explained what Aine was and exactly where I'd been. Then I told him what Aine had revealed to me about my dad's – and Nate's – side of the family and what I had inherited from our undine ancestor. Aine had told me to be careful, but she didn't say I couldn't tell anyone what I was. Not that I would have kept it from Nate. I was done hiding things from him.

Nate was on his third glass of scotch by the time I got to Aine bringing me home. I swirled the liquid in my own glass while I waited for him to speak.

He inhaled deeply. "I honestly don't know what to say."

"But you believe me?"

"Yes."

My body sagged in relief. "You're taking all of this a lot better than last time."

He set down his empty glass. "Well, a lot has happened since then, and I've had some time to come to grips with it all." He eyed the glass in front of me. "Are you going to drink that?"

I slid the glass across the table to him. "Are you trying to get drunk?"

He gave me a lopsided smile. "No, but this is a special occasion. It's not every day your niece comes back from the dead."

"I guess not." I watched the emotions play across his face – relief, joy, awe as color filled his pale cheeks again.

"This is going to be quite the shock for everyone," he mused out loud. "You've been gone so long, and we obviously can't tell people you've spent the last three weeks in Faerie land."

"We can't tell anyone. I mean, we have to tell Roland and Peter and the rest of the pack. And the Mohiri too, though I have no idea how to contact them since I lost my phone. But we can't tell anyone else. Eli's master is looking for Madeline's daughter, and if he finds out I'm still alive, he'll come after us again. I'm sure the Mohiri are looking for him, and if anyone can find him, they can. We can't let anyone know I'm back until they take care of him."

Nate frowned unhappily, but he nodded. Neither of us wanted to risk another attack. I hated putting him in this spot, but what other choice did I have?

I stared nervously at the phone. "I need to let Roland and Peter know I'm back, but I have no idea what to say to them."

"Do you want me to call them?" I nodded, and he wheeled to the counter and picked up the phone. "I'll be in the living room. This is going to be one hell of a call."

Sitting alone in the kitchen, I listened to the murmurs from the other room and tried to imagine Roland's reaction, the look on his face at that moment. I'd freak out if I thought he was dead and then he showed up out of the blue. Even for supes, coming back from the dead was a big deal.

I laid my head down on my arms and wondered what the heck I was going to do now. I'd missed almost a month of school – though it wasn't like I could go back while pretending to be dead. A teenager who falls off a cliff and supposedly drowns and then shows up alive and well weeks later would draw a lot of media attention. I couldn't stay cooped up in the apartment either because I'd go insane in a few days. There weren't a lot of options available. I could leave New Hastings and find some small, out-of-the-way place where no one would think to look for me, but a teenager on her own would raise eyebrows. Or I could try to contact the Mohiri. Before I'd disappeared, I'd already agreed to go stay with them for a while. I wondered where Nikolas was now. *Probably off rescuing some other unfortunate orphan,* I thought with a sad smile. Although after the trouble I'd put him through, I wouldn't be surprised if he'd washed his hands of that occupation for good. What would he say when he found out I was back? Would he come for me or send someone else to deal with me this time?

I raised my head when I heard Nate by the kitchen door. "How did he take – ?"

My eyes fell on the man standing frozen before me, his dark gaze burning into mine. "Nikolas," I breathed, stunned by his sudden appearance. How had he known?

My breath caught at the play of emotions across his face – despair, anger, joy, and something deeper that wrenched my heart and was gone before I could name it. His body was rigid as he filled the small doorway, looking like he couldn't decide whether to yell at me or hug me. It shook me a little to discover how happy I was to see him. Ever since I woke up in Faerie, I had felt adrift between the two worlds. Seeing him was like finding an anchor to hold me in this one.

"Where were you?" he asked harshly, and in those three words I heard pent-up frustration, relief, and a strong dose of anger.

"Don't look at me like that." I wrapped my arms around me, thinking that at least some things hadn't changed. "It's not like I stabbed myself and jumped off the damn cliff!"

His eyes widened at my outburst, and to my mortification, my own filled with tears. Before I could move, he was in front of me, and I sniffed as he knelt and lifted my chin so I was forced to look at him. The tenderness and regret in his eyes were my undoing. I began to cry in earnest, and I was unable to protest when he pulled me against his chest, and held me while my body shook and my tears soaked his shirt. I wanted to tell him he could let me go, that I was okay, but I found myself reluctant to leave the warm comfort of his arms even after the tears subsided.

"*Pozhaluysta, prosti menya.* I promised to keep you safe, and I didn't," he said thickly against my hair. "I'm sorry."

"No." I made myself pull away from him. "If you hadn't shown up when you did, Eli would have…"

He flinched. "Don't think about that." He stared at me like he still could not believe I was there. "We've been searching that area ever since you disappeared. Where were you?"

"Seelie."

"Come again."

"Turns out I have friends there." I gave a watery smile at his puzzled expression. "It's kind of complicated."

Nikolas ran a hand through his dark hair. "Why does that not surprise me?" He pulled out the chair behind him and sat in front of me, almost close enough for our knees to touch. Warmth spread through my belly, and I tried to shake it off. My emotions were pretty high right now and the last thing I needed was to add to them.

Crossing his arms, he watched me expectantly. "Well, let's have it. I'm dying to know how a Mori demon ends up in a world where no demon would dare to tread."

"Well, it all started the day I met a sylph… Actually no, it started before that with my great, great, great, great grandmother."

He quirked an eyebrow impatiently, and I scowled at him. "Look, I told you it was complicated."

His sigh was barely audible. "I'm sorry. Please continue."

The apology was so surprising, so out of character for Nikolas, that I forgot what I was talking about and it took me a moment to remember. I told him everything I'd told Nate about Aine and what I had learned about my undine ancestor. To give him credit, his face betrayed no reaction as I revealed my unique heritage. I ended by repeating Aine's warning to be careful because there were some who would not be happy about my existence.

"You didn't tell me that part," admonished Nate, who had come in halfway through my story. "Does this mean you're in more danger?"

"No," Nikolas told him decisively. "Because we will keep her safe this time."

Nate visibly relaxed. "So she's safe here?"

Nikolas faced Nate. "I have not lied to you since we met, and I won't start now. Until we track down Eli's master, Sara is not safe anywhere except with the Mohiri." Nate started to speak, and Nikolas said, "I know you don't know much about us, but Sara has family among the Mohiri and they would never harm her. And you would be welcome there as well."

"Really?" I asked. If Nate could come with me, going to live with the Mohiri might not be so bad.

Nate shook his head. "Thank you, that is very generous, but I can't just pick up and leave. I have a new book coming out and a book tour to plan. And truthfully, I don't think I would be comfortable living among people who all look like twenty-year-olds."

My heart sank. "But you could be in danger if the vampires come back."

"Everyone – including the vampires – thinks you are dead," Nate pointed out. "If they were coming back, they would have done it by now."

"He's right," Nikolas said. "As long as we get you out of here before anyone discovers the truth, Nate should be safe."

I looked at Nate. "But I just got back. I don't want to leave you."

Nate gave me a reassuring smile. "I don't want you to go, but I would feel better knowing you're safe. And it's not like we can't talk on the phone whenever you want. I'll even come for Christmas if the Mohiri celebrate it."

"We do, and Thanksgiving too," Nikolas informed us. He shook his head at my look of surprise. "We are not as different as you think we are."

I stared at my clenched hands, but they held no answers for me. After everything we'd been through, I didn't want to leave Nate, but if I stayed here, I risked putting his life in danger again. He had already been kidnapped and almost killed by someone trying to get to me. My decision had to be about his safety as much as it was about mine, and the weight of it rested heavily on my shoulders.

I'd gotten what I wanted: the truth behind my dad's murder, and the vampire who had killed him was dead. But looking back at all the terrible things that had happened directly or indirectly because of my selfish crusade made my skin prickle with self-loathing. I pushed my chair back and stood, avoiding their eyes. Neither of them spoke as I went to the sink and stared out the window at the bay. I loved this view as much as I loved our apartment. I always knew one day I'd have to leave here to go to college, but that had seemed so far away. Now my chest ached at the thought of leaving it all behind, of the prospect of never seeing it again. But I would do anything to never again put Nate through the hell he had suffered.

My hands gripped the edge of the countertop as I made the only choice I could.

"I can't believe you're really leaving."

I set my bag down next to the suitcases and boxes cluttering the hallway near the front door. Forcing a smile, I turned to face Roland, who had barely left my side since he and Peter burst into the apartment yesterday, fifteen minutes after Nate's call. My ribs still ached from their crushing hugs, but it was nothing compared to the pain in my heart.

We had spent the first hour of our reunion crowded together on the couch while I retold the story of that day and my incredible journey after I fell from the cliff. Then I listened while they told me how the events of that day had unfolded for them. As soon as Maxwell had hung up from his call with Nikolas, he had organized the pack to scour the town for my scent. It was actually Francis who had picked up my trail and found Tarek's body – or what the vampires had left of it – near the car. Francis, Maxwell, Brendan, Roland, and Peter had followed the trail to the cliff where they found Nikolas in a standoff with Eli and his coven. When I fell, the wolves and Chris took down the remaining vampires and made sure none escaped, while Nikolas dove straight off the cliff after me. When I heard that, I looked at Nikolas, who stood, staring out the living room window like he was watching for danger. As if he felt my eyes on him, he turned his head and met my gaze briefly before turning back to the window.

Everyone grew somber when Nate, Roland, and Peter told me about my memorial service and how many people had crowded into the small church beside the school. The entire pack had come along with most of the school, and it was eerie and surreal hearing about the eulogies given by some of my classmates who I hadn't even taken the time to get to know as well as I should have. Roland told me that Greg drove up from Philly for the service, and he had never seen my tough friend looking so heartbroken.

Nikolas took one look at my face and said it was too dangerous to let anyone else know I was alive. I told him I would not let Greg think I was dead and that was that. In the end, we made a compromise. I would not contact Greg until I was safely ensconced at the Mohiri stronghold.

That turned the conversation to me leaving, and Roland and Peter's joy over my return from the dead dimmed when I told them where I was going. Well, not where exactly, since I still didn't know where the Mohiri lived, but that I was going to live with Nikolas's people for a while. My friends spent another hour trying to talk me out of leaving, insisting that the werewolves would protect me and Nate. But the memory of Roland almost dying and the fear on Nate's face when Haism took us scared me too much to take a chance of it happening again.

"I want to go," I lied. "Nikolas says they can train me and teach me to defend myself." At least that was one thing I could look forward to. It would be nice to not have to depend on someone else for protection.

"But how long will you be gone? And how will we know if you're doing okay?" Peter asked.

I laughed as I walked back up to my room to grab my laptop bag and backpack. "Guys, I'm not moving to the Antarctic." At least I hoped not. "They have phones and computers. We'll talk so much you'll be sick of me."

"That's not the same," Roland protested, following me. "We were all supposed to go to prom together, remember?"

"I know." I looked around my bedroom at the bare walls and found it suddenly hard to swallow. Once I'd made up my mind to leave, I had started packing before I could change my mind. Roland and Peter had insisted on staying overnight, and between the three of us, my room had been stripped bare of everything that made it mine. Now all my belongings were crammed into boxes or suitcases or sitting in piles waiting to be packed and sent on to me later.

The old couch looked lonely without the books that usually littered it. Now Oscar and Daisy lay on it, watching me with sad eyes as if they knew I was leaving. It hurt to think of leaving them behind, but I had no idea where I was going. It wouldn't be fair to uproot them. I knew Daisy was content here with Nate, but Oscar would miss me. Hopefully, once I was settled in my new home I could send for him.

I'd gone up to the roof a few times to call to Harper, but there was no sign of the crow and I hated to leave without saying good-bye to him. He wouldn't understand what had happened or why I'd left him. I'd left a window open up here all night and this morning in the hope that he might show. I wished I could wait until he came back, but it might be days before he put in another appearance. I was gone so long he might have given up on me and never return.

Even the imps were quiet and strangely absent, and I found myself missing their shuffling and chattering behind the attic wall. I couldn't believe I was going to miss those thieving little fiends.

There was one big part of my life that I could not give a proper good-bye to, and every time I thought about it my heart ached. I knew Remy was forbidden to see me, but leaving without seeing him one last time left a little hole inside me. I wanted to go to the cliff in the hopes that he might come out or even to leave him a message in the cave in case he ever went back there, but Nikolas said it was too dangerous and everyone else agreed with him. Roland paled at just the mention of it. The only one not uncomfortable going back to the place where I had almost died was me.

"It's time."

The three of us turned to Nikolas, who stood at the top of the stairs. He had insisted on staying here as well, so our normally roomy apartment had felt pretty crowded last night. Roland and Peter were not happy about it, but Nikolas had left us alone for the most part, letting us have our last night together. I'd barely seen him today because he'd spent most of it outside on his phone – most likely making arrangements for the pickup. I didn't expect him back so soon, and my heart began to race. *I can't do this!*

Nikolas must have seen my panic. "I'll bring your bags out. Take all the time you need."

I nodded stiffly. As soon as he left, I turned to Roland and he wrapped me in another suffocating embrace, probably trying to make up for all the years I had refused to be hugged. I was still trying to catch my breath when Peter pulled me in for his hug. None of us spoke because we were too afraid of the tears that would follow. *This is not good-bye*, I reminded myself as I pulled away from them and turned toward the stairs.

There was one thing left to do, and I dreaded it more than anything else. I put on a brave face and went downstairs to Nate's office where he sat behind his computer pretending to work. The silence from his keyboard betrayed him, and when he looked up I saw that his eyes were a little red. We had spent a couple of hours together earlier this morning and I thought it would be enough to say our good-byes, but looking at him now, I knew it would never be enough for either of us.

"It's almost time to go."

He sighed. "I know." He wheeled around the desk, and before he even brought the chair to a stop I wrapped my arms around his neck. "I love you, Nate."

"I love you, too." He held me while I cried and then while I composed myself enough to pull away. Then he took my hands in his. "Nothing we say is going to make this easier for either of us. I just want you to know how proud I am of you and how proud your father would be if he was here. You've been through things that would break a grown man, and I know that wherever you go, you'll be okay. If I didn't believe that, I couldn't let you go."

I cleared my throat. "And you will take the Ptellon nectar like I told you, three drops every month? Nate had not reacted well when I called the vial of dark red liquid *Ptellon blood*, and it had taken some convincing to make him believe it really was just nectar.

"I won't forget."

"I'll call you as soon as I get there. And you promise to come for Christmas?"

"Nothing could keep me away."

"I'm gonna hold you to that." I refused to say good-bye so I said, "I'll see you soon."

Roland and Peter walked me down to the black SUV parked beside Nate's car. Behind the SUV was a white van loaded with my possessions. Two Mohiri I recognized from Portland stood beside the van talking to Nikolas, and I saw Chris leaning against the driver's-side door of the SUV.

I turned to give my friends one last hug when I heard a loud caw and the rustle of wings overhead. "What the hell?" Chris uttered, and the four Mohiri instantly went on alert as a large blackbird zoomed toward me. I saw a flash of silver in Nikolas's hand and knew he had a weapon ready to handle the new threat.

"Stop!" I ordered loudly as I extended my arm to Harper, who landed easily and cocked his head at me like he was waiting for me to explain myself. I brought him close to my chest and stroked his head.

"Um, Sara?" Roland called from a safe distance. "Why are you cuddling a crow? Are you some kind of bird whisperer, too?"

With everything that was going on, it felt good to smile. "You remember the crow I saved from Scott and his friends back in third grade? This is him." I held the crow away from me. "Harper, these are my friends."

The crow blinked and regarded Roland and Peter with intelligent black eyes that made the boys shift nervously. "He looks like he's thinking about pecking my eyeballs out," Peter muttered, taking another step back.

"Don't be ridiculous. He's just curious because I've never introduced him to people before."

Someone cleared their throat behind me, and I turned to Nikolas and Chris who watched me with cool appraisal. If they had been surprised by Harper, they certainly hid it well.

"What do you plan to do with that thing?" Chris asked in a tone that said he was not happy about the idea of sharing a car with a crow.

"Harper just came to say good-bye." As soon as the words were out, a lump formed in my throat. "Excuse me," I managed to say before I walked a dozen yards away to make my farewell to my old friend.

"I have to go away for a while," I explained as he stared at me intently. "You be careful, and don't go too far into the woods where the hunters will get you. And watch the cars on the road. I know you and your friends act like road kill is an all-you-can-eat buffet, but don't be stupid about it, alright?"

He shifted restlessly, and I stroked the back of his head, knowing this could be the last time I ever saw him. My future was so uncertain, and there were lots of dangers to a wild bird, even one as smart as Harper.

Never one to stay still for long, Harper lifted his wings preparing to take off. "I'll miss you," I said to him before he left my hand and circled me twice before flying away. I watched him until he disappeared from sight. Then I walked resolutely back to the waiting vehicles.

Ignoring all the stares, I hugged Roland and Peter and told them I'd call as soon as I got wherever I was going. Then I got into the back of the SUV. The windows were tinted, and I felt invisible to the rest of the world and more alone than I had ever been. I shivered and pulled my small coat tighter around me.

The front doors opened, and Nikolas and Chris climbed in. "Okay, that was one for the books," Chris declared as he started the car. His eyes twinkled when they met mine in the rearview mirror. "All set?"

"As much as I ever will be."

Nikolas turned in his seat to look at me. "Are you alright?"

Was I? I was heading off to God knows where to live with strangers. My future was uncertain, a vampire Master wanted me dead, and I was leaving everyone I knew. But the way Nikolas looked at me reminded me of that night in the alley when he silently assured me that I was not alone. There was something between us I couldn't define, but I'd felt it when I thought I was dying *and* the moment I saw him standing in the kitchen doorway yesterday. It was more than a truce; it was like we were connected somehow after everything we'd been through together. Whatever it was and whatever was waiting for me, I knew I could trust him to be there with me like he had been through all of this. Maybe we could even be friends. Stranger things had happened.

I gave him a small smile. "No, but I will be."

~ The End ~

293

ABOUT THE AUTHOR

When she is not writing, Karen Lynch can be found reading or baking. A native of Newfoundland, Canada, she currently lives in Charlotte, North Carolina with her cats and two crazy loveable German Shepherds: Rudy and Sophie.

Printed in Great Britain
by Amazon